THE LOST WOMAN

Feisty, hard-working Catherine McDonald knows what's best for everyone and tries to make it happen. To keep her aristocratic family's heads above water, she's turned their Scottish Highland home, Annat House, into a hotel, but it's a struggle. And things don't improve when a woman goes missing in the nearby mountains and the media moves in. Successful businessman Haydn Eddlington-Smith has had enough of fitting in with other people's wishes. He's moved to the Highlands so he can do exactly what he wants. So why is he spending so much time with his interfering neighbour Catherine? And what exactly has the missing woman to do with the McDonalds?

THE LOST WOMAN

THE LOST WOMAN

by

Gilly Stewart

Magna Large Print Books
Long Preston, North Yorkshire,
BD23 4ND, England.

British Library Cataloguing in Publication Data.

A catalogue record of this book is
available from the British Library

ISBN   978-0-7505-4432-0

First published in Great Britain by Accent Press Ltd 2015

Published in Large Print 2017 by arrangement with
Accent Press

Magna Large Print is an imprint of Library Magna Books Ltd.

Printed and bound in Great Britain by
T.J. (International) Ltd., Cornwall, PL28 8RW

Acknowledgements

Thanks to all my writing friends who have done so much to help me learn my craft, especially to Pia Fenton who has supported me through so many years of writing and from whom I've learnt so much.

I would like to give particular thanks to my late agent Dorothy Lumley for her wise advice and her belief in my writing. I'm so sorry she is not here to see this book in print.

Thanks to Hazel, Cat and all at Accent Press, without whom this novel would never have made the final step to publication – or been as good as it now is.

I would also like to give a shout to the Romantic Novelists' Association and express my appreciation to them for teaching me so much about writing, and introducing me to so many wonderful writing friends.

And last, but definitely not least, special thanks to my (mostly) patient husband and my two amazing, supportive sons. They told me I was a 'real' writer even when I was sure I was not – and so allowed me to become one.

To my mother, who loved to read.

Chapter One

The Lost Woman was a source of serious aggravation to Catherine McDonald. There had been no peace ever since she had put in her appearance – or should that be disappearance? First it was the police, then the journalists. Even the locals seemed to be obsessed. And it wasn't the sort of publicity you wanted when you were on the verge of launching a major tourism venture.

Catherine watched grimly as yet another stranger walked up her private driveway. She swung open the massive front door before he had time to ring the bell.

'I've got *nothing* to say,' she said.

The man paused with one hand raised to knock. 'Haven't you?' He was a tall man, forty-ish, with neatly cut mousey-brown hair and amusement in his eyes. 'How fascinating. What is it about which you have nothing to say?'

Catherine glared. He was one of the clever-clever ones, was he? 'About the Lost Woman, of course.'

'Ah. Of course.' He smiled down at her. 'And the Lost Woman would be...?'

For the first time Catherine began to doubt her assumption. The man wore smart black trousers, a dark jersey, and a long dark woollen coat, not normal journalist attire.

'I suppose there's no point asking if you're a

journalist? They all deny it.'

'It's true, I would deny it. It's *not* a profession I'm very fond of.'

Catherine sighed. She really didn't have time for this. 'OK, supposing you tell me what it is you do want?'

'What I want *now* is to learn all about the Lost Woman. You've got me enthralled. Is she really lost? Is it an ancient myth or a modern tragedy? Do tell.' He leant one shoulder against the door jamb, apparently settling in for a long conversation.

'Everyone knows. That's why they come here, isn't it?'

'It is?'

'Look, the Lost Woman is some *stupid* woman who parked her car at the bottom of our track and went walking in the mountains.' She gestured to the range which rose in peak beyond misty peak behind Annat House. 'And she hasn't been seen since.'

'How interesting,' he said. 'And was this recently?'

'Look, please stop pulling my leg. Everyone knows about the Lost Woman.'

The man gave this some thought. 'I don't think *everyone* can know, if I don't. Although, to be fair, I have been out of the country for several weeks, perhaps that explains my ignorance.'

'It was five weeks ago. Six this weekend. You can't have heard no news for that long.'

'You don't think so?' A frown marred his rather handsome face. 'I've never been an avid reader of newspapers, and I find the sort of coverage one gets on television these days a trifle vulgar, don't you? Perhaps that would explain my lamentable lapse.'

Catherine began to laugh. The man was mad, but amusing with it.

'OK. So if you're not here to ask about the Lost Woman, how can I help you?' She recalled that in the old days strangers did come knocking on the door, in need of information or directions. 'Are you lost?'

'No, I don't *think* so. I saw signs for Annat School a little way back, so I know roughly where I am.'

'Ah, you're looking for the school.' Catherine was relieved to be getting answers at last. 'It's not far away. You need to go another couple of miles and you'll see a large Victorian-gothic building on your right, can't miss it. Distances are deceptive, aren't they, on these winding roads? A lot of people turn back thinking they've gone too far.'

'It's a popular school, is it?'

'I believe so. A healthy outdoor Scottish education is apparently quite the thing. We haven't had much to do with it since my brothers left, but it was very well thought of then.' Catherine thought briefly of the time when her mother had still been alive and they had been an almost happy family. She shook her head to clear her thoughts. 'I suppose you have a child you're considering sending there?'

'I have a son, yes.'

'Just the one? How old is he?' Catherine felt obliged to add, 'I'm not a great fan of boarding schools myself.'

15

'Richie's ten. Or is it eleven? I tend to forget.'

'I believe they prefer to take them from eight. Most prep schools do. Didn't they tell you that on the phone?'

'I haven't spoken to them on the phone.'

In Catherine's opinion this man was rather too lackadaisical, and she was sure the head teacher would agree. 'I don't think they are very keen on people just dropping in,' she said severely.

'No, I can see that might be inconvenient.' He smiled. 'People can be so inconsiderate, can't they? When all it would have taken is a mere phone call in advance...'

Catherine was beginning to feel she was losing control of this conversation, an unusual experience. 'Is that it, then?' she said, making an effort to get back on track. 'If you do decide to take a look at the school it's two miles further on. You'll have no problem finding it.' She moved as if to close the door.

'Actually,' said the man, leaning forward confidentially, 'Actually, I was hoping to use your telephone.'

'The phone?'

'Yes. Did you know that mobiles don't work out here? I need to call the AA.'

'Of course I know that mobiles don't work. This is the Highlands, you know.'

He nodded politely. 'I should have realised.'

'So your car has broken down?' said Catherine slowly.

'Yes. At least, it appears to have. The engine died and it's certainly not starting when I turn the ignition. I've an inkling it might be the starter

16

motor, or spark plugs, something like that. I don't suppose you know about these things?'

'Absolutely not,' said Catherine, exasperated. 'Look, come in. You can use the phone here.' She stood back abruptly to allow him into the wood-panelled hall.

'Perhaps I should introduce myself before I cross your threshold? Seems rather bad manners not to. Haydn Eddlington-Smith, at your service.'

Catherine gave a snort of laughter. She couldn't help it. Nobody like this had appeared on her doorstep before. 'I think it's our phone that is at your service,' she said crisply. 'It's on the table over there. I'll leave you to it, shall I?'

She went back into the tiny room that was now her office, leaving the door ajar so she could keep an eye on him. He did, indeed, make a call to the AA. She also noted that he described the where-abouts of his car, a black BMW 7 Series, with great precision. He wasn't lost at all.

'Everything in order?' she said, reappearing as soon as he replaced the receiver. 'It's a fairly quiet time of year, you shouldn't have to wait too long for someone to reach you.'

'The lady assured me it would be between thirty minutes and an hour.'

'Ah.' Haydn Eddlington-Smith might be odd and annoying, but the Highland custom of hos-pitality prevented her sending him back out on a winter's afternoon. 'Perhaps you would like a hot drink while you wait?'

'I wouldn't say no,' he agreed.

Suppressing a sigh, she led him across the hall and down the stairs to the basement kitchen. With a bit of luck, Mhairi would be around and she could leave him in her assistant's capable hands. The few moments in the office had reminded her of the mass of things she still had to do.

Unfortunately Mhairi wasn't there. Instead, Catherine's youngest brother Malcolm was sitting at the large wooden table, eating his way through a packet of chocolate biscuits. Pip, the Jack Russell, raised his head from the rug by the Aga to give a token bark.

'Hi, Mal, this is, er...' She couldn't bring herself to repeat the name, even if she could have remembered it correctly.

'Haydn Eddlington-Smith,' said the visitor, stretching out a hand affably. 'Spelt like the composer but pronounced *hay-dun*. Pleased to meet you.'

'This is my brother Malcolm. And I'm Catherine, Catherine McDonald. Mal, this, er, gentleman's car has broken down and he's going to have a coffee while he waits.' She put the kettle on and set about finding mugs and milk. She might as well make herself a drink at the same time. 'You could offer those biscuits around,' she said severely to her brother. 'If you've quite finished.'

'I haven't, actually,' he said cheerfully, 'But always happy to share.' He proffered the packet but Haydn declined. He took a seat on one of the mismatching chairs and gazed around the kitchen.

'What a wonderful place you have.'

'It's not bad, is it?' said Catherine. This was a topic she was happy to discuss. Since winning the battle with her father about launching her new business, she had overseen the redecoration of the house herself. She had been longing to do it for years, and once set loose, with money not too much of a problem, she had been unstoppable. Now it was almost finished and she *loved* it.

'It's a bloody sight nicer than it used to be,' said Mal. 'Pity we're not going to get the benefit.'

'There's a perfectly good kitchen in the Lodge,' said Catherine quickly, remembering all the difficulties still ahead. 'Where you are supposed to be living now, *if* you remember.'

'This is my home,' protested Mal, through crumbs. 'I like it here, you know?' It seemed he really meant it. Unlike his older brothers, he hadn't used university as a stepping stone to the outside world. He had come straight back after graduating, and seemed, for the moment, intent on staying.

'*Was* your home. Now the Lodge is. Don't you start, you're getting as bad as Father. This house is now a business.'

Haydn listened to the conversation with interest. 'I hate to appear curious,' he said, 'but what kind of business venture? I didn't notice any bed and breakfast signs. In fact I was a little intimidated by the "Private" notice attached to your rather smart gates.'

'Don't pay any attention to that,' advised Malcolm. 'Nobody else does.'

'Especially not journalists,' said Catherine, who still harboured her suspicions. 'I would have taken it down before now if it hadn't been for this Lost Woman business.'

'Yes, of course, the Lost Woman.'

'Something very fishy about her if you ask me,'

said Malcolm conversationally. 'They'll probably find it's a false insurance claim or something. The Woman is probably sunning herself on some foreign island as we speak.'

'Last week you were sure she'd been murdered.'

'But if she had been, where's the body? They've had more sniffer dogs through these hills than at Heathrow Airport. And they didn't find a thing, did they?'

'Didn't they?' asked Haydn. 'I grow more and more interested.'

'You're not another of those journalists, are you?' asked Malcolm, paying him more attention. 'Or just a thrill seeker? I'm surprised Catherine let you in if you are.'

'I told you, his car's broken down,' said Catherine, quick to defend herself.

The visitor finished his drink and pushed his mug to one side. 'Thank you so much for that. Now I suppose I should brave the elements and go and await my knight in shining armour.'

Catherine rose as well. She had meant to leave him in the kitchen with Malcolm, but somehow hadn't got around to it. 'And I had better get back to work,' she said crisply.

'Before I go,' he said, his tone pleasant as ever. 'I wonder if you can tell me how far it is to Annat Cottage?'

'Annat Cottage?' said Malcolm. 'Why, it's just round the corner. You could have walked there as quickly as walking up the track here.'

'Why do you want Annat Cottage?' said Catherine with a sense of foreboding.

'Because I'm going to live there,' said the man,

taking a key from his pocket and waving it before them, as though they might need proof. 'I'm the new owner, as of yesterday. I was fairly sure it wasn't far away but as the phone isn't connected it wouldn't have been any use. Excellent news that it's so close. We'll be neighbours, won't we?'

'But,' said Catherine. 'But I was told the place had been bought by a Mr...'

'Smith? Yes, that would be right. These double-barrelled names can be such a bother, can't they? I tend only to use it on first meeting.'

Catherine noticed that almost thirty minutes had now passed since his phone call and hustled him back up the stairs and out of the door as quickly as she decently could. Then she returned to the kitchen.

'Aa-agh.'

'What?' Malcolm looked up from a yoghurt.

'*That* is our new neighbour.'

'So he says. Seems pleasant enough. English though. He'll probably just use it as a holiday home.'

Catherine's mood brightened slightly. 'I'll have to find out. I hope so.'

'Why?'

'Because – because I was rude to him when he first arrived and then I laughed at him and then I only grudgingly offered him coffee. What kind of start is that to a neighbourly relationship?'

Malcolm snorted. 'Sounds like Father couldn't have done better himself. You're more like him than you realise.'

This was not something Catherine wanted to hear.

Chapter Two

'You're coming home *tonight?*' said Catherine to her father. 'Couldn't you have let us know sooner?'

'It didn't occur to me. Arrange for someone to meet me at Pitlochry, please. I believe the train is due in at eight, but you had better check.'

'I suppose Malcolm could come and get you, if he hasn't anything else planned. If you'd phoned earlier, I could have asked Mhairi, or even Stewart. It's really not very convenient. And now I'll have to get your room in the Lodge ready. Honestly...'

'I won't be using the Lodge. I'll have my usual room in the house. I know you've no guests at present so no need to pretend you have.'

'But Father, you've got to start using the Lodge. I'll have it very nice for you.' Catherine changed her tone to coaxing. If she could get Malcolm and her father to sleep there tonight it would be quite a coup.

'Don't be ridiculous,' said her father. 'And by the way, I haven't eaten. Arrange some supper, will you? I do prefer home-cooking.' He rang off.

Catherine scowled. She was determined not to let her father win this time. She had to get him out of the habit of thinking Annat House was his home. It was the East Lodge or nothing. On a sudden inspiration, she went and switched off the boiler and, with only a moment's regret, the Aga too. She had let the oil tank run rather low, so why not conserve what she had left?

'Malcolm!' she shouted, wandering through the rooms. She found him eventually in the guests' drawing room, lying full length on one of the sofas, without having removed his shoes.

'This has got to stop.' She grabbed the remote fractionally before he did and switched off the television. 'Look at the mess you've made. Out!' She brushed down the velvet cushions with fierce strokes. Malcolm moved reluctantly to a seated position. Pip jumped hastily off his chair and hurried to ingratiate himself with Catherine. She said to her brother, 'And you know Pip's not allowed in here.'

'He comes in here with you.'

'When I'm in here I'm doing something useful, like cleaning windows or hanging curtains. I'm not loafing around. And he's *never* allowed on the furniture.'

'Try telling him that.'

'Father's on his way home. You've to go and collect him from Pitlochry.'

'Ah, no. I was going to wander down to the Foresters Arms and see if anyone fancied a game of pool. Why does he have to come home tonight?' He frowned. 'And why do I have to go and get him?'

'Because you're here,' said Catherine. She ignored the first question. It was inconvenient to have their father turning up just now, but Annat was his home. 'And until you find yourself a job you can make yourself useful.'

23

'I think I'll go and stay with John Hugo in Edinburgh.'

'No you will not. You'll just spend money you haven't got. Now, when you bring Father back, take him straight to the Lodge. I'll be there waiting.'

'He won't like it.'

'That's where his supper will be, and yours too. And, do you know, the heating in the house seems to be on the blink, so I really think you'd both prefer it down there.' Catherine smiled encouragingly. This was as good a time as any to evict her family. She had to have everything sorted for a week on Friday, when the first clients of Exclusive Activity Holidays were due to arrive. Setting up this business had been her dream for years. She *wasn't* going to let her father mess it up. After all, he had agreed to it – after a fashion.

Gordon McDonald was as irate as his children had anticipated at being delivered to the East Lodge.

'You're overstepping the mark here, Catherine, let me warn you.'

'Father, you know how you hate the cold, and the house is *freezing* without the heating on.'

'And why is there no heating on? Don't think I can't guess.'

Catherine looked shamefaced. 'I have to admit it's my fault. I forgot to order oil and we've run out. But I'll get some in tomorrow, or the next day at the latest.'

'I'm sure it will all be magically sorted before these precious guests of yours arrive,' said her father, regarding her with displeasure from pale blue eyes.

Catherine glared back. 'Father, you agreed to me, us, setting up this business. I'm going to make this house pay its way.'

'Time will tell.'

Sometimes Catherine thought her father actually wanted her to fail. He definitely resented the idea of having strangers in Annat House being waited on hand and foot. If his daughter was going to have to wait on anyone, it should be him.

'How long do you think you'll be home?' she asked, casually.

'Trying to get rid of me already, are you?'

'Of course not, Father. But I do need to plan meals.'

'Not your problem. I presume if we do have to live in this hell-hole we can at least have Mrs Mc-Whirter here to look after us?'

'Mrs Mac is on holiday. I told her to take this week off. She's been working like a star helping me get the house ready and she needed a break before the guests start arriving.'

'I'll have that girl Mhairi, then.'

'Mhairi's busy helping me; I'd really rather you didn't impose on her. Malcolm is quite capable of preparing a meal if pushed, and I'm happy to do some cooking when I can. The two of you are just going to have to learn to fend for yourselves.'

Her father looked at her blankly over the top of his half-moon spectacles. The truth was, he was spoilt. First he had had his mother putting herself out to meet his every whim, then his long-suffering wife, then Catherine had taken on that role. If she hadn't actually met every whim, she had done her best to make his life comfortable. Now she was too busy for that, because she was doing something *she* wanted to do. His life was going to change and he had better get used to it.

She decided, however, not to provoke him further just now. She turned to Malcolm, who had been leafing through *The Scotsman*. He said quickly, 'Don't look to me. I don't even know how to work the dishwasher.'

'About time you learnt,' said Catherine. 'I'll see if I can spare five minutes to show you that and the washing machine in the morning.'

'Can't you send Mhairi down?'

'And you think she would do it for you? No chance.'

'No but she could show me.' Malcolm's expression brightened.

'It's about time you found yourself a job, my boy,' said his father, transferring his dissatisfied gaze to his youngest son. 'It's a year since you finished that damned useless degree of yours and you haven't earned a penny since.'

'It's more like six months than a year,' said Malcolm resentfully. 'And I have earned some money. I worked as a barman in the Foresters Arms the whole of the summer.'

'Not a suitable career. And if you're going to hang around at home, why don't you help your sister? Plenty for you to do here.'

This was a sentiment that Catherine shared, but for once she held her tongue. Instead she said to her father, 'I don't think you said how long you would be home?'

26

He grunted. 'A week at the most, then I'm off back to the States.' Gordon worked in the oil industry. Since his move to an American-based company a couple of years ago he seemed to spend more and more time in the US. On the whole, Catherine thought this was a good thing. 'I hope you have my office set up exactly as instructed? Two telephone lines, computer? Yes?'

'Everything's ready,' said Catherine soothingly. 'The old cart shed lent itself very well to the conversion.'

'I still think it's ridiculous, having to go outside every time I want to move from office to house. What happens if it's raining or, worse, snowing?'

'It's only a couple of yards,' said Catherine. 'I don't *think* you'll get lost.' She was rather pleased with the arrangement. It meant that her father would spend most of his time out of the Lodge, giving him less opportunity to argue with Malcolm.

When the meal was finished her father took himself off to smoke his after-dinner cigar in the sitting room but Malcolm remained in the kitchen. 'I'll show you how to use the dishwasher now, if you like?' said Catherine, hopefully.

'I've been thinking,' he said, stacking the dishes for her to take from the table, but otherwise offering no help. 'About the Lost Woman.'

'Don't you start.'

'I'm not starting, I'm carrying on. You have to admit it's a mystery.' His expression was serious. 'Why did she leave her car here? Why did she disappear?'

'What I would like to know is why she didn't

choose to disappear somewhere else.'

'It was a hire car, did you know that? Mhairi says it was rented under a false name, too, although I don't see how she can know that. They still haven't identified the woman.'

'So bang goes your insurance theory,' said Catherine. 'If she was trying to claim life insurance money she'd want everyone to know who she was.'

'And if she was committing secret suicide she wouldn't want anyone to follow her, so why leave the car in such an obvious place? It doesn't make sense.'

'She had to leave the car somewhere... Anyway, I do not want to talk about this.' Catherine was annoyed at finding herself drawn in to the discussion.

'I think I'll make some enquiries of my own,' said Malcolm. 'It'll keep me out of the way while Father is home.'

'Finding a job would keep you out of the way and be far more useful.'

Malcolm shrugged. With his too-long curly hair and pink cheeks he looked far younger than his twenty-two years. Catherine wondered when he would grow up. Of all of them, he seemed to have suffered most from their mother's death eight years before. He had lost his sense of direction, and she sometimes worried he might never find it again. Perhaps taking an interest in the Lost Woman would be good for him, after all.

Chapter Three

The following morning, Catherine rose early to bake bread, using the Lodge kitchen as the Aga in Annat House was still switched off.

Her mum had baked bread regularly. She could turn her hand to anything, from fancy plaits and brioches to rye and seed bread. All effortless. All delicious. Catherine stuck to the more straightforward wholemeal, which she made only occasionally. Her reason for making it today was to take a loaf down to her new neighbour. That way she might erase that first embarrassing meeting from his mind.

She put on her Barbour jacket and took the path across the fields. It was still early and a mist drifted over the grey waters of the loch, obscuring the hills on the far side. She paused on the ridge to look back through the faint dawn light to her home, and smiled. Annat House rose three storeys high, pale grey stone walls beneath the darker grey slate roof. It belonged completely in this bleak grey and green and brown landscape. From a distance, it seemed to huddle into the hills behind. The vast windows on the ground floor were testament to the lovely, light drawing room and dining room within. Upstairs were eight beautifully redecorated bedrooms, all now en-suite. And then on the top floor, the smaller attic rooms. It was going to be perfect for wel-

29

coming her select groups of guests.

She strode across the short winter grass until the cottage came into view. It was built of the same grey stone as Annat House and the East Lodge, and had presumably once belonged to the estate. It was a rather quaint building, with fancy wood-work around the porch and eaves, and windows that gave magnificent views over the loch. Haydn Eddlington-Smith must have paid a pretty penny for it. Properties like this were snatched up almost before they came on to the market these days.

She knocked loudly on the front door. After a moment or two it was opened by her new neigh-bour, wearing a rather luxurious knee-length dressing gown.

'Miss McDonald!' he said, eyebrows raised. 'How nice. Do come in.'

'I hope I'm not disturbing you,' said Catherine, hoping she wasn't going pink. She hadn't ex-pected to find him in a state of undress. 'I just wanted to do the neighbourly thing, which I'm afraid I, er, rather failed to do yesterday, and drop by to say welcome. I've brought you a loaf of bread.' She handed him the still-warm package.

'My goodness! You don't get neighbours like this in London. That's exceptionally kind. Your own baking, possibly?'

She had wondered, yesterday, if he always spoke in this strange way. Clearly, he did.

'Yes. It doesn't take long when you've got into the routine.' She didn't want him to think she had baked especially for him.

'Do come in. Tell you what, I'll nip upstairs and dress while you put on the kettle.'

Catherine had been about to decline the invitation, but he was already ushering her through the sitting room to the kitchen at the rear. 'It struck me after I had left you yesterday that I hadn't made the most of your local knowledge. I want to pick your brains about one or two things. You won't mind, will you?'

He left her before she could reply so Catherine shrugged and busied herself filling the brand new chrome kettle. Then she looked around surreptitiously. Haydn didn't appear to have done much in the way of unpacking. There were two boxes on the floor, one of food and one of crockery. The furniture, as far as she could see, was identical to that used by the previous occupants, an Edinburgh couple who had used the place as a weekend retreat. He must have bought it with the house.

She leant against one of the kitchen counters and surveyed the weed-infested garden with disapproval. The Edinburgh couple had had no desire to spend any of their precious free time (or money) on it.

'Are you interested in gardening?' she asked as soon as her host reappeared dressed now in jeans and a black jersey. He hadn't shaved.

He followed her gaze and grimaced. 'No, I couldn't say that was one of my talents.'

'It needs attention. We have a very good gardener at Annat House who might be interested in doing some hours for you. Shall I tell him to pop by?'

'Er... If you wish.'

'Excellent. His name's Stewart. He's dour, but a hard worker.'

31

'Ah... Right.' Haydn made a pot of tea and cut some slices of the fresh bread. 'I haven't had breakfast yet. Perhaps you'll join me?'

'Just tea, black,' said Catherine, although she was pleased to note that the bread smelt delicious. She was trying to lose weight. Again. You would have thought all that rushing around getting the house ready would have helped.

She followed Haydn through to the sitting room. 'It must have been handy, buying the place ready furnished,' she said, taking a seat on the polyester settee.

He grinned. 'Pity the previous owners didn't have better taste. But it was a snap decision, and this is convenient for now. I'll refurnish at my leisure.'

'Won't you be bringing up your own things?'

'I won't.'

Catherine sighed. 'So Malcolm was right, this is just a holiday home? I had hoped that we might get a permanent resident this time. You know, it's not nearly so beneficial to the local economy...' She had thought this through. Despite her own reservations about having Haydn Eddlington-Smith as a neighbour, she knew it was best for the area if he wasn't just another summer visitor.

'I'd hate you to labour under a misapprehension. It is indeed my intention to live here on a permanent basis.'

'Oh,' said Catherine, wishing she had kept her mouth shut. Yesterday's experience should have taught her not to make assumptions about this man. 'Ah. Good.' So why he didn't have furniture of his own to bring up? She wondered if he was recently divorced; that might account for it. How could she find out?

'Will your wife be joining you?'

'No, I don't think so. I am not, presently, exactly sure of Esme's whereabouts, but I am not expecting her to join me here.'

Catherine wondered if he was once again having a joke at her expense. 'And is your son, who may or may not be ten, and who you may or may not send to Annat School, also missing?'

'Now now. It was your idea that Richie might go to Annat School.'

'You do have a son, I suppose?'

Haydn nodded, his expression more serious. 'Of course I do. He's at prep school just outside London. A very good prep school,' he added, as though he expected Catherine to criticise him.

As if she would. 'I hope you'll be very happy here at Annat,' she said.

'So do I, so do I.' He glanced out of the window and at that moment the sun rose above the eastern hills and lit up the waters with a pale golden light. 'If the view is like that every day, I shall be very happy indeed.'

'The view is never the same two days running, or even two hours, but it's always wonderful.' Catherine smiled at him. 'I never tire of it.'

'Have you lived here all your life?'

'Yes. Born and bred at Annat, and my father before me and his before him. I've never lived anywhere else and never wanted to.' Catherine loved this place. She loved not only the house but also the history, the fact that the McDonalds could trace their time here back to the fifteenth

33

century. She had to make sure they could stay.

'Didn't you say you went away to boarding school?'

'No, I said my brothers went away to boarding school. I, being a girl, could be satisfactorily educated in the local schools.' She couldn't keep the bitterness from her voice, even though she had never wanted to go away to school. Annoyed at revealing so much, she hurried on, 'Actually, to be totally truthful, I did go away to university. I spent four years in Edinburgh, but as I came home most weekends it didn't feel like living away.'

'A waste, surely, of all the magnificent opportunities a university city like Edinburgh can offer?'

'My mother wasn't well,' said Catherine shortly. 'Now, what local information did you want me to provide?'

Haydn considered her thoughtfully for a moment, as though about to enquire further into her family, then he rubbed his chin with one hand and grinned. 'Ah, yes, local information. As soon as I've shaved I thought I'd try the village shops. Or is it shop? Can you advise where one goes for food produce in the vicinity?'

Catherine relaxed. She loved promoting local businesses. She told him about the post office-cum-café and the small supermarket. 'We support the local shops as much as possible; the last thing we want is for them to close down.'

'And do they have local eggs? Salmon? Venison?'

'In season you can get venison, pheasant, and grouse from some of the gamekeepers. I can give you their names. And you can get fresh eggs at a number of farms.'

'That's very kind. Perhaps you can put me on your list for bread?'

Catherine frowned, wondering if he was teasing. 'I don't sell my bread.' His smile broadened and she added, 'And before you ask, no, I'm not offering to supply it free.'

'A shame, but never mind.' When he smiled there was a gleam in his green eyes that was very attractive. 'Which brings me to my next question. What is this business you are so secretively establishing at the big house?'

'There's nothing secretive about it.' Catherine wondered why he had to introduce that mocking tone when he asked questions. For a moment, when he'd smiled, he had seemed so much nicer. 'On the contrary, we've been advertising widely for the last few months. The signs will go up this week, now the Lost Woman fuss is dying down. What we're doing is starting a centre for exclusive activity holidays. I've been thinking about it for some time. I'm confident I've discovered a niche in the market.'

He considered this for a moment. 'I don't like to contradict,' he said, which was clearly a lie. 'But aren't there already hundreds of activity holidays on offer in Scotland, exclusive and otherwise?'

'Mine will be different.' Catherine spoke firmly, trying to rediscover the certainty she had felt when she first developed her ideas. Then they had seemed brilliant. The only difficulty had been persuading her father to agree. Whereas now... 'Luxury lodgings, excellent cuisine, staying in the house of a well-known local Scottish family, with daily instruction in the subject of their choice. Our

35

first two courses are *An Introduction to Water Colours* and *Geology of the Central Highlands.*'

Haydn grinned, his lip quirking up slightly higher on one side than the other. 'Very active.'

'Activities come in all forms. In the future we are offering courses in sailing, salmon fishing, and hill walking. And then there's *Traditional Scots Cookery* and a botany course, and...'

'Goodness, your talents are endless.'

'The whole idea of the project,' said Catherine, getting into her stride, 'is to employ as many local people as possible. We don't just want to bring our guests into the area, we want their visit to benefit the local population. I've found a cook who stays not too far away, the artist is a young man living at the head of the loch and struggling to make a name for himself. For the fishing...'

'I get the idea,' said Haydn hastily. 'And very commendable it is too. I wish you the best of luck.'

Catherine once again felt those unwelcome doubts threaten to engulf her. 'It's going to succeed. It has to.' Haydn nodded, watching her without comment, which made her feel un-accustomedly nervous.

She rose to her feet. She had stayed far longer than she had intended. Mhairi would be wondering what on earth had happened. 'I'd better get back,' she said. She gave him her best smile. 'I hope you'll be very happy here. Feel free to pop by any time, we'll be glad to help in any way we can.'

'Thank you. I'll bear that in mind. My main priority just now is installing my computer.'

'Ah,' she said. He had asked enough questions, so why shouldn't she? 'And will you be working from home?'

He hesitated, as though caught out. 'Well, not work per se.'

'You don't work?' Catherine was puzzled, not to say disapproving.

He smiled. 'I'm in the fortunate position of being retired.'

That made her frown all the more. Retired? At his age? That was ridiculous. He couldn't spend all day playing on his computer. It wasn't good for people not to work – look at Malcolm. She'd have to do see what she could do for this Haydn Eddlington-Smith. But not just now. She said her goodbyes and headed back to Annat House to begin her own day's work.

Chapter Four

Mhairi Robertson was rinsing the breakfast dishes when her mother limped into the small kitchen.

'You should be sitting down,' said Mhairi, frowning over her shoulder. 'You know you're not meant to walk without your crutches.'

'It's so annoying.' Her mother sighed. Being a nurse herself, she didn't make a good patient. 'I still can't believe I was so stupid as to break an ankle falling down two steps.'

'It happens,' said Mhairi, drying her hands. 'Right, I'm off. Try and rest, OK? Maybe Dad could do lunch for you?'

Her mother's lips tightened but all she said was,

'You have a good day.' She looked tired, as though she was still in pain, which she probably was.

Mhairi wished her father would be more helpful, but she didn't have time to worry about that now.

She wheeled her bike out of the lean-to shed and set off on the short journey from Kinlochannat village to Annat House. It was a lovely ride along the banks of the loch. She enjoyed it, would have enjoyed walking more, but that would take longer and time was precious. She had hardly touched the surface of the chores at home and there was always so much to do when she arrived at Annat House. She grinned suddenly. It was a good thing she wasn't afraid of hard work.

She pedalled as fast as she could against the wind. The leafless trees bowed before it and little white-crested waves scurried down the loch. She had been *very* lucky to get this job. Chances like this didn't come up often around Kinlochannat. Her mother was full of encouragement, of course, and her father's grunts at her bits of news could be taken as interest. Catherine really seemed to trust her, which was brilliant. It was only Catherine's brother Malcolm who was a problem. Once upon a time he had been a friend of Mhairi's, had attended the village school like any of the local children. Then he had departed for the world of boarding school, and now he was a stranger.

It was odd how often he seemed to be there when she least wanted him, watching over her shoulder, making her nervous. This morning he had appeared when she was having a coffee at the massive kitchen table, a sheaf of Catherine's notes before her.

'Catherine's out, is she? While the cat's away and all that. Make a coffee for me, too, will you?'

'No, I won't.' Mhairi glared at him. She had decided to stand up for herself. 'Make it yourself. I'm working.'

'Oo-oo.' He grinned at her in that annoying way he had. He was very good-looking, you couldn't deny it, but his posh accent and sulky face made her wary. During her teenage years she had been hurt that he ignored her, but she was over that now.

He hooked out a chair with one leg and sat down. The grin was replaced by his more usual gloom. 'Is my father about?'

'Not as far as I know. Is he back?'

'Yeah. Arrived last night. Hopefully he's still down at the Lodge.' He sighed and went to collect the four slices of bread that had been toasting on the Aga. 'Thank goodness Catherine's turned this thing back on.'

'Why would she turn it off?' said Mhairi, puzzled. She had wondered why the kitchen was so cold this morning.

'Can't you guess?' said Malcolm with a faint sneer. After a while, when she didn't respond, he said abruptly, 'D'you think this holidays idea of Catherine's is going to work?'

'Aye, I do. And so does she.' One of the things Mhairi admired about Catherine was her boundless confidence.

'She's willing to put in the hours, Catherine, I'll give her that. But I don't know how she's going to make a profit. Taking people like you on the payroll before she's even up and running won't help.'

'Catherine wants to do things properly,' said Mhairi, defensively. 'There's been a lot to get ready. And I don't see *you* offering to work for her.'

'I will if she pays me. I'm not working for nothing.'

Mhairi shook her head and returned to the papers. Did he think she didn't need money? Because she was living at home in that tiny house, wasn't she worth paying? She could feel prickles at the back of her neck as her anger rose.

Malcolm McDonald thought she wasn't good enough, did he? Well, she'd show him.

'He's retired,' said Catherine as she, Malcolm, Mhairi, Stewart, and her father sat down for lunch in the Lodge kitchen. 'How on earth can someone be retired at his age?'

'Why didn't you ask him?' asked Malcolm, spooning down his soup as though he hadn't eaten all day, which she knew from Mhairi was far from the truth.

'I will, but I didn't have time just then. I'd stayed far too long already.'

'Who, may I ask, are we discussing?' asked her father.

'Our new neighbour, Haydn Smith. Didn't I tell you he moved into Annat Cottage?'

'Haydn *Eddlington*-Smith,' said Malcolm. 'Although one doesn't like to use a double-barrelled name after first introductions, does one? He's a bit odd if you ask me.'

His father ignored him. 'Catherine, tell me more about our new neighbour.'

40

'There's not much to tell. He's forty-ish, comes from London, says he intends to live here permanently. We'll just have to wait and see.'

'Decent class of person?' asked her father.

'I couldn't possibly say.'

'He spoke posh,' said Malcolm helpfully.

His father sniffed. 'I wonder if he plays bridge? Invite him for a drink one evening this week and I'll look him over.'

'I'll see if I have time,' said Catherine. She turned to Stewart, who, as usual, had said not a word during the entire meal. 'By the way, Stu, I said you'd give him a hand sorting out his garden. Think you could call in and see him, get it arranged?'

'Aye,' said Stewart in his measured way. 'I don't see why not.'

'Make sure you clear out all those thistles and docks, they're an eyesore. And the old greenhouse will have to come down. I wonder if the pig sty is worth saving?'

'You've enough on your plate, my girl,' said her father. 'You don't need to start worrying about some newcomer as well as everyone else in this godforsaken place. And are we having anything more to eat or is soup your limit these days?'

'There's cheese and biscuits, and fruit,' said Catherine, not rising to his bait.

'I'll get it,' said Mhairi.

'I've been thinking,' said Gordon as he helped himself to a large piece of brie. 'Ask that new chap round on Friday. Kerr and John Hugo are coming up. We can all look him over.'

'Kerr and John Hugo?' said Catherine in dis-

41

may. She was, of course, fond of her brothers, but still. 'This Friday? When was it arranged? I really don't have the time.'

'I invited them,' said her father.

Catherine made a few token protests, but she knew it was in vain. Obviously, this visit was already a fait accompli. Her father must have arranged it a while ago; Kerr was a doctor and couldn't get time off at short notice.

'And we'll need to move back into Annat House,' said Gordon, looking pleased. 'There isn't enough room for us all here, is there?'

Catherine glared some more, but couldn't deny it. Also her father had seen the oil lorry make a delivery that morning, so she couldn't use that as an excuse, either. It looked like getting him to spend one night in the East Lodge had been a false dawn.

Later on, as she thought over her father's announcement, she felt a shadow of foreboding unconnected to the inconvenience. Why on earth did her father want all his children together? He wasn't normally keen on family gatherings.

Haydn didn't make his trip to the village until after lunch. It was amazing how long it took to unpack and explore his tiny new domain. Prior to his arrival, he had only seen the cottage via a virtual tour on the internet, but he wasn't disappointed. The rooms, although few, were reasonably sized.

He knew if he told any of his acquaintances that he had bought a two-bedroomed cottage in the Highlands of Scotland they would think he had gone completely mad. Everyone knew that a rather nice flat in Kensington should be complemented by a weekend house in the home counties. But he had sold the (massive, pretentious) weekend house as soon as he and Esme had separated. And now he no longer needed to be near London he could do exactly as he liked.

One of the best things was that no one here knew anything about him. That was such a relief.

He smiled as he admired the views and the silence. He kept pausing to look out of the window of whichever room he was in. From the front there were views of silvery-grey Loch Annat, but even from the kitchen the outlook was spectacular, up to the range of snow-topped mountains. And he couldn't see another house, another person.

He drove his car, now cured of its mystery illness, into Kinlochannat village. On another day he would walk it, or, when he managed to get a bike, cycle. He wondered if it would be possible to persuade Richie to take up cycling.

Haydn found the small supermarket with no difficulty. He filled his basket with what he felt was a sufficient number of items to please the shop keeper, and then made his way to the counter.

'Admirable place you've got here,' he said. 'I didn't expect such a wide selection of goods.'

'Aye, we do no' so badly,' said the woman who was serving. She was about his own age, and, by the accent, local.

'Perhaps I can introduce myself,' said Haydn, proffering a hand. 'Haydn Smith. I've just moved into Annat Cottage.'

The woman shook the hand gingerly. 'Nancy,' she said, but once she had her hand back she

43

became more friendly. 'Mr Smith, is it? We were wondering when you'd move in, like.'

'I arrived yesterday.'

The woman nodded, examining him with open, friendly interest. 'Aye, I'd have heard if you'd been here any longer.'

Haydn wasn't surprised. 'My neighbour, Miss McDonald, was kind enough to come by this morning with a welcoming loaf of bread.'

'She'll keep an eye on you, will Catherine.' The woman grinned. 'If you don't watch yourself she'll have you on half a dozen committees before you can blink. She's what you might call the organising type.'

Haydn grinned back. It was nice to have his first impressions confirmed.

'The McDonalds are one of the big local families, are they?'

'They're *the* local family,' said the woman, looking offended. 'Been at the big house as long as anyone can mind. You know that times have changed, don't you, when they've had to move into the old East Lodge.'

'You do?'

'Aye. I don't think Mr McDonald is that keen, nor the boys. John Hugo has had a few words to say, and although Malcolm's more on the quiet side you can see it's not what he wanted. I thought Miss McDonald would take it badly, like, but she just laughed when I offered my sympathies.'

'She doesn't mind, then?'

'Seems not. But she's always been one to go her own road. They say when she took the job at the village school her father wasn't happy at all, but she never bothered.'

'She's a teacher, is she?' Haydn was surprised.

'Was. An' a good one an' all. Some of the bairns there today could do with her skelping their backsides. I mind her skelping my brother's, aye, and mine too once or twice. She wasn't one to go light on the girls, Miss McDonald. And it never did us no harm.'

'I take it we're not discussing Miss *Catherine* McDonald?'

'No, of course not.' Nancy looked at him as if he was stupid. '*She* was never meant for a teacher. Her dad had higher plans for her. Marrying Sir George Farquharson from over Erricht way, that would have suited him just fine, but Catherine was having none of it. She came home to nurse her mother and she's stayed ever since. Mind, she's a good girl, so she is.'

Haydn had hoped that the shop would prove a useful source of information, and he wasn't disappointed. 'And the other Miss McDonald...?'

'That's Miss Georgie McDonald, Catherine's aunt. Her father's older sister. She must be going on seventy now but she's spry for all that. Lives in a cottage by the Black Wood.'

'Fascinating. Now, how much is it I owe you...?'

Haydn felt he had learnt enough for one day. It seemed he had made a favourable impression on Nancy, for the shop door hadn't quite closed when she turned to shout to her colleague in the back. 'That was that Mr Smith, frae Annat Cottage. Bit of a nob, like, but he's friendly enough.'

Haydn smiled to himself. Not a hint of the old gossip there. There was a good chance this move would turn out to be a success.

He really hoped Richie was going to feel the same.

Chapter Five

Once again Catherine opened the front door of Annat House before Haydn had knocked. This time it was because he had paused on the doorstep to turn and absorb the vista.

'I never knew mountains could be blue,' he said, looking out across the fields and the loch to the range beyond.

'They're not blue. They're mauve and grey and crimson, peach and amber where the sun touches them, and so brilliantly white where there's snow you wonder why the world isn't always perfect.'

'I see you've given this some thought.'

'Yes, well, um, why don't you come in?' said Catherine, embarrassed now.

'Thank you. It's very kind of you to invite me.'

'Yes. And don't start thinking we're always going to be entertaining in this style. This is The Very Last Time. Father insisted. Kerr and John Hugo are both home and the Lodge would be just too crowded.'

She took Haydn's coat, the same dark, expensive-looking garment he had worn on his first appearance, and was relieved to see that he wore a shirt and tie beneath it. Father shouldn't find anything to object to.

'This way. We're in the drawing room. I've completely revamped it for our paying guests, so if anyone spills so much as a drop of wine I'll have something to say.'

'I'll bear that in mind.'

'Sorry. I didn't mean you. My brothers, you know.' Catherine wished he didn't always take her so literally. She drew him into the room, pleasingly illuminated by the newly cleaned chandelier, with a good log fire burning. It was a beautiful room, if she did say so herself, with the walls a pale pink and the ornate cornice picked out in cream and gold.

All four McDonald men turned as one. She wondered if it wasn't just a little intimidating.

'Come in, come in,' she said quickly. 'This is my father, Gordon.' She indicated the tall, patrician man with the shock of white hair, who nodded a faint acknowledgement.

'And my elder brother, Kerr. He's up from London for the weekend.' Kerr was the image of his father thirty years ago. Shining blond hair swept back from his brow, pale blue eyes, and a disdainful expression. This look was no doubt useful in hurtling him through the medical ranks in London's prestigious teaching hospitals, but Catherine did wish he wouldn't use it at home.

'This is John Hugo, my second brother. He lives in Edinburgh so he manages to get home a little more often.' John Hugo was another blond-haired, blue-eyed beauty, but his hair was shorter and the newly acquired moustache meant he would never be mistaken for a younger version of Gordon. Unlike his father and older brother, he

47

smiled and came forward to shake hands.

'And this is Malcolm, who you've met already. Right, what would you like to drink? Mal will get it for you.' As her youngest brother went about his duties Catherine was struck once again by how divided her family were in their looks. She and Malcolm favoured their mother, with dark hair and eyes. They could almost be cuckoos in the nest, amongst the fair McDonalds. Except that they *weren't*. And it was her mother's money that allowed them all to stay here, never forget that.

'Come sit down,' said her father, waving their visitor magnanimously into a seat at his side. 'Do tell us about yourself, my boy. Eddlington-Smith, I believe Catherine said your name was? Sounds vaguely familiar. What's your family background?'

Catherine thought she had outgrown being embarrassed by her father, but apparently it wasn't so. She scarcely dared glance at Haydn. Would Gordon never learn his attitudes simply weren't acceptable these days?

She needn't have worried. Haydn was quite able to look after himself. 'Odd name, isn't it?' he said affably.

Gordon looked over his half-moon glasses, waiting for more. When none was forthcoming he said, 'I see. And what part of the country are you from? Hampshire? Surrey?'

'Yes, thereabouts,' said Haydn.

Gordon pushed his glasses up his nose so that he could look through them. Catherine realised he was examining the tie in the hope it would provide him with some clues. Honestly! Didn't he realise no one wore their old school tie these days?

48

'Went to Harrow, did you?' he barked, removing the glasses in a gesture that indicated to his family that he was satisfied with what he had seen.

Catherine and Kerr sat up with a start. Kerr looked at the visitor with renewed interest, Catherine with suspicion.

'Yes, I was a scholarship boy,' said Haydn, smiling. 'Good school, of course. We would never have been able to afford it otherwise.'

Gordon harrumphed. 'And what did you do then,' he paused for effect, 'before you retired?'

'Oh, this and that.' Haydn smiled and took a small sip from his glass.

'Weren't you involved in finance?' asked Kerr, eyes narrowed as though trying to recall something. 'Or one of those dot-com businesses?'

'No. I've worked mostly in the engineering field.'

Gordon's ears pricked up. He liked to think of himself as an engineer, although as far as Catherine could see he was nothing more than an up-market (and not entirely successful) salesman. 'What sort of business? Who did you say you worked for?'

After a moment's hesitation, Haydn said, 'Actually, I worked for myself.'

Kerr leant forward. 'Eddlington-Smith? Why, I know who you are.' His slim face was now alight with interest. 'Don't you run your own company? Something or other Engineering Solutions? Been developing some very interesting micro-technologies in the medical field. Anything to do with you?'

Haydn gave a small smile. 'Yes, I suppose you

could say I was involved with that. But as I said, I've retired now.'

Kerr didn't seem to notice that Haydn wasn't keen to pursue the subject. 'You sold out, didn't you?' he said. 'I read about it in the papers. You were doing good work. I hope the new owners take as much interest in these technologies as you did.'

'I'm sure they will. There's money in them, so why wouldn't they?'

Catherine turned to study Haydn a little closer. From what Kerr said, this man was – or had been – a successful businessman. A rather well-known one. What on earth was he doing up here in that tiny cottage?

'And how do you all occupy yourselves?' asked Haydn, looking around at his hosts. He seemed keen to move the conversation away from himself.

Catherine said, 'Kerr's a doctor, John Hugo is in banking, and Father works in sales.'

Her father frowned at her. 'I market specialist machinery to the top end of the oil and gas industry. We do not call that sales.'

'All very interesting occupations,' said Haydn.

'And Malcolm does nothing at all,' said John Hugo, smirking when Malcolm glared.

'Yet,' said Haydn. 'Still plenty of time.'

'Not when he's living at my expense,' said Gordon.

'Actually, I thought it was Catherine who paid most of the bills these days,' said Malcolm. 'Seeing as she was the one Mother left all the money to.'

'She didn't leave it to me,' said Catherine quickly, glancing at Haydn. His expression re-

50

mained politely disinterested. 'We've been through that a hundred times and we're certainly not going through it again now.'

'Absolutely not,' agreed Kerr. 'Now, Mr Eddlington-Smith...'

'Haydn, please. An unfortunate eccentricity of my mother's.'

'Haydn. What is it that has brought you to this part of the world?'

'Who wouldn't want to settle here?' said Haydn. 'It's beautiful and it's peaceful. I'll keep on my flat in London, but I intend to spend most of my time here.'

'My sons don't seem able to appreciate it. They seem to prefer the city life, said Gordon, as though he spent all his time at home. 'Catherine seems to be the only one that has inherited the McDonald passion for the land.'

'Not the land, exactly,' said Catherine. 'Seeing as we don't have any left. But I'm determined to put the house to good use.'

'Time will tell if you succeed,' said her father. 'And think of all the damned money you'll have wasted if you don't.' He narrowed his eyes as he surveyed the beautifully restored ceiling rose. Catherine wanted to point out it wasn't *his* money, but managed to hold her tongue.

Haydn seemed about to speak, and she wondered if he intended to defend her. It would have been rather nice, although of course she didn't need defending. However, John Hugo got in first.

'I want to hear more about this woman who disappeared near here. I've read a little in the papers, but what's the local angle? Always best to

51

hear things firsthand.'

'Ah, the Lost Woman,' said Malcolm, perking up. 'And it will be firsthand, if she'll talk. Catherine was the last person to see her.'

Catherine favoured him with a glare. She really wished he hadn't brought that up now, when she had been doing so well at forgetting.

'Really?' said her father, eyebrows raised. 'How unfortunate.'

'It was,' said Catherine.

'The police have been here to question her I don't know how many times.'

'Twice.'

'And hundreds of journalists have tried and failed.' Malcolm was grinning.

'Seems an ordinary story to me,' said Kerr. 'Although the press did get rather obsessed. Still, if we have such a personal angle, why not fill us in?'

'I'd rather...' Catherine looked around at the five pairs of eyes fixed upon her and sighed. She might as well give in, and then maybe people would leave her alone.

She paused for a moment to collect her thoughts, letting them drift back.

'One Saturday morning a few weeks ago I noticed someone park a maroon car at the foot of the track. You can see the entrance from my office, and it's very irritating when someone parks there. Why can't people park at the picnic site down the road? They've no idea how dangerous it is, the way it blocks your view of traffic coming down the loch... Anyway, let's just say I noticed this woman. She got out and walked slowly up the track, staring at the house the whole time. She stopped at our gates, as though she might be about to come in.' Catherine frowned and couldn't help glancing at Haydn. 'People do, despite the Private sign. Anyway, Pip started barking so I thought I'd let him out to stretch his legs. I've found that if you put in an appearance it tends to make the sightseers hurry on.'

'Unless they're the chatty kind,' said Malcolm, with feeling born of experience.

'I know how to deal with the chatty kind. Pip and I were just coming out of the side door as she passed and she sort of started, and stared at us in a furtive way. I called 'Good Afternoon' and she said the same, then stared again, then hurried on. The last I saw was her opening and closing the deer fence gate at the back. I was pleased to see that she did close it, some people don't bother despite all the signs... And that was it.'

'What did she look like?' asked Malcolm.

'Late forties, I'd say. Shortish, greying blond hair. Wore a kind of old-fashioned anorak and rather silly pink mittens. That's about all I noticed.'

'Did she look unhappy?' Malcolm's questions made Catherine recall his intention of looking into the disappearance and she frowned.

'Look, I only saw her for a moment. I don't remember any expression at all.'

'You said she was furtive,' pointed out Malcolm.

'That was just the impression I got, which annoyed me. It was the staring thing all over again, like when she was looking at the house, but she wasn't so open about it when she saw me.'

'So what happened next?' said John Hugo.

'When did you realise that she had disappeared?'

'I noticed her car was still there the following morning, but I didn't think much of it. Sometimes people walk all the way to Loch Erricht and get a friend to meet them there. They eventually get around to picking their car up.'

'Did she have a rucksack?' asked Malcolm quickly. 'You'd expect her to have had one, for a long trek like that.'

Catherine frowned and for the first time in weeks made an effort to recall the woman properly. She thought she remembered a stolid figure, slightly hunched. 'I don't think she was carrying anything.'

'Not very practical for the mountains in winter,' said Kerr.

'So was it you who reported her missing?' said John Hugo.

'No, it wasn't.' Catherine wasn't sure whether to be relieved she wasn't the one who had put the whole search into action, or feel guilty that she hadn't started it sooner. 'It was Colin McConnell. He keeps his eyes open, does Colin. He'd apparently noticed the car in the car park of the Foresters Arms, and then saw it had been left here longer than was normal, so he came up to the house to ask what I knew about it.'

'Good old Constable McPlod,' said Gordon disdainfully. He had no time for the local bobby since he had been caught speeding on the road from Pitlochry. 'Glad to know he's good for something.'

'It started off as just an enquiry into an abandoned car. And then they started worrying about the woman. She'd spent the night before at the Foresters but hadn't said anything about plans for a walk. And that was it. They never found any trace of her.'

'She could have walked through to Loch Erricht, got a lift back to the A9, and disappeared to wherever she came from,' said Kerr. 'Why are they so sure she didn't?'

'They're not sure about anything,' said Catherine. 'Anyway, it's not that big a story. It must have been a slow news week, early January. The tabloids picked it up and decided to run with it. Unfortunately.'

'It was the mystery aspect that got them hooked,' said Malcolm. 'The use of what turned out to be a false name and address. Nothing that could identify her left in the car. And no body.'

Catherine suppressed a shudder. She didn't want to think about the Lost Woman. She was busy launching Exclusive Activity Holidays. She hated to think she might have been at fault. Had something bad happened to the woman? Was there something she could have done to prevent it?

'Very interesting, I'm sure,' said Gordon. 'Now, tell me Haydn, do you play bridge?'

After a couple of drinks, Haydn politely took himself off. Catherine walked with the visitor to the door.

'Thank you for a very pleasant time,' said Haydn politely, looking down on her with that slightly amused expression he had.

'Thank you for coming. I'm sorry about Father. I should perhaps have warned you...'

55

'An, er, fascinating character. Indeed, you have a very remarkable family.' He hesitated and then said, 'And if you could all keep quiet about the whole business being sold off thing, I'd appreciate it. It's not really of interest to people round here, is it?'

'Oh... Of course. No problem.' Although Catherine couldn't really see why it should matter.

She wanted to prolong the moment, to stay and chat with him and not to have to deal with the cross-currents of her family. But the food was almost ready and her father hated to be kept waiting. And he had been hinting all day that he had *something important* to tell them. Better not to upset him just now. She smiled her goodbye to Haydn and went back inside.

Chapter Six

The family took their seats at one end of the gleaming dining-room table, with food brought up from the kitchen by Catherine and a reluctant Malcolm. The room was filled, like the rest of the house, with solid Scottish furniture, Edinburgh copies of fashionable London designs of the late eighteenth and early nineteenth centuries. The covered dishes were set out on the mahogany sideboard that Gordon claimed to be a Chippendale original but probably wasn't.

John Hugo busied himself with the wine and Kerr made polite conversation with their father, but the atmosphere was strained. They were all waiting.

And Gordon seemed to be having difficulty bringing himself to speak, as though he was nervous. Catherine wasn't used to him being nervous.

'You'd better start eating,' she said as she sat down with her own plate. 'You know how cold everything gets, having to trek it all the way up here from the kitchen.'

Her father looked at her through narrowed eyes, guessing correctly that this comment was aimed at him.

'Venison?' said Kerr, inhaling with pleasure. 'There's one thing I have to say for you, Catherine, you're a very good cook when it comes to the more traditional cuisine.'

'Why thank you.'

'I've found this rather good South African pinotage,' said John Hugo to his father. 'I bought a case. I'd be interested in your opinion.'

Kerr immediately raised his own glass to sniff and taste. He fancied himself rather a wine buff too, an opinion not shared by his father and brother. 'Passable,' he said.

Gordon reached for the bottle and made a show of examining the label. He was definitely playing for time.

It was Malcolm's patience which snapped first.

'So, Father,' he said. 'What's the big occasion? Why have we all been summoned here?'

His father gave him a cool look. 'I was under the impression that *you* were here whether you were summoned or not.'

'Well, I meant Kerr and John Hugo.'

'It is good to have my family around me again,' said Gordon. They all looked at him in amazement. 'It's a long time since we were all together.'

'We were all together at Christmas,' said Catherine.

'That was entirely different. Georgie was here as well, and that strange young woman Kerr had in tow. She seemed to be there every time I looked around. I prefer guests who keep themselves to themselves.'

'Marguerite was making an effort to get to know you,' said Kerr with a frown. 'It's a shame she was unable to come this weekend. She had been asked to cover for her consultant.'

'She wasn't invited,' said Gordon. He took a swallow of his wine. 'Rather good,' he said after a long pause. 'Possibly do with another year in the cellar. But not bad at all.' He gave his second son a nod of approval, while Kerr still glowered at the slight to his girlfriend.

'Your food's getting cold,' said Catherine to her father.

'I'll eat when I'm ready. And I thought you were all desperate to hear what I have to say?' He paused and surveyed them.

No one spoke. Kerr took another forkful of food and pretended to be bored. The others waited anxiously.

'I'm pleased to be able to tell you,' said Gordon. 'That I shall shortly be remarrying.'

Catherine felt the blood drain from her face. 'Marrying?'

She took a large swallow of wine which did nothing to calm her. 'You're getting *married?*'

'Yes, that is what I said.'

She couldn't take it in. 'Who to?' He had never seemed interested in any particular woman, had certainly never brought one home. And now, suddenly, this. She felt as though she had been struck.

Gordon cleared his throat. 'As you know, I've been working in the States a great deal over the last two years. I've got to know a few people, and one of them is this wonderful woman. She has done me the honour of agreeing to be my wife.' Now the announcement was made he seemed able to relax. He began to attack his food.

'But who is she?' asked Kerr.

'Have we met her?' said John Hugo.

'What's she like?' said Malcolm.

Gordon swallowed his mouthful before replying. 'The lady's name is Phyllida Blenheim, or Phyllida Dubrovsky as she has reverted to. Blenheim was her first husband. Texan. In the oil business. Know him slightly myself.'

'But this is such a surprise,' said Catherine. She felt a cold, horrified amazement. 'You never said anything, you've never even mentioned her.'

Her father met her gaze coldly. 'My life is my business. And I don't see why you should be surprised. Your mother was a very...' he caught Catherine's expression and changed whatever he had been going to say. '...a very special woman. But it is eight years now since she passed away.'

'Yes, but...' To Catherine it sometimes seemed like only yesterday, at others an eternity. Life would never be the same without her mother, but she had tried so hard to carry on. How could her father replace his beautiful, clever, long-suffering first wife? She swallowed. 'Tell us more about this ... Phyllida.'

'She's a lovely lady. You'll all like her. She's looking forward to meeting you.' Catherine wondered if he realised this told them absolutely nothing.

Kerr was tapping his fork on the table in a very irritating way. 'And when might we have that pleasure?'

'I shall bring her home after my next trip, probably about mid-March. I want her to get to know you all.'

Catherine thought of what she planned to be doing in a month's time. Her first two courses would be over, and there would be a short break before the third. She was hoping to embark on an orgy of publicity in preparation for the summer. She was even prepared to be interviewed by those intrusive women's magazines, if that was what it took. She didn't have time for *this*.

'You're bringing her to Scotland?' She felt suddenly sick. He did realise this was impossible, didn't he?

'Correct.'

Catherine stared at him. 'Father, we really want to meet her, of course, but, but ... I have to remind you that I'm on the brink of launching a new business. You can't bring her here, to the house. I'm really not going to have much free time.'

'You will make time for my fiancée.'

'I don't think you realise how much work Exclusive Activity Holidays is going to take. I can't neglect it at this crucial stage.'

Her father persisted, as ever. 'I told Phyllida you were trying your hand at a little paying hospitality. She's very impressed with your resourcefulness. But I won't accept that as an excuse not to make her welcome.'

'Of course we'll make her welcome,' said Catherine automatically. How could her father do this to her? If he had to remarry, which he didn't, he really didn't, but if he had to – why now? 'You'll be using the East Lodge, of course.'

'Phyllida is looking forward to seeing Annat House.'

'This house is a *business*,' said Catherine.

'I'm sure we can work something out,' said John Hugo, always the one least happy to upset his father.

'Of course we can,' said Gordon, smiling at him. He suddenly changed tack, which was another annoying habit. 'Well, I suppose Malcolm can show Phyllida around a little when Catherine is busy. He might as well make himself useful.'

Catherine glared. 'I'm hoping that Malcolm is going to help me.'

For once Malcolm didn't contradict her. Any number of 'exclusive' guests were clearly preferable to his prospective step-mother. He kept his head down and ate quickly.

'Phyllida and I will stay in the house here, of course,' said Gordon, continuing as though Catherine hadn't spoken.

'Father, *no.*'

'This is my ancestral home. It is *right* that she should stay here.' Her father fixed her with a glassy stare. 'The new blue room will suit very well. I

61

want everything of the best for dear Phyllida. She's so excited to be visiting the home of the McDonalds. I won't have her disappointed.'

'Father, I'll just have started taking guests. You agreed...'

'This is my house. I want Phyllida to enjoy it at its best.'

Catherine didn't know whether to scream or to cry. Of course the house was at its best. She had done her utmost to ensure that. And not for the benefit of some American woman who had caught her father's eye.

'I'll be more than happy to show her the sights of Edinburgh,' said John Hugo. His siblings glared at him.

'Does this Phyllida have any children?' asked Kerr. That was one of the questions Catherine had been planning to ask herself. Like how old was this woman, how long had marriage been on the cards, how could she possibly, possibly match up to Rachel Catherine McDonald, his first wife?

She had never understood her parents' marriage. Perhaps the children never do. In the wedding photos they had both seemed so happy, her mother darkly pretty, her father fair and handsome, looking genuinely in love. Or was that just for the camera? She tried to remember back to her childhood, but her father hadn't featured much. In the later years he had been away even more, and she had assumed that her mother was, like the children, relieved.

Gordon looked around the table. 'Phyllida has no children, fortunately. I think I have quite enough for both of us.'

62

'It's not as if we're a great burden on you,' said John Hugo.

Gordon's expression was grim. It was not the burden of the children, but what had happened to his late wife's money that really rankled with him.

Sometimes Catherine suspected he thought Rachel had died just to spite him. It was her money that had enabled them to live the life he felt he was due. His own salary, although reasonable, would never have supported a place the size of Annat House. Now the money was in trust for the children, and Catherine had had the *audacity* to turn his home into a business.

'And when are you getting married?' she asked. Best to know the worst.

'We're thinking of a spring wedding, but we can agree the details once Phyllida is here. We'll marry in Kinlochannat kirk, of course. She's so excited about coming to Scotland.'

Catherine's spirits fell as her father's words began to sink in. He was re-marrying. Replacing her mother. This woman would be arriving in a few weeks time. How long would she be staying at Annat? Until the wedding? Forever?

Kerr raised his wine glass and said, 'Well, this has been a bit of a surprise. How about a toast to Father and his bride-to-be? I don't think we've even said congratulations yet.'

Gordon nodded. This was more like it. Her brothers lifted their glasses willingly enough, probably to ready them for a much-needed refill. Catherine sighed and followed suit.

The remainder of the meal passed far too slowly, with occasional snippets of information about

Phyllida Dubrovsky leaking out, despite Gordon's apparent reluctance. Catherine gathered that the woman was about ten years his junior, very handsome, and, probably, very rich. She could see how attractive that would be for Gordon. Her heart sank even further. Did this mean he would have enough money to take over the running of Annat House?

After they had finished, Catherine took a tray of coffee to the drawing room. Malcolm had disappeared but Kerr and John Hugo remained with their father.

'Father,' Catherine said, as she handed him a black coffee in one of the beautiful porcelain cups that she was planning to use for her paying guests. 'You agreed to move to the Lodge. Phyllida can't come to live in the house. It's just not possible.'

'I'll say what's possible.' said her father.

Catherine tried to soften her tone. 'You won't like it, Father. There'll be all sorts of people around.'

'I don't want anyone else here for Phyllida's first week,' said her father. 'Remember, this is still *my* house. This is where she will be welcomed.'

'But I've already taken bookings, I've employed staff, I can't stop now.'

'All I'm asking is for one week of peace. Is that too much? Why do my family always want to thwart me?'

'Of course we don't want to thwart you,' said John Hugo.

Gordon ignored him. 'I want everything to be perfect for dear Phyllida.'

'You think your ... this Phyllida is going to be

64

happy living in the East Lodge?' said Kerr. 'One week of luxury is hardly going to hide the reality from her.'

Gordon observed them over the top of his glasses. 'Oh, it's not a permanent arrangement. After the wedding we will be making our home in the States.'

There was another very long silence. Kerr and John Hugo looked thoughtful, but Catherine felt as though she had received another blow. Instead of feeling relieved, she now felt hurt. Her father was not just remarrying, he was moving out, leaving the country. What did that say about her?

As soon as she decently could, Catherine picked up the tray and escaped to the kitchen. She had to think. All that wine followed by too much strong coffee was making her head spin.

Had she driven him away? Catherine knew she hadn't turned out to be the daughter he had wanted. She hadn't made a good marriage to the right sort of man. But with her parents' marriage as an example, did he really think she wanted to go down that road? And then she had refused to fall in with his second choice role for her – that of devoted daughter staying at home to keep house.

And now he was going. She wouldn't be lonely without him, of course not, she'd be far too busy for that. She would concentrate on sorting out her plans that, yet again, he had disrupted, and she would *not* feel guilty.

Chapter Seven

'Have you found out anything else?' Malcolm asked Mhairi the following morning. He'd rather speak to her than anyone in his own bloody family.

He perched himself on the edge of Catherine's desk in the office. Catherine had gone to Pitlochry, so it was safe to come in here.

Mhairi looked up from the pile of papers on her own desk. 'Found anything out about what?'

She was frowning, not pleased by his interruption. He should have thought to bring her a coffee, that would have been a better start. Why did he never think about these things beforehand?

He gave her his best smile. 'About the Lost Woman, of course. We got Catherine to talk about her last night.' He hurried on, he didn't want to think about what else had been discussed last night. 'It's the first time I've really heard about Catherine's sighting. You know how secretive she's been.'

Mhairi had turned back to her work, but after a moment she looked up again. 'So, what did she say?'

'Not a lot,' admitted Malcolm. It was nice to have Mhairi looking at him like that, interested. Her short, oddly-coloured hair was gelled up in its best peak, the jewels in nose and ears glinting piratically, eyes narrowed as she waited for him to

66

say more. He had to think of something else to say. 'You know, I wonder if Catherine's feeling guilty that she didn't take more interest.' He told Mhairi what his sister had said, as best as he could remember. It wasn't much. The description wasn't even as good as the one he had got from the receptionist at the Foresters.

'It's odd, isn't it? Apparently she asked at the hotel for directions to Annat House.'

'I know. I wonder why.' Mhairi narrowed her eyes in thought. 'She must have been planning something, to be so careful to leave no clues. But if it was suicide, where is the body? And if it wasn't, then what was she doing?'

'I'm going to have a look myself,' said Malcolm impulsively. 'I know these hills as well as anyone does.' He looked out of the window. The clouds had settled on the mountains beyond the loch and a drizzle was beginning. 'Not today, though. The forecast is better for tomorrow, I'll go then.' It would also get him out of the house.

'You think you'll be able to find something when Mountain Rescue, the police, and the sniffer dogs couldn't? Aye, that's likely.'

'You never know,' said Malcolm, determined not to be distracted now. 'And it might give me some ideas, just walking the path she took.'

'But you won't know which path she took, will you?'

'Paths, then. I can check them out.'

'Why are you so interested?' said Mhairi, examining him with her head on one side.

'I don't know. It just … doesn't feel right. And anyway, it'll give me something to think about

67

other than wondering why Father has got it into his head to marry again.' Shit. He hadn't meant to bring that up.

'He's *what?*'

'Haven't you heard?' Malcolm pretended to be surprised. It was true that Catherine usually told Mhairi all the news, but this morning she had been tight-lipped and desperate to get out of the house. 'It's no big deal,' he said untruthfully, but Mhairi looked so interested he provided her with the few details he had.

'And he's going to live in the States?' asked Mhairi.

'Apparently.'

'I should think that will make Catherine's life a wee bit easier. How did she take to the idea of a step-mother?'

For once Malcolm considered before he spoke. 'She wasn't happy. She mostly seemed worried about how it would impact on her business. That's what she said, anyway.'

'Mmm,' said Mhairi. 'Well, well, well.' She smiled into the distance, probably thinking of the mileage she could get out of this gossip in the village. Then she straightened up. 'Look, I really need to get on here. You're interrupting me.'

'I don't see why you have to work on a Saturday.'

'Because there are things to do.' Her smile disappeared. 'If you're not going to help, leave me be.'

Malcolm hesitated. 'Look, why don't you come exploring with me tomorrow? You know the hills nearly as well as I do.' He held his breath. He had phrased the invitation casually, but that didn't mean it wasn't important.

'*Nearly* as well as you? I know them a bloody sight better.'

'All the more reason for you to come.' Malcolm wondered why she had to take everything he said the wrong way. 'It'd be good if you did. Two heads are better than one.'

'I don't know.'

'Wouldn't you like to try and find out what happened?'

'Well...' She pursed her lips and Malcolm waited. 'I s'pose it might be interesting. As long as we don't have to get up at the crack of dawn. Sunday is the one day I get to sleep in.'

'Brilliant,' said Malcolm, his smile widening. 'I'll see you at the Foresters tonight and we can make arrangements. OK?'

'I must be mad.'

Malcolm left quickly. He thought he had done pretty well there, getting in the idea of a drink as well as the walk. Perhaps things were looking up at last.

Catherine had gone into Pitlochry because she couldn't bear to be in the same house as her father. She had lain awake most of the night, furious with him. She knew it was eight years, she knew her father had probably had girlfriends since then. But she had never thought he would let anyone take her mother's place.

She kept her head down as she stalked around Pitlochry. She had no time to chat with her all-too-numerous acquaintances. The only way to avoid these was to keep her eyes fixed firmly on the pavement. This was why she didn't see Haydn

Smith until the very last moment. He had to put a hand out to prevent her walking straight in to him.

'Hello there,' he said cheerfully. 'Goodness, you were worlds away. How are you doing?'

'I, er...' Catherine focussed on him with an effort. He was so much taller than her she had to look up and the drizzle fell into her eyes over the brim of her natty little hat. She rubbed it away. 'I was thinking. Sorry.'

'Miserable day, isn't it?'

'I've seen worse,' said Catherine, wondering if he was going to be one of those English people who moaned at every drop of rain. If so, she thought grimly, he was going to have an awful lot of moaning to do.

'I'm sure you have. Look, why don't we go and have a coffee? Then I can thank you for your hospitality yesterday evening and you can tell me the best places to shop here. You know what a premium I place on local knowledge.'

Catherine hesitated. She didn't feel like making polite conversation, but then she didn't feel like going home either. Eventually she acquiesced, indicating the long low building at the south end of the shopping street which was her own preferred café.

After they had placed their orders Catherine said, with forced cheeriness, 'And how are you settling in? I don't think I got a chance to ask you yesterday.'

'Rather well, as it happens. The folk in the village are very friendly, and the cottage is just as I hoped it would be.'

'You hadn't seen it before you bought it, had

70

you?' Catherine found that amazing.

'No. I was over in California. Sometimes one has to go with one's gut instinct. I knew it wouldn't stay on the market long. It seemed to be just what I'd been looking for and so it has proved.'

'You haven't seen any really bad weather yet, remember.'

'I'm sure it won't be the weather that will put me off.'

He sat back while their coffees and muffins were placed on the table, regarding both with approval.

'Now,' he said, smiling across at her. 'What was it that had you so lost in thought? From the expression on your face you might have been trying to decide on the best way to dispose of the body.' He grimaced. 'Oops, sorry, possibly not a good analogy in the circumstances.'

'I wasn't thinking about the Lost Woman,' said Catherine.

'You weren't'?'

'I've a lot on my plate at the moment, what with staff to train and the first guests arriving.'

'And, of course, you have your father and brothers at home just now. That could either be a big help, or a hindrance.' He smiled and waited.

Catherine scowled at him. He probably wasn't going to give up, so why not do what she really wanted to do and talk about the news her father had broken the evening before? Perhaps discussing it with a stranger would help.

She said abruptly, 'After you left last night, my father told us he is planning to remarry.'

She frowned at the bowl containing little paper twists of sugar. When he didn't reply immediately she glanced up and found an expression of polite, slightly amused interest on his handsome face. 'And you don't like it,' he said.

'Of course, it's his decision and there's no earthly reason he shouldn't... No, I don't like it at all.'

'I wonder why that is,' he said.

'Because...' said Catherine. How could she possibly put it into words? 'Because he shouldn't! Because he wasn't a good husband to my mother. He should mourn her, she was worth so much more. And he should think of his children, not go off to live in the States. He is our *father*, for heaven's sake.'

'He's moving to the States, is he?'

'Yes. His wife-to-be is American, and wealthy. We've never met her, hadn't even heard of her before yesterday, but what do we matter?'

'Will you miss him a great deal?'

Catherine was horrified to feel a cold wave of loss threaten to overwhelm her. 'Of course not. He's hardly here as it is. It's just... It's all so sudden. And he's making me change all my arrangements.'

'Hmm...' Haydn stirred sugar into his black coffee and leant back in his chair to study her. 'And you don't like being forced to change your arrangements.'

Catherine glared at him. Of course she didn't. Who would? 'He's bringing this woman over in a few weeks' time. It's going to mean a lot of hassle.'

'I'm sure it's difficult, thinking of someone taking your mother's place.'

'No one could take my mother's place,' she said grimly.

72

'Of course not. I would have liked to meet her. Your family is very … interesting.'

'I *loved* my mother,' said Catherine. She could feel the tears prickling in her eyes as she said the words. 'She was special. You would have liked her, everyone did.'

'It's often struck me as strange how many more perfect dead people there are than perfect live ones,' said Haydn.

His tone was bland, he smiled lazily at her, and it took her a moment to work out his meaning. 'My mother *was* amazing,' said Catherine with an angry toss of her head, tears forgotten. 'Ask anyone. I didn't say she was perfect, but she was...' She ran out of words and said, again, 'Special.' Her mother had made her feel special, too.

'Are you like her?'

Catherine frowned. 'People say so. To look at, at least.'

'Then she was clearly very attractive.' Before she could respond to this surprising comment, he had continued. 'Did you lose her recently? If so, I suppose one can understand your feelings.'

'Well, no, not that recently. It's eight years ago, actually. Eight years last month.'

Haydn took a sip from his cup and allowed the silence to stretch a little. He was probably waiting for her to admit how immature she was being. Well, there was absolutely no chance of that.

Eventually he said, 'People do remarry, you know, whether after a death or a divorce. And eight years is a long time.'

Catherine glowered at him. Eight years didn't feel like a long time to her. 'It's not right,' she said.

He smiled faintly. 'Really, do you think you should take this so much to heart? Your father is an adult, and so are you.'

This was not the sort of advice Catherine needed. She took a bite of her very good muffin, so that she wouldn't have to speak for a while.

After that Haydn changed the subject. He chatted about London and California and how different it was here. Catherine allowed herself to be distracted, but as she drove the meandering road back to Kinlochannat the anger and hurt returned. She turned the radio on, and then off again. She couldn't help going over everything in her mind, wondering if things could have been different. She remembered how delighted and amazed she had been when her father had finally agreed to let her have her way with Annat House. Had he been planning this, even then? Or had her plans pushed him into it? Haydn pondered on the fact that it was eight years since Esme had walked out on him. He had got over that, hadn't he? So surely Catherine could get over the loss of her mother. He was surprised she was so upset at her father remarrying.

Gordon McDonald hadn't struck him as an easy person to have around. He would have thought Catherine would be pleased to be rid of him.

Haydn felt a vast relief that he no longer had to put up with people he didn't like. He didn't need to seek finance, to manage staff, to find new markets. Those shackles had been removed. And it was now so long since he and the *honourable* Esme had separated the press were no longer watching his every move.

Yes, he was free of it all. He drove back to the cottage and prepared to do exactly what he wanted with the rest of his life. He just needed to decide what that was.

Chapter Eight

The sky was a very pale blue and a light breeze was already blowing away the last of the morning mist when Malcolm and Mhairi set off the next morning. True, the streams were torrents of brown water and the flattened grass and bracken bore witness to a fierce storm the night before, but just now all was bright and peaceful.

'Bloody good day for it,' said Malcolm with satisfaction. 'I brought coffee and sandwiches. We can stay out till dusk if need be.'

'Hmmph,' said Mhairi. She was not at her most cheerful first thing, although she looked very fine in her multicoloured woollen jacket with a rainbow-hued crocheted hat pulled low over her short hair. The jewel in her nose glinted. She looked like a grouchy ornamental bird amongst the washed-out browns and greens of the hills.

They strode briskly up the broad stony path that marked the beginning of the climb.

'I don't know what you expect to find,' Mhairi said.

'We're just looking, OK?' Malcolm surveyed the landscape. To their right was a stone dyke that stretched for miles into the hills and mountains above. To their left a slope of rust-coloured bracken fell to the tumultuous stream. At this point there was only the one path, so she would have had to come this way. Once they reached the open expanse of the heather-covered slopes above it would be a different matter. 'We should have brought Pip,' he said.

Mhairi sniggered. 'Pip as a sniffer dog? I cannae see it.'

'I didn't mean that, stupid. I meant to give him a walk. Catherine never takes him for long walks these days.'

'She doesn't have the time. And anyway, Pip doesn't like long walks. He likes nothing better than to sit by the radiator in Catherine's office, and snore.'

'We should get a proper dog,' said Malcolm. He remembered the two Labradors they had had in his childhood, one black, one yellow. Tinker, the older one, had loved to range over the hills. She always chose the path that led away from home, full of a boundless energy that his mother had adored. The dogs had died one soon after the other while his mother was ill, and nobody had bothered to replace them. 'I wouldn't mind another Lab.'

'Oh, aye, and who'll look after it when you go away?'

'Who says I'm going away?'

Mhairi sniffed. 'Well, you're not doing a whole lot here, are you? I presumed you were just biding time until you decided what it is you want to do. If you ever do.'

Malcolm pushed the dark, wavy hair from his eyes and glared. Why did everyone, absolutely everyone, have to get on his case? He *hated* being forced into things. 'I'm helping Catherine.'

'Hardly. If you helped her more there wouldn't be so much for me to do.'

'So it's a good thing I don't, or you'd be out of a job.'

Mhairi thrust her hands into the pockets of her bright coat. 'I just don't get it, how you can hang around and do nothing for so long.'

'I don't do nothing.'

'Near enough.'

'Look who's talking about hanging around,' said Malcolm, stung. 'At least I've been away, gone to university. You've never lived anywhere but Kinlochannat your whole life.'

'There's nothing wrong with Kinlochannat,' said Mhairi, but her tone was less certain and Malcolm took the opportunity to push his point home.

'You had brilliant grades at school, I know you did. Why didn't you go away and do something with them? Why are you still living at home with your mum and dad?'

'You're still living at home.'

'Ah, but I've been away and come back. That's different.'

'You were made to go away, weren't you? To boarding school and that.'

'Yes, well.' Malcolm didn't like to think about boarding school. That was something else he'd been forced to do. It had meant he was away from home as his mother grew more and more ill. And he didn't like to think about that, either.

Bloody Mhairi, why did she have to bring it up?

They walked on in silence for a while. Mhairi concentrated on picking her way across a slippery section of tree roots, her head bowed. Once they had emerged from the little copse of Scots pine she said suddenly, 'Anyway, I didn't want to go away.'

Malcolm could sympathise with that. He was so relieved to be back. But at least he could say he had been somewhere else.

'It would do you good to travel a bit.' He nodded knowledgeably. 'Perhaps that's the disadvantage of being brought up in such a small community. You're kind of sheltered here. It must make it scary to go out into the big bad world at seventeen or eighteen.'

'I was not scared,' said Mhairi.

After another long pause, she returned to the attack. 'I've earned my living for the last four years, which is more than can be said for you. How can you still rely on your father for everything? It's degrading.'

Malcolm kicked a stone. 'I have an income of my own,' he said, and then immediately wished he hadn't. Mhairi wasn't to know that the money he got from the trust was negligible.

On cue, she snorted. 'You've got an income without working? That's even worse. You should be ashamed.'

'It's not much,' said Malcolm hastily. 'It was Mother's idea. We all get some, even Kerr and John Hugo, and they don't need it. But only Catherine can draw on the capital, or something like that.'

78

Mhairi blew air out loudly through puckered lips and scowled.

The conversation wasn't going the way he had intended at all. He held his tongue with an effort, determined not to be the one who provoked further argument. Then they reached a fork in the path, which brought his mind back to the job in hand. 'OK, onward and up over to Glen Erricht or do we branch off west towards the Annat Moor?' He looked one way and then the other, seeking inspiration. The mountains were closer now, white topped and glittering in the pale sunshine. 'I vote for Erricht.'

Mhairi paused, hands on hips. 'No, I disagree. If she was going for a really long hike like that she would have had a backpack with her. Catherine never mentioned a backpack, did she? I'd say she was going for a stroll for the views, in which case she'd go left here. You can see back down to the loch, it's a really pretty walk.'

'But how would she know that?'

'She'd guess. That's what she would think. Struggle up to the high hills, or follow the contour and get some views of the water. I know what most people would prefer.'

'How come you've got such a strong opinion all of a sudden?'

'It was your idea to come out here and see what we thought. And that's what I think.'

'We-ell.' Malcolm looked about again. He didn't have any better ideas. 'OK, have it your way. Now, this is when we really need to start looking for clues.'

Mhairi snorted again, but she did start looking

about more closely. Although what they would find, six weeks after the disappearance, and following countless other searches, was anyone's guess.

The day did not live up to Malcolm's high hopes, either in finding 'clues' or getting a bit closer to Mhairi. As they began to descend the hills in mid-afternoon, they were bickering once again, and they had not found one piece of evidence that might indicate the Lost Woman had passed that way before them.

'I said it was a stupid idea,' said Mhairi.

'You didn't have to come, did you?'

That put paid to any further conversation for a while. Malcolm did his best to look purposeful, scanning the ground to the left and right of the path, narrowing his eyes as he tried to picture what she might have done if she had come this way. They had found nothing along the contour path and had looped back up to the higher corries and trailed over a number of possible routes up there. Now they were back down among the bracken of the lower slopes.

'Let's walk along the banks of the burn,' he suggested.

'Why?'

'Why not?' His reason, if he had one, was a fascination with fast-flowing water. The churning brown of the burn today was as wild as anyone could wish. They scrambled down through the dead bracken, sliding over wiry mountain grass to the water's edge, and then continued their descent beside it.

They were almost back on familiar paths, with the trees above Annat House just coming into view, when Mhairi stopped so suddenly that he bumped right into her. He had been watching the dancing water of the burn, eyes drawn almost irresistibly to the whirling torrent, and so, apparently, had Mhairi. 'Look,' she said, pointing at the water's edge still hidden from his view. She clambered down over the stones and reached for something that had been caught by the eddies and deposited in a little side pool amongst leaves and twigs.

She rose, holding a sodden pink object between her finger and thumb.

'Bloody hell.' Malcolm almost fell into the burn in his eagerness to get to her side. 'What is it?'

Mhairi held the thing away from her, so that the drips didn't fall on her trousers, and frowned. 'I think it's a glove,' she said. 'It's sodden and filthy...'

'It's hers!' yelled Malcolm, hardly able to get the words out in his excitement. 'That's what Catherine said she was wearing – pink gloves or mittens or something. That's what it is, isn't it? We've found something of hers!'

'Do you think so?' Mhairi held the thing up higher, so they could both see. The water drained out of a bulky pink mitten. She was about to move it to her other hand when Malcolm grabbed her arm.

'No, don't do that, best not touch it any more. We've got to take this to the police. Immediately.'

'It's wool. It's hardly going to have finger prints on it, is it?' said Mhairi.

'You never know. DNA and ... stuff. Come on, I've got a bag we can put it in.'

He reached into his knapsack to find the plastic

bag that had held the sandwiches. He turned it inside out and held it open for Mhairi to drop in the specimen.

She rubbed her hand on her coat to dry it and then held it against her cheek. 'Phew. Wouldn't have wanted to hold on to that much longer. The water's icy.'

Malcolm tied a knot in the top of the bag and they set off down the hill once again, now at a much quicker pace. Then he paused. 'Perhaps we should look for other stuff, if we found this?'

'It'll get dark soon.'

'Just quickly then.'

They went back to the location of their find, which Malcolm had been careful to memorise, and looked rapidly about, along the banks of the burn, in the bracken. There was nothing else of interest.

'She could have dropped it on her way up, it could have been here since then,' said Mhairi.

'Or it could have been washed down from somewhere higher up, given the amount of rain over the last day or so.' Malcolm looked longingly up the route of the burn, but even he could see the sense in Mhairi's words about daylight. The afternoons were short at this time of year and the last thing they needed was to twist an ankle clambering over wet rocks in the dark.

They returned to their descent, their mood more harmonious than it had been all day. It was almost as if, with the find of the glove, Mhairi believed for the first time that the task might not be fruitless. She, too, began to produce all manner of improbable explanations for the disappearance. Her slim, pale face, that so often looked at Malcolm with faint dislike, was now lit with excitement.

Chapter Nine

'How could you?' demanded Catherine of Mhairi the next morning.

'How could I what?' said Mhairi, but she looked sheepish.

'Go off looking for clues,' Catherine said, adding with mounting annoyance, '*And* finding them. For Chrissake, the whole thing was just dying down nicely. This will have the police crawling all over us again, and our first visitors arrive on Friday. And then we've got this ... this American woman coming.'

'I didn't think we'd actually find anything,' said Mhairi apologetically.

'It's Malcolm. He has the luck of the devil. How many times does he win a raffle? I should have known not to let him go off like that.' And she would have stopped him, if she had thought for a moment anything would come of it. But it had seemed a good way to get the boy out of the house, and if it rekindled his friendship with Mhairi, so much the better. 'And don't you go talking about it to anyone. Mention it to one person in the village and the whole world will know.'

'I haven't said anything.'

Mhairis answer was too quick. Catherine

pounced. 'But Malcolm has?'

'Well, he didn't do it on purpose. But someone had seen the police car up here yesterday and when they asked him about it in the Forrie Arms, well, you can imagine.'

'He couldn't wait to regale them,' said Catherine bitterly. 'No doubt we'll have journalists and everyone up here before the morning is out. In which case, best to get to work now, there's no time to lose. Bring that clipboard, I want to do a tour of the bedrooms.'

Mhairi moved quickly to do as she was told. She was a good girl, Catherine didn't really blame her for this new inconvenience, even if it was she, apparently, who had first spotted The Clue. Now she hurried in Catherine's wake, pen in hand, waiting eagerly to note down all that still needed attention.

Catherine had hoped today she would feel in control once again. Her father and older brothers had departed, bookings were coming in nicely for *Scottish Geology* and *Botany of the Highlands*, a new member of staff had started, and the much-delayed furniture had been promised for the following day. She had put that Phyllida woman to the back of her mind, to be dealt with after the first guests had been and gone. Yes, she had had high hopes of things getting back to normal. And now this.

She sighed and turned her attention to the task at hand. It was the detail that was so important. 'We still need a mirror to hang in the Rose Room,' she said, looking about. 'Stewart will do that. And I don't think those pictures look right in here.

Let's take them down and see what else we have.'
She suited actions to words and lifted the two
gloomy portraits from the wall. The bedrooms
were looking beautiful, with their pale patterned
wallpapers and bright new curtains. But she didn't
want to lose the original, family-home feel of the
place, and it wasn't easy getting the balance right.
'Perhaps those sea views that are hanging on the
landing? Can you go and get them?'

Mhairi went dutifully off and Catherine moved
back to the doorway to review the room once
more. Yes, it definitely looked good. This had
been her mother's room, where she had collected
together some of the Hepplewhite furniture. The
clear lines and elegant proportions had appealed
to her. Catherine appreciated them, but to be
honest she felt the heavier pieces suited the house
best. She had left the Hepplewhite here although
she wasn't sure how she felt about strangers
using her mother's things.

She suppressed a sigh at the thought of how
much her mother would have liked the conveni-
ence of one of the en suite bathrooms in her last
months. Whatever happened, she was going to
make sure that Dubrovsky woman didn't sleep in
here.

She and Mhairi spent a very satisfactory morning reviewing all the accommodation and, except
for a few small tasks for Stewart, Catherine felt
they were just about there. Ha! So much for her
father's doubts. The whole place looked magnificent. They needed flowers for the hallway and
drawing room, and then she would to turn her
attention to food. She was about to ask Mhairi to

85

note these points when the phone went for the twentieth time that morning. It was, of course, excellent news to have so many enquiries, but sometimes she could do with a bit of peace.

'It's for you,' said Mhairi, holding her hand over the mouth piece. 'It's a Detective Inspector Cowan of Tayside Police.'

Catherine groaned. This was just what she had feared. They were taking the discovery of the pink mitten all too seriously.

The detective inspector announced he would be visiting Kinlochannat himself. He wanted to speak to Malcolm and Mhairi. He also wanted to see Catherine, which she felt really wasn't necessary. With an audible sigh, she agreed to his calling at Annat House the following afternoon.

'Perhaps he won't stay too long,' she said gloomily to Mhairi. 'He wants to talk to you, too. Your mother had told him you were here. Which reminds me, how is your mum feeling now?'

'She's much better.' Mhairi's small face lit up. 'The plaster comes off next week.'

'That's excellent. Now she's more mobile, I was wondering if she might do something for me.'

'Erm,' said Mhairi, the smile immediately replaced by that cagey expression so familiar to Catherine when she mentioned the things she would like people to do.

She was long inured to it, and continued brightly, 'It's the School Council. We need another non-parent member and I think she would be ideal. Mention it to her, will you?'

'I'm trying to get her to take things more easily,' protested Mhairi.

'Attending one meeting every couple of months won't do her any harm at all. It'll keep her in the village, might even stop her dashing out to all her wounded waifs when she's not on duty.' And give her a break from your father, thought Catherine, but didn't say it.

'Well,' said Mhairi, not convinced.

'And while I think about it,' continued Catherine. 'There's a meeting of the Community Council coming up and I said I'd try to get more young people to come along. It's your community too, you know, but all you youngsters do is complain about the lack of facilities. Why not use some of your energy to think about what facilities we do want, and how we might get them?'

Mhairi's expression changed from unenthusiastic to horrified. 'I'll probably be working at the Foresters,' she said quickly. 'I'm still doing a couple of evenings a week for Bob.'

'I'll find out which evening it is and let you know tomorrow. That'll give you enough time to change your shift, if need be.'

'But–'

'And, anyway, didn't we agree that with things getting busier here you wouldn't have time to keep helping Bob out?'

'I, er...'

'You're keeping other people out of a job.' Catherine could feel her mood improving as she set to putting the world – or at least her corner of it – to rights. 'I know Bob likes you because you're quick and reliable, but he really needs to take the time to train up one of the other girls in the village.'

'He could always take Malcolm on again,' said

Mhairi maliciously.

'No, I've got other plans for Malcolm. What about the O'Connor girl? She's still looking for work.'

'That's because you wouldn't take her on.'

'That was different. Here she'd have to work unsupervised, whereas Bob could keep an eye on her the whole time. It's not as if she's dishonest, just lazy.'

'Well, that's all right then,' said Mhairi.

'Yes, isn't it? You know, I think I'll have a word with Bob myself.'

Chapter Ten

A couple of days later Haydn Smith appeared at Annat House as Mhairi was packing up for the day. He thanked Catherine for sending Stewart down to see him.

'You can rely on Stewart,' said Catherine happily. She liked it when her plans worked out. 'Have you time for a drink?' When he nodded, she took him down to the kitchen which had almost completed the transition from family sanctuary to hotel workplace.

'Tell me how preparations are going for your grand opening. Everything in hand?'

'I hope so. There's still a lot to do, but I've no doubt we'll get there.' Surreptitiously, she crossed her fingers.

'I've no doubt you will.' Haydn paused, studying her thoughtfully. 'And how have you decided to cope with the advent of your father's fiancée?'

Catherine put her glass down. 'I've agreed to them staying here.' She scowled. She was still hurt and resentful. 'I decided it would be for the best, in the long run. We managed to rearrange the bookings for the week in question. We only had two people confirmed and I phoned them myself and apologised profusely and offered them a very good discount on the rearranged course. They were very nice about it. Most people are nice, you know.'

'That'll help your profits.'

'If this is really the last rearranging I have to do for the benefit of my father, it'll be well worth it.' Catherine realised she was hunching her shoulders and made herself relax.

If only it was all over. If only she could pin her father down to what would happen after that first week. He *had to* move out of the house and into the Lodge. The fact that Gordon had implied agreement didn't mean he would be willing to oblige when the time came. And once they were in the Lodge what was she going to do with them? The date of the wedding hadn't been fixed, nor the length of their stay specified.

'Everything will be fine,' she said firmly. 'By the way, we're planning a party to welcome Phyllida and introduce her to everyone. I hope you'll be able to come.' She mentioned the date. 'I'll send out official invitations, of course.'

'That's very kind of you. Although I expect to have my son staying with me as it's the Easter holidays.'

'Bring him along,' said Catherine easily. 'There are usually a few people with youngsters in tow. We'll put them in the television room with a stack of DVDs. They'll be fine.' If she was going to let her father back into Annat House for that week, they might as well make full use of the facilities.

'Most kind. Actually, that was another thing I wanted to consult with you about.' Haydn hesitated and for the first time he looked unsure of himself. 'How do you keep children occupied around here? I suppose I should introduce Richie to some boys his own age. I wondered if you knew anyone?'

Catherine stretched out and considered. 'Tell me a bit about him,' she said.

'He's eleven, as I said before.' Haydn paused. 'I suppose he's very much like any other eleven year old, not that I know much about them myself.'

'I'm sure they're all different,' said Catherine. 'What sorts of things does he like doing?'

'He likes computer games. And computer games. Oh, and football. Can't think why, never could stand it myself.'

'There are more than a few football-mad kids in the village. I'll get Mhairi to think of who is the right age. And I know someone else who might suit. Miles Hamilton. He might be a bit older but I'm pretty sure he's interested in that kind of stuff. The Hamilton family will be coming to the party, I'll introduce you.'

'That's very kind.'

'You're welcome. And I'll see what else I can think of.' Catherine was still wondering about the unease in his tone. Was there a problem with the

90

boy, or between him and his parents? She couldn't help asking, 'And Richie's mother, any news of her?'

Any information on Haydn's wife had so far eluded even the keenest of village gossips, although the general consensus was that they were separated. It was practically Catherine's duty to ask outright.

Haydn pressed his lips together. 'I believe she's in Spain.'

'Ah,' said Catherine, nodding sympathetically, hoping for more. 'Spain?'

'She moved there with her second husband a couple of years ago.' His tone was grim. Was he still upset by the split?

'So you're divorced?'

'Yes, that generally has to happen before one of the parties can remarry.'

Catherine glared. No need to be sarcastic. 'And your son lives with you, does he?'

'I have custody, yes. In principle, Esme has access rights but in practice she doesn't bother. Which is why it's important for Richie to be happy here during the holidays.'

This conversation gave Catherine a lot to think about. She looked forward to meeting Richie Eddlington-Smith and introducing him to the children of some of the local families. What worried her more was his father. Haydn was, apparently, single. And very attractive. And just possibly keen to spend time with her. It was more than two years since she had had a steady boyfriend, and that had been a satisfactorily long-distance relationship. Simon had lived in Edinburgh, and when his work required him to move to London things had fizzled out with no hard feelings on either side. That was the sort of relationship she liked.

She wished now she hadn't been so pleased to see Haydn. She certainly shouldn't have invited him in for a drink. She really didn't have time for him just now.

The detectives from Tayside duly appeared and spent a couple of days asking questions in the village. They then returned to Dundee, to the relief of Catherine and half the males of the village.

'That Detective Inspector guy thinks he's so cool,' said Malcolm in disgust. 'You'd think he would have better things to do than sit at the bar and chat up Mhairi.'

'You would indeed,' said Catherine. 'And I thought Mhairi wasn't going to work any more shifts in that pub?'

'Ah, well,' said Malcolm looking guilty. 'Don't look at me like that. I offered to do them for her but she wouldn't have it: seemed to think you needed me here which is a joke if ever there was one.'

'It's not a joke at all. In fact, I've made you a list of your very own. All the things you need to do before the famous Phyllida arrives.'

'Look, I'll help with the paying guests if I have to, but I'm having nothing to do with *her*.'

Catherine suppressed a sigh. She felt the same, but you had to be sensible. For some reason, seeing Malcolm's resentment made it easier for her to behave in a grown up way.

'We'll all have to help,' she said firmly. 'Now,

what I'd like you to do today is act as Fergus's assistant. Mrs McWhirter is going to give the house a final clean with the help of Susan from the village. I'm going to go over the course content for a last time with this artist man. I'm not a hundred per cent sure about Fergus, I'd like you to keep an eye on him.' Fergus was the newly appointed chef.

'Can't Mhairi do that?'

'No. Mhairi' s got to work on the bookings for the next few courses.'

'I could help her with that.'

'I need you in the kitchen.' Catherine was having serious doubts about her new cook. Normally she didn't regret her decisions. This time she wondered if she hadn't been a little too impressed with Fergus's training in French cuisine and not observant enough about his attitude. He had been officially on their books for two days now and as far as she could see he had done nothing but find fault. 'Fergus says he's used to having an assistant, so that's what you are.'

Malcolm pulled a face. 'He's a tosser. All show and no substance.'

That was what Catherine feared too. 'All the more reason for you to keep an eye on him.' Malcolm opened his mouth to object further and she said quickly, 'I'll pay you, OK? I'll add you to the payroll as assistant chef or something. Just do it, OK?'

'Well … OK,' said Malcolm. He must be badly in need of money.

The first party of visitors to Exclusive Activity

Holidays was, fortunately, a small one. Seven elderly men and women with a desire to learn about water colours and money to spare to indulge this interest in luxury surroundings. Catherine welcomed them herself, and spent most of the first day popping in to the studio to check that everything was going well. It was Malcolm who pointed out that this was making the young artist more than a little nervous, so she controlled her own anxiety and tried to relax.

She kept telling herself that there were always going to be teething problems. It was difficult to keep even so small a group to time for meals and lessons. And it felt stranger than she would have thought possible to have all these people in her home, and to know that she was there to serve them. Thank goodness her father wasn't around.

It only took her a couple of days to realise that she would need to review her priorities when it came to creating the successful holiday experience. She needed to worry less about the course content and more about the food in general and the type of refreshments offered with afternoon tea in particular. Could the over sixties not live without their scones?

Fergus's cooking wasn't bad, not bad at all. His CV must have been mostly accurate, for he produced the most exquisite main meals, even if always a little later and a lot more expensive ingredient-wise than Catherine would have liked. His manner, however, continued to be a problem. He had upset Mrs McWhirter and Susan by treating them as kitchen skivvies and even Mhairi had had an argument with him when she found he was ordering supplies without going through the proper channels (that is, through Mhairi). Malcolm, surprisingly, was the most tolerant. 'He's a total wanker,' he said frankly. 'But he is a good cook. I quite like watching him.'

And it was Malcolm who came to the rescue when Fergus had refused point blank to produce still more food for afternoon tea. 'Three meals a day is what we agreed,' he said belligerently. 'In the afternoon I need to rest.'

'I could try and do rock buns,' Malcolm had said doubtfully, when the little dark-haired man had walked out of the kitchen, leaving Catherine speechless. 'They used to be my speciality at uni.'

Catherine stared at him and he said defensively, 'We made them at school three times with three different teachers, even I couldn't forget how.'

She agreed to his trying, although she had her doubts. She had to go down to Perth so there was no way she could do anything herself. And, apparently, the buns had been a resounding success.

So that first course had had its ups and downs, but on the whole, the guests had expressed themselves well satisfied. And Catherine had learnt a lot, which was the main thing.

Now she had to turn her attention to preparations for Phyllida. She wished her father was more communicative. Informing the family of his plans (as opposed to merely expecting them to fall in implicitly with them) had never been his strong point. He and Phyllida were flying in to Glasgow on the third Friday in March. He expected at least one of his children to meet them at the airport. More information than that he hadn't provided.

Catherine decided John Hugo could take the day off work and undertake collection duties, as he was always keen on keeping in his father's good books. This would also mean that he was coming to stay for the weekend. Her father always liked a house party and John Hugo's presence would dilute the impact of Phyllida. Catherine was still trying not to think about the woman. She *knew* she would hate her.

To plump up the numbers still further, she invited Aunt Georgie, her father's older sister, to move in for a few days. 'It'll be the ideal chance for you to get to know your future sister-in-law,' she said.

'Catherine my dearest. I don't imagine that I will have anything in common with a wealthy American divorcee.'

'Nor will I,' said Catherine gloomily. 'Please come. I need at least one other sensible person around.'

There was a silence, then Georgie sighed loudly. 'All right, I will.' Thank goodness Georgie, unlike her brother, took family obligations seriously. 'But only if I can bring the dogs with me. Milly is too old to be left with strangers and I'm doing some training with Batty which I don't want to interrupt. I don't suppose this Phyllis? Phillipa? is interested in dogs?'

'Phyllida. Somehow I don't think so. You're wonderful, Georgie.'

'I know.'

Relieved, Catherine turned her thoughts to the School Council meeting due to be held that evening. She had successfully persuaded Mhairi's mother to attend. Mhairi had also been talked – or bullied – into coming to the Community Council meeting the previous week, which meant that Malcolm, too, had put in an appearance. The usual elderly attendees had been suitably impressed. Some things, at least, were progressing well.

Catherine heard the car draw up on the gravel at the front of the house and steeled herself to be welcoming. She glanced in the hall mirror, sighing at the untidy dark curls and wishing she had taken the time to change out of her sensible navy trousers, which made her look fatter than ever. Then she put on her best smile. Why was she so nervous? Just think of the woman as a guest, it would be perfectly all right. No going back now, so she just had to get it over with.

Phyllida Dubrovsky was not at all what Catherine had expected. She was exquisitely turned out, with hair carefully tinted myriad shades of blonde, hiding any sign of grey, and her make-up was perfect. Her smart pale-blue suit was uncrumpled despite the hours she had been travelling. None of this was surprising: Gordon did not trouble himself with anyone who was not both rich and beautiful. It was her manner that threw Catherine.

The American regarded her future family with what might almost be trepidation. Her brown eyes examined Catherine's face carefully before she took her hand and kissed her briefly on the cheek. 'I'm so pleased to meet you,' she said, her voice low and her tone nervous. 'It's so good of you to invite me.'

'I, er, you're very welcome,' said Catherine, wrong-footed. 'I hope you'll be very happy here. That is, I hope you'll enjoy *your stay*. And now, let me introduce you...'

Georgie came forward and took the new-comer's hand with an equally grave, questioning expression, and seemed to like what she saw. Only Malcolm spoilt things by murmuring something that might have been a greeting and then disappearing downstairs, behaviour which was guaranteed to infuriate his father.

'He's helping out in the kitchen,' Catherine said quickly, at which Gordon raised an eyebrow in blatant disbelief. Exasperated, she said, 'He is, really. You'd be surprised. This new chef isn't the speediest of workers so Malcolm's acting as a kind of right-hand man.'

'That doesn't hold out much promise for the food,' said John Hugo.

Catherine bit back a retort, and led the way upstairs. Annat House always pleased her father in a way that his family failed to do, and today was no exception. The blue bedroom, with its king-size four-poster bed and double windows overlooking the loch was his favourite. He looked calmly self-satisfied as Phyllida said all the right things about the décor and the wonderful views.

'It's rather a nice place,' he said, as though he was responsible for keeping it that way. 'Now, we'd like a little time to unpack and sort ourselves out, then we'll meet in the drawing room for drinks. Shall we say at six?'

When Catherine made her way to the drawing

room forty-five minutes later, she found Aunt Georgie already settled in. The older woman had a whisky in hand and her two dogs and Pip snoring at her feet. 'Not what I expected,' she said bluntly as Catherine began to rearrange the logs on the fire. 'Sometimes that brother of mine appears to have good taste despite himself. As you know, I always liked your mother, so different to some of his earlier, er, liaisons. But I didn't expect him to get it right a second time.'

'She does seem pleasant,' said Catherine reluctantly. 'But it's a bit early to say.' She went over to the drinks cabinet and poured a whisky for herself.

'Didn't know you drank the stuff,' said her aunt.

'Today I need it.' Catherine surveyed the room and then set about plumping up cushions and straightening the heavy velvet curtains. 'Well, everything is ready in here. What's the betting that John Hugo is the next one down?'

'And Malcolm the last.'

'If he arrives at all. I wish he'd make an effort.'

'You have to remember he was your mother's baby,' said Georgie. 'This isn't easy for any of you, but it's hardest of all for him.'

'I don't see why,' said Catherine. *She* had always been closest to their mother.

'With a bit of luck – and a few sharp words if necessary – I think he can be made to behave.'

John Hugo arrived and frowned at their glasses. 'I don't know why you're drinking that stuff. I've brought a rather nice champagne to toast the happy couple. You'll have spoilt your palette.'

'What a shame,' said Catherine. She sighed and rose once more to get out the champagne flutes.

She glanced at the clock.

Georgie, as though reading her mind, put her own glass aside. 'You sit down and put your feet up for a moment,' she said firmly. 'I'll go and winkle out that younger nephew of mine. If we're to have a toast he will have to be punctual.'

Catherine gave a sigh of relief. Nobody, not even Malcolm at his sulkiest, was a match for a determined Georgie.

'What's wrong with the boy?' said John Hugo. 'Not quite the thing to slope off like that with scarcely a word to Phyllida.'

'At least I got him to come to the door,' said Catherine. 'That wasn't easy.'

'I do wish he'd grow up,' said his older brother in a superior tone.

'He's getting better,' said Catherine. To her surprise, Malcolm was proving very useful in the kitchen.

Chapter Eleven

Haydn had purchased Annat Cottage with the intention of keeping himself to himself, doing exactly what *he* wanted. For years he had hankered after solitude, especially after the very public nightmare of his divorce. Now he had sold his controlling interest in HES Engineering Solutions, he was in the fortunate position of being able to go where he wished.

So why, when he was in the retreat of his dreams,

did he find himself so willing, so, if he was honest, eager, to socialise with his nearest neighbour? He had been warned about the encroachingness of the community in rural areas, but had laughed it off, sure of his own ability to keep himself to himself. And yet here he was, striding up the driveway to Annat House for the third or fourth time in as many weeks, about to participate in what was to all accounts the biggest social event of the year.

'Why do I have to come?' said Richie, dragging behind.

'Because I say so.'

Richie kicked at the gravel with the toe of the brand new designer trainers that Haydn had unaccountably found himself purchasing the day before. Pieces of gravel skittered onto the grass.

'Don't do that.'

Richie made another movement with his leg which was just slow enough that he could claim it wasn't a kick. Haydn sighed. He and his son had only been together for two days and already they were at loggerheads. He loved the boy, of course he did. He just wished he *liked* him more.

'There'll be other children here,' he said encouragingly. 'Catherine is going to introduce me to their parents. We'll see if we can invite them round for you to play with.'

Richie said nothing.

Unsurprisingly, it was Catherine who opened the door to welcome them. Haydn had considered her an attractive woman from the moment of their first meeting, but tonight she was beautiful. Her dark curls were more glossy than ever and for once she had made a definite effort with her appearance. She wore a pale green dress in some material that showed off her curves, with a long, loose jacket of darker green over it. She also wore high-heeled shoes and carefully applied make-up that made the dark eyes larger than ever.

Forgetting that their acquaintance was no more than casual, he bent to kiss her cheek and smelt the faint musky perfume she wore. Catherine took the kiss in her stride, as she seemed to take everything. It was Haydn who pulled back abruptly.

'Your son?' asked Catherine, indicating the boy who trailed reluctantly in his wake.

'Ah, *that's* who he is,' said Haydn, clumsily affecting irony. 'So easy to forget when you see them so rarely.'

Catherine frowned at him and drew the boy forward with her ready smile. 'It's Richie, isn't it? Do you want to come and meet some of the other youngsters or would you rather stay with your father for a while? I know Antonia and Miles are here already; they're ten and twelve, about your age...?'

She glanced from father to son. Richie was looking at the toes of his shoes. Haydn hoped his manners were going to improve sometime soon. 'I'm sure he'd prefer to be with the other young people,' he said. 'He's had quite enough of me over the last couple of days, haven't you?'

Richie shrugged. The school insisted on cutting his hair unflatteringly short, leaving his ears large and exposed. Haydn sighed. How had he and Esme managed to produce such an unattractive child?

Catherine's younger brother Malcolm appeared and she instructed him to show Haydn to the drawing room. She took charge of Richie herself. Haydn watched the boy go with her, appreciating the sway of the soft green material over her hips, as well as the adept way she handled his son.

Malcolm was noticeably less adept at introducing Haydn to the party. 'You know Father, don't you? He's somewhere around.' He gestured vaguely and seemed to consider his duty done. He went to put plates from the tray he was carrying onto a table in the large bay window and fell into conversation with a young woman with striped blonde and burgundy hair who was engaged in the same task.

Haydn paused near the doorway and took stock of the room. The party had been billed as 'Open House from 7 p.m.' and although it was now only thirty minutes past that time the room was already almost full. There were a reasonable contingent of 'the great and the good', men and woman with greying hair and loud voices, expensively turned out in their good suits and frocks. He spied Gordon and a slight, attractive woman who looked to be in her fifties, presumably his fiancée, receiving congratulations from the group gathered around them. Time enough to give them his good wishes later. He looked further, and noticed a tall thin woman on one of the settees signalling him to approach. It seemed as good a place as any to start the evening.

He bent to shake her outstretched hand. 'Haydn Smith. I've just moved into Annat Cottage.'

'I thought so,' she said, patting the seat beside

103

her. 'I was hoping to make your acquaintance. Ah, you haven't got a drink. Mhairi dear, could you furnish Mr Smith with a glass of something? And top up my whisky while you're at it?'

The girl with stripy hair came over to take his request.

'Excellent. Now we've got that sorted, I should introduce myself. I'm Gordon's sister, Georgie McDonald.'

Haydn looked at her with renewed interest. 'Pleased to meet you.'

'Can't stand parties like this myself,' she said cheerfully. 'But Gordon is in his element. Look at him. You'd think he was really excited to be marrying again, wouldn't you?'

'Isn't he?'

'Who knows? Most likely relieved to be escaping Catherine's control. I hope that American woman knows what she is getting in to.'

Haydn didn't see why he shouldn't be blunt, if she was. 'I don't understand why Catherine appears to be the one who holds the purse strings.'

'Because her mother was a sensible woman. She was the one with the money, you know. The McDonalds have been losing theirs for centuries until this house is practically the only thing we have left. Gordon had to marry money to keep it. But the way Rachel left things, Catherine won't have to do the same. And I wouldn't be surprised if she doesn't make it pay its way with this new business.'

'The house is hers, too, is it?'

'No, of course not, the house is Gordon's. But it'll come to her eventually. None of the boys want it and even Gordon has realised if he wants

104

McDonalds to stay here, Catherine's the one.'

'I thought the younger boy, Malcolm, was still at home?'

'Malcolm wouldn't do,' said Georgie McDonald decidedly. She took a large drink from her replenished glass. 'Now, tell me about yourself. Divorced, I hear, with one son? What has brought you to this part of the world? Are you liking it?'

Haydn smiled blandly and picked out the questions he was happy to answer. He rather liked the woman, but that didn't mean he was prepared to tell her any secrets. When he decided the interrogation had lasted long enough, he said, 'Seems like a good turnout this evening. I presume the McDonalds know anyone who is anyone in this part of the world?'

'We know *everyone*,' said Georgie firmly. She reviewed the room from hooded, pale blue eyes. 'That's Jamie Campbell there, you know, of the Erricht Campbells? And the large chap in the unpleasant checked suit is Angus McLearly: he owns most of the land between here and Pitlochry. But it's not just gentry, you know. I'm pleased Catherine has managed to mix things up, there are a good few from the village, and more to come yet. I believe the Mountain Rescue people have been up in the hills looking for that dratted Lost Woman yet again; none of them seem to be here so far.' She sighed. 'We're rather an elderly gathering, aren't we?'

'It's a shame there is still this tendency for the young to move away from rural areas,' said Haydn, testing the water.

'Yes, and totally unnecessary. If Catherine has

105

her way we'll soon have a booming local economy, with more than enough jobs to bring them back.' She paused and pursed her lips. 'Of course, it might just bring English incomers like yourself.'

'Wouldn't we be welcome?'

'You're better than nothing,' said Georgie. 'If you intend to stay. Wait until you've lasted a whole winter before you answer that.'

Haydn noted the crowd around the happy couple had thinned and decided now was as good a time as any to offer his congratulations. He excused himself and made his way through the throng.

It was easy to say the right things to Gordon, because he took on so much of the conversation himself. Haydn allowed his attention to wander to the woman at his side who seemed to be that most unusual of beings, a quiet American. She was beautifully turned out in a pale silk suit and seemed content to allow Gordon to do the talking too.

'And when is the wedding to be?' asked Haydn.

'Soon, we hope,' said Gordon. 'We haven't yet set a date. We're planning on marrying in Kinlochannat kirk.'

'Gordon took me to see it this morning,' said Phyllida softly. 'It's the quaintest place.'

'But first we need to get the Reverend to see sense,' said Gordon tartly. 'I don't know what he means in this day and age, *reservations* about marrying divorcees. What has it to do with him, that's what I'd like to know.'

'I'm sure I can sort it out,' said Catherine,

coming to join them at that moment. 'I can usually persuade the Reverend John, although it does take time.'

'Absolutely ridiculous,' said her father.

Haydn was just wondering how to extract himself from this conversation when Catherine said, 'Ah, look, there are Miles and Antonia's parents. I said I'd introduce you, didn't I?' She placed a hand lightly on his arm and drew him away.

'The fiancée seems very pleasant,' he said, pausing so she couldn't insert him into the other group just yet.

'Yes, very pleasant.'

'Hard to dislike.'

She gave him a look that was no longer polite interest, and he smiled. He didn't want to be just another guest.

Then Catherine returned determinedly to hostess mode. She introduced him to the couple who lived just this side of Pitlochry and had two children close in age to Richie. They were the sort of people Esme would have adored. Well-spoken, well-dressed, and very clearly well-heeled. Haydn tried to put his own initial dislike to one side and make an effort for Richie's sake. The child was objecting to be taken so far from his London friends, so it behove Haydn to make some effort to find replacements for them. He just hoped these youngsters were less interested in Playstations and more in the great outdoors.

Haydn had been deftly extracted from that conversation and introduced into another group, his glass topped up yet again, when the mood of the room underwent a slight but definite change.

107

One or two late arrivals had come in and something they had said was passing from group to group, causing other conversations to falter and heads to turn. It took a moment or so before the whispers reached Haydn. 'They've found a body,' someone said. 'Up in the hills. They've found *her*.'

Haydn looked about for Catherine and saw her slipping out of the room. Putting aside his glass, he followed.

Chapter Twelve

Catherine was very put out. Why did they have the find the body *now?* It was bound to disturb her meticulously planned party and she didn't even want to think about the additional, unwanted publicity.

Malcolm, on the other hand, was delighted. 'Didn't I say she was still up there? It was us finding the glove that set them looking again. If they hadn't done a proper search soon I was going to go out again myself.' He was already pulling on Wellington boots and reaching for his waxed-cotton jacket.

'What are you doing?'

'Going to see if I can help. They're taking the Rescue Land Rover up the track behind us, to bring the body down or something. I can show them the way, open gates and so on.'

'They won't need you to show them the way,' said Catherine. 'And I do need you here to help

108

with the food. Who's going to serve it if you disappear?'

'Mhairi will manage.'

'No she won't.' Catherine's mood was not improved by the sound of the drawing room door opening and closing behind her. Some nosy do-gooder, no doubt.

'Anything I can do to help?' said Haydn.

'No, no, not at all. Everything's fine.'

'So it's true?' said Haydn, indicating Malcolm's outdoor attire with the nod of his head. 'They've found something?'

'We're not sure...' said Catherine.

'Yes,' said Malcolm.

'I really don't see why they have to bring her down this way,' said Catherine. She couldn't suppress a shudder. So the poor woman was dead. She felt suddenly squeamish, the thought of the long-cold body being carried past her door... She'd rather concentrate on other matters.

'Malcolm. I need you here.'

'I won't be long, I promise.'

'Who's going to help Fergus in the kitchen?'

'Mrs McWhirter's there, they'll manage without me.'

Catherine glared, but she could see she was losing the argument. Malcolm's face was alive with excitement and before she could say more he had let himself out of the door. She rounded on Haydn and said fiercely, 'Well, isn't this just what we needed?'

'It's rather a shame,' he said. 'Although it will doubtless add to the memorability of what is already a very pleasant party.'

'Hmph!' Catherine realised this wasn't a very ladylike response. 'Mmm. If you'll excuse me, I'd better go and check on the food.'

'I'll come with you. If Malcolm isn't back in time I'll be only too happy to offer my services. I always feel that one should keep one's waitering skills in practice, don't you?'

Catherine shook her head and suppressed a smile. She didn't think it was worth arguing. She needed to check on progress with Fergus and, after indicating politely that Haydn should rejoin the party, turned to hurry down the stairs to the kitchen.

Unfortunately, she had forgotten she was wearing these ridiculously high shoes. She rounded the corner a little too quickly, felt the heel turn, and went down with a crash. By chance she fell across rather than down, but nevertheless she landed hard. At first all she felt was shock, and then sudden, excruciating pain.

'Are you all right?' Haydn was immediately on his knees beside her.

'I'll be fine,' said Catherine, fighting to keep down the tears that had sprung to her eyes. 'Serves me right for wearing such silly footwear. Vanity, you know.'

'And you looked remarkably fine in them.'

'Mmm.' Catherine tried to stretch out her leg and winced. God, what a fool she was.

'Don't try to get up yet. Take a minute to catch your breath.'

Catherine really did need a moment to recover, so she took his advice. She leant back against the wall and closed her eyes.

Haydn removed her silly strappy shoe and manipulated the ankle with gentle hands. 'Does that hurt?'

'A – a bit.'

'See if you can bend it this way. Yes, I think it's just a sprain, nothing broken, but it'll be sore for a while.'

'I haven't time to be ill,' said Catherine through gritted teeth. She was trying to ignore the strange sensation she was feeling at Haydn's warm hand on her leg.

He smiled down at her, his eyes warmly sympathetic. 'If it's a sprain you'll have to take it easy for a day or two. Something that I don't imagine comes naturally?'

'Absolutely not.' Catherine tried to gather her thoughts. 'And we certainly can't sit here all evening. Do you think you could help me down to the kitchen?'

When she said help she didn't mean lift her bodily, but that was what Haydn seemed to consider necessary. He was a tall man but rather slight and she wouldn't have expected him to be able to carry her weight. Clearly she was wrong. They arrived in the kitchen, Haydn not at all dishevelled from his exertions but Catherine rather pink.

'That was fun,' he said as he put her down.

'Goodness,' said Mrs McWhirter. 'Whatever have you been doing?'

'I turned my ankle on the stairs, it's nothing.'

'I don't know how many times I've told you to take your time on they stairs. The way you rush aboot it's surprising you havenae done it afore. And it couldnae happen at a worse time...'

Catherine sank onto one of the kitchen chairs, glad to put a distance between herself and Haydn. He was still grinning at her in a most annoying way. 'Mrs McWhirter, this is our new neighbour, Haydn Smith. I don't know if you've met him before? And Haydn, Mrs Mac is the mainstay of Annat House; we don't know what we'd do without her, and this is Fergus, our very talented cook.' Fergus had ignored their arrival in his kitchen, where he always made Catherine feel an intruder, but now he wandered across to give his opinion on the injury.

Catherine hated people to fuss over her. The worst of the pain was subsiding and she was keen to concentrate on the tasks at hand. Her father might have agreed to a 'finger buffet' for the evening, but the number and variety of dishes he had requested made Catherine wonder if a sit-down meal wouldn't have been easier. She began to remind Fergus of all that still needed to be done and he quickly withdrew to his range.

Haydn brought her a glass of water from the sink. 'Sip that. Brandy might be better but that'll do for a start.'

'Thanks,' she said grudgingly. She wished he wouldn't look as though he were just about to laugh. It wasn't exactly amusing to be marooned in the kitchen when you were supposed to be in charge of the evening. 'Perhaps you could go and see if you can find Mhairi for me? A small girl with odd-coloured hair and lots of earrings? I'd be grateful if you could get her to come here.'

'My pleasure,' said Haydn. He leant down and added in a low voice, 'I'll be back myself, too. I can't wait to see how you manage to make that little man do anything he isn't inclined to.'

The next quarter of an hour was not one of the most enjoyable Catherine had ever spent. Her accident seemed to have put her even more at a disadvantage when it came to getting Fergus to take instructions, and Mrs McWhirter wouldn't settle to anything, so impressed was she that her dire predictions had come true. Catherine was ready to scream by the time Mhairi appeared, with Haydn in tow.

'You should go to bed,' were Mhairi's first words. 'Mum says rest is the only thing for a sprain, and the shock will have quite taken it out of you.'

'I always said you should have been a nurse,' said Catherine sourly.

'Do you want me to help you upstairs?' asked Haydn.

'I'll go up to the drawing room shortly, and although I'd appreciate your help, I certainly don't want to be carried. If I sit by Auntie Georgie for a while hopefully no one will notice. But Mhairi, this means you'll have to be in charge of getting the food on to the table at the right time, as well as keeping your eye on drinks and all the rest of it.'

'I can do that,' said Haydn.

'You're a guest. John Hugo will help with drinks, Mhairi, if you ask him nicely.'

'Malcolm's gone out, hasn't he?' said Mhairi, eyes narrowing. 'The ba ... brat. Have they brought the body down yet?'

Mrs McWhirter and Fergus then wanted to know what she was referring to, and more time

113

was wasted while explanations were made and theories aired.

'How could he go without telling me?' said Mhairi.

'You're working, remember? Now, I've made a list of the order in which I want the food served. Fergus, I think the filo baskets are burning; get them out now! Mrs Mac, I am *not* going to bed. Mhairi, run up to my room and see if you can find my brown sandals; there's no way I'm wearing these strappy things again. Haydn, if you would be so kind as to take my arm while I stand?'

These orders were obeyed with varying degrees of speed and willingness. Catherine closed her eyes tightly as she put weight on her left foot. She didn't want Haydn to see how much it hurt, but reluctantly allowed him to put his arm around her waist and help her back up those damn stairs. It was slightly better than being carried, but not much. There was something about Haydn Smith that made Catherine prefer to keep her distance.

As they paused in the hallway to gather their breath, he said in that easy drawl, 'While I have you on our own, I wondered if I might invite you to dinner? I still haven't returned your very kind invitation to drinks. I'm not much of a cook, but if you could recommend somewhere local I would very much appreciate your company.' He was looking directly into her eyes in a way which Catherine found unnerving.

'There's no need. You, er, bought me coffee,' she said, feeling off-balance.

'Coffee doesn't count. I'd like to take you out for an evening.'

114

'I don't know, Phyllida has only just arrived and...'

'I don't mean immediately. How about we say next weekend? You can let me know which evening would suit you best.' He smiled down at her. She was sure he would have an answer for whatever excuses she came up with. She might as well just give in.

'Oh, all right,' she said gracelessly and glared when he laughed. Didn't he know how busy she was just now? She didn't have time for going out. She would explain to him this was just a one-off. 'I'll manage on my own from here,' she said firmly, limping towards the drawing room door. Haydn ignored her and took her arm once again.

It was quite a feat, but she managed to reach the seat beside Georgie without drawing too much attention to herself. Her aunt regarded her from calm blue eyes. 'I see you've been getting very, er, friendly with Mr Smith. How nice.'

'I've hurt my ankle. He was being helpful.'

'I wouldn't have put him down as the helpful type.'

'Georgie,' said Catherine warningly, as Haydn returned with the brandy he was determined she should have.

Georgie immediately raised her own glass. 'Another whisky, please. Two fingers. No water.'

Haydn grinned and took the glass away. Catherine sighed. What was the point in objecting to his help, if he was so determined? She supposed she should be relieved he left them alone after returning with Georgie's glass.

Georgie also allowed her peace for some

115

minutes, as though aware of how much pain the ankle was causing. Then she said abruptly, 'Have they brought the body down yet?'

'How should I know?' Catherine scanned the room for Malcolm and found him still absent. 'Probably not.'

'I wonder if they'll be able to identify her now.'

'Surely they will? She must have something with her to tell them.'

'Not necessarily. Don't you remember that body they found further north a few years ago? Youngish man, had cut all the labels out of his clothing, left no ID whatsoever. Turned out to be French, eventually. Or was it Spanish?'

'I don't see why people have to come to the Highlands to commit suicide,' said Catherine sourly. 'And I especially don't see why they have to come to this bit of the Highlands.'

'I wonder if she had a special reason for coming here,' said Georgie soberly. 'Always assuming it was suicide.'

'Of course not. Why should she?'

Georgie looked thoughtful. 'The arrangements she made and so on. I could be wrong. Time will tell.'

Catherine took a sip of her brandy. The idea made her very uneasy.

Chapter Thirteen

Once a selection of dishes had been laid on the sideboard, Georgie levered herself off the sofa for the first time that evening and said she would bring a plate for Catherine. It was, however, Phyllida who brought the food back.

'Catherine, you should have said. Your aunt has just told us about your fall.' The American woman hesitated and then took the seat beside Catherine. 'How are you feeling?'

'I'm fine,' said Catherine for the umpteenth time. She watched her aunt talking to her father and saw the displeasure on his face. He looked across at Catherine and frowned. She felt tears rise in her eyes. Silly to get so emotional. It was just the pain, and being tired. She forced herself to turn her attention to Phyllida. 'This is very kind of you, but really you didn't need to. And you don't have to sit with me, everyone is dying to meet you.'

'They sure are. I think I've spoken to every single person in the room at least once.'

'Of course, it must be difficult, confusing, so many new people.'

Phyllida sighed softly. 'Your father is an excellent host. I hope he won't mind me taking a few moments out.'

Catherine was fairly sure that her father would, but didn't say so.

'The food is delicious,' said Phyllida after a

long pause. 'It's mighty kind of you to arrange this party for us. You've gone to an awful lot of trouble.'

'No, no problem. I'm glad it's going so well.' Catherine just wished the woman would leave her alone, that the party was already over.

She didn't see Malcolm re-enter the room, but suddenly he was at her side, his dark eyes alive with excitement. He dropped to his knees, ignoring Phyllida. 'I'm back. Do you want to know what happened?'

'Not nearly as much as you want to tell me.'

'It was cool. You wouldn't believe... What've you done to your foot?'

Catherine sighed. There was no ignoring the swollen ankle now propped up on a little stool. She explained what had happened. Malcolm did not waste any time on sympathy.

'You stupid thing. Shows what happens when you rush around too much.'

'Where have you been?' demanded Mhairi, appearing at his side. 'We've all been working like mad to keep this bloody show on the road and you...' She noticed Phyllida sitting beside Catherine and realised that it might be infelicitous to complain about the workload. 'Tell us what happened,' she said instead. 'And quickly. There's still masses to do.'

Malcolm turned back to Catherine, as his main audience. 'They let me go with them in the Land Rover. GPS is all very well but a knowledge of the terrain is handy on a night like this. Quite wild it is, out there. Guess where they'd found her?'

'I've no idea,' said Catherine with a sigh. She

glanced at Phyllida. She couldn't recall how much of the background their visitor knew. Her expression gave nothing away.

'She was hidden at the back of the Craig Dubh waterfall. Did you know there was a little cave there? They think she walked upstream in the water for ages, that was why the sniffer dogs couldn't get a scent. She really didn't want to be found. Quite impressive, isn't it?'

Catherine shuddered and Mhairi said, 'I didn't know there was a cave. How did she know? And how did they find her?'

'The body must have been dislodged by the heavy rainfall. Initially, she would have been totally hidden, and probably dry, too. They're pretty sure it was suicide. I wonder why she did it.'

'They didn't let you see the body, did they?' asked Catherine.

'No.' Malcolm sounded disappointed. 'They'd decided not to move it yet and had it kind of cordoned off, waiting for forensics or something. I was hoping to have a glimpse but no luck. Once the high-heid-yin police arrived we were told to leave. So unfair. *And* I had to walk down which is why I've been so long.'

Catherine put her unfinished plate on the floor. Malcolm's interest was positively ghoulish. The truth was, no one knew what would happen next, and while Malcolm and Mhairi eagerly discussed the possibilities Catherine closed her eyes and wished they would all go away.

'Now that they've found the body, maybe the publicity will subside,' suggested Phyllida gently. Catherine nodded. She doubted if the older woman was right, but she appreciated the attempt to give comfort. She didn't want to like this woman, but she couldn't help softening towards her. Malcolm had no such problem. Once the euphoria wore off and he realised that she was part of this group, he withdrew.

'Clean yourself up and get back to helping,' Catherine called after him.

'He's a very handsome boy,' said Phyllida, watching as Malcolm stopped at one group and then another to spread his news.

'Mmm.'

'In fact, you're a very good-looking family. Your father is just so lucky to have you.'

'I'm not sure he would agree.'

'Oh, he does, he's very proud of you all. He has spoken a lot about you, and about Annat House.'

Catherine could believe that the latter, at least, was true.

'Tell me about your part of the States,' she said, determined to make up for Malcolm's lack of manners. It wasn't Phyllida's fault her father had sprung his marriage on them. 'Didn't Father say you were from Texas?'

Catherine listened as Phyllida spoke about her homeland in her soft voice. It sounded a very different place from the one she saw on television or heard about from her father. For the first time, she felt a stir of interest in the country. Phyllida smiled cautiously. 'When we're married, we'll be living near Dallas. So useful for Gordon's work.' She patted Catherine's hand briefly. 'I do hope you'll come out and visit.'

Catherine surprised herself by saying, 'Perhaps

I will, thank you. But I need to get the first season of my holiday business out of the way before I even think about it.'

Soon after that, her father came to whisk Phyllida away. He frowned down at Catherine's ankle. 'People are starting to leave. I suppose you can't stand so Phyllida and I had better do the honours.'

'Don't worry about him,' said Malcolm slumping down beside her. 'He'll be happy to stay the centre of attention for as long as possible. What was that woman saying to you?'

'We were just chatting. She's really quite nice.'

'I don't know what she sees in *him* then.'

'You should try to get to know her a bit.'

'Thanks but no thanks.'

Malcolm looked set to relapse into one of his sulks when Georgie appeared and sent him off to help Mhairi clear the table. 'I don't know what staff are coming to these days,' she said, settling down in Malcolm's place. 'I've been down to the kitchen to have a word with that cook of yours and I can't say I'm impressed. His pastries are delicious but his manners leave a lot to be desired.'

'He's a bit temperamental.'

'Get rid of him. Temperamental staff are never worth the trouble.'

'I can't. I'll never find anyone to take over in time for the next course.' Catherine shook her head grimly. 'It's going to be hard enough with me scarcely mobile.'

'You'll be fine in a couple of days, as long as you don't do anything silly. And I've decided I'll stay until then, keep an eye on things for you.'

'Thanks.' Catherine felt absurdly grateful. Then she said, hesitantly, 'Have you heard they found a body? Behind the Craig Dubh waterfall?'

'Yes, I heard.'

'I didn't even know there was a cave there.'

Georgie pursed her lips. 'I knew. Used to go there with your father when we were children.'

'But how did this woman know?'

Georgie shrugged. 'No idea. Now, I suggest you take yourself off to bed and get a decent night's rest. Best thing for you.'

The idea of bed was tempting, but who would make sure the clearing away was done properly if she wasn't here? And, even if she did agree to go, how was she to get there? For the first time she wished she hadn't allocated herself a bedroom in the attics.

'Shall I call that neighbour of yours to give you a hand?' asked Georgie, as though reading her thoughts.

'No, really, I'm fine. John Hugo or Malcolm can help me later.'

'You wanted me?' said John Hugo, drifting across.

'Not just now,' said Catherine.

'Yes, she needs a hand to get up to her bedroom,' said Georgie. 'Go on, off with you. I'm going to take charge down here. And, you know, I think I'm going to enjoy it.'

Faced with the resolute gleam in her aunt's eye, Catherine decided to give in gracefully.

Chapter Fourteen

'You know, I think that Haydn guy fancies your sister.'

'Huh?' Malcolm was propping up the bar in the Foresters Arms, as he did nearly every evening when Mhairi was working. Usually he was the one trying to engage her in conversation but now he was annoyed at being distracted from the paper. 'What did you say?'

'I said Haydn seems quite keen on Catherine. Aren't you interested?' Mhairi was polishing glasses with a white towel, but he knew from the way she kept darting looks at him that she was hoping for a reaction.

'It's nothing to do with me.' Malcolm turned over the idea of Catherine and Haydn in his head, and didn't like it. 'And what makes you suddenly come out with that? Catherine won't be interested in him.'

'Why not? He's a very good-looking man.'

'He's too old for you.'

'But not for Catherine. There can't be more than ten years between them, which is nothing at their age.'

'Forget it. It's not going to happen. Don't you want to know what the papers are saying about the Lost Woman?'

'Haydn's asked me to babysit on Friday. He didn't *say* he was taking Catherine out but I bet

123

he is. Mum invited her to meet the cousins who're over from Canada and she said she was busy that evening. So you see...'

'No, I don't see,' said Malcolm.

'You would if you were interested. Anyone would put two and two together. Except her baby brother, of course.'

Mhairi went to serve someone further down the bar and Malcolm tried to return to the article he was reading. It didn't bother him who Catherine went out with, it was just that he resented Mhairi gossiping about her.

After a while, Mhairi wandered back. She was wearing jeans and a low-cut top striped like a candy stick. She didn't have much of a chest to flaunt, but when she bent over, as she was doing now, to share his paper, it gave her a very tempting cleavage. Malcolm looked at it and then away. 'You shouldn't lean across the bar like that,' he said.

She glanced down and pulled a face. 'Oo-ooh. Don't look if you don't like it.'

'It's not me I'm worrying about. You'll have all these old men trying to paw you if you're not careful.'

'Malcolm, fuck off, OK? I can look after myself.'

They glared at each other for a moment. Mhairi had strange eyes, brown shot through with hazel like a cat's. It was Malcolm who looked away first.

'Have you read this?' he said, lifting the paper fractionally.

She hesitated so long he thought she was going to walk away, then she said, 'Not today's I haven't. What does it say?' She glanced again at the page but this time, for all her protests, she was careful not to lean over too far.

'It was definitely suicide. She'd taken an overdose.'

'Oh. Poor thing.'

'They still haven't identified her.' Malcolm had been scouring the news channels and the papers ever since the body had been found. 'She hadn't cut out the labels on her clothes, contrary to Aunt Georgie's suspicions. But she did almost as well. Everything she was wearing had been bought at a UK chain store. It doesn't give a thing away.'

'She knew what she was doing. She didn't want to be found. And, if she was found, she didn't want to be identified.'

'But why not? What could make someone want to do something like that?' Malcolm shook his head in disbelief.

'I've no idea, and I don't suppose we'll know until they find out who she is. Have they published a sketch yet? Surely then someone would recognise her.'

'I haven't seen one. The body had been there quite a while. I suppose it had, you know, decomposed a bit. She might not be very recognisable.'

'Oh, yuck,' said Mhairi, wrinkling her small nose. She noticed Bob glaring at her and hurried away to serve more customers. After she had done a trawl of the room, collecting empty glasses and chatting with the clientele, she returned to Malcolm.

'Why don't you let the O'Connor girl do that?' he said. 'If she's working here she needs to be useful.'

125

'I'm not quite sure she's realised that yet,' said Mhairi. 'Bob is definitely regretting taking Catherine's advice.'

'Catherine? What? Well, never mind. Look, don't you think they should be able to do an artist's impression?' He was far more interested in this than the staffing of the Foresters Arms.

'Can't they do DNA tests or something? Find out who she is that way?'

'Dunno. Anyway, she'd only be on a DNA register if she'd committed a crime in the past, wouldn't she? I don't get the impression she was the sort.'

'Just because she was a middle-aged woman? Well, if that isn't a generalisation I don't know what is.'

'It's true. I'm sure you'd be the first to tell me that the majority of crimes are committed by men between the ages of eighteen and twenty-five.'

'Aye, especially those who are unemployed,' added Mhairi with a smirk.

'Well, I'm not unemployed any more, am I? I'm working for Catherine just like you.' Malcolm pushed the paper to one side. 'I wish I'd done journalism at uni. Journalists are the first to know everything. I think it might be quite a fun job.'

'The *police* are the first to know things. And there are thousands of people wanting to get into journalism and the initial pay is crap. I can't see it being your kind of thing. Why don't you do something sensible?'

'It was just a thought,' said Malcolm. Why did everyone have to be so negative about his ideas?

He took himself off soon after, instead of waiting to walk Mhairi home as had become his habit. Perhaps she would appreciate him a bit more if she saw him less.

What Malcolm had forgotten was that returning home early meant risking bumping into his father and that American woman who were still staying in Annat House. It would almost have been worth moving back to the Lodge to avoid them. But the way Catherine's bookings were going, he wasn't going to have many more chances to sleep in his childhood home.

He parked the ancient runabout at the back of the house and entered through the kitchen door. So far so good, he was unlikely to come across his father here. Now he just had to negotiate the stairs to his room without being summoned into The Presence.

All would have been well if it hadn't been for Pip. The stupid dog must have been asleep by the fire in the drawing room and in that unfortunate way he had of only hearing something when you didn't want him to, let off a volley of barks as Malcolm tried to sneak past. Father was at the door at once.

'Oh, it's you.' He looked his youngest son over with the usual distaste. The generation gap was just too great for him to be able to appreciate torn jeans and hooded T-shirts. Malcolm hoped he might be so disgusted he would let him go, but he wasn't so lucky. 'You might as well come in and have a drink with us,' his father said, holding the door wide. 'Phyllida was just saying she has hardly seen anything of you.'

Malcolm didn't like to refuse outright. His way

was to avoid confrontation, swerve before it happened. So far he had been swerving very successfully for the five days since Phyllida's arrival.

'Get yourself a drink,' said his father, gesturing towards the cabinet. 'I hope you didn't have more than a half down at the public house? You know how hot they are on drink driving these days.'

Malcolm thought this was a bit much, coming from his father. 'I just had a shandy,' he muttered.

'I'd like to visit the village pub one day,' said Phyllida in her soft, little girl voice. 'I don't think I've ever been in a real British pub.'

'It's nothing special,' said Malcolm.

'But it is our local,' said his father, who rarely set foot in the place. 'Perhaps you could take Phyllida there for a drink tomorrow evening? I find I have to go to Aberdeen and I don't know when I'll be back.'

Malcolm could feel himself blanching. 'I'm sure she'd rather go to Aberdeen with you.'

'It isn't convenient this time. I'll take her when I'm not in such a rush. Tomorrow would be a good time for you to show her around.'

Malcolm looked hopefully at the woman sitting so neat and tidy on the edge of the settee. Surely if she expressed a preference to go with him, his father would have to give in? She merely smiled, showing even, white, American teeth and said, 'Why, don't worry about me. I'll have a quiet day here, if Malcolm is busy.'

'Malcolm won't be busy.'

Malcolm made a vague sound that could be

taken for agreement, but wasn't. He would make sure he was occupied with Fergus the whole of the following day.

'Malcolm has always been a difficult child,' said Gordon to his fiancée. 'Not nearly as able as the other two boys.'

Malcolm had heard this so many times before, he wasn't even upset.

'Given any more thought to your future career?' asked his father, turning back to him.

'Of course I have: can hardly avoid it with you lot going on at me all the time.'

'It's ridiculous, your hanging around the house and Catherine like this. John Hugo said he could put in a word for you with his Group, might get you an interview for a traineeship.'

'I don't want to be a banker.'

'You could do much worse.' His father regarded him over the top of his glasses. 'It was very good of John Hugo to offer to help.'

Malcolm didn't want help, especially from John Hugo, who was always his father's blue-eyed boy.

'I can see why you might want to stay at Annat House,' said Phyllida softly. 'It sure is a wonderful place.'

'It's OK,' said Malcolm, resenting her opinion.

'Annat House is now a place of business,' said his father. 'What you need to remember, if you insist on staying here, is that your home is now the East Lodge, young man.'

'And yours isn't?'

'We are talking about you, not me.' Gordon's tone was icy. He never could cope with backchat. 'If you don't like the Lodge, do something about it. Get up off your lazy backside.'

'I'm not lazy!' Why was everyone always getting at him? No one understood. 'At least *I'm* helping Catherine. *You* still treat the place like a hotel, somewhere you have to be waited on hand and foot. Do you think you would all be getting fed if I wasn't helping in the kitchen?'

'Malcolm,' said his father ominously.

Malcolm's temper, slow to rouse, had reached its limit. 'It's the truth! Have you any idea how much trouble you've caused having this little week's *holiday* here?'

'Don't you speak to me in that tone of voice.'

'I'll speak how I like! I'm not beholden to you. It's Catherine who pays my wages.'

'Perhaps it's time I had a word with Catherine.'

'It's nothing to do with you,' said Malcolm, tripping over the words in his fury. 'This is Catherine's business, that's why it's going to be a success. I'll be so pleased when you move to the States. So will Catherine. That's probably why she hasn't made too much of a fuss about, about...' Malcolm glanced at Phyllida, whose pretty face was puckering. He turned quickly back to his father. 'You've always been the same. I don't know how Mum put up with you, coming and going at a moment's notice, bringing visitors, never showing appreciation. Criticising everyone. It's about time someone faced up to you.'

'How dare you speak to me like that?'

Gordon was shouting and Malcolm felt that all too familiar quiver of fear at having provoked his father. 'You don't care about us,' he said, but less vehemently, his anger beginning to wane.

'Apologise to Phyllida for causing such a scene!'

'I will not. *I've* nothing to apologise for.'

'Then go to your room!'

Malcolm rose quickly, glad of the excuse. 'I was just about to.' He was shaking. He'd always disliked shouting matches, which was why he avoided them. And this one was all bloody Phyllida's fault. Malcolm hated her for coming here and causing trouble. Trying to take his mother's place. As if!

Chapter Fifteen

Haydn and Catherine drove in silence to the Glentoul Hotel. Catherine was thinking of all the things she should be doing and wondering why on earth she had agreed to this evening out. What Haydn was thinking she had no idea, and that fact disturbed her even more.

She began to relax, however, when they drew up outside the massive stone building, a relic of the nineteenth century when wealthy city dwellers from the Central Belt had begun to frequent the Highlands. Everything about the place was overdone, from its too-numerous turrets to its double-legged staircase. The current owners had gone with this mood, accentuating the sumptuousness with thick carpets, many-swagged curtains, and masses of squashy chairs. Catherine had conscientiously visited all the local hostelries before setting up Exclusive Activity Holidays at Annat House, and this had been one of her favourites.

'You're very quiet,' said Haydn as they took their seats in the gold and green lounge.

Catherine felt defensive. 'One doesn't need to talk all the time.'

He smiled across at her. 'Absolutely not. But one of the things I have learnt about you is that you are more than capable of holding your own on the conversational front.'

Catherine made only a vague murmur in response.

Haydn continued, chattily, 'You know, I was quite misled by your first words to me. You opened your magnificent front door with a flourish and announced "I have nothing to say". Now, I wouldn't want to imply that you are a chatterbox, far from it, but I have to admit you have had rather a lot to say ever since.'

'Really?' said Catherine in what was meant to be a crushing tone. She smiled gratefully at the waiter who brought her gin and tonic.

'Arranging the gardener for me, advising me on the local shops.'

'Isn't that what you wanted?'

'Making sure I met the right people.'

'I thought you asked to be introduced.' She tried to remember whether he had or not. Certainly he had asked for advice, and now he was implying that she had been interfering.

'You've been very helpful.'

'I've only done what anyone would do.'

'Hardly. But please don't think I'm unappreciative.' His expression was serious but she couldn't help suspect that laughter was lurking in those green eyes.

Unlike any man she had known, he did not seem put out by her managing ways. This was not necessarily a good thing. She adjusted the neckline of her dress, wishing she had worn something less revealing, and changed the subject. 'Where's Richie this evening?'

'There you go, checking up on my childcare arrangements. Very wise.'

'I'm just showing a polite interest.'

'I'm surprised you don't already know the answer. That remarkably versatile young assistant of yours, Mhairi Robertson, is babysitting for me.'

'Mhairi?' Catherine was doubly put out, firstly that he had asked one of her staff to help him, and secondly that she hadn't known about it. They might have been busy at Annat House today but that was no excuse for Mhairi not telling her. She wondered if Mhairi knew where Haydn was going – and who with. That was the kind of gossip she really didn't need. She put on her best smile and said, 'You're quite right, she's a very versatile girl. And she's excellent with children. I'm sure she and Richie will have a great time. How is Richie taking to life in the wilds of Scotland, by the way?'

Haydn's smile faded. 'As well as could be expected, which isn't very well. He doesn't, er, like change.'

Catherine nodded sympathetically. 'Has he had a lot of change to deal with?'

'Not particularly.' For once Haydn's tone wasn't jokey. 'If you're thinking that Esme and my divorce has been a problem for him I can assure you otherwise. He was only three when we, er,

133

separated and after the initial, er, arguments he has lived with me. He's been at the same prep school since he was six; that's surely enough continuity for anyone.'

'Does he like his school?'

'He complains, but don't all children?'

'There are complaints and complaints,' said Catherine, wondering if she shouldn't make time to get to know Richie herself. He hadn't struck her as a happy boy. In fact, he had been entirely unexpected as the son of the suave and handsome Haydn. If she hadn't been so occupied with Phyllida, and the finding of the body, and arrangements for Exclusive Activity Holidays, she might have given him more attention already. 'Some children don't settle well at boarding school.' She thought of Malcolm.

'He's only been boarding since he was eight. Before that I employed a nanny and he was a day pupil. He's been very well looked after.'

'Of course,' said Catherine quickly. She hadn't meant to imply criticism. 'My father would approve. He's very impressed by the Harrow connection.'

Haydn raised an eyebrow. 'These things matter, do they?'

'They certainly do to Father and Kerr. They have both checked you out. Kerr seems to think you're something of a genius, but Father can't understand why you decided to sell the business. He said you could have had a knighthood if you'd hung in there.'

She had hoped to discomfort him by these disclosures but he merely said, 'How fascinating to be the source of such interest.' His tone was cool now.

Catherine looked down at her shoes (sensible ones tonight, no danger of tripping) as she remembered the reason her father had given for his enquiries. 'You're a good catch now, my girl. You need to be on the lookout for fortune hunters.' She shook her head. So many insults rolled in to one.

'We're a very nosy family,' she said.

'Oh, good,' said Haydn. 'I do like nosy people, allows one to be the same, don't you think? So, tell me, how old are you, if you don't mind me asking?'

Once again, Catherine felt caught out by the sudden change of subject. She felt she should be insulted by the bold enquiry, but then she caught the glint in his eye and had to smile in return. He was just waiting for her to rise to the bait.

'How old do you think I am?' she demanded instead.

'Mmm. Now do I flatter you by saying mid-twenties, which I'm sure you aren't? Or would you object to that because it would imply I thought you just a girl, whereas you are clearly a woman of standing?'

'How about telling the truth?'

'Thirty, I'd say then. You're older than John Hugo and younger than Kerr, isn't that right? I'd say about thirty.'

'Not bad. Thirty-one last November.'

He raised his glass to her. 'A November birthday? I'll have to remember that.'

Catherine said nothing. If he did, he would be the first man of her acquaintance to remember without prompting. Not that she minded, of course, and a birthday party was always better if you arranged it yourself.

The waiter came over and indicated their table in the restaurant was ready. They followed him through to the even more ornate splendour of wood-panelling, gilt cornices, and hundreds of mock-candle chandeliers. Haydn stared around appreciatively. Catherine was pleased he could enjoy it.

'Now, the next question,' he said, after they had taken their seats and placed their orders. 'Do you have a boyfriend at present?'

Catherine felt the ground dip suddenly beneath her. He couldn't be implying a serious interest; this was ridiculous. She could feel herself colouring as she tried and failed to produce a cool reply.

Haydn continued unperturbed, 'From the discreet enquiries I have made in the village I am led to believe that you are single, but it's always best to be sure, isn't it?'

'Is it?' Catherine glared. She took a sip of the rather nice white wine. 'That depends on your motive.'

'My motive is that I appreciate your company, of course.'

She blushed deeper. 'I'm glad you do. But why should it matter to you whether I am single or not?'

'Catherine, don't be obtuse.' He looked un-nervingly serious, laying his hand over hers on the table. 'You're a very lovely woman.'

'Rubbish.' She moved her hand away. His touch was warm and she felt chilled without it.

'I can assure you it's not rubbish.' He studied

her for a long moment through narrowed eyes, making her more annoyed than ever. 'You must learn to accept compliments gracefully, my dear.'

'Fortunately I don't get enough for that to be a problem.'

'Ah-ha. That's what you need, practice. Shall we start now? You have the most beautiful eyes, so dark that in some lights they look black.'

'Ha ha.'

'And eyelashes that lie like dark spikes against your creamy skin – especially when you bother to put mascara on them – making your eyes huger than ever.'

Catherine began to laugh. How could she not? 'Yes, and you're not bad looking yourself. Now, what are we having to eat?'

To her dismay, she found herself enjoying the evening very much. Haydn was fun to be with. She had thought it would be easy to go out with him this once, surely impolite not to do so, and then she could get back to the real business of her own life.

But as she readied herself for bed that night she found her thoughts dwelling on him; how attractive he was, how he was the only person she knew who really appreciated irony. And what had he meant by asking if she was single, saying he enjoyed her company? He hadn't pursued that line of conversation so she really didn't know.

This wasn't good. She had decided long ago how her life was to be. She loved Annat and she adored her independence. These things she would not give up. A relationship on her terms, with someone not close at hand, was all very well.

She just couldn't see Haydn in that light. He would want to have his way. My God, he might even want to be involved in her business. It would never work. She punched her pillow and tried to settle for the night.

Chapter Sixteen

Malcolm found himself, unaccountably, escorting Phyllida on a trip to Pitlochry. He didn't know why she couldn't drive herself, he knew she had a licence. But everyone seemed to think poor Phyllida needed looking after.

His father was still trying to get him to apologise to her for the row a few nights before. Malcolm had managed successfully not only to avoid that, but also any attempts to make him spend time with her. Now, on the last day before moving back to the Lodge, when he just happened to get up late, he had lowered his guard.

It was Catherine's fault. When he'd asked to borrow the runabout she'd nodded. And then said, 'Why don't you take Phyllida into town with you? She said she would like the chance to wander around.'

'I don't really think...'

'No Phyllida, no car,' she had said quietly.

Weirdly, the American woman wasn't difficult company. She didn't chatter or pry or make ridiculous pronouncements. She took herself off to trawl the shops and didn't try to interfere in his life, as anyone else in the family would have done.

Phyllida even didn't complain when he arrived late at their meeting place and he actually felt bad. So bad that, without being prompted, he found himself offering to make a detour on the way home to show her the local beauty spot, Queen's View. The way Phyllida thanked him in her soft voice you would think he had offered her the lottery prize.

'Queen Victoria is supposed to have visited, hence the name,' he said as he drew the car into the steeply sloping car park. He led the way up the short path to the viewpoint and they gazed together down the length of Loch Tummel. The water shimmered into the distance where the strange conical shape of Schiehallion hid its head, as so often, in cloud. 'My mother used to like it here.' He wished, then, he hadn't brought her.

'I can see why. It's very beautiful.'

Malcolm said nothing. Personally, he preferred the bleaker uplands.

'It's very kind of you to bring me,' said Phyllida, touching his arm.

Malcolm stepped away, not even trying to hide his distaste. He kept his eyes on the water far below and wondered what would happen if he jumped. Had his mother ever thought of jumping? He screwed up his eyes, thinking of the pain she had been in during those last weeks. God, he wished he had been home more, been able to help more.

'I'm sorry if it reminds you of your mother,' said Phyllida gently.

Her niceness infuriated Malcolm. 'How do you

know what it reminds me of?' He swung around to face her. 'You know nothing about any of us.'

'I'd like to get to know you, honey.'

'Don't call me honey.' Malcolm was pleased to feel anger. He'd hated himself for starting to like her. 'I don't know what you're doing here. I don't know why you bother with Father.'

'Don't you want your father to be happy?'

'Why should I? He's a pompous idiot.'

'I respect your memories of you mother,' said Phyllida, taking advantage of his silence. 'She sounds to have been a truly lovely person.'

'She was,' said Malcolm shortly. Sometimes he almost couldn't remember her and the pain of that was unbearable. But now, through the argument, she was there in his mind, laughing dark eyes and dark hair, so like Catherine, teasing in her faintly Lancashire-accented voice. 'She was perfect. You couldn't be her even if you tried.'

Phyllida swallowed. His mother's voice in his head wasn't laughing now. *Malcolm,* it said quietly. *Remember your manners. You can't control how others behave but you can control yourself.* He turned away and clenched his fists.

'Perhaps we should go back,' said Phyllida nervously.

'It's not you!' said Malcolm, turning back to face her. He took a deep breath. 'It's not you I resent. It's him. Come on. Have you seen enough of the view? We might as well go home.' He knew he should apologise but he couldn't. 'Why do you put up with him?' he said.

'Your father is good to me.'

Malcolm stared at her in amazement.

'I had a difficult first marriage,' said Phyllida in her soft voice. 'I couldn't have children. My husband left me for someone who could have been his daughter. He made me feel worthless. Your father makes me feel important.'

'Oh,' said Malcolm, because he couldn't think of anything else to say. What on earth did she mean? He almost felt sorry for her. And, strangely, he resented both her and his father far less.

When they returned to Annat House he went in search of Mhairi. She was counting sheets in the airing cupboard. 'Did you have a good trip?' she said, sparing him a brief glance.

'It was OK.'

'I told you it would be.'

Malcolm sighed. 'You were right. She's not bad, really.'

That made Mhairi smile approvingly. At least she thought he was doing something right for once. He waited until she had finished counting, making neat little ticks on her list. 'Look, I wondered what you were doing this evening? There's still a half tank of petrol in the car, we could go into town.'

'Ah,' said Mhairi, folding her list. ''Fraid I can't. I promised I'd watch a DVD with Mum. By some miracle she's persuaded Dad to join the darts team, so we have control of the remote for once.'

Malcolm scowled. That wasn't even a proper excuse. She preferred watching a DVD with her bloody mother to going out with him? He didn't know why he bothered. 'Fine.'

Even when he tried to do things right, they weren't right. He swung round and left her.

Chapter Seventeen

Catherine was working on a spreadsheet and it was making her head sore. Surely there couldn't be quite so much money going out and so little coming in? This was her bloody father's fault for distracting her from what she should really be doing, which was drumming up business.

She looked up at a tap on the window of her office and frowned to see Haydn standing there. Really, did he have no manners? He could perfectly well have rung the front door bell.

He smiled and indicated the window catch and with a sigh she reached across and opened it.

'How are you this fine morning?' he said cheerfully. 'I was considering a walk and wondered if you and Pip would like to join me?'

'I'm busy,' said Catherine, looking at the figures on the screen and the piles of paper on her desk.

'Surely nothing that can't wait for an hour or two? I always think you should make the most of the good weather when we have it, don't you?'

Catherine sighed again. 'I didn't know you were back,' she said. He had travelled south to return his son to boarding school, but surely that didn't take so long? She hadn't seen him for more than a week.

'You missed me?' he said with his lopsided smile.

'Noticing and missing are two entirely different things.'

'Exactly. Now hurry up and get your coat. Leaving the window open like this is letting all your valuable heat escape.'

Catherine gave up the pretence that she didn't wish to go with him. She closed the window and went to find suitable outdoor wear.

Haydn was right about the day. It was a bright breezy April morning, with little white clouds chasing each other across the sky and the smell of new growth in the air. She could hear the lambs in the home field of the neighbouring farm, a sound that definitely meant the worst of winter was over. Catherine pulled her hat low over her ears, pushed her hands into the pockets of her jacket, and prepared for a good stride out. Pip capered about her heels as though he hadn't been offered the chance of a walk for weeks, but that was just for show. When she had taken him out first thing, he had tiptoed through the dewy grass with a look of great disgust on his little face, and darted back to the kitchen door as soon as permitted.

'Shall we go up the hill or down by the loch?'

Catherine hesitated. She preferred the paths through the hills, the views were so much better, but since the discovery of the body she had chosen other routes. 'Let's go up,' she said finally.

'Have you seen the photograph the police are showing round?' asked Haydn.

Catherine couldn't even pretend not to know what he was talking about. 'Of course. Detective Inspector Cowan was *kind* enough to come up to the house and show it to me himself.'

'Recognise her?'

'As far as I can tell, it's the same woman who

parked her car at the road end.' There had been something vaguely familiar about the face, that was probably why.

'But you don't recognise her from anywhere else?'

'No, I don't. And nor does anyone else in the area. We've all been asked I don't know how many times, but the whole point was, she was a stranger. That's why she came here, wasn't it? Because we didn't know who she was. And we still don't.'

Haydn walked steadily up the steep slope, his long legs covering the ground with apparent ease. He wasn't the least bit out of breath and Catherine was determined to show that she wasn't, either. It was more annoyance at the choice of subject than the strain of the climb that was getting to her.

They paused beside a stand of Scots pine in the lee of a small ridge. Catherine rested a hand on the rough bark. These were her favourite trees, not tall but sturdy, and with that lovely reddish colour.

'I suppose if you have to die, it's a beautiful place,' said Haydn, scanning the mountains behind and then the loch far below.

'We all have to die.'

'And we don't all get to choose when. Or where.'

'Well, I suppose we could, if we wanted. Most people don't want to die at all, do they? That's why they don't choose where to do it. Too busy avoiding it.'

'Did your mother want to die here?'

Catherine looked all around, her eyes finally coming to rest on the chimneys and slate roofs of

144

Annat House. The answer was, she supposed, yes. 'She was too young to die.'

'Cancer?'

'Yes.' Catherine turned to walk on. Her mother had loved to walk these paths. Woolly hat pulled down over her curls, drowned by one of her husband's jackets, she would go out in all weathers. She had loved it if her children would go with her. Catherine wished she had gone more often, but it wasn't the sort of thing that appealed to teenagers. She hadn't known then how little time they would have.

'How are the wedding plans progressing?' Haydn said after a while.

'Oh, brilliant, fantastic, couldn't be better.'

'I'm so pleased.'

'My bloody father's gone away for at least a week. So guess who that leaves in charge of everything.'

'And there was I, thinking you liked to be in charge.'

She glared. It was better to be angry than upset. 'I've got quite enough to be in charge of at the moment with our next two courses running back to back. I could really do without the hassle of arranging a wedding to my father's specifications.'

'Demanding, are they?'

'You might say. My father isn't speaking to the minister who is to perform the service because he expressed reluctance to marry a divorcee. And it hasn't helped that we've changed the date three times already because of Father's so-called business obligations, although I think it's really because he wants the date to suit his wealthy

American friends.'

'Always good to have one's friends attend this kind of occasion.'

'Hmmph. Anyway, we've settled on the last weekend in May. Let's hope he doesn't change his mind again.'

'Useful to have a date to work towards.'

'Yes. But that wasn't the only problem. First he refused to have Fergus cater for the reception, even though he wants to have it at Annat House. Then, when I've given Fergus the weekend off, he changes his mind about that too, because *our chef* does such marvellous canapés. He isn't speaking to Kerr because after the third change of date *he* refused to change his rota yet again in order to attend. And Father isn't talking to Malcolm because – oh, goodness knows why, they've never got on.' She really should work harder at bringing them together.

'I do so like happy families.'

'And it's not as if I haven't enough to do already. I mean, the whole thing is absurd, why do I have to do everything?'

'I'm sure you don't *have* to.'

Catherine ignored that. 'And why does it have to be here, and why now?'

'Surely the sooner the better. Won't your life be easier once you get him off your hands?'

'Yes,' said Catherine. 'But...' But what? But she didn't want Gordon to leave? She was afraid she would miss him, or at least miss being needed by him. Haydn would quite rightly think her mad if she admitted to any of that.

'Poor you.' Haydn put an arm about her shoul-

146

ders and pulled her close. They had paused once again to admire the views, and he left his arm around her. She didn't want to make an issue of it by pulling away. In fact, part of her didn't want to pull away at all. It felt so comfortable to stand there, sheltered from the brisk breeze.

'What you need is a break,' said Haydn after a while.

'Ha. And when am I likely to get that?'

'Of course, a few days away might be difficult just now, but surely you could manage one?'

Catherine shrugged uneasily. She was much too busy to consider taking time off. She moved away from him.

'I was going to ask you a favour,' he continued. 'I still haven't got around to re-furnishing the cottage and I thought I would go down to Edinburgh for a day sometime soon and make a start. The whole process would be so much more enjoyable if you would come with me.'

He regarded her calmly as he waited for a reply.

'I'll treat you to lunch and dinner,' he said coaxingly, as though that would make all the difference.

'I really don't have the time...'

'And we could maybe take in a theatre performance in the evening?'

'It's very kind of you, but I don't think just now.'

'You know what they say: a break is as good as a rest.'

'They say all sorts of things, most of them rubbish.'

He smiled, not looking in the least offended.

'You would be doing me a huge favour.'

Catherine could feel herself weakening and took another step back, pushing her hands deep into the pockets of the disreputable Barbour jacket. 'Talking of favours,' she said, with sudden inspiration. 'There's something I've been wanting to ask you.' There, that was better, now she was back on her own territory.

'Ye-es?'

'Yes. We have a very active Community Council in the village.' She eyed him cautiously. 'I wondered if you would come along to a meeting.'

Haydn's smile broadened to a grin. 'Well done! That was a very clever way of turning the conversation.'

She smiled but said nothing. Sometimes waiting got you the answer you wanted.

'You know,' he mused, 'It's taken you longer than I expected to get round to inviting me.'

'I don't know what you mean.'

'I've heard all about you and your Community Council. Why, I believe they've been taking bets in the village on your chances of getting me to join.'

Catherine glared. 'It would be good for you to be involved in the community. And your entrepreneurial skills would be a real asset.' And if this distracted Haydn from inviting her to spend a day with him, all to the good.

Haydn sighed, then smiled. 'I'm really not quite sure what a Community Council involves, but I'm willing to give it some thought.'

'Excellent.'

'We would need to talk it over.'

148

'Yes, if you want.'

'I do want. In fact, I think this is just the sort of thing we could discuss at our leisure on a trip down to Edinburgh.' He met her eyes calmly. 'What do you think? I'd be willing to give it a try if you were.'

There was a long silence. The reddening of Catherine's cheeks had nothing to do with the wind. 'I suppose we could,' she said at length. She felt a curl of excitement or fear in her stomach, which was ridiculous. He was only inviting her for a day out, because he wanted her help.

He took her hand and swung it lightly as they turned back down hill. 'Now, which day would suit you best?' he said. 'As long as it's not too far in the future, I'm happy to let you choose.'

'So how was the DVD?' Malcolm asked, the words coming out more abruptly than he had intended.

Mhairi looked up briefly from her interminable lists. 'It was a chick flick. You wouldn't like it.'

'How do you know?' he said grumpily, although he was pretty sure she was right.

He took a deep breath and decided to start again. He gave Mhairi his best smile. 'If I invited you to a smart restaurant like Haydn took Catherine, would you come out with me?' He was determined to make a real effort this time.

'Oh, I don't think so.'

'But Mhairi, why not?'

She wrinkled her nose at him, not smiling any more. 'What do you think?'

Malcolm's mood slipped. 'Look, what's wrong

with me? You've been out with practically every boy in the village, or so I hear. Why not give me a try?'

'Who I have and havenae been out with is no business of yours. But I'll tell you for nothing I've no' been out with most of the lads in the village.' She glared. 'Only the good-looking ones, and there aren't so many of them.'

'I'm not bad looking,' said Malcolm hopefully.

'Says who?'

'Lots of people.' Malcolm glanced at his reflection in the darkened glass of the window. They were sitting at the kitchen table, having a coffee while Mhairi worked. What was wrong with him?

Mhairi turned and studied him. 'I suppose you're OK. If you like that long-haired girly look.'

Malcolm sighed. He wished he hadn't made the invitation now. He and Mhairi had been getting on OK recently. Maybe it would have been better if he'd built up to this slowly.

'Piss off,' he said, doing his chances no good at all. 'Why are you always so horrible?'

'I'm just honest. People like me are.'

'What do you mean, people like you?'

'The lower classes, you know? What your father calls *commoners*. We're lazy and ignorant and we don't have the jolly good manners of someone of your class.'

'What on earth are you talking about?' Malcolm was puzzled. There was an anger in Mhairi's voice that belied her smile. Before, she had been brushing him off as she brushed him off every time, giving no clue as to her reason. And now...

'You really think this class thing is important?'

'*I* don't.'

'Well, nor do I.'

Mhairi gave another brittle smile. 'But you don't deny that there is a difference between us.'

'For God's sake, what century are you living in?'

'This one. So just leave me alone, OK? I've got a job to do for Catherine. It's the best job I've ever had and I don't want to mess it up. Having you hanging round interfering isn't exactly helping.'

'I'm not interfering.'

'But you're always there, aren't you?' Mhairi pushed herself up from the table, and at that moment the phone rang. She looked relieved as she pressed the button on the portable handset, turning away from him.

Malcolm watched in silence. It must have been one of the local suppliers. She smiled as she chatted, dropping into a broader dialect, relaxed as she cajoled them to do exactly what she wanted. Did she really think something like class was important? That he thought it was?

'Best get back to work,' said Mhairi, when the call finished. She took her lists and the handset and headed for the stairs.

Malcolm was about to give up, again, when it occurred to him that there was one reason she *hadn't* given for not going out with him. She hadn't said she didn't fancy him.

He jumped up and followed her, taking the steps two at a time. 'Look, just give it a try, all right? Give me a chance and if it doesn't work out, it doesn't.'

Mhairi paused and turned. Three steps above

151

him, she was for once the taller. It was strange looking up to her small, sombre face. 'Malcolm, forget it, OK? It wouldn't work.'

'I'm not forgetting it.'

'You're only interested because I keep saying no.'

This time Malcolm grinned. 'There's only one way to test that – say yes.'

'God, Malcolm! Look, if I go on one date with you, will you leave me alone?'

Malcolm considered, hope rising. 'No, one date isn't long enough.' He didn't think so highly of his attractions. 'No. How about a ... a month? Let's give it a go for a month, and if it doesn't work out, it doesn't. I won't pester you again.'

Mhairi pulled a face, disbelieving. 'Are you serious?'

'Absolutely. Go on. A month starting from, say, Friday.'

She shook her head, but she was smiling now. 'You're mad.'

'Go on. I'll take you out somewhere. Where do you want to go? You choose.'

There was a long silence while Mhairi looked him up and down thoughtfully.

'Well, there is a movie on in Pitlochry I'd like to see...'

Malcolm wanted to punch to air. Yes! She was weakening. 'That's it then. We'll go into Pitlochry.' He moved up another step. 'You let me know what time the movie starts and we can maybe have a meal before or after. How about it?'

'Well...'

'It'll be fun.'

'Well... OK then. I'll check the times.'

She looked so cute, frowning at him with narrowed eyes, he couldn't resist kissing her lightly on the lips. He'd wanted to do that for so long. It was only a touch, but it made him want more.

'A month starting on Friday, then? It's agreed?' He leant in for a second kiss.

'If you're going to do that, I think the month should start now,' said Mhairi, stepping away. Before he could argue she added, 'Go on, off with you. I really have got work to do and – well, what do you know, there's the phone again.'

Malcolm let her go without protesting that time. She had agreed, actually agreed, to give him a chance. And this was one thing he wasn't going to mess up.

Chapter Eighteen

'I've foun' oot mair aboot yer neighbour,' announced Nancy when Catherine called in for the Sunday paper. 'Did you ken he was famous?'

'Famous?' said Catherine, playing for time. Fortunately there was no one else in the shop just then.

'Aye. His name's no' Smith, it's some hyphenated thing. Look, here it is, Eddlington-Smith. Did you ken that?'

'He might have mentioned it.' Catherine felt uncomfortable. Haydn had wanted to keep quiet about his successful past. People wouldn't mean to, but it would change the way they acted towards him. She was just surprised Nancy had found out. It wasn't like her to read the business pages.

She waved a paper at Catherine. 'Look, here it is.' Catherine saw with a sinking heart it wasn't the business section at all, but one of Nancy's favourite gossip columns. *Lady Cavanagh, daughter of Lord Milby and former wife of multi-millionaire Haydn Eddlington-Smith, is back in the UK for the first time in years...* There's a picture of her, and of him, that's how I realised. Who'd have thought it, someone like that moving up here? I mind now there was a great fuss a few years back about the two of them.'

'A fuss?' asked Catherine, surprised.

'Aye, it was one of they big fancy divorce cases. A while back now, which is why I didnae realise at first, and the name being different an' all. Sir Harold Cavanagh has some kind of connection with royalty, it'll come to me in a minute, so it was all over the papers. And Esme Eddlington-Smith was in the magazines a bit herself, you know, *Hello* and the like, pretty, isn't she? The divorce was big news, 'specially with the husband fighting for custody of the child.'

Catherine was dismayed that Haydn had said nothing about all this. Did he just assume they knew? 'It was all a long time ago,' she said discouragingly.

'Aye, but it was a big story, you'd have known if you read the right papers. I'm sure there was more to it but I cannae mind just now.'

Catherine tried to discourage Nancy from discussing the story with anyone else, but she didn't think she was very successful. She was happily

154

regaling Mrs Morris from The Close with details before Catherine had even left the shop.

Catherine had made this journey down to Edinburgh many, many times. Edinburgh had been her mother's favourite city, which may have been why Catherine chose to do her degree there. During her first year at university she and her mother had had happy times exploring the galleries and shops, attending the theatres, doing all the things that it was so hard to do living in a place such as Annat.

And then her mother became ill, and everything had changed. Then it had been trips to the hospital, and finally the ever more frequent journeys home so that Catherine could be with her mother. But she wasn't going to think about that now.

Traffic on the A9 was quiet for once and Haydn drove his smart, sleek car at a good pace through the hills and winding valleys. When they dropped down to the flatter lands beyond Perth, he asked if she wanted to stop for a coffee. She declined. They would find parking more easily the earlier they arrived. Since the Scottish Parliament had opened, traffic in the city was worse than ever.

'City centre first?' said Haydn as he turned off the ring road and finally slowed to join a long queue of traffic. 'Princes Street, is that right? Where do you suggest we park?'

Catherine realised this wasn't a place he would know well. His confident driving and light-hearted conversation had made her think that for once she didn't need to be the one taking decisions. Now she would have to concentrate.

He took her instructions without complaint, which was a point in his favour. Neither her brothers nor her father could bear to be told where to go.

The morning was spent having coffee in a lovely place with views of the magnificent Edinburgh Castle, and then wandering around the galleries on George Street. This was not shopping as Catherine knew it. Haydn had insisted they start here. He said that a piece of original artwork would give him just the inspiration he needed for the mood of the house. Catherine wasn't convinced, but decided not to tell him that, yet.

'My God, you're decisive,' she said sarcastically, when they went back to the first gallery for the third time, to see if he still liked the tiny seascape he had seen there.

'If I still like it, I'll buy it,' he replied cheerfully. 'And I'd like to see what else this artist has done. I think she's a real talent.'

'The gallery owner said she's not long out of college, I can't see why her stuff is so expensive.'

'Because it's good.'

'The guy who did my watercolours course could have done you something similar at a fraction of the price.'

'Something similar isn't enough.'

Catherine smiled. She knew exactly what he meant.

'We'll look at furniture in John Lewis's after lunch,' he said. 'And then check out Ikea. Have you got the stamina for that?'

Catherine harrumphed. 'I don't understand why you want to spend a fortune on a painting and then buy your furniture at Ikea.'

'Good design doesn't have to be expensive. I'll get the basics there, then I'll see.'

'It's not that I don't like the stuff,' she added, wondering if she had come over as a snob. 'I just wondered.'

'I suppose being brought up in a house of antiques, it's different for you. You won't ever have had to consider how to furnish from scratch.'

'Not from scratch, no, but I've had enough to do in that line recently.' Catherine thought about all the fights with her father, about which furniture should stay in the big house to be 'ruined' by the guests, and which should move with him to the Lodge. 'I wonder if Father will want to take anything with him to the States when he goes.' She frowned. She hadn't thought of that before.

'Is the furniture his?'

'Oh, yes, all the assets belong to him. It's money he's short of.'

'Perhaps Phyllida won't like antiques?'

'What will it matter what Phyllida likes?' Catherine frowned some more. 'Well, he definitely can't take any of the big pieces from the house. He promised to back me in this business and I'll bloody well see that he does.'

'You do that,' said Haydn, regarding her, as ever, with amusement.

Catherine had laughed off his comments about stamina, but by six o'clock even she was beginning to flag.

'Time to stop for a drink and plan the evening?' suggested Haydn. She was more than happy to agree. She wouldn't have admitted it to him, but the ankle she had sprained a few weeks back was paining her again. Even the little black boots she had chosen to wear had too much of a heel for comfort just now.

A glass of good red wine revived her somewhat and she persuaded Haydn to give up his idea of a theatre performance and opt instead for trying the new Provençal restaurant that John Hugo had raved about on his last visit home.

It was down on the waterfront in Leith, still a very trendy part of town although no longer so up and coming as it had been in her student days. Haydn took her hand as they strolled along the water's edge, pausing to watch the reflected lights.

'Not a bad place to live if you have to be in a city,' he said, looking up at the converted warehouses.

'Could be worse,' agreed Catherine. She could see it had a charm. Each flat had its own little wrought iron balcony from where you could look down on the buzz of city life or out over the water. She could have put up with it for at least a week.

Catherine took a sip of her second glass of wine and decided to take the plunge. He would know soon enough that his secret was all over the village. 'Nancy from the shop mentioned there was something in the papers about your wife being back in London.'

He paused with his glass half way to his lips, his expression absolutely blank. 'My wife?'

'Ex-wife. Lady Cavanagh? Is that right?'

He sighed and put the glass down without tasting it. 'Yes.'

'I'm sorry to bring it up, but I thought you should know people have, er, made the connection. I presume she's pretty well known if she's in the papers? Or her new husband is? Perhaps I should have realised sooner.'

'Thank God you didn't.' His lips were pressed together, his expression grim. 'I suppose it was too much to hope it wouldn't come out. God knows why people are so obsessed with *fame*. What has my life got to do with them?'

'I'm sorry,' said Catherine again.

'There's no need for you to be sorry. It'll be Esme blabbing to the press, being seen in all the right places. I knew this move to Spain was too good to last.'

Once the waiter had brought her first course, a small portion of an extremely spicy bisque, she couldn't resist asking, 'How is Richie getting on?'

'Fine.' Haydn's face took on a guarded expression, as it did so often when his son was mentioned. 'As far as I can gather, school is the same as it has always been.'

'He might feel isolated, being such a long way away from you.'

'He's been a full boarder for a while. My being here makes no difference.'

'It probably *feels* different. Especially if his mother is out of the country a lot.'

Haydn took a sip from his glass. He had moved on to fruit juice, as he was driving. 'But not, as it happens, at the moment.' He sighed.

'Will she visit Richie?'

'I have no idea.'

'How long is it since she saw him?' asked Catherine. Haydn might accuse her of improper curiosity but she couldn't help it. It seemed impossible to her that a mother would not want to spend time with her children.

'Let's see... Over two years? Yes, he spent Christmas two years ago with her and Sir Harold.'

'That's a long time.' Catherine felt sad.

'She's been away. She and *hubby* wanted to make a new life for themselves in Spain.'

'Spain isn't so difficult to get to, or from.'

'I know.' He was still looking uptight, but at least he was talking. 'Esme was very bitter when she wasn't awarded custody. She hates having to ask me if she can see her son so contact has been sporadic. I suspect second husband isn't particularly fond of Richie. The boy doesn't fit his idea of the sort of offspring he wants to show off.'

Catherine felt guilty for knowing exactly what Haydn meant. 'Hmm. Has he any children of his own?'

'No. Harold isn't sufficiently grown up himself to see the value of children. Sorry, I shouldn't have said that.'

'You don't like him?'

Haydn's expression had darkened but now he smiled determinedly. 'One doesn't normally have warm feelings for the man who was instrumental in the ending one's marriage, but I don't want you to think I'm broken-hearted.'

'I'm sorry. I shouldn't have intruded...'

'Think nothing of it. I've come to realise that the man was doing me a favour. Esme and I could never have been said to be well-matched. Now she's spending his money rather than mine,

160

and if she has to pander to his every whim in the process, well, that's not my problem, is it?'

'It's a shame for Richie.'

'Yes. Richie.'

'Will he be coming up here again soon? I'd like to get to know him.' Catherine was sure there was something she could do to help.

'Half term's in a few weeks' time, but it's a long way for him to come for such a short break. I'll have to see...'

An idea occurred to Catherine. 'You could always move him to Annat School. That would be so much more convenient.'

He raised an eyebrow. 'I'm grateful, of course, for your interest, but he's only got the rest of this year and then one more left at prep school.'

'A year is a long time to a child. Annat is considered to be a very good school.' She smiled encouragingly. 'Why don't you go and look it over?'

'Richie is already at a good school.' Haydn seemed, unusually, annoyed.

'Yes, of course.' Catherine was determined not to give up. 'Or you could send him to Kinlochannat Primary. It's very well thought of, small classes, you know, and if Richie was a day pupil you'd see so much more of him.'

'I'm not sure that would be good for either of us,' said Haydn repressively.

'Ah, well. Annat School does weekly as well as full boarding...'

'Thank you for your thoughts,' said Haydn. 'How about dessert?'

Catherine decided to give up for now.

They spoke little on the journey home, although Catherine did extract an agreement from him to attend a Community Council meeting. She lay back and closed her eyes, tired from the unaccustomed day's shopping, followed by good food and even better wine. Haydn had been the perfect companion, funny and interesting. Apart from that touchiness over Richie's school, the day had been perfect.

And soon it would be over, this little escape from the pressures of Exclusive Activity Holidays, and wedding preparations, and the rest. A cloud of depression seemed to settle softly around her as they passed Kinlochannat and turned onto the even narrower road home. She had never before felt depressed to be coming home.

She shook herself resolutely, physically as well as metaphorically. Haydn asked, 'You all right?'

'Yes, fine. I wanted to thank you for a wonderful day out.' There, that was the right tone.

'My pleasure.'

'It was really very kind of you. I'm sorry I wasn't more help with the furniture, and then suggesting that rather expensive restaurant...'

'As I said, it was my pleasure.' They were almost at the entrance to Annat House and he slowed the car right down. 'I don't suppose I could persuade you to come back to the cottage with me?'

Catherine had been watching his profile, thinking how good-looking he was even in this light. His mouth lifted in that half-smile. 'To the cottage? Oh, for a coffee.' Her heart was beating uncomfortably. She was no good at this kind of thing. 'We can have a coffee at the House, if you'd like.'

Haydn didn't turn up the track to Annat

House. Instead, he drew the car to a halt, so that the decision still had to be made. 'I didn't mean for coffee. I meant for the night.'

'Oh...' Catherine was breathless. Her heart was thumping and there was that quiver of excitement in her stomach. She just stared at him, trying to make out his expression. She thought he was smiling still.

'So that's what it takes to make you speechless,' he said, and leant across and kissed her. It was a gentle kiss, warm lips on warm lips, the hint of the day's stubble brushing against her skin. She hesitated and then leaned in and kissed him back.

After a while, Haydn pulled away. 'Not really very comfortable here,' he said. 'Do I take that as a yes?'

'No. Yes. No, no.' Catherine shook her head as if that would clear her thoughts. 'No, no, I need to think.'

'Thinking is often overrated.'

She put out a hand and squeezed his gently. 'I'd like to go home, please.'

She had known he wouldn't push her, and he didn't. It would have been so much easier not to like him if he had.

Chapter Nineteen

Catherine was taking trays of scones from the oven the following morning when Malcolm came flying down the stairs to the kitchen. She was baking to distract herself from thoughts of Haydn.

'They've identified her,' he said breathlessly. 'Her name's Jean Lawson. She was from somewhere near London. They were right about that.'

'I take it you mean the Lost Woman?' she said, her tone determinedly mild.

'Of course. Who else? Nancy at the shop told me and I've just looked up the details on the internet. The internet's brilliant for getting up-to-date information. There's a statement from the police and a wee bit on some newspaper websites.'

Catherine put the oven gloves tidily away and smoothed down her shirt. She wasn't sure if it was good to know the poor woman's name.

'How did they identify her?'

'Oh, they've had sketches in all sorts of papers, it was bound to happen at some point. The statement says she was forty-two years old and from Reading, or was it Surbiton? Croydon? One of those places near London. She hadn't even been reported as missing.'

'Anything else?'

'Not much. She had lived alone since her mother died. I bet there'll be more in the papers tomorrow. They'll be trying to find out all about her, won't they? I wonder if they'll find some dark secret.'

'I wonder if she had any other family,' said Catherine.

'The papers didn't seem to think so.'

'So that's that,' Catherine said after a moment. The woman had looked older than forty-two. She couldn't have had an easy life. 'I suppose they'll bury her now.'

'I suppose so.'

Catherine shook her head, wondering. How could someone be so alone that their disappearance was not even noticed? Her family had a lot of bad points but at least they were *there,* interfering, making demands.

'Oh and Nancy said she's remembered more about Haydn's divorce, something about Richie. Seems to think you might want to know?'

Catherine wrinkled her brow with distaste this time. Why did Nancy think she would want to know? 'I'm not interested in gossip,' she said repressively.

Later that morning Aunt Georgie phoned looking for Gordon.

'He's still in Aberdeen,' Catherine said. 'At least he took Phyllida with him this time. And your guess is as good as mine as to when they'll be back. Can I take a message for him?'

'No, no, I don't think so.'

'What is it about?' she asked bluntly.

'Just one or two matters I'd like to discuss with him.' Georgies tone was cold, but as she and her brother were often on bad terms Catherine didn't think anything of it. 'Do you think he'll be

165

back later? I could come over and see him.'

'As I said, I don't know. I was under the impression he was returning yesterday, but he never turned up. Shall I give you his mobile number and you can ask him yourself?'

'No, no, that won't be necessary.' Georgie was very active for her age, but she had an old person's dislike of new technology. 'Just let me know when he does reappear.'

Catherine sighed. 'I hope he doesn't come back today. Malcolm and Mhairi have the afternoon off and I've a new party of guests just arrived.'

Thank goodness Catherine had said no. Being with that woman affected Haydn's judgement. He did not want to get into a relationship again. He'd managed to put the fiasco with Esme to the back of his mind for years, but having her back in London brought it all too much to the forefront. He'd had two phone calls already this morning, supposedly about Richie, but with the barbed comments and intrusive questions – oh yes, he could remember all too well what a failure he was at relationships.

He had been pleased with his move to Scotland. Despite the stares he was now getting in the village, things had worked out pretty well – the location was spectacular, the house small enough for him to manage, and the isolation was just what he needed. For the first time in a long time, he didn't think a major decision he'd made was the wrong one. Looking out at the cool, hazy grey dawn he had been sure all those mistakes were behind him. New home, new start. He felt positive about life, even about Richie. Why shouldn't he and his son be able to build a better relationship? Maybe he just hadn't approached things the right way up to now.

So why had he insisted Catherine go to Edinburgh with him, invited her back to spend the night, for godssake? He needed to be more careful. There was something about her that drew him. She was very attractive, and she wasn't impressed by his wealth or looks, nor intimidated by his brains. When he was with her, he wanted more. He sighed. *Thank goodness* she had had the sense to say no.

He turned his mind firmly back to his new project, revising some rather tricky computations of the aerodynamics of large vehicles. He had this idea for designing attachments to fit to vans and lorries, to reduce wind drag and improve fuel consumption. He'd seen it done before but no one had come up with a design flexible enough to suit all vehicles, and now he understood why. It was taking forever to do the calculations. He didn't know why he had got interested in this; it wasn't anything like his previous projects. It was nice to play around with the idea for the fun of it, he definitely wasn't thinking of taking it on to market or anything like that.

When the phone rang he grabbed the receiver without checking caller display and barked, 'Yes?'

'Haydn, darling, so lucky to catch you.'

Haydn groaned. 'Esme.'

'Yes, darling, it's me.' She gave a little girlish laugh that must have charmed him once.

'Is there some reason for this third phone call?'

'Actually, there is. I've been phoning darling Richie's school to arrange to take him out and they're being most unreasonable.'

'You know you have to make arrangements through me,' said Haydn, trying to keep his tone level. 'You just make it difficult for the school if you try and contact them direct.'

'It seemed the sensible thing to do. He is my son.'

Haydn paused so that he could get a rein on his temper. 'Yes, but you still have to arrange access via me.'

'I've missed him so much. I don't know when we'll be here again so this seemed the perfect opportunity.' She gave another little laugh.

When Haydn said nothing, Esme rattled on, 'It would be so lovely if he could spend some time with us, and it would be a break for him, wouldn't it? School can be so dreary.'

'I suppose I could get him a meal pass,' said Haydn reluctantly.

'Oh, pooey. A meal wouldn't be long enough. Surely we could have him for the weekend?'

'The school doesn't like children being out overnight,' said Haydn, not quite truthfully. 'Especially not this close to half term. And he's coming to *me* for half term, that's already arranged.' He was relieved, now, he had decided this.

'I wonder how he feels about this move of yours. He's not really a country boy, is he?'

'He's perfectly happy about it,' said Haydn. 'Do you want me to arrange a meal pass or not?'

'I suppose so, if that's all we're allowed.'

'Tell me what dates suit and I'll see what I can

168

do. And can you be quick about it? I'm rather busy at the moment.'

'Darling, you always are rather busy.'

Low-level irritation with Esme hung over him after he put the phone down. He didn't like the thought of her being in London, close to Richie, when he was so far away. Catherine's suggestion about Annat School suddenly seemed a whole lot more appealing.

Maybe he should take a look at the place. It might even be a good idea to get Catherine to come along and give a second opinion. No, stop thinking about Catherine! He really had to get out of the habit of asking her to go on outings with him.

With a conscious effort, he turned his thoughts to the relative benefits of various poly-carbon materials. Then he had the beginnings of an idea how to reduce wind drag even further, with one small but very clever tweak. He put down his mug and went up to his study.

'Where are we going?' said Mhairi as she and Malcolm climbed out of the car in the centre of Pitlochry.

He took her hand. 'Wait and see.' Her hands were small and slight, like the rest of her. He liked the feel of her cool fingers against his own. She glared at him and slid her hand away, burying it deep in the pocket of her multi-coloured coat. Not to be denied, he put an arm around her shoulders. She couldn't push that off without causing a scene. And, after all, she had agreed to a one-month trial, hadn't she?

When he had kissed her after the movie on Friday he had thought he felt the quiver of a response. Surely it wasn't just his own heart that beat a little faster? It had been the hardest thing to do, pulling back light-heartedly, not pushing her. He had a month to make this work and he was pretty sure rushing wasn't the right way with Mhairi. That's what she would expect, so he had to show her something different.

When they reached the doorway of the coffee shop Mhairi stood still. 'We're going *here?* I thought you said we were doing some investigating.'

'We are.' Malcolm felt smug.

'So we're going to investigate our coffee cups, are we?'

'Don't be silly. I've agreed to meet someone here. You know I said to you I was interested in journalism? Well, I got talking to one of the journalists from the local paper, sounding her out about the possibilities. I'm not sure I'm actually that keen any more, but that's beside the point. This woman was quite friendly and she knows I'm interested in the Lost Woman. She phoned earlier and said she'd got some new information and did I want to come and meet her this afternoon. So here we are.'

Malcolm was rather pleased with himself. He had quite liked the journalist, a woman called Annie Grieve. She wasn't his normal idea of a reporter, being female and quite old, at least fifty, but that had made it easier to approach her. And she had obviously taken to him, phoning him up like that.

As they queued at the counter, Malcolm spotted her at the back of the room and raised a hand. The woman acknowledged him with a nod of her grey head. When he put the tray down on her table and introduced Mhairi, he realised that she was looking none too pleased.

'I'd expected you to come alone, like,' she said, her voice soft with the local accent but her eyes sharp.

'Mhairi and I've been looking into things together,' said Malcolm. He hadn't wanted to miss the chance to spend time with her on one of their rare free moments. 'It was Mhairi who found the glove.'

'I remember.' The older woman frowned some more as she poured herself another cup of tea.

Malcolm and Mhairi took sips of their own drinks, then Malcolm hinted, 'You'd found something else out about Jean Lawson?'

'I have,' said the woman.

'That's good.' Still the woman just looked at him, consideringly. 'I hope it's going to explain once and for all why she chose to die on Annat land.'

'It wasn't Annat land,' murmured Mhairi, who never seemed to be able to resist contradicting him.

'It used to be.'

'Did it?' said Annie, writing something in her notebook. 'Interesting.'

'Is it? Look, are you going to tell us what this is about or not?'

'I've found something I thought you might like to see,' said the woman slowly. 'It'll be in the

171

paper tomorrow but I thought you might like to have a look first.'

'Ye-es?' said Malcolm. Her tone was making him uneasy.

The woman bent to the capacious bag at her feet and pulled out a brown envelope. From this she drew a sheet of paper which she placed on the table in front of Malcolm. 'Have a look at that and tell me what you think.'

Malcolm looked down at what appeared to be a photocopy of a birth certificate. 'Is it hers?' he asked, excited.

''S'not very easy to read,' said Mhairi, leaning against his shoulder. 'Why did they have to hand-write everything in those days?' She peered closer. It was great to feel her so warm against him. 'OK, date ... seems about right.'

Malcolm followed her finger as it moved along the grainy paper, and when she paused he took over the reading. 'Place of birth some street I can't make out, but it's in Croydon, that seems right, doesn't it? Name, Jean Sarah Lawson. Ever heard of a middle name before? No? Sex, girl. Name of father...'

He stopped reading. Then he swallowed hard. He leant closer to be absolutely sure he was seeing right. 'Name of father. Gordon...' He paused again. 'Gordon Hugo...' He cleared his throat. 'Gordon Hugo McDonald.'

'And how do you feel about that?' said the journalist, pen poised.

Chapter Twenty

'I need to speak to Father,' said Malcolm as he burst into the Lodge kitchen.

'Join the bloody queue,' said Catherine.

'I need to speak to him *now*.' Malcolm's face was ashen and his eyes hard and staring. Catherine had never seen him like that before and the disquiet she had been feeling all day deepened. In the morning her thoughts had all been of Haydn, but after calls from Georgie and the police, both looking with increasing urgency for her father, she had been forced to worry about other things.

'Where is he?' Malcolm's tone was sharp. There was no hint of the petulant child. This was real anger. 'I know he's back, his car's here.'

'Have a seat,' said Catherine, gesturing to the kitchen table where Phyllida and Georgie were already sitting.

Malcolm glanced at them briefly, and then a second time, as though only just taking them in.

'Hello, Malcolm,' said his aunt. 'What's all this about?'

'I'll speak to my father first, but it won't stop there. Oh, no, it won't stop there. You'll all hear soon enough.' His eyes rested on Phyllida and Catherine's apprehension grew. Why was Phyllida the one he looked sorry for? He swung back to Catherine. 'Where is he?'

'He's ... with someone at the moment. For

heaven's sake, Malcolm, sit down, you're making me nervous.'

And he was. His wide-legged stance and fierce expression were so unlike her younger brother.

'Have some tea,' she said, lifting the pot to test whether she could squeeze out another cup. 'What's happened to Mhairi?'

'Mhairi?' He looked as though he had no idea who she was talking about.

'Mhairi. Wasn't she going into Pitlochry with you?'

'Oh, Mhairi. I dropped her at home.' He removed his jacket abruptly and draped it over the back of the chair. 'What are you doing here, anyway? Shouldn't you be up at the House looking after your guests?'

This was exactly where Catherine should be, but she wasn't leaving yet. 'Fortunately this afternoon they're having a talk by Charlie Andrews, our local plants enthusiast. I'll go and see how they're getting on presently.'

Malcolm sat down but this didn't lessen the waves of anger that emanated from him. He didn't actually beat out a tattoo of impatience on the table, but he might just as well have done.

'You were telling us about your trip to Aberdeen,' said Georgie to Phyllida. 'Not a bad place, is it, despite all that grim grey stone.'

Phyllida took the cue and continued her soft-spoken praise of the northern city. Catherine managed to wonder, briefly, if Phyllida would ever find something about Scotland that didn't please her. 'Aren't you missing the States?' she asked, abruptly.

'Of course. But I've been made so welcome here and it is *such* a beautiful country.' Phyllida smiled her gentle smile, and Catherine felt bad.

Then a door in the hallway opened and her father's voice could be heard showing Detective Inspector and his colleague out of the front door. She didn't know why she had been reluctant to identify the visitors to Malcolm, unless it was because she didn't want to admit their presence even to herself.

Malcolm rose without a word and stepped out into the hallway.

'Father!'

'Why, Malcolm...'

'I need to talk to you.'

'Why, what a lot of people,' said Gordon. His voice sounded oddly high-pitched.

'That was the police, wasn't it?' said Georgie. 'I was hoping to get to you before them.'

'Ah, yes.'

Malcolm rounded on his aunt. 'You *know?*'

'Of course I know,' she said flatly. 'I'm just wondering how on earth you do.'

'For Chrissake, stop talking in riddles,' said Catherine, her eyes darting from one face to the next. Her father looked dazed, Malcolm still angry, Georgie sad. Only Phyllida looked as bemused as Catherine felt. 'What on earth is going on?'

Gordon took a seat. It was at the head of the table, but he made no effort to take charge. Instead, he looked down, not meeting anyone's eyes. After a moment, Malcolm sat down too.

'Well?' said Catherine.

Neither her father nor her brother would look at her. It was Georgie who spoke.

'I think the police probably came to tell Gordon they have found out more about the identity of the so-called Lost Woman.' She glanced at her brother who was still staring blankly away. 'You all know from the press that her name was Jean Lawson. What you didn't know is ... who Jean Lawson was. Who her parents were.'

'Who was she?' said Catherine.

'She was our sister,' said Malcolm hoarsely. 'That's who she was. Our sister. *His* daughter.'

Catherine felt an almost physical jolt of shock, and at the same time saw how it all now made sense. The vague familiarity of the face, the strange connection with Annat...

'I don't understand,' she said, putting out a hand to steady herself.

'She was Gordon's daughter from a relationship that happened a long, long time ago.' It was Georgie, once more, who took up the story. 'Long before he married your mother. As you may or may not know, he lived in London for a few years when he was younger. It happened at that time.'

'And we never knew?' said Catherine, collecting herself enough to stare at her father. 'You had another child and you never told us?'

'There wasn't any need,' said Gordon, raising his head for the first time. 'These things happen.' He cleared his throat. 'Really, I don't know why you're all making such a fuss about it.'

'She was your *daughter*,' said Malcolm. Catherine didn't know how he had managed to find out this fact, but clearly he had had longer to think about it than she had. Malcolm was glaring at his father. 'So you did know she existed?'

'Of course.'

'You knew it was her? That the Lost Woman was your daughter?'

'No.' Gordon still looked stunned. 'No, it never crossed my mind.'

'When did you last see her?'

Gordon frowned, as though struggling to remember. 'I only saw her once, as a baby.'

'You abandoned her.' This was Malcolm.

His accusing tone seemed to rouse Gordon a little. 'I did not abandon her. You don't think I would shirk my responsibilities, do you?'

'Did Mum know?' said Catherine.

'No, of course not, it was all well in the past.'

'I thought you said you didn't shirk your responsibilities? You just deserted her – and her mother I suppose – you...'

'I provided for them,' he said stiffly.

'Did you keep in touch?' Catherine didn't know which would be worse, that her father had turned his back on his own child, or that he had kept in contact, secretly, behind her mother's back.

'Of course not.' When he saw her expression he added, 'Things were different in those days.'

'I can hardly believe this, even of you,' said Malcolm, his voice filled with pent up rage. 'How could you abandon your own child? Did you never even think...?'

It was Georgie, not his father, who interrupted. She put a hand on his arm. 'I hate to agree with my brother,' she said in her down-to-earth way. 'But these things do happen. No point in making a song and dance about them after the fact. Things *were* different in those days.'

'What happened?' asked Catherine, trying to collect her thoughts. 'When was all this? Why didn't we know?'

'Nothing much to tell. It wasn't a serious relationship.'

'It was a relationship that created a child!' snapped Malcolm.

'Audrey and I had already parted before I knew she was pregnant. As I said, I saw her once after the child was born. I have had no word from either of them since. Contrary to what you and the police seem to think.'

'Didn't you want to know her? Didn't you *care?*'

'Her mother and I agreed it was for the best,' said Gordon stiffly. 'It was what Audrey wanted.'

Malcolm snorted. 'How can we trust a word you say?'

'I don't have to answer to you, young man.' Gordon spoke coldly, sounding like his normal self for the first time since he entered the room.

But Malcolm was not to be stopped. 'How do we know you didn't drive her to her death? Because you abandoned her. Or maybe she was trying to blackmail you, maybe...'

'You're letting your ridiculous imagination run away with you.'

'Don't you have a conscience? Where were you when she needed you? Did you care?'

'I gave her mother plenty of money...'

'Money!' Malcolm banged the table, making them all jump. 'God, you make me sick.'

There was a silence, this time broken by

Phyllida. She put a hand across the table to touch Malcolm's hand. 'It's been a shock for you,' she said gently, as if it hadn't been a shock for them all. Then she turned to Gordon. 'Would you like a drink, darling? I think we could all do with something – something stronger than tea.'

Catherine had to go back to Annat House and her guests. Even reeling from the news she had just received, she couldn't forget her duties, and she had an awful feeling that, unsupervised, Charlie might be boring her guests rigid about the significance of heath bedstraw or whatever plant was his current obsession. She heaved a long, wavering sigh and pushed herself to her feet.

'I'll come back and see you later,' she said. Her head was spinning. The Lost Woman was *her sister*. A sister she hadn't even known she had.

Catherine walked slowly as she returned from Annat House to the East Lodge. She had a torch with her but tonight she didn't need it. The moon was almost full and lit the landscape with a faint, silvery light in a way that she would normally have admired. Now she sighed heavily and wondered what she would say to her father. I have a sister, she kept thinking. I *had* a sister.

She hesitated before entering. Part of her really didn't want to go back in there. The other part knew she had to. She called Pip to heel. Poor dog, he was confused by all this to-ing and fro-ing between House and Lodge. He wasn't the only one.

Only her father and Phyllida were in evidence. They had retired to the sitting room, her father fingering an empty whisky glass and Phyllida with a coffee mug beside her. She didn't think they had been talking when she came in, but for a moment she felt like an intruder.

'Where are the others?'

Her father stared at her blankly for a moment, then collected himself and the familiar dissatisfied frown settled on his high forehead. 'Georgie had to get back to her bloody dogs. Malcolm's gone to sulk in his bedroom.'

Catherine listened for a moment and decided from the sounds overhead that Malcolm had decided to take his sulks for a long bath. He was probably using all the hot water in the house. That would serve Father right.

'Why did the police want to see you?' she said. This seemed as good a place to start as any.

'Tying up loose ends is the expression I believe they used. Like Malcolm, they had traced the woman's father's name and made the obvious connection.'

'They must've been surprised you hadn't made the connection yourself, earlier.'

'I've been busy. Unlike some, I don't have time to waste on the gutter press.'

'I can't believe it,' said Catherine, for the umpteenth time. 'That you had a daughter and didn't tell us. And she's now dead. That the Lost Woman was *our sister.*'

Gordon reached for the whisky bottle and poured himself a large tot.

'It's been a shock for him,' said Phyllida.

'It's been a shock for all of us,' Catherine snapped.

'Less than a month until the wedding, then you'll have us off your hands,' said her father after taking a long swallow of his drink. 'You'll be able to put all of this behind you.'

'Don't you *care?*' demanded Catherine. 'Don't you care that your eldest daughter was so alone and unhappy that she took her own life? Aren't you sad? Ashamed? Don't you have any regrets?'

'I suppose it's too much to hope that the news won't become public knowledge.'

'For fuck's sake!'

'Language. Catherine, please.'

'I'll speak however I bloody like. Because you *don't* care, do you? Not about her, not about us. All you care about is what people might think of you.' Catherine prided herself on rarely losing her temper these days. Now she was shouting, her face surely red, her hands shaking. She could have done with a whisky herself, but didn't want him to see it. 'You deserted her! If you hadn't, maybe this wouldn't have happened, maybe we could have helped...'

It was Phyllida who interrupted her. 'Catherine, honey, we can't change the past. We all have things we regret, and shouting won't change them. Now, how about I get all of us a hot drink?'

Chapter Twenty-one

What was life? A duty, a burden, a privilege? If you didn't want it, did you have to endure it? Catherine couldn't stop thinking about her poor half-sister.

Whose fault was it Jean hadn't wanted to live? She probably hadn't had an easy time. An illegitimate child when such things were neither normal nor acceptable. But she *could* have fought through it, couldn't she? If family was so important to her that she came all this way, why not come sooner, make an effort to contact them?

So many questions, and she would never know the answers.

'How punctual you are,' said Haydn, interrupting these thoughts. He had come to collect her for the visit to Annat School he had so inexplicably arranged, and even more inexplicably insisted on her going on. 'I wish everyone was so reliable.' It was the first time she had seen Haydn since the trip to Edinburgh which now seemed like ancient history. It was also the first time since the news had been broken. He had called by once, but she simply hadn't had the energy for him. She had been busy with guests and trying to make sense of it all in her head. Now, looking at his unusually grim face, she wondered if he was annoyed with her. Well, too bad.

'I expect the journalists have been hassling you

again,' he said after a while.

'Yes.' She tried to keep her tone light. 'You'd think we'd have got used to it by now.'

'One never does,' he said.

After a short silent journey he turned the car between granite gate posts and up a long gravel driveway. She had forgotten just how enormous this place was: three or four times the size of Annat House and not nearly so old, a folly that by some great good fortune had found a new lease of life when it became a school.

'Looks well cared for,' she said, trying to concentrate on the job in hand. She nodded at the neat lawns and weed-free parking area. 'Always a good sign.'

'Didn't it used to be?'

'I don't remember. It's not the sort of thing you notice as a child. And I wasn't here often, only for sports days and prize-givings.' She remembered suddenly and very distinctly one long-ago visit with her mother. It had been a brilliantly sunny day and they had watched race after race, giggling at the pernickety teachers and the sweating youngsters. They had sat under a sunshade and sipped iced lemonade which wasn't nearly as good as they made at home. Malcolm came second in the four hundred metres and Catherine smiled to remember his joy and consternation at her mother's rowdy celebrations. Gordon, as usual, hadn't been there.

She wondered what Jean had been doing that day.

The current head teacher, Mr Congleton, came bouncing out to shake their hands. He was younger than Catherine had expected, certainly much younger than the aloof, black-gowned man he had replaced.

'Integrated education is the way forward,' he said enthusiastically, as he showed them around. 'Children can learn in the hills and on the loch as well if not better than in the classroom. And learning to learn is what education is all about at their age, developing an openness to experiencing the world, a confidence to face it and an enquiring mind to learn from it.' It might have been hype straight out of the school brochure, but his zeal was genuine.

'It sounds great,' said Catherine.

Haydn frowned. 'My son is not particularly an outdoor type. Not really the sort to go running in the hills before breakfast.'

The man paused. 'Then we'll start him off by walking. And never before breakfast. Good nutrition is essential to any developing youngster.'

'Indeed.'

'And if you – and your wife? – have any questions, feel free to ask.'

'I'm a friend, not his wife,' said Catherine quickly.

She could feel Haydn's gaze resting on her and she wondered again why he had invited her. Just meeting his eyes sent a totally inappropriate shiver down her spine, even when his expression was guarded. She really needed to speak to him, tell him she didn't have time for personal things just now.

She tried to concentrate on the tour, and it was, indeed, impressive. A swimming pool had been built since her brothers' time and there was a brand new games hall. The boys and girls (it was now co-educational!) seemed well behaved. The casual sweatshirts and black trousers or skirts were far preferable to the stiff white shirts, ties, and grey shorts she remembered.

'I had expected a more formal set up,' said Haydn at the end of their conducted tour. He eyed a group of rowdy youngsters. 'I presume you have a blazer and tie for trips into town?'

'No, we've done away with all that.' Mr Congleton himself wore chinos and an open-necked shirt. 'Some parents were a little reluctant to accept the changes but I think they've come to see the sense of them now. Tools should be fit for purpose and clothes are just another tool. We want the youngsters to be comfortable in what they wear.'

'Preparing them for the world ahead?' said Haydn. He seemed determined to be displeased.

'I think it's an admirable strategy,' said Catherine, frowning at Haydn. Richie had struck her as a very uptight little boy. Maybe this was what he needed, a little more freedom, a new approach. 'How long is it since you started taking girls? That must have changed the atmosphere quite a bit.'

'Eight year – or nine year come September. We feel it has been a very positive move.'

Haydn grunted. He was beginning to irritate Catherine. If he was going to be like this, why had he bothered to visit?

They said very little on the drive back to Annat House.

'Well, I was very impressed,' said Catherine as the car drew to a halt. She felt duty-bound to try.

'You will give some thought to moving Richie, won't you? Maybe even straight after half term? I always think if you're going to make a new start you should make it, you know? Not let things drift.'

'I'm really not sure it's my kind of place. But thank you for your time. I appreciate you coming with me.'

'It was your idea to visit.'

'Actually, it was your idea. I merely allowed myself to be persuaded.'

Catherine stared ahead, for once not seeing her surroundings. This was ridiculous. Why were they arguing? Richie was his problem, not hers. She had problems enough of her own.

'You could discuss it with Richie,' she suggested. He raised an eyebrow and said nothing. He seemed annoyed with her, although whether over her enthusiasm for the school, or the silence that preceded it – or both – she had no idea.

Suddenly, Catherine's thoughts coalesced. She wasn't going to worry about Haydn. It was her family who needed her. Her *sister* needed her. She had been unable to do anything for Jean in her lifetime, but she could and would make sure she had the very best send off in her death. That's where her energies should be focussed.

She thanked him politely for the lift, slammed the car door rather harder than was necessary, and strode up the steps, prepared for action.

'Watch out, Catherine's on the warpath,' said Mhairi coming into the kitchen thirty seconds before his sister. Malcolm jumped up guiltily.

Fergus was yet again on days off and he was supposedly making sure all equipment was cleaned and put away, and making out lists of ingredients for the next guests. He didn't even have a sheet of paper in front of him.

'Good to see you're so busy,' said Catherine.

He shrugged. 'I was thinking. We don't all feel the need to be running round in circles every minute of the day. And anyway, where have you been? Was that Haydn Smith's car I saw you go out in?'

'I went up to Annat School with him. He's thinking of sending Richie there.'

'So that's why he was asking about the place.' Malcolm smiled at how easily Catherine had been diverted. 'Has it changed much?'

'More than you'd believe. Now, I've been thinking about the funeral. It's really time we started getting it organised.' She folded her arms and waited for a response.

For a brief, mad moment Malcolm wondered if she had done away with their father and they were now arranging a funeral, not a wedding. Then he realised. Jean. Their sister.

'I hadn't thought about that.'

'I have. I'll contact that DI person to find out, but we are her next of kin, so we can and should make all the arrangements. Yes?'

'Well, yes, I suppose.' Malcolm's thoughts were still on all those lonely years that had led up to the death; on his father keeping her existence a secret. He hadn't got around to thinking of funerals yet. But Catherine was right. 'Yes, definitely, that's what we should do.'

'Good, I thought you'd agree. I'll start looking into it.'

'Yes, I...' But she had turned and was already out of sight up the narrow staircase. If she wasn't careful she'd be twisting her ankle again. Since the news of Jean's parentage had been broken, Catherine hadn't seemed to be able to sit down.

He looked after her in silence. It was a moment before he realised that Mhairi was still in the room. She was leaning against the Aga, watching him.

'I'm just off home,' she said, after a pause.

'Oh. Right.'

Another silence while Malcolm thought of his sister Jean and what kind of funeral could possibly be appropriate. Mhairi was still watching him.

'Do you want to do something tonight?' she said abruptly.

'Do something?'

'Aye, like go out. To the movies, or for a drink.'

'Oh. I don't know. Do you want to?'

'Yes, actually, I do.' Mhairi now had her hands on her slim hips, glaring at him. Part of Malcolm's mind registered that she looked very cute, but mostly he had other things to think about.

He said, 'I think I might go down to Croydon.'

'Croydon?' Surprise replaced irritation. 'Why on earth?'

'I just think I should go.' Malcolm had been mulling over the idea for a few days but this was the first time he had spoken of it. Catherine's intention to arrange a proper funeral was good, he was pleased she had thought of that, but there were other things they should do too. 'I want to see where she lived.'

'Why?' said Mhairi. She was examining him like a puzzle.

'She was my sister.'

'Half-sister.'

'She was my half-sister. We are – were – her next of kin. As you all keep pointing out, I'm not essential here, so I think I should go.' He frowned. 'I wonder if I can get into her flat.'

Mhairi gave a slight but visible shudder. He knew how she felt. Going into the home of a dead person wasn't something he exactly looked forward to, but it might tell them something. He had been trying to find out more about Jean Sarah Lawson, questioning Georgie, contacting the police, but either they couldn't or wouldn't help.

'The police have been in already, they say there isn't a suicide note or anything like that.'

'It's so weird,' said Mhairi.

'I know.' He sighed. 'My father is such a bastard.'

Mhairi considered. 'He's not my favourite person, as you know, but you can kind of see his point of view, can't you? I mean, it must be a bit embarrassing, having something out of your past come back at you, with all this publicity. He isn't the only man to have had and left children, a child, behind.'

'I know.' But he was Malcolm's father. 'I *despise* him.'

'Look, Malcolm, everyone's got problems in their family, don't think you're special. What about my dad, for a start?'

Malcolm thought of Mhairi's father, and then

189

wished he hadn't. He had always found it inexplicable that this grey wisp of a man could have such a beautiful daughter, that his clever, hard-working wife had stayed with him. 'I don't really know your dad.'

'Exactly. Because he scarcely moves from the house and in the house he hardly moves from the bloody settee. I know what everyone thinks of him.' Her face was grim. 'I'm not complaining, OK? I'm just saying don't think you're the only one with problems.'

'I don't.' Malcolm was, momentarily, shaken out of his preoccupation. This was the first time Mhairi had mentioned her father to him. 'I'm sorry, I didn't think. It must be tough for you.'

'It's not tough, it's fine. We cope. Look, I said to Mum I'd be home for tea, I'd better go. Do you want to meet up later or not?'

'Mmm, I don't know.' Malcolm wished his brain would work more quickly. It seemed to have been in a daze ever since he had seen his father's name on that birth certificate. 'Not tonight.'

Mhairi shrugged, a faint flush coming to her cheeks. He thought for a moment she was going to argue with him, but fortunately she didn't. She just said, 'See you, then,' and turned on her heel and left.

Chapter Twenty-two

Malcolm took the sleeper down to London and then made his way slowly and with only one or two mistakes to the address his father had been given on the outskirts of Croydon. Catherine had arranged for him to have the keys. He didn't know what he had expected. Certainly not a place of luxury. But this drab block of 1930s brick was utterly depressing. Even as he walked up the stairs, key in hand, he thought of Annat, the mountains and loch, the space, and felt sick.

He opened the front door of number eleven and swallowed and took a deep breath before forcing himself to go in. The air smelt stale. Someone, possibly the police, had half-drawn the curtains, so that the whole place was cast in gloom. He found the sitting room and pushed back the faded brownish curtains. The view was of the row of shops and offices opposite. He looked at that for a while, and then turned around to examine the room.

What on earth was he doing here? There was nothing wrong with the flat as such. It wasn't filthy or tiny – not extreme in any way. It was just dull.

The contrast with the size and style of Annat House was almost painful. He wondered what Jean had made of it herself, when she stood at the gates and stared at the house. Had she stood there long, maybe even made the trip more than once? *Why* hadn't she taken that small extra step and knocked on the door?

He began to look methodically through drawers and cupboards, in the pockets of clothes hanging limply in the wardrobes, trying to find some indication of what his sister had been thinking in those days leading up to her death. He knew the police had been here before him, but they had been looking for a suicide note and a will. Probably it had been a local constable with lots to do and no particular interest in a distant suicide. Malcolm wanted something, anything, that would give him a clue to his sister.

He didn't find much. He was dismayed by how little he found. A couple of old letters from and to her mother; a few more photographs of mother and daughter, no one else; a folder of school reports, a confirmation certificate. Either she had been exceptionally tidy, or had cleared away the debris of her life before setting off on that final journey.

Malcolm felt crushed by the emptiness of it all.

He didn't sleep well. He had a pint and an over-salted, fat-laden lasagne in a nearby pub and then retired to one of the single beds with his sleeping bag. It was hard to get comfortable and even when he did drift off, strange snatches of dreams woke him again, dreams of women just out of reach, or his mother coming to visit, of his father not being there.

When he woke at five the next morning he knew he wouldn't get back to sleep. He lay looking at the white ceiling in the grey dawn light. And as he did so he thought of all the places he hadn't yet looked. Under the mattress, under the carpet. If she wanted to hide something she wasn't going to leave it in an open drawer, was she?

He spent the next hour looking, at first haphazardly and then more methodically. Surely, surely, there had to be something here?

He found no damning photograph, no letter from the heart. But he did come across a bank statement. It hadn't even been hidden, but merely fallen down between the fridge and a cupboard in the kitchen. It was a savings account, and contained more than fifty thousand pounds. Whatever had driven Jean to despair, it wasn't a lack of money.

After speaking on the phone to Malcolm, Catherine's thoughts were filled more than ever with questions about Jean. A sister more than ten years her elder. A sister she had never known, who had walked past her on that day not so long ago. Why hadn't Catherine called out, started a conversation? Maybe that would have been the one little gesture Jean was waiting for.

Malcolm had gone to search for answers in his own way. But Catherine suspected, if she was persistent, she might find some closer to home. After breakfast, she set out for Georgie's.

Her aunt must have seen her arrive. By the time she had climbed out of the car, Georgie was at the crooked latch-gate, the two dogs tumbling in her wake.

'We were just going out,' she said abruptly.

Georgie had been avoiding them all for days but Catherine was not to be put off this time.

'Where are you going?'

'Up the hill. Need a good stretch of the legs.' Georgie opened the gate and the dogs raced through. Barty gave Catherine a perfunctory greeting, but the woods at the back of the cottage clearly held far greater interest.

'I'll come with you,' said Catherine.

'You're not dressed for it.' Her aunt looked down disapprovingly at Catherine's footwear. The shoes were flat, but more suited to house than hills.

'I'll manage,' said Catherine firmly.

Georgie set off at a brisk pace, leading the way up the grassy path through trees dripping with lichen. The Black Wood had always seemed to Catherine to be well named. It was dark in here, the broad-leafed trees crowding close together, gnarled and twisted with age. Even on the path, sunlight struggled to filter through.

To begin with, Catherine was silent. She knew this route well, and after a steep climb it turned to follow the contour of the land. Here, when she had regained her breath, she spoke.

'Tell me what you knew about Jean.'

Georgie shot her an unfriendly glance from hooded eyes, so like her brother's. 'Why don't you ask your father?'

'I have. He won't tell me anything. Please, Georgie.'

'I didn't know Jean at all. Your father and Audrey had split up before the child was born.'

'But you knew Audrey?' Catherine had suspected as much.

'I met her,' said Georgie reluctantly.

'Tell me what she was like. Was it a long relationship? Did the family know about her? Did they approve?' From the little she and Malcolm had gleaned, Catherine was fairly sure her grandmother would have disapproved strongly. Audrey had been a secretary in the office where Gordon worked. And she hadn't even been a rich girl playing at work. She would not have been Sarah McDonald's idea of a future daughter-in-law.

'Gordon didn't bring her home,' said Georgie.

'So how did you meet her?'

'I went to London occasionally. As a teacher, I had the long summer holidays and I wasn't averse to using my brother for accommodation.'

'What was she like?'

'Pretty. Small, slight, blonde. Not at all like your mother.'

'And he got her pregnant and left her.'

'Catherine, I don't think he did it *on purpose*. These things happen.'

'This was the swinging sixties. For goodness sake, they must have known about birth control.'

'I believe Audrey was Catholic.'

'Catholic?' Catherine's mind went blank. What did that have to do with it?

'That's why she wouldn't have an abortion. I admired her for that, I must say.' Georgie carried on walking, not looking at Catherine, but at least she was giving answers.

'Did she want to marry my father?'

'I don't know.'

'But you knew she was pregnant? What did Grandma think? I bet she had something to say.'

'My parents never knew. Your father didn't

think there was any point.'

'Why didn't he marry her?'

'Catherine, the relationship was over before they even knew she was pregnant. Audrey really wasn't the sort of girl Gordon would marry. He had some money of his own, he gave her that. He moved back to Scotland soon after.'

'I can't believe he never kept in touch.'

'It would have been more surprising if he had,' said Georgie. 'However.' She paused. 'However, I did stay in touch.' She stopped then and sighed heavily. 'That is to say, I tried to. As I said, I admired Audrey for being brave enough to keep the child. And I was concerned about her. She was – fragile.'

'You kept in touch? You've been in contact with them all these years?' Catherine paused to take in this new shock.

'No, unfortunately not. We exchanged letters, but after a few years Audrey asked me to stop contacting them. It was about the time of your father's marriage. I wish I'd been more insistent. Perhaps if I had...'

Catherine allowed them to walk on in silence. Things were becoming just a little clearer. Her father had had a fling with a pretty office junior, a social nobody. It hadn't done him any harm, but it had changed Audrey's life for ever. Had she hated him? Had she spoken of him to her daughter? All they knew for sure was she had never married and had had no more children.

'I don't think I can forgive him for this,' said Catherine, speaking very quietly. They had come out of the trees now. She could see the roofs of

Annat House on the far side of the loch, half hidden by a fold in the land.

'Don't be ridiculous,' said Georgie brusquely. 'What is there for you to forgive? This doesn't change his relationship with you.'

'Yes it does. If he could do that to her, he could do it to us. It shows me how little I knew him.'

She turned to walk back.

'Think about it sensibly,' said Georgie. Now it was she who was trying to keep up with Catherine. 'This is exactly the way you would have expected Gordon to behave, if you had known about it. It's not the least bit out of character. And you four are different. He married your mother. There was no possibility he would disown you.'

'He deserted his own *daughter*. He prevented me even knowing I had a sister.'

'Catherine, he is still your father.'

Catherine said nothing. She walked quickly, watching the cavorting dogs through eyes blurred with tears.

Chapter Twenty-three

Catherine was so preoccupied, it took her a while to realise there was something different about Mhairi. They had been busy, Mhairi in the office and Catherine checking the guest rooms, so they hadn't seen much of each other until lunchtime, which they ate in the kitchen with Mrs Mc-Whirter, Stewart, and Fergus.

'You're not wearing any make-up,' she exclaimed, examining her young colleague with a frown. It was years since she had been aware of Mhairi's freckles.

'Aye, I noticed that,' said Mrs McWhirter. 'You all right, hen?'

'I'm fine,' said Mhairi flatly. 'Just couldn't be bothered this morning.'

'Partying too late last night?' sniggered Fergus.

Mhairi shrugged and said nothing, so that Catherine was surprised on two counts. One, that she hadn't immediately snapped back, and two that there really was something different about her appearance. She was clean and tidy enough – too tidy, in fact. Gone was the normal short skirt, woollen tights, and brilliant, layered tops. She was in jeans, but smart jeans, with a plain, fitted shirt. The effect was to make her look, suddenly, grown up.

'Are you really all right?' she said.

'I'm fine.' Mhairi glared.

Later in the afternoon, Catherine cornered Mhairi in the office. She had more chance of getting answers if the others weren't around. 'How are things?'

'Fine.' Mhairi barely looked up. 'Taxis ordered to pick up the next lot of punters tomorrow. I've checked with Rory who's running the course and he'll be along first thing in the morning. That's the first course that's been fully booked, good sign, hey? And I'm now dealing with enquiries for the *Traditional Scottish Cookery* and *Flower Arranging.*'

'Well done.'

'We really need to start thinking of producing a proper brochure to send out for future courses.'

'Ah, yes, we do.' This had been Catherine's original intention, but life had rather taken over in the last few weeks. 'We'll get on to that after the wedding.'

'And all the food orders for the wedding are confirmed.' Mhairi looked up briefly. The diamond in her nose glittered oddly against the pale, freckled skin. 'Anything else you want me to do for that?'

'I think we're just about there. Thanks for all your help. You've been a star.'

Mhairi shrugged. 'I'd like to get off work a bit early today, if that's all right with you. Mum's got tickets for some show in Perth. Not really my kind of thing, but I said I'd go with her.'

'No problem. That's an excellent idea. What show is it?' Catherine was pleased that Shirley Robertson was getting out and about.

'Dunno. Mum chose it. She wanted Dad to go with her but he wouldn't.'

'Ah.' Catherine was surprised that Shirley still tried to get her husband to go out. She had thought such optimism was long past.

'And she asked me to pass on to you her thanks for her invitation to the wedding reception, but she won't be able to come as she's on call.'

'That's a shame.'

'I don't think I'll come, either,' said Mhairi, looking away out of the window. 'It's very good of you to invite me and all that, but it's really not my kind of thing.'

Catherine had been leaning on the door jamb.

Now she sat down on her own office chair. 'What's all this about? I thought you were looking forward to coming? Didn't you say you were going to get a fascinator, go a bit over the top?'

'Aye, well. I've changed my mind. Mrs Mac and Fergus aren't coming, why should I?'

'They're working, so they can't come as guests. I thought you were a friend as well as a colleague,' said Catherine. frowning. Had the other staff been saying things to Mhairi? It was quite possible that Fergus, at least, had been making digs at her. It wasn't like Mhairi to care.

'I'm an employee. I'll come along in the evening to help with the serving staff, if you want.'

'You were invited as a guest,' said Catherine.

'Aye, well, as I said, thanks very much, but no.'

'If you don't want to come, of course that's fine.' Catherine studied the girl's thin back, thinking hard. She wasn't surprised at Shirley Robertson declining the invitation. She had nursed Rachel McDonald during those difficult last months and had not kept to herself her opinion of Gordon's behaviour. There were others in the village who might feel the same, but would come along out of curiosity, or simply for the party. Not that many villagers had been invited. Gordon had kept a close eye on the lists.

'Malcolm will be disappointed,' said Catherine thoughtfully.

Without the cover of make-up, Mhairi's blush was clear, even with her face averted. 'He won't even notice.'

'He's coming back tomorrow, why don't you ask him yourself?'

200

'It's nothing to do with him,' said Mhairi, stabbing at her keyboard with savage fingers.

'He's finding this whole business of a lost sister a bit difficult.'

'I wouldn't know, he hasn't talked to me about it.'

'I thought you were there when that crafty journalist produced the birth certificate? She certainly got some good copy out of it.' Catherine shuddered at the memory of the 'skeleton in the family cupboard' stories that had appeared for days in the local – and national – press. Thank goodness her mother hadn't been alive to see it.

Mhairi shrugged and said nothing.

Catherine folded her hands together and considered.

She said, 'You don't need to decide yet about the wedding. Think about it a bit more, OK? And you haven't forgotten the meeting tomorrow night, have you? That's the one you and Malcolm were chairing, to launch Youth Aye.'

'Youth Aye?' said Mhairi blankly.

'Yes. I know we've been busy, but we can't neglect the community because of that. And I'm counting on you. You won't let me down, will you?'

Mhairi shook her head but she didn't actually say no.

'Now, off you go. You don't want to make your mother late for the theatre.'

Mhairi banged the door of the village hall viciously with her shoulder. You needed to bang it to make it open, but she also did it for the enjoyment. She wanted to hit something.

She still couldn't quite believe she had got herself involved in this. Going along to the first Community Council meeting had been a bit of a laugh, and she had still been sufficiently in awe of Catherine to want to please her. And Malcolm had come along too. For all his annoying ways, the presence of another 'young person' had made the whole process kind of all right. And now here she was, magically in charge of the whole Youth Aye project, when she still had only the haziest of ideas what it was about. How had that happened?

Her mother must have sensed her unease, for she had offered to come along to the meeting. Mhairi had declined. She didn't need anyone looking over her shoulder, or thinking she wasn't up to the job.

That was one thing about Catherine McDonald; she never gave you the impression she thought you weren't up to the job. She simply expected masses of you and left you to get on with it.

Mhairi sighed. It was because she was such a sucker for approval that she had let herself be drawn into this. She switched on the fluorescent lights and looked around the cavernous hall. It was cold in here and smelt, as always, of sawdust and old paint. She started setting out a few of rows of chairs, wondering if anyone would actually turn up.

She was pretty sure Malcolm wouldn't. She didn't even know if he was back from London yet. His train was supposed to get in mid-afternoon, but if he had arrived at Annat he must have gone straight to the Lodge. She had certainly seen nothing of him.

She was furious with herself for having got involved with him. Hadn't she known he was too bloody gorgeous for her? Kissing him had been torture, trying not to show how much she wanted more. But she had been right all along, she was just a passing interest, someone to distract him until something else came along. She was not going to think about that now.

It was a bit of a shock how many of the youth of the village drifted into the hall as the official meeting time came and went. She tried to chat to them as she might do in the park or the shop, but it felt all wrong. She had set up a table and chairs for herself and Malcolm at the front, which made her feel horribly like a teacher. The ages of the youngsters spanned from about seven to seventeen, which meant she could, actually, be their teacher. Awful thought.

'Right,' she said, ten minutes after the official starting time, when the trickle of arrivals seemed to have tailed off. 'Shall we get started?'

The chatter continued unabated.

She raised her voice. 'OK yous, I said shall we get started?' They looked at her blankly but at least they were only murmuring now. 'Thanks for coming. It's good to see so many of you.'

'Nothing else to do in this bloody place,' said one of the youths, and the others laughed.

'Exactly,' said Mhairi. 'That's why we're here. You think there's nothing to do here? We want to change that, and need your ideas as to how we do it. So, what do you think we should do?'

That brought absolute silence. She wasn't expecting *a contribution* from them, was she? Mhairi

203

was getting into her stride now. 'I'll start by telling you a bit of the background to Youth Aye, shall I? The Community Council has got a grant, about a thousand pounds to start with, and the money has got to be spent on something that you lot want.' She didn't think they'd want to hear about the money being to promote community involvement and all that kind of crap. 'The only criteria is that it should be spent in Kinlochannat...'

'Hows about a pairty?'

'And that it should be on something lasting.' That silenced the laughter. 'Malcolm McDonald, who's supposed to be here but isn't, and me, we've come up with a few ideas. See what you think.' She took a deep breath and looked at her slip of paper. She didn't know if it was a good thing to give them too much of a lead, but she had to get the ball rolling somehow. 'Extend the wildlife walk down by the river.' Blank looks. 'Replace the football nets in the park.'

'Aye, that'd be all right.'

'Buy equipment for indoor games in here.'

'Like what?'

'Carpet bowls and skittles ... no, no, I'm joking. Badminton, maybe, or indoor hockey. Nothing too rough, though, or you'd never get permission.'

'We'll never get permission anyway, not unless we have an *adult* with us the whole bloody time.'

Mhairi thought this was probably true so hurried on. She definitely did not want to find herself running a weekly youth club.

'Look, that was just a few ideas to start you off. If you don't like those then why not come up with something better?'

There was another silence, then some low muttering.

'You cannae dae nothing with a thousand quid,' said one girl.

'What would you like to do?'

'Start a café, something where we can go in the evening. It's OK for you, you can go to the pub, there's nothing for us.'

'Well, I'll write it down,' said Mhairi doubtfully.

She heard the outer door open with its signature bang, and paused to allow the latecomer to join them. The inner door swung open and Malcolm slouched in. He was wearing ancient jeans and a leather jacket and just looking at him made her heart skip a beat.

'You started already?' he said looking around without any apparent interest.

'Yeah. We started at seven.'

'Thought it was half past.' He paused as he neared the front, seeming inclined to slip into the end of one of the rows.

Mhairi was having none of that. 'Come and sit here.' She pushed the seat with her foot. 'I'll tell you the ideas people have come up with.'

He slouched into the seat beside her and frowned as she read through them. 'Not very original, are they?'

She swallowed her irritation. 'We're only just getting going.' She smiled at the audience. The teenage girls were suddenly looking a lot more alert, and she realised now what had motivated them to come. 'Look, why don't we have a ten-minute break and you can chat among yourselves, see what you can come up with. That OK?'

Nobody answered but from the way they turned to their neighbours and began to chatter she presumed they liked the idea. She just hoped some of them were talking about Youth Aye.

She turned to Malcolm, who was examining his boots. 'Thanks for your support. You must have known it was seven.'

'I wasn't sure.'

'If you weren't sure why didn't you ask?'

'Actually, I wasn't going to come. But I'd forgotten how fucking dire the atmosphere at the East Lodge is.'

Mhairi hesitated. 'How was Croydon?'

He carried on staring moodily at his feet. 'The place she lived was awful.'

'Did you find anything?'

'Depends what you mean.'

Mhairi sighed. They really couldn't talk about this now. And she had promised herself that she wasn't going to get interested. 'Fine. Got any more ideas for Youth Aye?'

'No.'

They lapsed into silence until Mhairi judged ten minutes had passed.

She raised her voice. 'OK, listen up. This is how we're going to do it. You can shout out any ideas you've got. I'm going to write them down. Nobody's going to comment on them yet. OK? It doesn't matter how mad they seem, we just want some schemes to consider. It's called...'

'A bloody stupid idea,' murmured Malcolm.

'Brainstorming,' said Mhairi firmly. 'OK, let's go.'

'A basketball court,' said someone hesitantly.

'Ah, naff...'

'I said no comments. Next?'

One of the smallest boys raised his hand. 'A new slide for the park, really big.'

'Flowering baskets for around the village.' Mhairi was familiar with the little girl's mother, so she knew where that idea had come from.

'A climbing wall.'

'A skate park.'

'A mountain bike track.'

They were off now, the ideas flooding in, some good, some ridiculous. Mhairi wrote them all down. She was surprised and relieved that they were getting into the mood. Even Malcolm began to look interested. He raised his gaze from the floor and started to listen.

Mhairi had filled three sheets of paper before the ideas ran out. 'I think you're brilliant,' she said, grinning round at them.

'Not that we would be able to do half of them,' said Malcolm.

'The next step,' said Mhairi, ignoring him, 'is to divide the ideas up. Into things like practical short term, practical long term, not practical, too expensive. Give Malcolm and me a few minutes to do that and then I'll tell you what we've got.'

'I think Catherine's got to you with her obsession with lists,' muttered Malcolm as she tore off more sheets from her pad and began to write headings.

'You take the original list and read them out to me. Can you think of any other categories?'

'Naff. Totally naff. Totally utterly...'

'Fuck off, Malcolm. You can leave if you're not

207

going to take this seriously, OK?'

He glanced at her, surprised. 'It was only a joke.'

After another three quarters of an hour they had achieved two things. Firstly, the group actually felt like a group, with a shared purpose and maybe even an intention to carry it out. Secondly, they had a shortlist of three possible projects.

Mhairi read them out. 'Replace the football nets. That's feasible but not very original and not everyone plays football. Two, a skate park, or at least some jumps in the park. Three, a mountain bike track. I think that'll have to be a longer-term goal; I know it's the favourite but it'll cost loads and we'd need to find a suitable piece of land. Now Malcolm and I will take these ideas back to the Community Council and the grant body and see what they think. I'm going to arrange another meeting for us in a fortnight's time.'

'They won't let us do nothing,' said Tommy McAllister, the boy who had suggested the 'pairty'.

'We won't let them stop us,' said Mhairi, caught up in her own optimism. 'Right, anyone got anything else to say before we finish?'

No one had so she called the meeting to a close and gathered her papers together with a sigh of relief.

'Want to go for a drink?' said Malcolm.

'No.'

'I'll tell you about my trip.'

Before she could answer, one of the youths had come up to talk mountain bikes with Malcolm and Mhairi found herself holding back a wave of admiring girls. 'Thanks for coming,' she said, trying to usher them towards the exit. 'Aye, it is good of Malcolm to give up his time. I'll see yous in two weeks, like, if not before?'

'Is he your boyfriend?' hissed one of the teenage girls, peering past Mhairi.

'No,' said Mhairi, hoping she wasn't blushing.

She glanced back and found that Malcolm was closer than she had thought. He grinned and looped an arm over her shoulders.

'Of course I'm her boyfriend,' he said. 'And she's coming for a drink with me in the Foresters right now. Aren't I lucky?'

Mhairi could tell who the girls thought was lucky. 'I can go for a drink quite happily on my own,' she said, shrugging off his arm, but feeling herself weaken all the same. The alternative was going home to spend the evening with her parents and the too-loud television.

Malcolm continued, 'And she's going to be my partner to my father's wedding.' The two girls who had been questioning Mhairi looked suitably impressed.

And, stupidly, Mhairi could feel herself weakening. It felt so good to be close to him.

And she'd already bought that spangly, sequined dress – where else would she wear it if not at Gordon McDonald's stupid wedding? She sighed, but didn't contradict him.

Chapter Twenty-four

Catherine was in a hurry as usual. She banged her knee on the corner of the wooden bed and swore. Now she would have a nice big bruise on the side of her leg, to go with her pale face and still-dicey ankle. Of course, all eyes would be on Gordon and Phyllida: it was their big day. No one would be looking at her. She had hardly seen Haydn since the visit to Annat School. She was far too busy for socialising.

Kerr and Marguerite had finally agreed to attend the wedding and had arrived the evening before. Their presence had added a new layer to the atmosphere of Annat House (yes, they had all, for the *final* time, moved into Annat House). Kerr had given Phyllida one piercing stare and apparently approved. Unfortunately, Gordon still didn't feel likewise about Marguerite, and blanked her completely.

Catherine wished very sincerely that it was all over. This day, which she had once viewed with such trepidation, had now arrived and she felt no emotion about it at all. It was just another task to get through. Her thoughts were more on Jean than her father. By tomorrow evening, Gordon and Phyllida would have departed for their short honeymoon on Skye and the rest of the family would disperse the following day. It wasn't too long to survive, was it?

Kerr and John Hugo were already in the dining room. Kerr was lifting the lids on the various dishes left on the warming plates and looking dissatisfied. 'Over-cooked and far too fatty,' he said.

'This is what Father wanted,' said Catherine, helping herself to egg, bacon, and mushrooms when she had only intended to snatch a piece of toast. 'And at least with these new warming plates it's not stone cold.'

'I would have preferred to eat in the kitchen.'

'Well, Father wouldn't. And it *is* his wedding day.' Catherine had to keep reminding herself of this. 'If you don't eat this there'll be nothing until the wedding meal. No one will have time to make lunch, even if you had time to eat it.'

Kerr chose a piece of bacon and brought it back to the table with a mug of black coffee. After a moment he said, grudgingly, 'Everything in hand, is it? You've had a lot to organise.'

Catherine felt it was a bit late for him to ask now. 'Yes, everything's fine.' She crossed her fingers beneath the table.

John Hugo said officiously, 'Church service at three, drinks and photos back here from four to six, followed by a sit-down meal and dance in the marquee.'

'Don't know how you got Father to agree to a marquee.'

'I didn't. Phyllida did. She has a way with her.'

'Mmm. And holds the purse strings.'

'She does it very subtly.'

They ate in silence for a while. Catherine was beginning to feel revitalised by all that protein, and a large drink of very strong coffee.'

'I'm glad you could get time off.'

It wasn't easy. There're a lot of staff off sick just now and everyone that's left is doing double shifts. It would have been better if I hadn't needed to come.'

'You didn't *need* to,' said Catherine.

'It was the right thing to do.' Kerr patted his mouth with a napkin. 'You know, it would have been a lot more convenient if you could have arranged the funeral for this week as well. I can't see Marguerite and I being able to come up again in the near future.'

'Oh, yes, that would have been really great,' said Malcolm, making Catherine jump. He must have been standing at the doorway, probably wondering whether he wished to spend time with his older brothers at this hour of the morning. Now he stalked in. 'Let's have a wedding and a funeral in the same week, just to suit you.'

'A day or two apart would have been perfectly satisfactory.'

'To who?' Malcolm was lifting and lowering the silver lids with exactly the same expression of dissatisfaction as Kerr had had. 'Bit congealed, isn't it? Whose idea was it to put the food out like this?'

'That's how Father wanted it. It's how it always used to be, he said.'

'I don't remember it. Think I'll have cereal.' He poured himself a massive bowl of cornflakes and brought it to the table, spilling milk on the clean linen cloth. He turned to his oldest brother. Anyway, we can't have the funeral until the Procurator

212

Fiscal agrees to release the body. You should know that.'

'These things are different in England,' said Kerr coldly. 'Although you probably wouldn't know that.'

'Not that different. In England they have a coroner. I looked it up, but otherwise...'

'Let's not discuss that now,' said Catherine. 'The point is, as Mal said, we can't arrange the funeral just yet, even if we wanted to. I'll let you know as soon as we have a date and if you can't come, well you can't.'

'It would be more fitting if I did. I am the oldest sibling.'

'Fat lot of interest you've taken so far,' said Malcolm bitterly.

'I've been busy, unlike some people.'

Catherine piled up the used dishes, noisily, and made her escape. Oh, happy days.

Catherine was in the kitchen discussing food with a reluctant Fergus when the phone rang. She paused and waited. Surely someone else could get it? And eventually, on the sixth or seventh ring, they did.

'Now, what was I saying? Yes, the smoked salmon. I see we've had the special delivery in from...'

She paused. There was some shouting overhead, a bang, then more shouting.

'I'll see you in a moment,' she said to Fergus, who was smirking, and headed for the stairs.

'Everything all right?' she shouted as she reached the wood-panelled hallway. There was no one in sight.

'Some problem with Phyllida,' said Malcolm from the dining room. He was still seated at the table, drinking another cup of coffee and reading his father's copy of the *Telegraph*.

'Oh dear.' Catherine climbed the next flight of stairs, and paused on the first floor landing. She could hear an argument through the half-open door of her father's favourite bedroom, the blue room. She hesitated. She didn't want to get involved if this was private. It was just she was so used to being the one who sorted things out.

At that moment, Gordon turned and spotted her. 'Oh, it's you,' he said.

'I heard the phone. Is there a problem?'

Phyllida came into view. She was still wearing her 'casual' clothes, a beautiful peacock blue skirt and matching blouse, but she had already begun the serious making up of her face for the wedding. One eye was carefully outlined in kohl, mascara, and delicate shades of brown, the other still untouched, giving her a clown-like appearance. She looked upset. 'I'm afraid that was my sister. Their connection from Ireland to Glasgow has been delayed and they won't be here in time for the wedding.'

'Oh, what a shame.' Catherine didn't know if Phyllida and her sister were close, but it must have been nice to think at least some of her family would be there. The McDonalds could be a bit overpowering.

'Told them they should have come over earlier, ridiculous leaving it to the last minute,' grumbled Gordon. 'And why choose to come via Ireland? I really can't understand it.'

'My brother-in-law has family connections in Ireland...'

'That's not the point. They are coming over to *Scotland,* for *our* wedding. They should damn well make sure they get here on time. My friends have all managed it.'

'I'm sure they're very disappointed too,' said Catherine, trying to soothe. 'Do they know when they might get here?'

'Probably not til early evening,' said Phyllida, looking worried.

'Could be any time this bloody year,' said Gordon.

'It's a shame.'

'I'll be fine without Vanessa,' said Phyllida doubtfully.

'It's not right,' said Gordon, still glowering. 'You should have a Maid of Honour. We want to do things properly.'

Phyllida swallowed. 'It's not as though it's a first marriage. I'll be all right, really.'

'Hmm,' said Gordon, his eyes resting on Catherine.

'I'd better get on,' she said, backing towards the stairs.

'*You'll* have to be Maid of Honour,' said her father. 'It's the only solution.'

'No,' said Catherine, her voice faint with shock. She would never betray her mother like that.

'Don't take that tone of voice with me,' said her father, fixing her with a hard stare. 'We all have to help out in an emergency.'

'Father, I can't.' Catherine met stare for stare.

How could he ask this of her? My God, she *would* be glad when he was gone.

'I'll be fine on my own,' said Phyllida.

Catherine flushed. She really didn't have anything against Phyllida. She quite liked her, if the truth be told. It was just that she didn't want to see anyone taking her mother's place. And if she was Maid of Honour, it would look like she *approved*.

'I don't think it would work,' she said, trying to sound conciliatory. 'I'm up to my eyes with all the arrangements...'

'It's really all right, I'll manage fine,' said Phyllida. The more she said that, the more Catherine felt herself weakening.

'Isn't there anyone else?'

'It's ridiculous,' said Gordon. Phyllida should have been better organised.'

'Like you,' said Catherine. 'You still haven't asked Kerr if he'll be Best Man, have you? You've just assumed, as always, that everyone'll fit in with you.'

A new voice broke in on the conversation. It was John Hugo, hurrying along the corridor, fastening his cufflinks. 'And what's this about Best Man? I offered a few weeks back but...'

'The eldest son is more appropriate,' said Gordon. 'But actually, you could come in useful. Phyllida's brother-in-law was going to walk down the aisle with her. You could do that, couldn't you? It looks like it's either you or Malcolm.'

Malcolm? Catherine was profoundly grateful when John Hugo agreed. And after that, she really couldn't refuse to be Maid of Honour, could she?

216

Chapter Twenty-five

Haydn and Richie were getting ready for the wedding. The boy's hair had been cut incredibly short again. Haydn was sure he had asked the school not to be so ruthless.

The McDonalds would all, naturally, be wearing kilts. As Haydn didn't think there was an Eddlington-Smith tartan, nor feel confident he could carry off showing his legs in public, he had opted for a morning suit. Catherine had said the wedding would be smart, so he had assumed some effort was called for. He had met Richie off the plane in Edinburgh yesterday and hired suits for both of them there.

'It looks stupid,' said Richie, wriggling thin shoulders inside the starched white shirt.

'It'll look great once you get the tie on.'

'I'm not wearing a tie.'

'Yes you are. I'll do the knot for you.'

'I can tie the knot myself,' said Richie sulkily. 'I have to do it at school every stupid day, and on Sunday for church.'

'Excellent. I'm glad they're teaching you something down there.'

Silence. Richie never coped well with irony. Haydn suppressed a sigh. 'There'll be other children there you'll know. What were the names of the ones you met at Easter? Giles and...?'

'Miles and Antonia. I bet they won't be wearing suits.'

'I'm sure Antonia won't. And Miles will probably be in a kilt.'

'Oh, gross.'

'Think yourself lucky then.'

Haydn changed quickly, wishing he had time for a second shave but deciding he really didn't. The grey suit looked all right, even if he said it himself, rather sophisticated. Esme would have approved.

'Ready?'

Richie rose slowly. There were crumbs around his mouth which Haydn dusted off, to the child's disgust. Once they were settled in the car, he said, still thinking of Esme, 'How did lunch with your mum go?' Richie had been uncommunicative over the phone.

Richie looked stolidly ahead. 'All right.'

'Is she looking well? I'm sure all that Spanish sunshine would agree with her.'

Richie didn't bother to answer. Haydn wished he knew how he should talk to a child. He had thought that as Richie grew up, it would start to come naturally. So far, it hadn't.

'Where did you go?'

'Dunno. A restaurant in a big shop.' Harrods, possibly, or Fortnum and Mason. Haydn knew Esme's taste.

'Was Harold there?'

'He came to pick her up afterwards.'

Haydn wasn't surprised. Harold wouldn't want to waste a whole lunchtime on his stepson.

'He brought me a present.'

'Did he?' That was unexpected.

'Mum had told him to.'

218

'What was it?'

'Gameboy game. I'd already got it.'

Haydn wished he could tell if this small gesture had improved Richie's opinion of his mother and her second husband, but no emotion was visible. He wondered if they had told Richie they had invited him for half term, and whether he would have preferred to go to them. He felt a shadow of fear that the child might have preferred to stay in London. Too late to sound him out about it now, they had already arrived at the pretty little church.

Haydn was looking forward to this wedding, in a strange sort of way. He had missed Catherine. He knew she was busier than ever. Maybe, when things calmed down, he could take her out again?

The small church was already nearly full. Haydn had been inside once before, because Catherine had told him it was his duty to show a face at the Sunday service. On that occasion the place had been half empty, rain rattling on the leaded windows. Today the sun shone through in golds and reds, and the plain wooden pews were filled with an exotically dressed, gaily chattering throng. Haydn preferred the gloomy charm of his first visit.

'Bride or groom?' said someone in a bored voice. 'Oh, it's you, Will you go on the bride's side? We're a bit overfull on the groom's. Who'd have thought it?'

'Always happy to oblige,' said Haydn, recognising Malcolm. 'Everything all right?'

'Fine.'

It didn't look like things were fine. The boy's expression was sullen, but Haydn thought it probably wasn't the right time to cross-question him.

He looked around for Catherine, but so far couldn't see her.

The organ music changed and a hush fell in the church. They turned to watch the arrival of the bride, dressed beautifully in an understated cream gown, one gloved hand resting on John Hugo's arm. He wore full kilted regalia and smiled smugly around. He clearly didn't share his younger brother's dissatisfaction with the whole event. Behind these two was the person Haydn really wanted to see.

Catherine was wearing a dress of deep rose pink. With her dark colouring, she could wear almost any shade, but mostly Haydn seemed to remember her in sensible navy trousers or skirts, light shirts, woollen jerseys. The evening of Gordon's engagement had been one of the few exceptions. Then he had realised how lovely she was. Seeing her now only emphasised that. The dark curls had been cut and styled, make-up used not merely to present a tidy appearance but to emphasise those lovely eyes and full, red lips.

He wondered why Catherine was taking such a high-profile role in proceedings. Surely that hadn't been the plan? Whatever the reason, she was carrying it off with her usual calm assurance.

He looked around to see how others were reacting. They seemed to be looking at Phyllida, which was good. Catherine had a strange invisibility in the neighbourhood, and he found he wanted to keep it that way. Esme had always been the centre of attention. She was the sort of groomed blonde who could be easily mistaken for a model. He had been flattered to be seen with her, once upon a time. What a fool he had been.

He looked at the gangly child at his side and felt a strange sadness. The poor boy. It couldn't have been easy for him. Why had Haydn never realised that before? Haydn wondered if the child remembered the divorce. He had never asked about it. They rarely discussed Esme. After all, *she* had left *them*, she was in the wrong. And that hadn't stopped her fighting a long and bitter battle for custody of their son.

Until now, Haydn hadn't thought it had had much effect on the child. Suddenly he wanted to know.

After the church service the wedding party returned to Annat House for photographs. Catherine thought she would be able to relax a little now. Her father was married, and the worst of this Maid of Honour fiasco was over. But the undercurrents flying around made relaxation impossible.

Kerr wanted Marguerite in the photographs, John Hugo wanted himself, Malcolm wanted Mhairi. Georgie watched, amused, from a distance and Gordon barked and fumed. 'Whose wedding is this? Bride and groom, that's who I want in the bloody pictures.'

'And now all the key participants,' said the photographer, apparently deaf to the conversations around him. 'Best man, yes? And bridesmaids, come on now...' He tried to round up Mhairi, who grinned cheekily but with a firm, 'Not me,' retired to Georgie's side.

'Malcolm and Catherine,' snapped Gordon. 'Hurry up.'

Catherine hoped the silly little hat she had bought specially for the occasion was still perched at an acceptable angle on her curls. There was one good thing. With the strain of the last couple of weeks she had actually lost some weight. Not that anyone would be looking at her. Phyllida was the centre of attention, as she should be. Her appearance was immaculate. She also looked amazingly happy.

'What's happening about the seating?' said John Hugo. 'Happy to move to the top table if required.'

'Hopefully Phyllida's relatives will have arrived by then.' Catherine was determined not to think about that problem until she absolutely had to. 'Thanks for walking in with her.'

'My pleasure,' he said.

'He loved it,' said Malcolm. 'He doesn't care about Mum.'

'Not now!' said Catherine, looking around quickly to see who was in earshot. She decided a change of subject was called for. 'I'm glad you persuaded Mhairi to come.'

That distracted Malcolm. 'What do you mean? I gave her the invitation ages ago.'

'But she never actually accepted. She mentioned while you were in London that she didn't really think this was her kind of thing.'

Malcolm frowned. 'That's not on. How could she do that?'

'Because you went to London without her?' suggested Catherine, watching him closely. 'I thought you must have talked about it, to get her to change her mind.'

'No. I just assumed...' Malcolm looked around to see what had happened to his partner and found she had disappeared. 'Where's she gone now?' Looking concerned, he hurried off. Catherine smiled. That would keep him busy for a while.

She was just about to do a circuit, make sure all was well with the guests, when Haydn appeared at her side with two glasses of champagne.

'Is that for me? You really didn't need to.' It felt odd to have someone looking after her.

She had seen Haydn with Richie in the distance. The pale grey suited him perfectly. She had been careful to keep away, as she had been careful to avoid him over the last few weeks. She had been preoccupied with the wedding and Jean. She didn't have time to think about Haydn. Now she wondered if that was true.

Haydn smiled his lopsided smile. 'I thought you might just possibly need it. Not that you don't look absolutely beautiful and totally in control. As ever.'

Catherine hoped she wasn't blushing. 'At least they're married,' she said. 'Thank goodness.' Who would have thought she'd be so relieved?

'It all went beautifully.'

'So far so good. Sometimes I thought today would never arrive. So much has happened it's been difficult to concentrate on the wedding.' She suppressed an image of Jean's hunched figure walking slowly away from her. It was one that filled her mind all too often. 'And then this morning when Phyllida's sister's family were delayed, I wondered what else could go wrong.'

'Best not to think of that,' he said with a smile. 'I find these things happen whether you've planned for them or not.'

'Yes.' Her spirits lifted just fractionally. Haydn was right. No point in worrying about what might or might not be, especially with Haydn standing so close, smiling down at her with that sparkle in his green eyes. She had missed him. 'I'd better go, circulate, you know.'

'Of course. I'll catch up with you later.'

Chapter Twenty-six

Very fortunately, Phyllida's sister and family arrived just after six o'clock. They looked distinctly jet-lagged but Catherine sent them straight upstairs to change. Plenty of time for resting later. Now they were here, she wouldn't need to alter her seating plan which was causing quite enough aggravation already.

The only McDonald at the 'top' table, apart from Gordon himself, was Kerr. He was not impressed, having wanted to spend this rare evening together with his beloved Marguerite. Marguerite wasn't in Catherine's good books at present, having used the very last of the hot water pouring not one but two baths for herself ('I can't bear tepid water, darling, so I had to start all over again'). She had been put at a table being hosted by Georgie. If Kerr intended to bring this woman into the family she had better know what she was getting into.

John Hugo was hosting a table of neighbouring landowners, including boring old George Farquharson who Gordon had once had in mind as a spouse for Catherine. As if that would have worked! She had also put Haydn there, which was rather a shame, but it was good for him to meet some other locals.

Catherine was hosting the table with people from the village. Malcolm was in charge of the young ones' table, which included not only all the children but also Mhairi, as she had far more idea than he of how to control the rabble. The promise of unspecified games for anyone who sat quietly through the meal seemed to be her main tool, along with a running competition for the world's worst joke.

Catherine poured herself an over-full glass of wine and began to unwind. Only the speeches to get through now. Her mother would have been proud of her. At least she hoped so. She felt her throat tighten and took another sip of wine.

Kerr proved to be a very competent Best Man. As well as giving his own speech – short and amusing, without any real emotion – he introduced Phyllida's brother-in-law, who told them more about Phyllida than they had learnt in the last two months, and then Gordon. Gordon had had way too much to drink, and spoke for far too long, but it was his wedding, and he was leaving the country soon, so no one really minded.

Kerr was about to propose a final toast to the bride and groom when Malcolm pushed himself to his feet.

'I've got something to say,' he said, his cheeks red and his speech slurred.

Catherine shook her head fiercely at Kerr who said, 'We're not expecting a speech from you, my boy.'

'Won't take long.' Malcolm put one hand on the table to steady himself and raised his glass in the other. 'Just wanted us to remember absent family.' He hiccoughed. 'Not everyone is able to be here with us this evening but I don't think they should be forgotten. Even if they are dead.'

A murmur passed around the marquee. 'First, a toast to my mother. She was a bloody brilliant mother, and wife, and despite everything she'd want *him* to be happy now. Here's to my mother.' He raised his glass and drank. A few people did likewise, but most looked around for guidance and stayed still.

'Thank you, Malcolm...' said Catherine, starting to rise.

'I've not finished yet. Next, I want us to raise a toast to the absent one among my father's children, to the sister we never knew, the daughter he abandoned. Here's to Jean Sarah Lawson McDonald, the Lost Woman who came home to Annat. May she never be forgotten.'

He drank again and the murmurs grew louder. This was the first time the Lost Woman had been acknowledged publicly. Gordon looked apoplectic.

'And one last thing,' said Malcolm, swaying now. Catherine was at his side but he ignored her. 'Jean deserves to be remembered. So I'm announcing that my father is going to give a legacy – get off, Catherine – Father is going to give fifty thousand pounds to set up a fund in the memory of his eldest daughter, to be spent in Kinlochannat, where she was never recognised but chose to return – nearly finished, Cath – and her funeral will be here and you are all invited!'

He sat down abruptly. There was no murmur this time, just absolute silence. All heads were turned to Gordon who, for once in his life, appeared speechless.

Kerr collected himself first. 'Fill your glasses, everyone, and let's raise them in a toast to the bride and groom.' Everyone except Malcolm rose. 'To the bride and groom. May they have a long and happy marriage.'

As soon as the dancing started, Gordon marched over to Malcolm's table, followed immediately by Kerr and John Hugo.

'...absolutely disgusting behaviour,' Gordon was shouting. 'Think of Phyllida if you can't think of me.'

'What's this about a legacy?' said John Hugo.

'Don't think you'll be welcome in our house in the States because you won't be.'

'It was very bad form, butting in like that,' said Kerr. 'If you wanted to speak you should have let me know earlier.'

'I didn't know, earlier,' said Malcolm. The shock of so much attention seemed to have sobered him. Either that or the pint glass of water that Mhairi had placed in front of him.

'I expected better from a son of mine,' Gordon hadn't finished yet. 'What is the world coming to...'

'If a father won't even attend his own child's funeral,' said Malcolm, raising his voice again. 'Everyone knows now. You'll have to.'

'I, er...' Gordon looked to his left and right. 'I never said I wouldn't. As long as it's convenient. As you are aware, we leave for the States in a fortnight.'

'It'll probably be before that,' said Catherine, touching the wooden table.

'Didn't know she'd left you all that money,' said John Hugo. 'Surprised she had so much.'

'She had at least fifty thousand in the bank, plus the flat with its mortgage paid off. She wasn't poor, you know.' Malcolm had obviously done more investigating than Catherine realised. 'And unfortunately as there's no will, most of it goes to Father.'

'What?' said Gordon. 'Why wasn't I aware of this?'

'Surprised you didn't promise the flat away while you were at it,' said John Hugo, regarding his younger brother with dislike.

'I didn't think of it,' admitted Malcolm. 'I wish I had.'

'Now really isn't the right time to discuss this,' said Catherine.

'What right had you to promise Father's money to the village?' said Kerr.

'It was the only way to make sure he did it.' Malcolm glared at his father.

'I didn't do it,' said Gordon, still looking thunderous.

'But you can't back out now.'

'We'll talk about this tomorrow,' said Catherine.

228

'Actually, I may agree to setting up a little fund,' said Gordon suddenly. His children turned and stared at him. 'Wouldn't want the village to be forgetting me, would we? The Gordon McDonald Fund. Yes, I could get to like the sound of that. Perhaps a building in my name? Or a nice little monument?'

'It won't be for you to decide,' said Malcolm, looking put out at this volte face. 'And it should be the Jean Lawson Memorial Fund.'

'If I'm giving the money I'll decide on the name. Yes, this might be quite fitting...'

Haydn had been observing the argument from afar and as the family drifted back to their tables, he appeared once again at Catherine's side.

'Everything all right?'

'I wouldn't go as far as to say that.' She glanced up at him. 'My bloody family.'

'Come and dance,' he said, and she did.

It was the first time she had danced with Haydn. Indeed, it was the first time she had danced in a long while. She had forgotten how much she enjoyed it. The band was concentrating on waltzes and other old-time music – Gordon's choice – and it felt totally natural to move into Haydn's arms.

'Are you good at everything you do?' she murmured against his shoulder.

'Definitely,' he said. 'And that makes two of us.'

She might have imagined it, but she thought he dropped a kiss on her hair.

Dancing with Haydn had made her light-headed and giddy, but eventually it had had to end. It was Haydn who drew them both off the floor. He looked at her strangely. She smiled back brightly, and then dutifully returned to circulating among the guests, making sure no one was without a drink or a companion.

Later, Catherine slipped out of the marquee in search of fresh air. She needed to clear her head of jumbled thoughts of her mother, and Phyllida, and Jean. And Haydn. She walked carefully in the high heels, inhaling the fresh beauty of it all, the sunlight still catching the distant mountains that she could name as if they were family: Ach Ruach, Cam Beag, Bein Meall. It lifted her heart to gaze on them.

She took off her shoes and padded softly around to the side of the marquee. Here the view was even better, and there was less chance of being disturbed. She was about to let out a sigh of relief when she noticed someone else had, unfortunately, had the same idea. Perched on a fallen log, which would do his pale grey trousers no good at all, was Richie Eddlington-Smith.

He had long since discarded the jacket, waistcoat, and tie but he still looked smarter than any child should have to do. Catherine sighed. She might never get a better opportunity than this to talk to the child.

He didn't look up as she approached and it was only when she was a few steps away that she realised what was engrossing him. With one of those new-fangled computer game things in his hands, he had no time for the view.

'Hello there,' she said brightly. 'What's that you've got?'

He jumped guiltily. ''S my phone.' He looked

up but didn't meet her eyes.

'Your phone? You won't get reception on it here. And I thought you were playing a game.'

'I was. You can play games on phones too.'

'Can you?' said Catherine, surprised. She bent and brushed loose leaves and twigs off the log, then sat down beside the child. She was probably ruining her beautiful silk skirt, but it was in a good cause.

'That's a nice phone,' she said.

'Dad bought it for me.'

'Lucky you.'

'He wanted to be able to phone me at school. All the boys have them.'

'Really?' Boarding schools seemed to have changed a lot since her brothers' days. Richie said nothing. He looked at the ground, clearly hoping she would go away, but she had no intention of that. The other youngsters were playing amongst the rhododendrons at the far side of the house, he would be much better off with them. First she wanted to chat.

'Do you like your school?' Catherine's cheery tones grated even on her.

'No.'

'Ah ... I suppose all children say that.'

Richie sat stolidly beside her, saying nothing.

'Did you know there's a school near here that you could perhaps go to instead? Has your dad mentioned it to you?'

He shot her a suspicious glance and she noticed he had his father's moss green eyes. 'No.'

'Ah, well. Shall I tell you about it?'

Richie didn't say no outright so Catherine spent

a few minutes extolling the virtues of active, child-centred Annat School.

'And they don't wear a shirt and tie, do they? Richie said.'

'That's right. It looks like a really nice, comfortable uniform. Miles and Antonia both go there, you should ask them about it. I think they're weekly boarders, come home for weekends.'

Richie gave a slight nod. It was hard to know if he was interested or not. Eventually, even Catherine ran out of steam. She wasn't going to leave him sitting out there on his own, though. Before she went back into the marquee she took him to where the other children were playing some complicated form of hide and seek, and stayed long enough to make sure they were including him.

Chapter Twenty-seven

Malcolm had been watching Mhairi all evening. He was sure she was avoiding him. Not in an obvious way, just sliding out of conversations, steering clear of groups which included him. That was one of the reasons why he had drunk so much and then said what he did after the speeches. He meant every word of it, but perhaps it hadn't been quite the right time to speak out.

Once the dancing had got underway and he had done his duty by Catherine and Aunt Georgie, and even Phyllida, he looked around for her, but she always seemed to be dancing with someone else. Then when the band started packing up he lost sight of her completely. At first he thought she had gone, then he realised she was helping clear the last of the tables. He caught her arm as she went past. 'That isn't your job.'

'Everything is everybody's job. I'm just lending a hand.' She shrugged him off.

'I wanted to dance with you.'

She didn't meet his eye. 'Too late now.' He watched as she walked away. She looked beautiful this evening, different somehow. True, the bright colours were still there, but the hair was now more blonde than anything else. Her dress was amazing, sewn from hundreds of scraps of shiny material, scattered with pearls and sequins. It had a high front and a very low back. She had exchanged her Doc Marten boots for spindly high-heeled sandals.

Malcolm swallowed the last of his glass of water – disgusting stuff– and followed her into the house. It seemed the only way to have a word with her was to start clearing up too, and he made a couple of journeys to and fro before he managed to accost her in the hallway.

'Come on, Mhairi, what's the problem? Stop avoiding me.'

'I'm not avoiding you.' She bent to rub one ankle. Those shoes clearly weren't meant for waitressing.

'Take a break, then. Look.' He held aloft a half-full bottle of champagne he had lifted from one of the tables, and two clean glasses. 'Let's find somewhere to drink this.'

'Why d'you bring it in if it's not finished? You

should have left it on a table.'

'I want some privacy. Come on, let's sit down for a minute.' With his shoulder, he pushed open the door of the small sitting room and found it was, thankfully, empty. After a pause, Mhairi followed him and he immediately closed the door behind her.

In silence she slipped off her shoes, folded her slim legs under her, and took a glass of the bubbling golden liquid from him.

Malcolm sat down on the same settee, but with her legs folded under her like that it was hard to get close.

'It's not gone too badly, the wedding thing,' he said cautiously.

'Would have been a wee bit better without your contribution.'

Malcolm chewed his lip. 'It needed to be said.'

Mhairi raised one slim eyebrow and looked away. During the course of the day her make-up had become slightly smudged, giving her strange gold-flecked eyes a vulnerable look.

'I'm sorry if it upset you,' he offered.

'It's no' me you should apologise to.'

Malcolm sighed. He certainly wasn't going to apologise to his bloody father. He took a long drink of champagne. He didn't particularly like the stuff but he needed to do something to fill the silence.

'Do you want to go out somewhere tomorrow evening? I don't know what movies are on just now. Or go out for the day? Hey, why not? We could go down to Edinburgh or Glasgow.'

'No thanks.'

'But Mhairi, I've hardly seen you...'

'That was your choice,' she said. 'And your month's up now. The experiment's over.'

He felt as though she had punched him in the chest. 'The month's up?' How could that be? He wracked his brains, trying to remember when the month had started. He had been a little distracted lately. 'That's not fair.'

'Life's not fair,' she said, raising her chin. 'When you grow up you'll realise that.'

'Look, I'm sorry we didn't see as much of each other as we should have. I got kind of caught up in the whole Jean thing.' He watched her with wide eyes. He couldn't believe she was doing this to him. She had been interested, he was pretty sure she had.

'I said it wouldn't work and I was right, wasn't I?' Mhairi put aside her untouched glass and made as though to replace her shoes.

He put out an arm to stop her. 'Please, Mhairi. Don't go yet.'

'That's you all over, isn't it? Please, Mhairi, go out with me when I want you to. Please, Mhairi stay with me – when I want you to. Well, life isn't like that, OK? I don't wait around for anyone.'

She pulled her arm away but he took hold of it again, his fingers tightening on the warm, freckled skin. Her eyes were no longer cold but flashing with anger.

Malcolm put aside his own glass so he had both hands free. 'And I don't give up just like that. I really like you Mhairi. We could have something – good.'

'You had your chance.'

Had he had his chance? Had he blown it? 'OK, then. Kiss me and see how it feels. Kiss me goodbye, if that's what you think you want, and then walk away.'

'Don't be ridiculous.'

She pulled back but he followed her movement so that she was leaning in the corner of the sofa with Malcolm towering over her. 'Just one kiss.' He bent and touched her lips. 'Or maybe two.' He kissed her softly again. She didn't respond but she didn't push him away either. He bent so that he could feel the warmth of her mouth against him, willing her to respond, forcing himself not to snatch her into his arms. You couldn't push Mhairi.

If she had held out much longer he would have had to back off.

She groaned and said, 'It doesn't mean anything.' Then threw her arms around his neck and drew him down to her.

Why on earth does he want to see me now, thought Catherine. She had been told by one of the temporary waitresses that the chef needed her in the kitchen. She wasn't pleased. It was that time of the evening when people were starting to take their leave and she needed to be around, not dashing off to the main house to sort out staff problems. But somehow, with Fergus, she wasn't surprised.

The dark-haired, edgy little man had never settled into the easy camaraderie of the other staff. Catherine wasn't happy with him, but his cooking was excellent, so she had turned a blind eye to his time-keeping and his manners. With so much on her plate she didn't need to go looking for problems.

Now she clattered down the steps in her wedding shoes, keeping her hand safely on the banister, and listening with alarm to the sounds from below.

Fergus was sitting in the ageing armchair beside the Aga. Mrs McWhirter was drying cutlery with fast and vicious movements while berating him in a very loud voice.

'Yer should never have come here, ye lazy wee sprat. Don't think I havenae seen through you long since. Aye, a tyke like you thinking he could take over in my kitchen...'

'You wanted a word?' said Catherine, loudly. She had addressed Fergus but both permanent members of staff turned to face her. The waiters and waitresses hired for the evening hovered in the background, fascinated.

'He wants a word with you! And I'd like a word too, so I would...'

'I can't be expected to put up with these working conditions any longer,' said Fergus

'Work? Yer don't know what work is...'

'I need proper assistants. This ... woman is worse than useless. I refuse to put up with her any longer.'

'An' I refuse to put up with you. I...'

Catherine took a deep breath. Whatever light-headedness she had been feeling from dancing with Haydn, or the alcohol, evaporated. 'Calm down, both of you,' she said coldly. She turned to the black-and-white-clad youngsters. 'Haven't you got anything to do? You can carry these cases of clean glasses out to the van, and the rest of you, back to the marquee and see what needs tidying away there.'

Once they had trailed up the stairs, she turned back to poor, plump Mrs Mac, whose chest was heaving, and the pale pointed face of her chef. He hadn't risen when she entered the room so she pulled up a chair and sat down herself.

'Now, what's all this about?'

'He's aye telling someone else what to do and never gets off his own bloody backside...'

'She won't follow instruction. She's no use at all. I've told you before...'

'Mrs McWhirter has worked for the family a long time and has always been very reliable. Very hardworking.' Catherine gazed at the man and realised that she really didn't like him.

'She's a real sook, that one,' he said. 'You don't know what she's like when you're no' here.'

'What she needs to know is what you're like when she's no' here,' put in Mrs Mack. 'Why, there wouldn't hae been half they starters if young Malcolm and I hadn't stepped in. You were late again this evening, and don't deny it.'

'It's her or me,' said Fergus dramatically, standing up to his not-very-considerable height. 'I don't need to put up with this. I can get a job anywhere I want. If she stays, I go.'

'Well,' said Catherine, adjusting her gaze and finding she perhaps wasn't quite as sober as she had thought. 'No need to be hasty.'

'I'm not being hasty. I've not been happy from day one and this is the last straw, her trying to lord it over me in front of all those youngsters. I'm the chef, this is my kitchen.'

'Actually,' said Catherine, 'it's my kitchen.'

'I came in today as a favour to you. This isn't in my contract, cooking for the family.'

Catherine decided that now wasn't the time to point out he was being paid extra for his trouble – or that the outside caterers had done most of the work. Fergus had only been asked to prepare the canapés. From what Mrs McWhirter said, and Catherine had never known her to lie, he hadn't even done that.

'I'm sorry you're unhappy, but I suggest we discuss this again on Monday, when we have all calmed down.'

'No.' He pressed his lips together. 'I mean what I said. I'm not coming back if she's here.'

'Well then,' said Catherine. She paused and he gave a snide grin, waiting for her to capitulate. 'Well then, I think we'll have to take it that you've resigned, won't we?'

The silence in the room was sudden and complete. Fergus went white, then red. Mrs McWhirter held her breath for a moment and then clapped her hands. 'You've aye bin a sensible lass,' she said to Catherine, then sniffed in Fergus's direction and went back to her drying.

'I'll just go then, if that's what you want me to do,' said Fergus, blustering. 'If that's what you want, I'll go. But you'll regret it, so you will. Who's going to cook for your wonderful guests if I'm not here?' He was shouting, spittle on his lips. 'I won't come back, you know. Don't think you can treat me like this and expect me to come running when you realise the mess you're in.' He stormed towards the narrow stairs.

Catherine hurried up after him. 'Where are you going?' She had visions of him running amok amongst the remaining guests.

'You think I'm going to scuttle out of the back door like some serving boy? You think that you're something special living in a big house like this! I came in through the front door on my first day and now I'm going out that way.' He shot her a final murderous glare, crossed the polished wooden floor of the hall, and slammed the massive door behind him.

Catherine stood still, waiting for her breathing to slow, wondering what on earth she had done. Oh, Jesus, she had just lost her cook. And the next course started on Monday.

'What was all that about?' said Malcolm, appearing from the small sitting room looking pink and rather tousled.

'That was Fergus. He's, er, left.' Catherine was still looking at the front door. She should have handled things better.

'Left?' said Mhairi, joining Malcolm in the doorway. 'You mean for good?'

'Yes, I think that's what I mean. Oh, shit!' The full impact of what had just happened was hitting Catherine. 'He's just walked out.'

'Who's going to cook?' said Mhairi. 'He can't do this. He's got to work his notice. We need him to. He might be a little weasel but he does know his stuff.'

'I won't have him back, even if he would come.' Catherine turned her head from side to side, to see if that would clear it. She could hear the faint sounds of jollity from without. She really should get back to the party. 'But what we're going to do, I don't know. I'll get on to the agencies in the morning, see if they can help...'

'Don't bother,' said Malcolm. He pulled off his already loose tie and stuck it in his pocket. He grinned. 'I'll do it. What can be so hard? I've been doing the ordering, choosing recipes, helping him out for weeks. You just leave it to me.'

Both Catherine and Mhairi turned and stared at him open-mouthed.

'It would certainly help, but...' Catherine wavered. 'I don't know.'

'Go on, give me a try. I can easily do the next course. The menus are all planned.' He sounded, unusually for Malcolm, full of confidence.

And Catherine thought, why not? From what Mrs Mac had said, he'd been doing far more of the work than she realised. Malcolm as chef! Who would have thought it?

It took Haydn ages to track Richie down. The last place he expected to find him, and therefore the last bloody place he looked, was amongst the rowdy group of youngsters playing among the rhododendrons.

'Richie! Where on earth have you been? I've been looking everywhere.'

The boy hitched up his suit trousers, which were now looking distinctly grubby. 'I've been playing. Catherine told me I could.'

Haydn pressed his lips together. He'd been worried about the boy, worried he'd been neglecting

him. He didn't need to hear that Catherine Mc-
Donald had once again taken charge.

Another boy, who Haydn thought might be
Miles, said, 'Richie was really good at seeking. We
go in pairs and everyone wants to be with him.'

Richie managed to look embarrassed and
pleased at the same time.

Haydn told himself this was good, the boy was
joining in. But he felt a small resentment that he
hadn't been the one to think of organising this.

'Time to go home now. Have you any idea
where you left your waistcoat and jacket?'

Richie trailed after him back to the marquee,
the happiness seeping out of the boy the longer
the two of them were together. His thin face took
on its usual anxious expression and Haydn wondered again why it had to be like this.

Trying to recover the mood, he said, 'You
seemed to be having fun.'

'Yeah. I was.'

'Was that Miles?'

'Yeah.'

And then, just when Haydn thought the conversation was going nowhere, the boy mumbled,
'Catherine said that, well, maybe ... that maybe I
could go to Annat School, with Miles. Do you
think...?'

Haydn came to a standstill 'Catherine said
what?' How could Catherine talk to his son like
that! Start talking about schools before he had
even broached the topic himself. Before he had
even decided whether he was going to broach the
topic.

'It's a school that's near here,' said Richie

doubtfully. 'But I suppose I can't, really.'

'No, you can't!' Haydn felt wrong-footed and furious to be put in this position. But it wasn't the child he should be angry with. He tried hard to keep his voice calm and murmured a few platitudes.

Just wait until he had the chance of a word with Catherine.

Catherine was helping Phyllida change into her going-away outfit. Even after her sister Vanessa had finally arrived, everyone seemed to expect that Catherine would continue in her Maid of Honour role. And she was, amazingly, willing to do so.

She held up the filmy peach-coloured suit. 'This is very pretty. Did you get it here?'

'No, I brought that from the States with me. My wedding dress I bought here.'

'Yes, I remember. With a little help from my father.' Gordon had marched Phyllida off to Edinburgh to oversee her selection, having no truck with that rubbish about not seeing the wedding dress before The Day.

'It's been a wonderful day,' said Phyllida. 'Thank you for all you've done.'

Catherine looked down, embarrassed. She could think of a few things that might have gone better, starting with her own clash with her father that morning. She thought of her mother. Strangely, it no longer hurt to see Phyllida in her place. Or not in her place, exactly, but married to Gordon. Rachel's place could *never* be filled.

She cleared her throat. 'You don't need to

243

thank me, I was happy to help with the preparations, and you did a lot of that. I'm sorry about the ... fuss.' She could feel herself blushing. Apologies had never come easily to her. 'It was just the way my father spoke.'

'He doesn't mean to annoy you,' said Phyllida.

Catherine wasn't at all sure about that, but she didn't say so. She hugged the older woman, feeling tears coming stupidly to her eyes. 'I hope you'll be very happy.'

Phyllida kissed her lightly on the cheek, so as not to smudge her own make-up. 'I sure hope so.' She turned back to the mirror. 'I think we will be. I can give Gordon something he badly needs.'

'Money,' said Catherine immediately. 'Oh, sorry...'

'Money helps, of course, but that's not what I meant. I can give him approval, put him first. That's what he needs, and I want to do it.'

Catherine didn't know what to say. She felt young and silly. No mention of love here.

Phyllida smiled her sweet smile. 'Goodbye for now. I'll look forward to seeing you again after the honeymoon. Gordon has promised to be here for this funeral.'

'Yes. Yes, of course.' Catherine realised this might not be very convenient for Phyllida. She hadn't considered her needs before. 'I'll get on to that on Monday. I believe that the Procurator Fiscal will sometimes release the body even if investigations aren't finished.'

Phyllida gave a small shudder. 'Let's not talk about that now.'

Yes, she was just right for Gordon. He never

244

liked to talk about unpleasant things either.

A few minutes later, Catherine waved her father and new step-mother off on their honeymoon. 'I hope they have a good time,' she said to John Hugo, who stood beside her. 'The weather on the islands can be so unpredictable this time of year.'

'Don't worry, they'll be fine,' he said bitterly. 'Father always lands on his feet.'

As the small crowd began to disperse, Haydn moved to her side. 'I'd like a word with you,' he said. His voice was hard, so different from earlier in the evening.

'What is it?' She squinted up at him but his features were in shadow and she couldn't read his expression. What on earth had happened?

'I'll only take a moment.' He guided her away from the group to the now-empty marquee. 'In here will do.' The staff had left for the night having stripped the tables of their white cloths and removed most of the flowers. It looked drab under the bare lights and smelt of damp grass and stale alcohol.

Catherine sat down wearily on one of the chairs that had not been stacked away. 'How can I help?'

'I've just had the most surprising conversation with Richie.'

'Oh?' Catherine felt confused, and really too tired to try and understand.

'Yes.' Haydn glared down at her. In this garish light, she had no trouble reading his expression. It was one of fury. 'I would just like to ask you not to interfere between my son and me.'

'But...' Catherine cast her mind back over the

evening. She had almost forgotten her brief conversation with Richie. She couldn't think what she had said to arouse such emotion. In fact, she hadn't said nearly as much as she had intended. 'Has he had a good time?' she asked, trying to deflect the conversation.

'As it happens, he's had a rather fine time. Getting filthy playing hide and seek in the undergrowth. Telling all the other children that he's going to be going to *Annat School* and won't ever need to go back to London.'

'But I never said that...'

'You clearly said enough. Don't you think it would have been polite to let me broach the subject with him first?' There were none of his ironic smiles and quirky innuendos. This was absolute upfront anger.

'I'm sorry. It just came up...'

'I bet you made sure it did. And I'm the one who has had to disappoint him, tell him it's not practical to move schools just now.'

'That's your decision,' said Catherine, feeling her own anger rising.

'That's right. It is.'

'What I mean is it's your decision whether to disappoint him or not. You don't *have to.*'

'Richie will stay at his current school until *I* decide otherwise. Perhaps you don't realise how much notice is required to change these things. His fees are already paid.'

'Is it about money?' Catherine was genuinely amazed. Of all the things she thought of Haydn Smith, she had never considered him mean with money. 'You're committed to paying his London school so you don't want to move him.'

The fees are a consideration, but they are not the main one. The main issue is that Richie is my son. I have his *sole custody*. I fought hard enough through the courts to ensure that was the case.'

Haydn prevented further discussion by turning on his heel and walking out.

Chapter Twenty-eight

Without Gordon and Phyllida, Annat House felt strangely quiet. There was no reason for this. They had been living in the East Lodge, and they had been away on a number of occasions previously, but somehow it felt different. As though a new era was beginning.

Catherine just wished she knew what the new era was to be.

She set about reorganising rooms and bookings with a vigour that had been lacking in recent weeks. It annoyed Mhairi and the other staff no end, but it made Catherine feel better. And she was constantly in the kitchen, hovering behind Malcolm, wondering if she had been mad to let him take on the task of cooking for ten people, fourteen if you included staff.

The meals on the first day of the *Wildlife of the Highlands* course were actually very passable, but they had been pretty easy. She didn't want her precious guests to have warm chicken salad and (bought) sticky toffee pudding every day.

247

She had seen nothing at all of Haydn and Richie. There was no sign of the smart black car going to and fro on the loch road, so either they were away or staying quietly in the cottage. She certainly wasn't going to walk over in that direction to find out. Haydn had made it clear what he thought of her 'interfering' in his life. If that was the way he felt, fine.

It didn't help at all that Malcolm and Mhairi were suddenly inexplicably and exuberantly happy. Just when she had been sure that relationship was floundering they appeared to have sorted out their differences. It was good to know Malcolm was not only busy and useful, but happy too. She just wished she didn't have to see it at such close quarters.

Catherine also found time to devote to arranging Jean's funeral. She didn't do this with quite so much vigour, but it was something else that needed doing.

'We've got to do something about Catherine,' said Mhairi.

Malcolm looked up warily. He didn't like the sound of that, but he was learning caution. He didn't contradict her outright.

It didn't make any difference. Mhairi continued as if he had disagreed vehemently. 'Yes, we have. Just because she's your big sister and you're scared of her...'

He snorted.

'You are. You've always been a bit overawed by your mother and now by Catherine.'

Malcolm frowned. That was a bit close to the

mark. Mhairi continued regardless. 'What you don't see is that they need help too. Catherine puts on such a good show of being in control of everything, but I know she's unhappy.'

'You're not going to tell me she's missing Father.'

'It's not your father, stupid.'

'So what is it? She's not shown nearly so much interest in Jean as I have, all she seems interested in is holding the bloody funeral at Kinlochannat.'

'Malcolm, it's Haydn that's the problem.' Mhairi stood before him, hands on hips, her bright eyes pinning him down, demanding attention. 'It's Haydn she's missing.'

'Well ... why doesn't she just go and see him? He only lives next door.'

'It doesn't work like that, does it? They've had some kind of argument and they're both too proud to back down.'

'How do you know that?' said Malcolm, impressed despite himself. He should be getting on with the Cullen Skink for lunch but he gave the pot a quick stir and then sat down to listen properly. 'Did she tell you?'

'Of course not. Catherine's a very private person. But something must have happened at the wedding. She's been quiet ever since. It's been over a week now and Haydn hasn't shown his face here. Yet I saw them dancing that evening and I thought they were getting on really well.'

'Did you?' Malcolm hadn't noticed anyone dancing except Mhairi. The slow, cold fear he had felt when he saw her dance with all those other men still made him shiver.

'You were too drunk.'

'I was ... otherwise engaged.'

'Yes. 'Specially towards the end of the evening.' She smiled suddenly and dipped down to kiss him, hopping back before he could pull her onto his knee. 'So, either we try and persuade Catherine to get down off her high horse, or we have to approach Haydn.'

'I don't really think it's anything to do with us.'

'Don't you want Catherine to be happy?'

'Ye-es.' Malcolm hadn't really thought about it before. Catherine, like his mother before her, was simply there. 'But I don't think it's a good idea to get involved. I mean, you don't even know what they had the argument about.'

'That doesn't mean we can't try and help.'

Malcolm shrugged uneasily. He could feel himself losing ground here. He stood up. 'I really need to get on with the food. And don't you have a job to do?'

'Fortunately I'm a wee bit better organised than you. That's why I came down here, to give you a hand.'

'Well why didn't you say?' He pulled her against him and for a moment she leant in, touched her lips to his. Eventually, she pulled away.

'OK, chef, what's on the menu?'

You, thought Malcolm, I wish it was you. But he had to be sensible now. Catherine was relying on him. He flicked open his notebook and began to give instructions.

It was fortunate he did so, for when Catherine came down the stairs ten minutes later it was to find both of them conscientiously employed,

Malcolm filleting pheasants in the back kitchen, Mhairi preparing vegetables.

'Something smells good,' she said, smiling at them. Malcolm watched her through the doorway. She looked tired, the skin around her eyes pale and drawn. Maybe Mhairi was right.

'Cullen Skink,' he said, nodding at the pan on the Aga. 'That's for lunch, with some of your bread, cold meats, and salad to follow. We're working on dinner just now.'

'That's good.' She smiled at him properly this time. 'I don't know if I've said how grateful I am to you. It's amazing what you've managed to achieve, and it's been a real life saver.'

'So are you going to stop checking up on me all the time?' He hadn't meant to sound so grumpy, but her lack of confidence was annoying.

'I know I can rely on you absolutely,' she said, which was maybe taking it a bit far.

'Well, thanks...'

'I was wondering whether you'd be prepared to carry on helping long term?' Catherine propped herself up against the table and considered him carefully. Apparently this time she hadn't come down to check on him, but questions about the future were even less welcome.

'I'm not really sure...'

'You're very good with food.' Catherine still sounded surprised about this. 'Have you considered this as a career?'

It made a nice change to be praised, but Malcolm did wish people weren't so keen to pin him down on a career.

'He's thinking of becoming a lawyer,' said

251

Mhairi helpfully.

'It was a solicitor, actually, and it was just an idea.'

'Oh. Well.' Catherine sounded amused. 'Father would be pleased.'

'Maybe I won't do it then.' Malcolm smiled to show this was a joke. At least, he had intended it as a joke. Catherine just sighed.

'What I need to know is whether I should tell that agency to carry on looking for a chef, or whether you'll stay on until – say the end of the summer? What do you think?'

'I could probably do that,' said Malcolm. He didn't have any other plans.

'Excellent. And, if so, do you want me to arrange any training for you during the times when we don't have visitors here? I know you've been doing brilliantly, but it is without any formal training. I could get Mhairi to look up some courses.'

Malcolm raised his bloodied hands from the pheasant carcases and looked at his sister warily.

'I'll pay,' she said encouragingly.

'I...' He felt a chill run through him. He was coping fine in this kitchen he had known all his life, copying the recipes he had learnt from the skilful if unpleasant Fergus. Being seen to take it all seriously, exposing his limitations in front of a group of strangers, was something else entirely.

'Think about it,' said Catherine. 'At the very least you'll need a Kitchen Hygiene certificate.'

'Mmm. I suppose.' Malcolm piled the pheasant fillets neatly to one side and bagged up the waste before putting it in the bin. He then washed his hands thoroughly at the sink and returned to the main kitchen. Still, Catherine remained leaning against the table. He caught Mhairi's eye and she gestured with her head, as though to say 'go on, ask her'. He widened his own eyes in disagreement but Mhairi ignored him and spoke herself.

'I was wondering how Haydn is,' she said, introducing the topic with no finesse at all. 'I haven't seen him for a while.'

Catherine pushed herself upright. 'I presume he's fine. I really wouldn't know.'

Malcolm could tell from that tone that Mhairi was right. 'Have you had an argument with him?' he said, deciding to join in. 'Is there a problem?'

Mhairi cringed and Catherine glared. 'I don't know what you're talking about.'

'It's just, er...' he floundered. Mhairi stayed silent, the coward. 'It's just, er, you've been a bit down recently...'

'If you think I'm missing Haydn Smith, you're quite mistaken. It's Jean I've been thinking about. In fact, that's what I wanted to say.' She took a breath and the brief flash of emotion that the mention of Haydn had caused disappeared. 'I've been thinking about Jean a lot. I've got the bloody Reverend to agree to the funeral next week.'

'That's good,' said Malcolm.

'Yes, it is. But it takes some organising. And another thing,' Catherine was getting into her stride now. 'Seeing as Malcolm was so insistent about the whole thing, the meeting of the Community Council next week is going to consider the format establishment of the Gordon McDonald Fund. You should at least show your faces. And didn't you say you wanted to get in early with your suggestion of using some for Youth Aye's skate park idea?'

'Shit, is it so soon?' said Mhairi.

'We can't be expected to do everything.' Malcolm's heart sank. He couldn't think, now, why he had been so enthusiastic to get involved in the project, unless it had been to spend his father's money.

'You won't have to do everything. But as it was your idea I think coming along to the meeting and mentioning your plans is the least you can do,' said Catherine, rubbing her hands together in a satisfied way. 'If you have any free time between preparing meals it wouldn't do any harm to think things through.'

Malcolm waited until she was out of earshot before muttering, 'Why does she always have to be so bossy?'

'She's right, though, we do need to get on with it,' said Mhairi. 'And you know what, I think the very person to advise us lives just on the doorstep.'

'Huh?'

'If you do have any free time between meals, as Catherine put it, I think we should pay a visit to Mr Eddlington-Smith.'

Haydn was surprised and not particularly pleased to find Catherine's youngest brother Malcolm and the girl Mhairi on his doorstep.

'Yes?' he said discouragingly. He'd been keeping himself to himself since the wedding, just the way he had always meant to do. Richie was back at boarding school and Haydn was relieved to be finding his studies of manufacturing using poly-carbon materials strangely absorbing

'We wondered if we could pick your brains,' said Mhairi. 'About a business idea. Well, not business exactly. Could we explain it to you, see if you have any suggestions?'

Haydn sighed, but politeness prevailed and he led them into his newly-decorated front room. Here he heard all about the establishment of the community fund and how it was essential most of the money went to something for the young people of the village, because nothing was ever done for them. And what the youngsters wanted was a skate park, so this was what they needed to plan for. Mhairi was keen and articulate, and Malcolm roused himself to join in with more sensible questions than Haydn would have expected.

'It sounds like you've already done a great deal of thinking,' said Haydn, finding himself interested. 'You won't be involved in the formal setting up of the fund? No? Then that makes it easier to put in a bid against it. You don't need to do anything long-winded at the moment, but I can give you the format for a simple business plan.'

It was amazing how good it felt to have the youngsters listening to him, taking his thoughts on board. Maybe Catherine was right and with a bit of encouragement all sorts of entrepreneurial activity could start up locally.

It was more than an hour later when the young couple got up to leave. 'Thanks so much,' said Mhairi. 'I think we really know what we should be doing now.'

'We just need to find the time to do it,' said

Malcolm, noticeably more cautious. 'And this is just the planning stage. It'll be a whole lot harder if we do get funding.'

'One step at a time,' said Mhairi firmly. She turned again to Haydn, 'Don't you miss being involved in this kind of thing? You're so good at it.'

'Well, actually, I've had a few ideas for projects myself.' Haydn had been reluctant to put this into words, but now he had it made so much sense. 'Maybe I'll approach one of the small enterprise groups, see if I can get one or two of them off the ground. Ridiculous, isn't it, when I've just retired...'

'Of course it's not ridiculous,' said Mhairi. 'You've got loads of skills so you should use them.' She sounded so like Catherine! 'It's been good to see you. A shame you haven't been around at Annat House recently.'

Haydn said quickly, 'No doubt I'll see you again at the Community Council meeting. It'll be my first one as a full member.'

'And you will come to the funeral Catherine's organising for Jean, won't you?' persisted Mhairi. 'I think she'd really like to see you there.'

Haydn was absolutely sure that she wouldn't, but when Malcolm added his own encouragement (after a glare from Mhairi) he found himself saying he would see whether he could manage it.

Chapter Twenty-nine

The atmosphere in Annat House was strangely quiet as they prepared for the journey to the little church for Jean Sarah Lawson's funeral. The wedding of Gordon and Phyllida might not have been welcomed by all members of the family but the atmosphere then had been lively at least – fractious at times, but animated.

Now there was not so much a sadness settled on them as lethargy. How to mourn someone you had never known? Catherine had agreed to read the eulogy, yet she didn't know her sister at all. Father Michael from Jean's church had sent a long, effusive, but not particularly informative letter. Two members of the congregation had sent cards of condolence. No one had made the long journey north.

Even the weather was wrong for a funeral. The sun shone from a cloudless, egg-blue sky, trees were lushly in leaf, the water of the loch lay like a sheet of silver, disturbed by not so much as a breath of air. Catherine fanned herself discreetly with the order of service and wished it were over.

Her mood wasn't improved by seeing Haydn entering the small church as their car drew up. 'What's he doing here?' she said to no one in particular.

Malcolm looked guilty. 'I invited, well, mentioned to him...'

'I don't see why he is interested,' she said, angry to find that she cared. 'Just nosy, like the rest of the bloody village.' The church was almost full. At least half of the village had made the effort to be present, along with a few local journalists and what were possibly a couple of national ones. DI Cowan was there, dressed correctly in a very dark suit, but with fair hair flopping over his face.

'Good turn out,' said the Reverend John, coming up to shake her hand. He looked very pleased about it. She wondered sourly if he had to submit records of church attendance to his superiors. If so, he should be grateful to the McDonald family.

The small notice that had announced the funeral in the local paper had invited anyone attending to return to Annat House for a light tea afterwards. As Catherine slipped into a pew beside Malcolm she whispered, 'Have we got enough food for all this lot?'

'Don't worry. I've just phoned Mrs Mac to tell her to double the ham sandwiches and get more vol-au-vents out of the freezer. Although hopefully they won't all come to the house.'

Catherine sighed. 'They'll want to see the new decor,' she said gloomily. 'And have a closer look at Phyllida.'

'So? Let them. Don't worry about it.'

Catherine would have been far less worried if she could have been sure that one guest in particular wouldn't be there. Haydn nodded to her from afar, but didn't approach. In dark suit and pristine white shirt he looked more stunning than ever. It hurt to look at him and know he disliked her.

Speaking was surprisingly easy when it came. She started from notes but then real emotion took over and she spoke from her heart. 'We didn't know you, Jean Sarah Lawson McDonald, and we never will. But we won't forget you.' As she came to the end, she raised a hand to dash aside the tears and looked out at the congregation. 'We miss you, Jean,' she said, meeting her father's eyes. He had deprived them of this sister. 'We won't forget you.' She looked at Malcolm, who nodded. 'We hope you are at peace.'

When she returned to her seat Georgie leant over from the pew behind and said, 'You did very well,' in a surprised voice.

Catherine shrugged. She would have done better if she had known more. The place in her life where her sister should be would always be empty now.

Haydn watched Catherine from the back of the church. He was trying to make up his mind. He had come along because Malcolm had been so keen that he should and he had wondered if Catherine had put him up to it. Seeing her now, he knew this was not the case. Catherine barely acknowledged him, her dark head held high. He could see she was close to tears, especially after she had spoken. And she didn't look in his direction once.

Over the last couple of weeks he had nursed his resentment about Richie and been determined not to think of her. Now, when they were face to face again, he couldn't even remember why he had been so upset. All that seemed to matter was that she was sad, and he wasn't there to make things better for her.

Catherine fought hard not to break down and cry during the wake. It was ridiculous. She hadn't known this sister, and yet today she suddenly felt close to her. She had still not forgiven her father, and yet today she wanted to weep at the thought he was going so far away. And always, hovering in the background, was Haydn. She didn't want to think about it. He had behaved in a completely unreasonable way. She was better off having nothing to do with him.

As she thought these things the tears seem to well up in her throat and overpower her. But she had to keep going, talking to the guests, welcome and otherwise, making sure everyone had tea, sandwiches, someone to talk to, and that they didn't wander all over the house, supposedly looking for a toilet but really spying on all the changes she had made.

She wasn't that successful in keeping everyone downstairs. She heard Nancy from the shop saying to one of her friends, 'You'll no believe it, it's got bathrooms in every bedroom, must've cost a fortune...'

Catherine got Mhairi to stand sentry on the stairs and moved on.

When she entered the drawing room she walked straight into Haydn, who was standing just inside the door, almost as though he was waiting for her.

'You've put on a very good show,' he said. 'No more than I would have expected, of course.'

'Thank you.'

'But you're looking tired. It can't have been easy...'

'I really have to go. Need to talk to...' Catherine glanced around desperately. The tears were threatening to choke her. 'To Phyllida.'

She hurried to her stepmother's side and felt oddly protected. Phyllida had been standing close to Gordon, content to let him dominate whatever conversation was taking place. But now she drew Catherine away. 'Are you all right, honey?' Her smile was gentle as always, but Catherine was beginning to suspect Phyllida saw more than she gave away.

'I'm fine. Just wishing it was all over.'

'You've done her proud. You should be pleased with yourself.'

'I've had a lot of help. From Malcolm especially.'

Phyllida nodded. It was impossible to know if she heard the unspoken criticism of Gordon. Phyllida didn't defend him, and her quiet acceptance was steadying.

'They won't stay too long, will they?' The older woman looked around at the crowd, which was starting to thin. 'And then you can get some rest. Gordon and I leave tomorrow, which I'm sure will be a relief to you. The last few months haven't been easy, have they?'

'It's not you,' said Catherine.

'You'll like to get back to normal,' said Phyllida calmly. 'I hope you don't have too many guests lined up for this month? What you need is a break.'

'I need paying guests for the money,' said

Catherine with a sigh. 'I'll be fine.'

Phyllida put a well-cared-for hand on Catherine's arm. 'Don't try and be too strong, honey.'

Catherine didn't have the chance to find out what that was supposed to mean. The kaleidoscope of guests revolved again and she found herself drawn into another group. But the few minutes with Phyllida had calmed her. The tears were in abeyance now and she concentrated on thanking people for coming and making it very clear that it was now time they departed.

John Hugo was good at this kind of thing, and seemed happy to help out. By six o'clock, most of the crowd had dispersed. Malcolm and Mhairi were ferrying used cups and plates down to the kitchen where Mrs McWhirter was loading and unloading the dishwashers with stolid efficiency. Since Fergus had left she hadn't complained about anything, not even working extra hours. Catherine was sure it couldn't last.

As she climbed back up the stairs she came face to face with Haydn.

'I thought you'd gone,' she said churlishly.

'I didn't want to go without saying goodbye.'

'Well. Goodbye then.' She almost offered to shake his hand, the words sounded so formal.

'And to ask why it is you're avoiding me.' He looked down at her from those green eyes, unblinking. She couldn't tell from his tone whether this was a statement or an accusation.

'I, well, I haven't really... I've been busy, you know...' Catherine looked down so that she could concentrate. She wished he would move away. Standing so close to him made her feel uncomfortably warm, but if she took a step back she would fall down the damn stairs. She hated to feel cornered and that made her hit out. 'I seem to remember that our last conversation didn't end on a very friendly note. I thought *you* were avoiding *me*.'

'You're right.' He smiled. 'I should apologise for that. I'm sorry.' He watched her closely and again she felt wrong-footed. 'If you haven't been avoiding me, then perhaps you'd like to come over for a coffee in the morning? I believe your father leaves first thing, so just say when is convenient.'

Catherine frowned, trying to work out what was going on. The last thing she had expected was a polite invitation to morning coffee. 'I really don't know...'

Gordon appeared in the doorway of the drawing room. 'Ah, Catherine, there you are,' he said, as if he hadn't seen her for hours. 'I've been wanting a word.'

'Shall we say eleven?' said Haydn, flashing her that amused half-smile she hadn't seen for weeks, and taking his leave before she could think of a reply.

She could feel herself blushing as she turned to her father. 'Yes, how can I help?'

'What was all that about?' He frowned after Haydn.

'Nothing. Nothing at all.'

'In that case, perhaps you could come in here?' He led her into the small sitting room and closed the door. Then he seemed, unusually, at a loss for words.

'Yes?' said Catherine. She was still confused by

Haydn's invitation.

'Catherine, I just wanted to say...' Gordon took off his half-moon glasses and polished them. 'I just wanted to say – you're a good girl. You've done well with the funeral. A proper McDonald send off.'

'Oh,' said Catherine, nonplussed. 'Thank you.'

'I wish things had been different,' he said gruffly. 'With Jean.'

She stared at him. It sounded as though he was apologising. For a moment, he wasn't her irascible father but an elderly man, unsure of himself, admitting he might have made mistakes. It was a side of Gordon McDonald she had never thought to see.

'I'm sorry too,' she said, forcing the words past the lump in her throat. 'But we can't change things now. We just have to go on.'

'That's right.' He took out a large handkerchief and blew his nose.

She wanted to hug him, something she hadn't done for years, but before she could make a movement he had taken a step back. He replaced his glasses and cleared his throat.

Speaking in his normal brusque tone, he continued, 'Right. We should go over the arrange-ments for sending my boxes to the States. They'll need to be carefully packed and I don't want you to forget about the insurance. And keep an eye on Jean's things when they come up from London, won't you? See if there's anything of value. I know I can trust you.'

Catherine smiled faintly. This was back to the old Gordon with a vengeance. But he had apologised, in his way. He had thanked her. She couldn't quite forgive him everything, but her heart did feel lighter.

Chapter Thirty

Catherine wasted a great deal of time during the evening and night trying to come up with reasons why she shouldn't go and see Haydn. Unfortunately, none of them sounded convincing, even to her own ears. It was cowardice, pure and simple, that would keep her away, and she refused to be a coward.

So she rose early to say a surprisingly tearful goodbye to her father, and receive a long list of instructions from him. She dealt with worst of the day's paperwork, and then told Mhairi she was going out. She put on an extra touch of make-up to bolster her confidence, and called Pip to go with her. Then she headed down the drive. She didn't tell anyone where she was going, but she had no hopes it would remain a secret. Someone would be watching to see which way she turned.

It was a beautiful morning. Yesterday's heat had been dispersed by a brisk breeze which rippled the water of the loch and sent high white clouds scudding across the sky. The trees swayed lightly, bright in their summer clothing, and all around the mountains reached up to the dazzling sky, a hundred shades of green and grey. Numerous cars passed her on the loch road, driving slowly so the occupants could ooh and ahh over the views. Tourists. Very useful people, of course, but she did wish they'd look where they were going. She had to keep Pip close at heel and was relieved when she had covered the short distance to Annat Cottage.

She knocked smartly on the recently repainted front door, and tried to ignore the hammering of her heart. This was a neighbourly visit, nothing more.

'Punctual as always,' said Haydn by way of greeting. His expression was guarded and she wished for once that she was a coward.

'Come in, come in,' he said impatiently, as she hesitated on the doorstep.

'I, er, thanks. Pip might be a bit muddy, do you mind...?'

Haydn didn't even bother to answer that. He moved aside and the Jack Russell shot past him. Catherine had no choice but to follow.

'Your new furniture has arrived,' she said, surprised out of her unease. 'It looks good.'

The heavily patterned suite and carpet were gone, replaced by sanded wood floors, pale rugs, and the simple lines of the chairs and tables she had helped him select. The small oil painting had pride of place, hanging above the fireplace on the repainted cream walls.

'Have a seat. I'll bring the coffee through.'

Catherine hesitated, then did as she was bidden. On her previous occasional visits she had followed him into the kitchen, had chatted as he prepared the beverages. Clearly, that was no longer acceptable. She felt a twinge of fear. What was he going to say? It hadn't occurred to her before, but looking around she saw how easy it would be for him to sell this place, making a tidy profit. Was he about to tell her he was leaving?

He brought through a tray containing a cafetière, two slim blue mugs, and a matching jug of milk. He put it down on the pale wood and glass table and took a seat at right-angles to her. For a moment he said nothing, just stretched out his legs and looked beyond her through the window to the loch. He looked handsome and remote in black jeans and a soft grey jersey.

Catherine opened her mouth to speak, to lighten the atmosphere as all well-brought-up ladies would do, and then closed it. He had invited her. Let him start the conversation.

It was almost as if he could read her mind. He glanced across at her and gave a slight, mocking smile. 'You're very quiet.'

'I'm sure that makes a pleasant change.' She couldn't help herself, she wanted to rile him.

He merely smiled, but to himself this time, and sat forward to push down the plunger on the cafetière. 'White coffee, is that right?'

'Yes, please.'

'I'm afraid I haven't any biscuits.'

'That's OK. I'm not hungry.' She was beginning to wonder if she would be able to swallow her coffee. The strange elongated silences were making her more and more edgy.

'I thought you might like to hear how Richie is getting on.'

Catherine started at the mention of the child's name. 'Yes, of course. I hope he's well.'

267

'Very well. The fact that this is going to be his last term at the London school appears to have cheered him up no end.'

'That's good.' Did this mean Haydn was moving the child to Annat School? Catherine steeled herself not to ask.

'Don't you want to know where he is going after the summer holidays?'

'I'm sure you and Richie's mother have made a sensible decision,' she said stiffly.

'I hope we have. Or that I have. It is my right to make these choices.' He smiled faintly. 'Esme was less than impressed at the idea of her child going to school in the wilds of Scotland, but there is, fortunately, nothing she can do about it.'

'He's coming to Annat?'

'That's right.'

'I'm glad.'

'So's he. So am I. So that's all right then, isn't it?' He was watching her carefully, eyes half-closed so she couldn't judge his expression. Not that she had ever been very good at judging his expressions.

'I'm sure he'll be very happy there,' she said, to break the silence.

'Time will tell. But I think he has a good chance. At least, for once, he's in agreement with a decision I have made.' He sighed. 'I'd never thought to consult him before.'

Catherine took a sip of her drink. It was hot and very strong, but she managed to swallow it. She nerved herself not to come out with any more platitudes.

'Your father and Phyllida get off all right?'

'Yes. John Hugo took them to the airport.'

'You'll miss them.'

Catherine shrugged at this blunt statement. 'It'll be different.'

'Easier?' He smiled briefly.

'Possibly.'

Catherine took another sip of her coffee. She didn't think this was going anywhere. She realised now how attracted to him she was, how important he had become despite all their arguments. But it was over. Just sitting here with him, so close and so distant, was awful. The sooner she finished and left, the better.

He had told her about Richie. They were friends. It was fine.

'Can I ask you something?' he said.

Normally, Catherine would have smiled politely and replied in the affirmative. Now she didn't want him to ask her any of those probing, difficult questions.

'I think I'd rather you didn't.'

That surprised him. The eyebrows were raised, the eyes no longer hooded. 'And I wonder why that is.'

She smiled brightly in return. 'Best to keep things simple.' A pause. 'You've, er, made a lovely job of the redecoration.'

'Yes, haven't I? I was fortunate to be able to call on the advice of someone with excellent taste.'

She took another sip and didn't rise to the bait.

'If I can't ask you a question, perhaps you would be prepared to listen to what I have to say?'

Catherine shifted uncomfortably. So he wasn't going to let things slip back to polite platitudes.

She could feel a lump at the back of her throat again. She shrugged, neither a yes nor a no.

He watched her for a moment, then sat back in his chair, legs outstretched. 'I want to tell you a little about me.' Once again he was looking past her, but his eyes weren't focussed on the view. She said nothing and after a while he continued. 'I have been married once, as you know. It wasn't a good marriage.' He shook his head. 'But that's not where I want to start. I want to tell you about my childhood.'

Again he paused and again she waited. She was desperate to hear what he had to say, and sure it was going to hurt her.

'I was an only child, perhaps I've mentioned that before. My parents had high expectations of me. Very high. You think you had a difficult childhood here, with your selfish father and your ambitious brothers. But you had your mother, who you clearly loved and were loved by. And for the most part, it appears to me, you were allowed to go your own way. I, on the other hand, had the full weight of two parents' hopes resting on me. I didn't mind at first. I was clever. I got scholarships. I was a star, and they were pleased. I went to Oxford. Everyone said I was brilliant. I worked hard. Everyone's expectations were fulfilled, again.'

He was still looking beyond her, his face expressionless. 'Then I left and started my own business, and they raised a few concerns. But that was a stunning success, more than even I had expected, and believe me I had never contemplated failure. I married Esme, beautiful and well-connected. We had a son. My parents were over the moon. I had done everything they ever dreamt of.'

He let his eyes rest on her face for a moment. 'Can you picture that?'

'Being everything my parents ever dreamt of? Absolutely not.'

'You have no idea of the burden.' He snapped his fingers in sudden exasperation. 'It sounds pathetic, doesn't it? Grown man, self-made millionaire, and all he worries about is what his parents might think. I loved my parents, don't get me wrong, but I was living the life they wanted me to live, not my own. And then things started to go wrong. Or maybe they had always been wrong and I just hadn't realised.

'Esme didn't enjoy being a mother and certainly didn't want more children. She passed her time spending the money I was earning, making sure she was *seen* spending the money. Going to the right parties, the right gallery openings. She loved being photographed. She didn't like my parents, too middle class, and didn't bother to hide it.' He sighed. 'Nobody was happy. Yet when it came to the divorce, my parents were appalled. They didn't believe we couldn't work it out. It was my fault, in a way, for letting them believe for all those years that I could do everything right. The divorce was ... messy. I had to fight Esme for custody of Richie.' His tone was bitter. 'Nobody supported me. They all thought it was right for a child to be with his mother, no matter that the mother cared *nothing* for him. But Richie is *my* son and I wasn't going to let him go. Fortunately, as she'd walked out on us, I won. Eventually. And she did things that didn't exactly help her case.'

He closed his eyes for a moment.

After a pause, in which Catherine said nothing because she could think of nothing to say, he continued. 'My parents died last year, a couple of months apart. For the last few years, things weren't so good between us. Richie wasn't the grandchild they had hoped for and I was too busy with work to see them as much as they thought I should. I stayed in London in order to be close but it wasn't enough. They were old and frail and ... well, you don't need to know about that. I'm just giving you the background.'

'And when they died, you sold the business and moved up here?' Catherine spoke slowly, thinking it through.

'That's right. I asked myself, what did I really want to do, with no one else's hopes and expectations riding on my shoulders? And this was it. So I did it.'

Catherine nodded uncertainly. She didn't think her approval was what he was looking for.

'You've no idea how proud I was of myself.' He smiled sardonically. 'You've never seen anyone so decisive. I sold the company within six months, bought the house up here sight unseen. It was pretty impressive. Here I was, starting my new life, with only myself to think about.'

'And Richie.' The words were out of Catherine's mouth before she could stop them.

The shuttered look came down on his face again. 'Absolutely. And Richie. Not that that occurred to me at the time. He was enrolled in a good school, one that I had chosen but my parents and Esme had approved of. His name was down for Harrow. For weeks at a time I hardly saw him. He was being well looked after and I wasn't going to live my life according to his demands any more than I was going to listen to anyone else's.'

This time he left a silence so long that Catherine shifted in her seat, and said, doubtfully, 'I see.'

'I haven't finished yet.' He went back to his staring out of the window. She allowed her eyes to rest on him, watching the expressions flit across the handsome face. She could guess now where this was going, and she wanted to remember every plane of his face, every inflection of his voice.

'What I hadn't realised was how selfish I had become. I was so obsessed with not falling in with other people's wishes I could think of nothing but my own. And my wish was above all things to be on my own, answerable to no one. Then, who should I meet on my very first day here, in the very first hour, but the bossiest, most interfering woman I have come across in my entire life.'

Catherine frowned. She thought that was a bit much. But he didn't even glance at her.

'At first I was amused by her. I liked her. I enjoyed spending time with her. She was undoubtedly attractive and never boring. I thought a little flirtation wouldn't do any harm, but I found myself drifting more and more towards a serious relationship. I hardly realised what was happening, but I was happy, and in her own inimitable way, she seemed interested.'

Catherine shifted in her seat again. She wanted to think of some way of making him stop. He was trying to explain why it would never work between them. He didn't need to do that, she could see it clearly enough for herself. She didn't want him spelling it out for her, and then apologising, and expecting everything to be fine.

She put her mug aside and glanced at her watch. 'Yes, well, I'm sorry things didn't turn out... I really think I'd better go.'

'Please don't.' He met her eyes squarely and she saw that his were as weary as her own. She wasn't the only one who had been losing sleep. 'Let me finish. It won't take long. And then you can make up your own mind.'

Catherine spread her hands uncertainly and he took the gesture for agreement.

'So here I was, falling in love with a woman I had barely kissed, without even being aware of it.'

Catherine made as if to speak and then didn't. No one had ever said they loved her before, even in retrospect.

'And then I start to have these niggling feelings. Am I losing control of my life again? Am I allowing someone else to decide my priorities? I start to have serious doubts about the relationship. And yet when I'm with her, the attraction is undeniable. I want to dance with her, to talk to her, to sleep with her so much I can think of nothing else. It makes me doubt my judgement even more.'

He sighed and shot her a quick glance, as though scared of what he might see. 'And then my difficult, prickly son, who will hardly speak to me, speaks to her. He tells me this woman is right, that he's unhappy in London, that he wants to move. I was – I know it's ridiculous, but I was shocked,

274

and, well, jealous, and that made me furious. I told you what a battle I had to get custody. This woman makes suggestions about his future and he says that she's right and I'm wrong... For you to dare to speak direct to him, by-passing me, well, it made me lose my head. I took it out on you. I'm sorry. I was probably very rude.'

He glanced at her again. She had never seen him nervous.

'Yes, you were,' she said. 'But no doubt I asked for it.'

He smiled faintly. 'You were only trying to help.'

'As you said, I was interfering.' When he said nothing, Catherine took a deep breath. 'I'm sorry too.' There, she had said it. They had both apologised, like two civilised adults. 'Thank you for explaining,' she said carefully.

Now he could bring this politely to a close and she could leave. Her throat felt stiff with not crying. She felt an immense sadness for him and his solitary upbringing. And she knew soon she would feel an even more immense sadness for herself.

'I'm sorry to be so long-winded,' he said with a wry smile. 'I didn't know how else to explain, except by starting at the beginning.'

'That's all right,' she said stiffly.

'And now I want to ask you that question.' He sat forward. Catherine kept very still, willing herself to agree to be his friend. 'It's better that I explained everything first.'

She nodded weakly.

He said, 'Will you marry me?'

Catherine opened her mouth then shut it again.

She was stunned, bewildered, confused – and very, very scared. She could feel the colour flooding over her face as she tried to capture her breath.

He put out a hand and touched her cheek tentatively. 'You could say something, you know.'

'I'm – speechless.'

'It's not often anyone achieves that.' He took one hand and raised it to his lips. The feel of his warm breath made her shiver. 'Will you marry me?'

She pulled her hand away so that she could think more clearly. 'I don't know what to say. I need to think.' She shook her head, bewildered. He had surprised her more than once in the past, but this was the biggest surprise of all.

'But you will think about it?'

'You don't even like me,' she said. 'You've just explained how everything I do is wrong.'

'No. I've tried to explain why I reacted like I did. Why I was annoyed.'

'So I'm bossy and annoying.' Catherine was fighting for time. 'That's quite some proposal.'

'And beautiful and bewitching. I love you.' He said it again, properly this time, and she felt that great surge of fear – or was it hope? 'Can't we give this a try?'

'I don't know,' she said, so quietly he wouldn't have heard had he not been leaning so close.

He bent and kissed her very gently on the lips. 'Think about it. Please?'

And then, when all she wanted him to do was take her in his arms and make her agree, he sat back and left her all the space in the world. 'Shall I walk up to Annat House with you?'

He accompanied her as far as the wide stone steps of the front door, where he left her with nothing more than a peck on the check. She felt bereft.

Chapter Thirty-one

Catherine sat down for lunch, various members of staff crowding haphazardly around the kitchen table. For once, her contributions to the conversation were minimal. She was hardly aware of the people around her and after Mrs McWhirter had asked her for the third time if she wanted tomato or lentil soup, they left her more or less alone.

She couldn't bring her thoughts to order. Haydn had asked her to marry him, but *why* had he asked her to marry him? And why had he done it so suddenly, taking her completely by surprise? Why couldn't he have suggested friendship, even becoming lovers? She blushed at that thought, but it would have been easier to handle than marriage. Marriage was enormous and serious and very, very scary.

And then he had walked home with her and left her at the door, making no arrangement for when they would see each other again. She wished she had thought to invite him in to eat, and then, looking around the table at all the interested faces, was glad that she hadn't.

'Is anything wrong?' said Mhairi eagerly as they made their way back up to the office.

'No. No.'

'How's Haydn?'

Catherine frowned down at the inquisitive young face and Mhairi had the grace to look away. 'I'm going out,' said Catherine, making the decision on the spur of the moment. 'Have you enough to be getting on with here?'

'Yes, of course.'

'I'll see you later then. Check up on that delivery of flowers, won't you? We can hardly run a flower-arranging course if the bloody things don't arrive on time. Keep on at them.'

'I will,' said Mhairi, looking more and more interested. Catherine wished she'd spoken calmly.

She thought she might drive to the west end of the loch and walk up into the hills there, except that meant passing Annat Cottage, which she didn't want to do. She headed for the village instead, meaning to pin Nancy down about the next meeting of the Women's Rural, but when she reached the shop she realised she couldn't remember either the dates or the topics for discussion. So she carried on around to the south shore of the loch, driving as slowly as any tourist, and when she found herself before her aunt's ramshackle home she realised this was where she had meant to come all along. Georgie might have kept Jean's existence a secret all those years, but she was still the one person Catherine trusted in her heart.

She parked the car on the weed- and gravel-strewn area at the side of the house and shouted greetings to the two black Labradors who were throwing themselves exuberantly against the fence. The rear of her aunt's ancient Land Rover could be seen poking out of the lean-to so there was a good chance she would find her aunt at home. She knocked on the door of the sunroom at the side of the cottage and, when she received no answer, let herself in. As always, it smelt of plants and dogs and the sort of cooking her aunt preferred – potting and bottling, smoking and pickling.

She inhaled the sweet, heavy scents, and began to relax. She ran her aunt to earth in the pantry, where she was rearranging shelves of jars and bottles, but seemed happy to be distracted.

'Camomile,' she said, after one look at Catherine. 'That's what you need. With perhaps a teaspoon of honey.'

'You know I hate camomile.'

'Yes,' said Georgie unsympathetically. She waved her niece to sit in one of the two ladder-back chairs that stood either side of the small scrubbed kitchen table and began to clatter about with mugs, boxes of herbs, and jars of honey.

'You could run a course on *Country Skills of Times Gone By*,' said Catherine, as she watched.

Georgie didn't bother to look round.

'It'd be very popular.'

Georgie grunted.

When her aunt brought two steaming mugs to the table, Catherine was grateful to cup her hands around the warmth. Outside, the clouds had gathered and in here it was definitely cool. Unlike Catherine, Georgie switched off her Aga at the first sign of summer.

'Aunt Georgie,' said Catherine, turning the strange, handle-less mug slowly around in her

279

hands. 'Why did you never marry?'

'Nothing to do with you,' said her aunt sharply.

'Was it to do with my father? Or my grand-parents?' Catherine had no memory of her grandfather and only a very faint recollection of her grandmother Sarah, after whom she – and Jean, she supposed – had been named. She had been a tall woman, straight-backed even in old age, with the pale eyes and high brow of the McDonalds, unsurprising this as she and her husband had been second cousins.

Georgie reached over for a cube of brown sugar and stirred it absently into her tea, despite the fact she had already added honey. Catherine began to be hopeful. If Georgie wasn't going to speak, she would have snapped at her again by now.

Catherine tried to remember things her mother had said. 'Did you have a boyfriend who was lost in the Second World War?'

'I'm not that old.'

'Oh.' Catherine was embarrassed. A quick calculation would have told her that much. 'The Korean War?' she suggested hopefully.

'I didn't marry because I didn't want to. Simple as that.'

'Did anyone ever ask you to marry them?'

Georgie examined her from narrowed blued eyes. 'This is about Haydn Smith, isn't it? I knew as much. I've seen the way he's been watching you, circling around at the wedding, coming back for more at the funeral. You need to think carefully, my girl, very carefully indeed.'

This made Catherine indignant. 'Why do you say that?'

'Think, my girl. Why is he pursuing you? What does he want?'

Catherine put down her mug suddenly so that it splashed pale, hot liquid over her fingers. 'I don't know what you mean.'

'Of course you do. You're not stupid, so you must be wondering. Is it your name? Your hands-off reputation? The big house? The trust fund?'

Catherine let all these accusations sink in, one soft blow after another. She let them reverberate through her mind. 'Why can't it just be – me?'

'It's not me you need to ask,' said Georgie, her expression closed. 'It's yourself.'

'Did you have a boyfriend who wanted you for those things?'

'Catherine, my dear, I had many boyfriends. It didn't matter what they wanted because I didn't want them. It's only when you want them that it matters. So – do you want Haydn?'

Catherine smiled wryly at this McDonald way of putting things. Not *do you love him* but *do you want him?* She said, 'He doesn't need my money. He doesn't need anything I've got.' That was true. It had taken this visit to Georgie to make her realise. She really had nothing to offer.

'Yes, I understand he's a very wealthy man. Your father couldn't find out anything to the contrary.'

'So he doesn't want my money. Which is fortunate, as I don't actually have any.'

'In a manner of speaking.' Georgie sipped her tea and waited.

Catherine chewed her lip. 'I really don't know what he wants,' she said at last. Then she dropped

281

her voice and sighed. 'He says I'm very bossy.'

'You are very bossy. There are not many men who could cope with that.'

'I'm enjoying Exclusive Activity Holidays. I like the challenge of that.'

'So, carry on with it. Has he asked you to do otherwise?'

'No, but...'

'You need to know your own mind, Catherine.'

'I always know my own mind,' protested Catherine. Wasn't this what she was always being criticised for, knowing her own mind too well?

'You know what you want for others. But do you really know for yourself?'

Catherine stared at her blankly.

'Think about it. You have to get down to the essentials, Catherine.'

Catherine picked up her mug and began to sip the sweet, unpleasant liquid. Georgie was right. She must concentrate on the essentials. She thought of Haydn and smiled. She would finish this drink and then she would go back to see him. When she saw him, she would know what he wanted, and, maybe, what she wanted too.

As she was leaving Georgie said, off hand, 'You mustn't forget, you're a very attractive woman, Catherine.'

'I am?' Catherine closed the flimsy glass door behind her, pushed aside the dogs, passed through the gate, and closed that as well. As she put her hand on the car door, she bent and looked at her reflection in the wing mirror. She frowned at it. The woman looking back at her had high colour, wild dark hair, and a resolute expression in her eyes. She remembered Haydn had said she should get used to accepting compliments, and that made her smile. When she smiled she looked almost – pretty?

She drove the long way around the loch to reach Haydn's cottage. The single-track road meandered along the water's edge on the south side, then took a loop away from the shore at the extreme western edge to take in Lochhead Farm. The farmer there was moving sheep from one field to another and Catherine raised her hand to him as she always did, and he regarded her impassively in return. It made her smile. Years, maybe decades, ago, her father had done something to annoy Bertie Menzies from Lochhead, and the family had never been forgiven.

Then she turned the car along the slightly wider road on the north side, driving east now, the sun in her mirror and her own special hills rising high on her left. She drove slowly, savouring the journey.

For a moment, when she arrived, she thought he had gone out. The black car was parked beside the cottage, but no lights were on and no one came to answer her soft knock. She waited a moment, taking a deep breath as she scanned the fields on either side, then knocked again.

She was just about to turn away when she heard footsteps, then the door was pulled open. She supposed she could have tried it herself, but that wouldn't have felt right.

'Hi there,' she said, her voice rather high. 'I thought I'd come to see you.'

Haydn's eyes had that unfocussed look of someone who has been staring too long at a computer screen and his hair was ruffled from fingers being run through it. 'Come in,' he said, standing aside to make way for her, his eyes not leaving her face, as though trying to read her intentions before she had even spoken.

She sat down on one of his new settees, and then stood up again. 'I've been thinking about what you said this morning.'

'Yes?'

'It was a shock to me.'

'I could see that. But you must have realised that I've been interested in you for a while.'

'Interested?' she said and gave a little snort, which reminded her so much of Georgie she sat down and decided to start again. 'I did think there might be – something between us. But after that – discussion – at Father's wedding, I thought that was that. So it's surprising when you come out with something like that.'

'Like asking you to marry me?'

'Yes.'

'I'm an all or nothing person.' He grinned. 'And so, I think, are you. I've been bloody miserable these last weeks and according to Mal and Mhairi so have you.'

'What have they…?'

'Don't blame them. They only had your best interests at heart. And they're right, if we are in love, why are we shillyshallying around wasting time? We're far too old for that.'

'I hope they didn't say that.'

'No, but I could guess what they meant.'

284

Catherine shook her head. Haydn was smiling at her and once again she was losing control of the conversation.

'Maybe I should have taken things more slowly,' he said musingly. 'But the fact is, I've realised I love you and I want to marry you, so why not get it all out in the open?'

Catherine could feel her colour rising at the words and the emotion that glowed in the dark green eyes. She cleared her throat. 'Now I've had time to think...'

He smiled broadly. 'That's what I love about you, Catherine. Other people might take days or weeks. With you it's an hour or two and snap! There's a decision.' When she didn't speak for a moment he said, softly this time, 'Are you going to tell me what the decision is?'

'Yes,' she said, and then hesitated. It was so difficult to expose herself. 'I don't know how I feel about everything. But I can tell you as far as I've got.' She took a deep breath. 'I don't know whether I love you. I find you – very attractive. Very. And I don't know if I'll marry you, but I'm willing to give the relationship a try, and if things work out, well, they work out.'

She held her breath. What if that wasn't enough for him? She wished she could offer more, but she couldn't, yet. It was strange to think that she did believe he knew what he wanted, but she wasn't sure about herself.

He smiled gently. 'I suppose that'll do for now,' he said. He leant forward and kissed her very gently on the lips. 'Now, where shall we start?'

Catherine was going to say, let's have a coffee,

there's a lot we need to talk about. But he kissed her again, and she couldn't help it, she was kissing him back, madly, pulling him towards her to erase those lonely weeks. She put her hand up to the thick, short hair, making it more ruffled than ever, so unlike the sleek and controlled Haydn. When he pulled back ever so slightly to smile down at her, her heart lurched.

'Maybe we should start in the bedroom?' she said, before she could throw herself at his feet and promise to love him forever.

Chapter Thirty-two

'Shall I come with you to Edinburgh? To meet Richie?'

Catherine felt strangely uncertain as she spoke. There were a whole lot of other questions: did Richie know about her and Haydn, would he mind, would she still be able to stay over at the cottage when the child was home?

So far they had literally taken the relationship one day at a time, one wonderful day at a time. She refused to enter into any discussions with Mhairi about what was going on and handled Malcolm's teasing by simply ignoring it. She worked as hard as ever on her fledgling business, but every minute she could spare she would slip away to the cottage and be with Haydn. It didn't matter if they talked or were silent, made love or merely looked, just to be with him was unbelievable bliss. Sometimes he came to see her at Annat House but she found this more difficult. She wasn't used to touching him when other people were around.

She had climbed the narrow stairs in the cottage and peered into his tiny office to speak to him. Haydn was hunched over his computer, engrossed, and it took him a moment to surface. 'Hmm? What?'

'Richie. You'll need to leave soon to meet his plane and I wondered ... well, probably I should get back to Annat House, see how things are going.'

'You don't have any guests in just now,' he said, sitting back and stretching, smiling at her in a way that made her heart race. 'Come with me. Maybe we can have something to eat after we've picked him up.'

'If the plane's on time,' she said gloomily, to hide the warm feeling his invitation had produced.

'I can check that.' He turned back to the computer and began interrogating the internet. Everything was so quick and easy, literally at his fingertips. She vowed yet again to get to grips with this computer thing. Clearly it wasn't just e-mails you needed to know about, there was a whole (web) world out there.

They drove south through the sort of summer evening that Catherine loved, the clouds high in the pale sky, the sun drifting slowly down to the hills behind them, flooding the world with pale golden light. It hadn't rained for days and the trees had a dusty look to them, the road unnaturally pale and dry. It wouldn't last, but it was another kind of beauty.

'Richie must be delighted,' she said musingly, turning her thoughts to the child. 'The beginning of the summer holidays and he's finished for ever with the school he didn't like.'

'Children rarely like school,' said Haydn.

Oops, perhaps she shouldn't have mentioned that. 'Er, no. This one does seem to be very good at supervising his transport. I suppose they see him onto the plane in London?' She'd only just thought of that.

'Of course. They'll even arrange an escort if you want, but Richie would hate that. He managed fine last time so I've no reason to think he won't do so again.'

I wasn't criticising, thought Catherine, but decided not to say it out loud. 'He seems a sensible child,' she said placatingly.

'At least I don't have to worry about him talking to strangers.'

The airport was quiet at this time of the evening. They stood in the arrivals lounge, waiting impatiently for Richie to appear. Haydn hadn't had his arm around her, but even so he seemed to take a step away from her when the child came into sight. She realised she still hadn't asked if he had mentioned their new relationship to Richie. Now she suspected he hadn't.

Richie and his father greeted each other awkwardly.

'Good journey?' Catherine asked cheerfully, careful to stop herself giving him a too-effusive hug.

He dipped his head in a kind of nod. For once,

288

his hair wasn't shaved to the skull and the summer weather had brought a faint colour to his pale skin, but he still looked far too thin, hunched inside his uniform. What kind of school made the children wear uniform for travelling home?

Haydn took his luggage and they headed back to the car. 'We thought we'd eat on our way home,' he said. 'We'll stop in Perth, that'll be easiest. As it's your first night back why don't you choose? Fish and chips, Indian, Chinese? I draw a line at a burger but otherwise the choice is yours.'

Richie shrugged. 'Don't mind.'

'If you don't choose I'll let Catherine make the decision. Come on, speak up.' Haydn's tone changed subtly when he spoke to the boy. He seemed ill at ease, which came over as either hearty or short-tempered. Catherine reminded herself the two hadn't seen each other for nearly two months, it would take a while for them to get used to each other again.

When the child looked at his shoes and still didn't answer, she said brightly, 'Why don't we go to a place I know called Dino's? It's Italian but they also do fish and chips and a few other things. We'll surely find something for everyone there.'

'Sounds good,' said Haydn, shooting her a smile. 'OK with you, Rich?'

'Yeah, OK.'

As they slid into the car Catherine's unease about her own position faded. She didn't think it was her presence that was causing the awkwardness. She suspected, rather, this was typical. But it wasn't right and if she was lucky maybe she might be able to do something about it.

Dino's was busy, this being a Friday evening, and the three of them had to squeeze in around a table meant for two. During the ordering of drinks and the choosing of food, Richie seemed to relax a little. He glanced at Catherine a few times, but didn't comment on her presence.

'I hope the school have sent everything home with you this time,' said Haydn.

'We're supposed to pack our own trunks,' said Richie.

Catherine pulled a face. 'That must be fun.'

'I'm sure Matron helps,' said Haydn. 'I'll certainly be on to her if we're short of five sets of underwear and I don't know how many socks, as we were at Easter.'

Richie looked uncomfortable and Catherine was glad when their drinks arrived, a Coke for him and a carafe of Italian red for her and Haydn.

'Better move some of this or there'll be no room for the food,' said Haydn, passing the menu, flower in a vase, and a serviette holder to his son, indicating he should put it on the windowsill behind him. When he turned back, Haydn fluffed his hair. 'I'm so glad they let this grow.'

'They said I had to have it cut,' said Richie, squinting up to try and see his fringe. 'They said they were sure my mum would want me to look neat and tidy, but I told them it was my dad's decision and he was letting me grow it.'

'Quite right,' said Haydn. 'I don't know how many times I've told them...'

'You can have your hair as long as you want at Annat School,' said Catherine, 'so that won't be a problem from now on.'

'Yeah, Miles said so,' said Richie, suddenly forthcoming. 'But if it's too long you have to tie it up for science and cookery. I don't think I'd like that. An' I don't know if I'm going to like cookery. I've never done it before.'

Haydn was looking bemused, so Catherine rushed in again. 'About time you started, then. You remember Malcolm, my brother? He's now the chef at Annat House. You can come over and watch him cook if you want.'

'Maybe.' Richie glanced doubtfully at his father.

'Excellent idea,' said Haydn heartily. 'The sooner you learn to cook the less likely I am to accidentally poison us both.'

At that, Richie sniggered. 'I'm going to check the sell-by dates on everything I eat from now on. That yoghurt I opened last time I was here was completely gross...'

To Catherine's relief, Haydn smiled. It was going to be all right.

And, from then on, the meal passed off cheerfully. Richie even giggled when the final plate of food arrived, his side portion of chips, and there was absolutely no room on the table. 'Where shall I put this?' he said. 'On my head?'

Catherine laughed. It wasn't a good joke but it was a joke. Haydn smiled faintly and said, 'Make some room on your plate.'

'And if you don't want them all, may I have a few?' said Catherine, realising that with the type of food that Malcolm now insisted on producing, it might be a very long time before she saw chips again.

In the car on the way home, Richie went quiet

again. Maybe he felt left out, with her and Haydn chatting in the front. She turned round to smile and say, 'Are you looking forward to the holidays?'

'S'pose so.'

'I've got a few things planned,' said Haydn. 'It'll be good.'

Catherine longed for Richie to ask questions, show some enthusiasm, but he just sat quietly in the back. She said, 'What kind of things?'

'Well, er ... I thought Richie and I might learn to sail, if he's interested. And didn't I promise you a day out at that adventure park with the water slides and climbing walls?'

'Mmm,' said Richie.

'We could invite Miles along if you like.' Haydn glanced at his son in the rear view mirror.

'Yeah. OK.'

'You'll have to look after yourself a bit this first week. I've been trying to arrange a visit to a specialist manufacturer, and unfortunately it's turned out to be this Friday. I've a lot of stuff to prepare before then. I might ask Miles's mum if you can go there for one day at least.' Catherine remembered now Haydn had been unusually excited about a meeting he had set up concerning his new 'idea'. She'd been pleased and approving. But it was a shame it had to be just after Richie came home.

Richie made a small sound that indicated he had heard. Catherine wondered if he was hurt at not being the centre of his father's attention.

'You can come up to Annat House any time,' she said brightly. 'I know we're all adults but half the time Malcolm doesn't act like one.'

Richie said nothing.

'That's very kind of you,' said Haydn. 'Isn't it, Rich?'

The child muttered something. Catherine remembered how he looked when he smiled and vowed to try harder. Haydn would need to learn to lighten up, too.

Mhairi marvelled at how brilliant her life was these days, and then touched wood. Maybe it was best not to think like that. Catherine said she had got this job because she was so capable, and Malcolm said he wanted her for his girlfriend because she was so lovely. But she couldn't help believing it had all been a fluke and might so easily be snatched from her.

She had vowed she would prove she was good enough for the McDonalds. Now they really seemed to think she was and she was the one worrying it had all been a mistake.

She closed down the computer for the night, touched the wood of her desk again for extra luck, and went down to the kitchen to tell Malcolm she was off.

It's all right for some,' he said gloomily. 'Knocking off at five.'

'Half past. And that's only when we don't have visitors.'

'While others of us have to carry on until the job's done.'

'That's because you're not so good at organising yourself,' she said, standing on tiptoes to kiss him. 'Or delegating. Where's Danny?' Danny was a local boy who they had taken on trial as Malcolm's assistant.

'He had toothache so I sent him home.'

'You're soft.'

'It takes twice as long doing things when he's here, having to explain everything. He's not exactly quick on the uptake.' Malcolm sighed and pushed the curls off his forehead with the back of one hand, leaving a trail of flour. He looked flustered and very beautiful. 'Still, only one more batch of shortbread to do now. Fancy meeting up later?'

Mhairi was amazed that he still seemed so keen to spend time with her. She had been so convinced this would be nothing but a passing fancy.

She hesitated. 'I said I'd go to the end-of-term school bingo with Mum. She's worried there won't be enough people there.'

'Do you have to?'

'I said I'd support her. Dad won't go and this is the first event she's organised since she joined the School Parent Council.' Mhairi felt the familiar irritation at her father's lethargy, at his total lack of interest in anything the family did.

'Serves her right for letting Catherine talk her into joining,' said Malcolm, but he was smiling. 'Tell you what, why don't I come along too, if you need to make up the numbers? It's years since I played bingo.'

'Really?' Mhairi was touched. 'You're brilliant. Seven thirty at the school, then?' She kissed him again.

'Fine. And maybe we can spend some time alone together, afterwards?'

'Maybe we can,' said Mhairi happily.

Chapter Thirty-three

Catherine and Richie were spending the day in Perth. It was the day of Haydn's big meeting and someone had to look after Richie. Catherine had volunteered and Richie had seemed happy at the time. Now he just seemed grouchy.

'Where are we going now?' he said. The occasional giggles of last Friday evening were gone. He had withdrawn into the silent child Catherine had first met, who spoke rarely and then only in a monotone. She tried to hold on to her patience. She was starting to feel some sympathy for Haydn.

'Just the cash-and-carry still to do,' she said. She had given up smiling and chivvying him along hours ago. It was Richie's choice to come with her.

The child sank back into his silence. Catherine tried to remember what Malcolm had been like at this age, but mostly she just remembered the stroppy teenager he had become, belligerent and unhelpful. She didn't think he had ever been quiet in the way Richie was.

Richie had not commented on the new relationship between his father and Catherine. Haydn insisted he had spoken about it to the child and he had been fine, but Catherine suspected that just meant he hadn't said anything. Catherine was a great believer in communication, but after nearly a week of having her cautious approaches rejected she wasn't sure what to do next.

'It's a shame Miles and Antonia had to go to their aunt's today,' she said.

Richie made that small sound that indicated he had heard, nothing more.

'And that your dad's busy.'

'My dad's always busy.' He lowered his chin into the neck of his fleece and stared ahead at nothing in particular.

Was that the problem? Did he resent how little he saw of his dad? Catherine wished she knew. But just now she was going to see if she could make him enjoy himself just a little bit.

'That's all my stuff done,' she said later as they exited the cash-and-carry car park 'It didn't take quite as long as I feared. We could either go straight home, or maybe you might like to do something else?'

He was silent for a moment, as though he didn't realise he was expected to answer. Then he said, 'Er, what?'

Catherine took this as encouragement. 'I wondered if you'd like to take advantage of the fact that we're in the "big city". We could, I don't know, see what's on at the movies? Go to that new park where they've got a helter-skelter and mazes? I'm told there's a karting place somewhere around here. We could try that if you wanted?'

'I don't mind.'

'Oh for godssake, Richie, liven up! I'm offering you a choice here. Do you want to do something fun or do you just want to go home?' Patience had never been Catherine's strong point.

Richie shifted marginally in the passenger seat, as though the raised voice had finally got through to him. 'Well,' he said after a moment, still not looking at her. 'I've never tried karting.'

From Richie, that counted as enthusiasm. Catherine reached across to the passenger cubby-hole and, after a moment's scrabbling, found the leaflet she was looking for. It showed an address in an out-of-town industrial estate and a crude map. She handed it to the child. 'Are you any good at map reading? I'll head in the general direction and we'll see how we get on.'

Richie took the piece of paper and turned it over slowly in his hands.

As soon as they were inside the warehouse, Catherine regretted her suggestion. It was a vast, gloomy space smelling of burnt rubber and exhaust fumes. The noise of the little carts hurtling round and round the track was deafening. The few hoardings on the walls were tattered, the coffee machine in the viewing gallery broken. It looked like a business that had been started on a shoe string and gone downhill ever since.

'Can I help?' asked a young man in very dirty red overalls. He didn't meet her eyes and didn't give the impression of wanting to help at all.

Catherine hesitated, looking at Richie and hoping he might have changed his mind. He stood stolidly by her side, giving no clue.

'I was wondering if Richie here could have a go.' Catherine gestured to the child and then to the carts.

'Age?'

'Sorry?'

'Age?'

'Oh. Eleven, I think. Richie? Yes, eleven.'

'Ever done this afore?' The youth addressed Richie directly.

The child shook his head and his expression wavered towards disappointment. It was the most emotion Catherine had seen all day.

'Does it matter?' shouted Catherine above the engine noise.

'Nah.' Suddenly the race ended and the silence was stunning. 'We'll just get this lot off, like, and he can hae a wee shot. No one else booked till five. Fill out the form.' He slid a poorly photo-copied sheet towards her and disappeared through a door into a back room.

It might be a lesson in how *not* to treat your customers, but at least they hadn't been turned away. And the youth hadn't hung around to listen to her questioning Richie as she completed the form, and notice how little she knew about the child. Date of birth, full name, next of kin ... she realised she didn't know half of it. She had to sign a disclaimer and almost lost her nerve. Should she really be agreeing to someone else's child participating in what might be a rather dangerous activity? Haydn didn't even know they were here.

Richie was watching her carefully, his hands clasped tightly together, as though expecting her to change her mind.

She signed with a flourish and after a few moments the youth returned and led the child away to be kitted up. He was unrecognisable when he reappeared, blue overalls rolled up almost to his knees, full-face helmet hiding any hint of expression. But somehow, she could sense how he felt beneath it all. He moved with a hesitant swagger and when the youth said 'Y'all right, pal?' Richie giggled – actually giggled – and gave a thumbs up sign.

Catherine went to the front of the viewing gallery to watch as the child was inserted into one of the smaller vehicles and instructed on its use. For a moment, she could see the warehouse through his eyes: a hugely strange and exciting place where he could rev an engine as loud as he wished, where he could smell the fumes and rubber and *drive*. She wished Malcolm was here. She suspected he would have enjoyed this, participated even, not been the outsider that she was.

Her phone began to ring as Richie started his second set of laps. She probably wouldn't have heard it if he hadn't stalled the engine, giving a small piece of silence. The person rang off before she had fumbled the phone out of her bag. She checked the 'missed calls', something she had only recently learnt to do, and found that it was Shirley Robertson who had been trying to reach her. Mhairi's mother. Why on earth would she be calling Catherine on her mobile?

Catherine glanced at Richie, who was now careering happily around the track, and then slipped outside. She pressed 'return call' and told herself to stop panicking. More than likely it would be something to do with the School or Community Council, although why it was so urgent she should ring Catherine right now she couldn't imagine. Maybe she had just dialled a wrong number?

'Hi, Shirley. Catherine here. 'Were you trying to call me?'

'Yes.' The voice that answered was low, muffled by tears.

'Shirley, what's wrong?' Catherine held the phone tightly against her ear, moving further away from the building and the drone of the engine.

She heard the older woman sniff and clear her throat. 'I'm trying to get hold of Mhairi.'

Catherine let out a very small sigh of relief. Not a problem with the McDonald family, then. 'Have you tried Annat House?'

'Of course. I only got the answer phone. Same at the Lodge.' She gave a half-hiccup, half-sob. 'I need to speak to her.'

Catherine's mind was racing. Why was no one answering the phone at Annat House, and what could be so serious that Shirley was desperate to talk to her daughter about it?

'Maybe she and Malcolm have gone for a walk,' she said carefully. 'They said they might. And this is Mrs McWhirter's day off. Shirley, what is it? Can I help?' She waited as the line hissed and crackled. She hated mobiles at the best of times, the connection with the other person so faint and unreliable. Shirley seemed a very long way away. 'Whereabouts are you?'

'I'm in Perth. At the Infirmary.'

'Why, I'm in Perth too. But what's happened? Are you all right?'

Shirley gave another loud sniff. 'They've brought Keith in here. He... I think he took an overdose.'

Catherine put a hand to the wall to steady herself. Shirley's reclusive, ineffectual husband had...?

'Is he all right?' she said. 'I mean, is he...?'

'He's still alive.' Shirley's voice was clearer now, as though saying the words had calmed her. 'But they don't know yet... I just need to get hold of Mhairi. And I can't use my mobile inside the hospital so I have to keep coming outside to try. Then I have to switch it off when I go back in so no one can get me. Mhairi'll be frantic when she hears, she needs to know...'

Catherine was back to her normal self, doing what she did best. 'I'll take care of it,' she said. 'I'll keep trying Annat House and the Lodge on my mobile. As soon as I get an answer I'll come up to the hospital to let you know. Where will I find you? A and E? Right, you go back inside. You can stop worrying about Mhairi, at least.'

She ended the call and hurried back inside the noisy warehouse. The small cart was zooming round and round the track and a red-overalled individual was sitting on a pile of tyres in the centre, picking his nails and occasionally watching the boy. All seemed well.

She went back outside and began the task of tracking Mhairi down. She tried both her and Malcolm's mobiles on the off-chance they had reception, but eventually when she got an answer, it was at the Lodge. She wished she had more information, but at least Mhairi knew now, and could head to the hospital herself.

Catherine went back into the warehouse. She felt she'd been away ages but Richie was still going round and round. The first youth appeared from the back room. 'Y'all right?' he said.

'I'm afraid I need to go. Can you finish the session, get the boy off?'

The youth chewed his lip. 'He's nearly finished, can't you wait?'

'No, I really need to go.' She was desperate to get to the hospital and speak to Shirley, to make sure that everything possible was being done.

'He won't want to come off,' said the youth, almost chattily. 'He's bloody good. You sure this is his first time? You should see his lap times, they're something else. You should bring him back, he's a natural.'

'Er...' Catherine looked at him blankly. 'I haven't time for this, OK? I have to go.'

The youth shrugged and disappeared through the doorway, coming into view at the track side a moment later with a chequered flag in his hand.

Richie must have been told what to do when he saw this and he drew the cart neatly into the 'pit lane' at one side. There was some chat, in which Richie clearly expressed the desire to continue, and the youth gestured towards Catherine. Then he said something else and patted the boy on the shoulder. This time Richie extracted himself from the cart and almost bounced up the steps to the changing room, laughing as he pulled of the helmet, his face one big grin.

When he was returned to Catherine he said, without waiting for her to speak first, 'That was brilliant. Can I have another go? They say I was good. Really good.' He waved a sheet of paper at her.

'That's nice,' said Catherine, hastily signing a cheque. 'Come on we've got to go.'

'I want to come again. Did you see me? I did one ginormous skid but I didn't crash. And look at my times...'

'We'll talk about it later.'

'I...'

'Come *on*, Richie, we have to go.'

She hurried him out to the car, phone already to her ear. Richie lagged behind, his smile already a thing of the past. He climbed slowly into the passenger seat. He was silent as she navigated the way to the hospital.

Mhairi felt dead inside. Not worried or angry or disgusted with herself, just nothing. When the phone had rung at the Lodge she and Malcolm had been in bed and had ignored it. But later it had rung and rung and after all they weren't *busy* at that moment, just lying lazily in each other's arms, chatting desultorily. Eventually, Malcolm had pulled on a pair of trousers and gone down to answer it. And then the nightmare had begun.

She didn't even have a car of her own to get down to Perth. Malcolm had offered to lend her the Annat House runabout, and then decided he had better come with her, as she was in no fit state to drive. So here they were, battling against the end-of-rush-hour traffic to get into the town and still with no further news. Mhairi had bitten her nails to the quick. Catherine had been good, very good, at phoning on her mobile, checking on where they were, keeping in touch. But she didn't have anything to tell them – or if she did she wasn't telling it.

'What if he's dead,' she said as they drew into

the sprawling car park.

'No point in worrying.' Malcolm's face was grim. He would probably prefer not to be here. It wasn't his problem.

'Just drop me off and get back home. I'll need to stay with Mum.'

He glanced across at her, dark eyes resting briefly on her face before flicking back to the road. 'I'll drop you at the door of A and E, then I'll go and find somewhere to park. I'll catch up with you.'

'There's no need...' She tried to think properly, be polite.

'You don't think I'm leaving you here, like this, do you?' He sounded angry and she didn't have the energy to argue. When the car stopped on the bright yellow lines outside Accident and Emergency, she slid quickly out and dodged between ambulances towards the door.

She took a deep breath. She had no idea what she would find inside.

What she found was Catherine, sitting neat and tidily on a plastic chair, sensibly keeping an eye out for her. She had Richie with her. Mhairi had forgotten all about him. She gave the boy a vague pat as she demanded, 'Where's Mum? How's Dad? Can I go and see them? What's happening?'

Catherine put an arm round her shoulders. 'They're just taking your dad up to one of the wards. They've, er, pumped his stomach or whatever they do and now they want to keep him in overnight.'

'He's – OK?' Mhairi staggered slightly and Catherine's arm helped to keep her upright. 'I couldn't help thinking...' She squeezed her eyes tight shut for a moment, fighting away her worst imaginings.

'I know. I'm sorry. But I told you not to worry.'

'You would have said that anyway.' Mhairi sat down abruptly on one of the hard chairs. Her dad was alive. 'What's happening? Is he conscious?'

'I don't know. Your mum just came out quickly to tell me they were going up to the ward. Look, let's speak to the nurses, see if they think you can go up.'

Mhairi looked at the doors, knowing there was something she was waiting for. Then she remembered. 'Malcolm's just coming. He had to park the car.'

If Catherine was surprised at her brother's presence, she hid it quickly. 'That's fine. Richie can keep an eye out for him while we go and find a nurse.'

Catherine always made everything so easy and straightforward. Mhairi let her lead the way, scrabbling in her pockets for a hanky to stem the flow of tears that had started now she knew the worst hadn't happened. She hadn't lost her dad.

When Catherine returned to the plastic seats Malcolm was sitting beside Richie, the two of them grimly silent.

Malcolm spotted her first and said, 'What news?'

He glanced doubtfully at Richie and Catherine realised she had been so caught up in this drama she had hardly given the child a thought. Now she wondered how much he had taken in, and whether the blank face was boredom or dismay.

'Er, things seem to be improving,' she said. 'I said we'd go down to the canteen and wait for them there.'

'That's good,' said Malcolm. He rubbed his hands over his face and let out a long breath. 'Yes, that's good.' He punched Richie lightly on the shoulder. 'You want something to eat, mate? I bet you're fed up hanging around here.'

Richie rose and they made their way along corridors until they found the hospital canteen, a large, low room occupied mainly by staff on their evening meal break. Catherine hadn't realised how late it was. She told Malcolm and Richie to join the queue while she phoned Haydn.

It was only when she was outside she wondered if she should have let Richie talk to his father himself. The child was so silent it was easy to forget he might have preferences. Maybe not knowing what Richie wanted wasn't all Haydn's fault.

She reported the latest news to Haydn and promised to have Richie home by nine, or to phone again if there was a problem. 'They don't really need me here now, but I thought we'd stay and eat. We might be able to give some moral support.'

'Stay as long as you think's necessary. Do you want me to come through and collect Richie?'

'No, not at all. We won't be long now and it isn't as if he's a problem. He's very quiet and well-behaved.' Too well-behaved. After his enthusiasm at the karting, he seemed more withdrawn than ever. He hadn't complained. It was like he was used to having his wishes thwarted.

'I'm glad to hear it. Don't let him be a nuisance.'

'He's not that. A bit too quiet, maybe, but we can talk about that some other time.'

'Mmm,' said Haydn noncommittally. She needed to remember that he was still touchy when it came to his son.

She and Malcolm and Richie ate their soup in silence. It was only when Richie went to get himself dessert that Malcolm said, 'Why do you think he did it?'

'Oh, Malcolm, who knows? I don't.'

'It's like Jean all over again.'

'No, it's not. We didn't know Jean, and she was alone and, well, this is different.'

'Yes. He had a family and a nice home. He had everything going for him although he never did anything.'

'He had his problems,' said Catherine, wishing she'd been more sympathetic. She had always been fond of Shirley and had never quite understood the marriage. 'I think he had an accident at work, or something, years ago. Shirley doesn't say. But he hasn't worked since.'

'I thought he was just lazy.'

'There's usually more to it than that,' Catherine realised, unhappily. She saw things all too often in black and white. 'And here's Richie. What did you get? Syrup sponge pudding? You know, I might try some of that myself.'

The stodgy dessert was comforting. She and Malcolm had coffee, sipping it slowly, wondering how long they would have to wait. Catherine didn't want to go and seek out Shirley and Mhairi, but she should really be getting Richie home. Poor boy, in the warm atmosphere of the canteen he was definitely drooping.

And then the two women appeared. Shirley half-raised a hand in greeting and made her way to the self-service counter. Mhairi came slowly over to the table.

She sat down on the chair that Malcolm pulled out, her arms wrapped tightly around her body. Her face was pinched, mascara smudged by tears.

'How's things?' said Catherine.

'Not bad, I think. They say Mum got him here in time.'

'That's good,' said Malcolm.

'Were you able to speak to him?'

'A bit. He was groggy. He's sleeping now.' Mhairi looked down so she didn't need to meet their eyes.

'That's good,' said Malcolm again. 'Maybe they'll keep him in a while, try and sort things out...? Give your mum a break.'

'We don't need a break,' said Mhairi fiercely.

'No, of course. It's just he's always there, and you never speak about him. I mean, I haven't even met him since we started going out. I wondered...'

Catherine tried to catch Malcolm's eye. This was no time for a heart to heart about Mhairi's father.

'I'm not ashamed of him, you know,' she hissed.

'No, no, of course not.' Malcolm looked surprised at what he had provoked.

Shirley brought a tray to the table and gave what little news she had in a dull, unfamiliar voice. It was the merest good fortune that she had called in at home in the middle of the day, and found her husband. If she hadn't ... it didn't bear thinking of.

308

Mhairi said nothing. When she wasn't sipping her black coffee she kept her arms wrapped tightly around herself, as though she was very cold.

Chapter Thirty-four

Catherine was alone at Annat Cottage when the phone rang. She hesitated before answering it. True, she spent a lot of time here these days, had even slept over the previous night, the first time since Richie's arrival, but it wasn't her *home* and she didn't want to be seen to be taking liberties. On the other hand, it might be Mhairi trying to get her from Annat House. She picked up the receiver.

'Annat Cottage, can I help you?' she said briskly.

'Oh, I say,' said a breathless voice at the other end. 'Have I got the right number? I was looking for Haydn. Mr Haydn Eddlington-Smith.'

'Yes, this is the right number,' said Catherine, wishing immediately she hadn't answered. She had a fairly good idea who this might be. 'Haydn has gone to drop Richie off at a friend's house. He'll be back shortly. Can I take a message?'

'Would you? That would be so kind.'

'No problem.'

'This is Richie's mother, Esme Cavanagh.'

The woman paused and Catherine struggled for something to say. Should she introduce herself? Would the woman even have heard of her? 'I'm Catherine, a neighbour of Haydn's,' she said, trying to keep her tone offhand. 'How can I help?'

'Catherine? Catherine. I think Richie has mentioned you.' Catherine said nothing, sure now the woman was fishing for information. When Catherine gave none, she continued, 'Jolly kind of you to take a message. Haydn's not the easiest person to get hold of.' Catherine remembered then that Haydn had call-screening on his phone, and wished she had used it. 'I'm phoning about darling Richie. It would be so nice if he came to Spain for a visit. Now we've organised his bedroom, I can't wait for him to see it. Do you know what Haydn's plans are for the summer?'

'No,' said Catherine. At least the woman was showing an interest in her son, which was good. 'Shall I ask Haydn to call you when he gets back?'

'Would you? So kind. I'll give you the number again, although heaven knows he should have it by now.' The woman laughed, although she hadn't said anything funny. 'Tell him we were thinking about the last fortnight in August. Do you know when Richie goes back to school?'

'No, I don't. But I presume it'll be September.'

'That would suit perfectly. So nice to speak to you, Catherine. Bye for now.'

Catherine glared at the phone, as though it was responsible for involving her in this. She hadn't liked the woman. After exchanging no more than a few sentences with her, she felt nothing but animosity. It was probably jealousy, she told herself firmly. Esme Cavanagh, formerly Esme Eddlington-Smith, was no doubt a lovely person. If she had booked to attend a course with Exclusive Activity Holidays Catherine would have had no problems dealing with her.

'Your wife called,' she said, as soon as Haydn returned.

He raised an eyebrow. 'I presume you mean my ex-wife?'

'Yes, of course. Esme. She wanted to speak to you about Richie going to visit.'

Haydn's expression darkened, as Catherine had known it would. He was far too protective, or was it defensive, when it came to his ex-wife and son. She wondered if she should try and get him to talk about it. 'I presume she was calling from Spain?'

'Yes. I wrote the number down.'

'I have the number,' he said crisply. 'I wonder what she's playing at.'

'I thought you said she had access rights to Richie,' said Catherine cautiously. She knew only too well Haydn didn't like interference, but she had to do what she thought was right. 'It can't be good for him to see so little of her. Perhaps a visit out there is just what he needs.'

'And perhaps it isn't. She saw him in London a couple of months ago, why does she need to see him again?'

'Maybe that made her realise how much she has been missing him?'

Haydn gave a grunt of disbelief and turned away, ostensibly to make himself a coffee.

'Well, I'd better be going,' said Catherine. 'Things to do, you know.'

'Fine,' said Haydn. 'I'll see you later.' He bent his head to return her kiss, but he didn't try to persuade her to stay.

'Maybe you and Richie could come over for dinner?'

'Maybe. He's been invited to stay the night at Miles's but I said I'd check how he felt later on.'

'I'll phone you then,' said Catherine, keeping her voice determinedly bright. She pulled on her jacket and let herself out of the back door.

It was pleasing to see how much progress Stewart was making with the garden here. The debris of years had been cleared away and the bones of a new beginning laid out. It just showed, thought Catherine as she jumped down the far side of the stone wall and set off across the field, that with a bit of determination you *could* make things better.

Mhairi and Malcolm were in the kitchen when Catherine arrived back at Annat House. She wondered if they were having a late breakfast or an early coffee break.

'...because I don't want to.'

'I don't understand you. Your father's getting better. What's the problem?'

'I just said I don't...' Mhairi stopped as she heard Catherine's footsteps and turned immediately to smile at her. 'Hi there, I was wondering when you'd be back. I've got one or two queries I want to go through with you.'

Her face was pale and her hair needed a wash. It was a week now since her father had been rushed to hospital, but the girl was still taking it badly.

'That's fine,' said Catherine encouragingly. 'Just let me get a coffee first.' She hadn't even had breakfast at Haydn's. She had been in the shower when he and Richie left, and had planned to wait for Haydn's return so they could have a leisurely breakfast together. So much for that idea.

Malcolm turned to her, his handsome face sulky. 'I wanted Mhairi to come to Glasgow with me. She's due some time off, isn't she?'

'Ye-es,' said Catherine doubtfully. 'Why are you going to Glasgow?' True, there was a four-day gap between this and the next course but Malcolm was supposed to be using the time to try out some of his new dishes, not go gallivanting.

'Fergus mentioned some restaurants there where the food is really good. He was a tosser but he knew his food. I want to go and try them for myself, get some ideas.'

'Goodness.' Catherine was surprised by his enthusiasm. 'Doesn't sound like a bad idea at all.'

'Excellent. So you'll sub me for it?'

'Well...'

'And Mhairi too. It'll be much more fun if she comes.'

Malcolm had remained wary of attending any courses other than the basic hygiene one, but this sounded like a positive step. 'I don't see why not,' she said.

'I can't go away just now,' said Mhairi quickly. 'Dad's only just come home, Mum needs my help.'

'You are due some time off, if you want to take it.' Catherine considered her young assistant. She didn't want the girl to make herself ill, worrying about her father. Perhaps a couple of days to think things over was just what she needed.

'Getting away would be much better for her,' said Malcolm.

'You didn't want me to go away with you last time. To London.'

313

'That was different.

'It was about your family. This is about mine. My family need me here.'

'I bet your mum would be happy for you to come.'

Mhairi narrowed her eyes and snapped, 'It's not up to her.'

Catherine lifted the kettle off the Aga and poured water into her favourite mug. Mhairi had departed for the office upstairs, but Malcolm remained, glowering at the doorway.

Catherine tried to suppress a sigh. 'She's having a difficult time just now,' she said. 'You need to try and be a bit more understanding.'

Malcolm turned his scowl on his sister. 'I don't get it. First she holds it against me that I go off without her, now she's acting like she's never heard of anything so unreasonable as coming away with me. What's her problem?'

'She's upset about her dad.'

'But he's fine now.'

Catherine shook her head. 'Just because he has survived this ... suicide attempt doesn't mean he's fine.'

'He's seen the psychiatrist. Did you know he'd been seeing a psychiatrist for years?'

'No. Not that it's anything to do with us.'

'They'd changed his medication. That's what Mhairi said. They think maybe that caused the problems.'

'Hopefully they can get it sorted out then. But it won't happen overnight.' Catherine didn't know much about depression, but she realised the problem Keith Robertson had was a serious one. It wasn't something that could be solved with a magic wand.

'I don't see why Mhairi is so upset.'

'She blames herself.'

'That's stupid. Why?'

'I don't know.' Catherine wondered if it was because Mhairi had been so often at Annat House, so happy with Malcolm.

'It might have been better all round if he had succeeded,' said Malcolm in a low voice.

'Malcolm! How can you say that!' Catherine put down her mug and bent to examine his face more closely. 'Think of Jean. Aren't you the one that keeps saying life couldn't be so bad? Why didn't she contact us? We could have helped her.'

'It was *you* who said we could have helped her.'

It was true. Catherine had been convinced of that, initially. Now she wasn't so sure. Some lives weren't so easy to sort out.

'Be gentle with Mhairi,' she said.

Malcolm grunted.

After Catherine left, Haydn went up to his little study and switched on the computer. For once he didn't look out of the window at the loch and the mountains beyond. He had felt so content as he drove back from dropping Richie off. Loving this place, knowing Catherine was waiting for him back at the house. Richie hadn't said anything about the amount of time Catherine was spending with them, hadn't commented on her staying overnight in the cottage. He seemed to have simply accepted her, and his behaviour was marginally better with Catherine around. Yes,

Haydn had definitely felt his life was on the right track. He was pretty sure that Catherine would agree to getting married soon.

And then Esme had to phone. He could feel the little hard knot of inadequacy and anxiety tighten within him. If he had his way he would never have to speak to her again. He couldn't forgive her for first walking out on him and their son, and then coming back and thinking she could steal the child from him. He felt cold every time he remembered how close she had been to winning custody. If she hadn't made the mistake of snatching the child from his nursery, who knew what the courts would have decided?

But he had to do what was best for Richie. Was Catherine right? Would it be good for the child to rebuild his relationship with his mother? The boy was pleased to be moving to the new school, even, possibly, to be coming home to his father every weekend. He really felt he was getting to know his son. And how could he do that if Esme was going to start interfering?

He sighed, realising he had been staring at the start-up screen for more than five minutes, and hadn't even keyed in his password. He lifted the telephone at his side.

Harold Cavanagh answered and Haydn could feel the sneer forming on his face.

'May I speak to Esme?'

'Who's calling?'

Haydn ground his teeth, sure the man knew exactly who it was. 'It's Haydn, returning her call.'

He waited and after a few minutes, heard the clatter of heels on a tiled floor and the receiver at the other end being lifted. 'Haydn, darling, so good of you to call back.'

Clearly she wanted Richie's visit – or was it something else? – very much indeed.

'I got your message. What can I do for you?'

'As I explained to your, er, friend?' She paused but he didn't elucidate. 'As I explained, Harold and I are dying to show Richie our new house now we're settled in.'

Haydn wondered why it had taken them two years to 'settle in'. 'Have you spoken to Richie about this?'

'I mentioned it last time we spoke. He said he'd ask you, but you know what he's like. Always so uncommunicative.'

'He hasn't.' It was true that Richie was un-communicative, except when it came to talking about karting, about which he had developed an inexplicable enthusiasm. 'I'll talk to him,' he said reluctantly. Should he involve the child in the decision, as he had about the change of schools? 'We'll get back to you.'

'That would be super. I'd phone him myself on his mobile, except the stupid thing rarely works up there. Tell him that Mummy would love to see him. The last two weeks in August. I'll get Harold to look into flights, shall I?'

'Don't book anything yet,' said Haydn quickly.

'It's a busy time of year, you know. Best to book soon. We don't want to miss out.'

'We'll phone you this evening,' said Haydn firmly. Or maybe he wouldn't. If Richie wanted to stay over at Miles's that would the perfect excuse for delaying.

Chapter Thirty-five

Malcolm had gone waltzing off to Glasgow, which was just like him. Thinking of no one but himself, out to have a good time.

Mhairi was in the kitchen at home, a room about a quarter the size of the one at Annat House, but perfectly adequate all the same. She was making a broth for her dad. He liked home cooking and she was just as good at it as Malcolm McDonald. When it came to the basics, at least.

Her dad was lying on the settee in the sitting room, watching Sky Sports. She used to wonder why her mum wasted all that money subscribing, but now she realised he had to have something to occupy him. Unlike Mhairi and her mother, he didn't enjoy reading. Apart from sleeping, watching sport seemed to be the only thing he actually liked. She'd started to notice a lot of things in the last few days. Like how his mood varied during the day depending on how long it had been since he'd taken his medication, and how worried about him her mother was.

When the thick soup was ready she took a bowl through on a tray, with a couple of slices of white bread, toasted, and a big mug of tea.

'Here y'are, why don't you try this?' she said, setting it down on the table beside him.

Her father was a small man who had been wiry in his youth but put on a lot of weight recently.

He turned his pale and puffy face towards her. 'What's all this?'

'I made you some soup. Scotch broth. I remembered you used to like it.'

He moved laboriously into a sitting position and sniffed the bowl gingerly. 'Your mum bin telling you to look after me?'

'No, not really. I just thought, seeing as I wasn't working, I'd do some cooking. Try it and see what you think. I made a big pot so there'll be plenty for Mum when she gets home.'

He sniffed and took a small spoonful of the soup. 'Mmm. 'S'all right.'

'Good.'

'So why aren't you at work? Don't tell me you've lost your job.'

'No, of course not. I've got a few days off.'

Her father continued to eat stolidly and said nothing. She didn't know whether to stay with him or not. Previously, she would have gone straight to her room. She used to spend most of her time up there when at home. Her mum complained about it but her dad never said anything.

'How're you feeling?' she asked tentatively.

He didn't look at her or cease the slow movement of spoon to mouth. 'Fine.'

'We could go out for a walk or something afterwards, if you wanted.' Mhairi remembered when she had been very young, before her father's accident, he used to take her for walks along the loch.

'Mum's put you up to this, hasn't she?'

'No, she hasn't.' Mhairi rubbed her nose, uncomfortable. Her mum had asked her to make sure Dad had some lunch, nothing more. 'I just

319

thought it might be nice. Make the most of the summer while it's here.'

'No' just now,' he said, glancing at her almost apologetically. He pushed the empty dish towards her. 'Ta for that.' Then he swung his legs back up on to the cushions and turned his attention back to the television.

Mhairi waited until she was in the kitchen before she squeezed her eyes together in a silent cry. She was filled with dread. She wasn't doing any good. He wasn't getting any better. Where would this lead?

She rinsed the plate and bowl, splashed water on her face, although she didn't think any tears had actually fallen, and left by the back door. If he didn't want to go for a walk, it didn't mean she couldn't.

She wandered along the banks of the small river that meandered down from Loch Annat. In winter it could be quite a torrent, but now the water was a gentle flow, flickering in the sunlight that filtered through the ash and birch trees. There had always been a rough path here, but the primary school had taken it on as a project a few years back, making it into a 'wildlife walk' with a route flat and wide enough for wheel chairs or children's buggies, benches dotted here and there along the way. If she ignored the graffiti on the benches, and the small amounts of litter in the undergrowth, it was a pretty good place to be. And so close to home. Not many people had somewhere so beautiful so near at hand. When the path came out of the trees she sat down on a bench. From here there was a view up the whole length of the loch.

The peace was shattered by the sound of bikes and voices. She sighed. One thing this path wasn't meant for was bikes, but nobody had managed to convince the local youths of that.

It was Tommy McAllister and a couple of other teenagers, two on one bike and one on another. They had been shouting to each other but fell silent when they saw Mhairi.

'Hiya,' she said.

They grunted a greeting and had almost passed her when Tommy muttered something to his friends and turned back. 'You know this skate board thing,' he said abruptly.

'The skate park? Aye.'

'Do you think it'll actually happen?' He stood with one foot on either side of the bike, leaning against the handlebars, frowning at her. He was a gangly youth of fifteen or sixteen, known to be a bit of a troublemaker. 'A bet it doesnae.'

'Well, I can't guarantee it or anything,' said Mhairi, realising she hadn't given the Youth Aye project a thought for weeks. 'But I don't see why not. If you lot really want it and if we can find a piece of land.'

'Is it true the McDonalds are giving us the money?' said one of the other boys.

'That's the plan.'

'A bet they don't,' said the boy gloomily.

'I think it's time I did some checking up and arranged another meeting, so I can report back to you,' said Mhairi. 'How'd that be?'

The boys pulled faces but didn't disagree.

'It should be for bikes as well as skate boards,' said Tommy. 'If we can't have a mountain bike

321

track, we'd want to use the ramps and that.'

'Maybe,' said Mhairi, trying to remember what she and Malcolm had discussed with Haydn. 'And anyway,' she continued, 'What are you lot doing here at this time? Why aren't you at school?' She groaned inwardly as she realised how much like an adult she sounded.

Tommy sniffed. 'It's the summer holidays. Are you stupid?'

'Still?' said Mhairi, confused. So much had happened recently she had been sure the holidays were over, for the local schools at least. It would be different for Richie at his posh private place.

'Aye,' said the other boy who had been silent up till now. He sniggered. 'An' what are you doing here? Should you no' be working?'

The others sniggered too and Mhairi was reminded of why she was having these days off. She was sure the boys would know what had happened. Everyone in Kinlochannat would know her dad been rushed to hospital like that.

'I'd better get home,' she said, standing up quickly. 'Thanks for reminding me about Youth Aye, though. I'll get that meeting organised.'

The boys moved off, not bothering to say goodbye.

As they disappeared from sight she heard Tommy say, 'You got the smokes, Jordan?'

She shook her head. OK, she and her friends had tried smoking at that age but it wasn't right, was it? It was because they were bored and had nothing else to do. The sooner this skate (and bike?) park became a reality, the better.

Catherine was sitting at her desk going over her accounts. She hadn't given Exclusive Activity Holidays as much of her attention as she would have liked, but maybe, just maybe, it was going to work out. She needed the courses to be eighty per cent filled to break even, and the next few were almost full. The cashflow was still pretty tight, though. She frowned and went over the figures one more time.

She was relieved when she heard a car drawing up on the gravel outside. It might be Malcolm, but he usually parked at the back. Or it might be the postie, early for once. But it might just be Haydn, returning from dropping Richie off at Edinburgh airport. She hadn't seen much of him lately. She sat back in her seat and waited.

After a few moments, there was a brief knock on the front door then it swung open and Haydn's voice called out, 'Anyone home?'

'I'm here.' Catherine rose and went to meet him. He took her in his arms and kissed her long and slow. 'Mmm, what was that for?' she asked, smiling as she leant back to look up into his eyes.

'To say hello.'

'Hello yourself.' She stood on tiptoes to return the kiss, thankful that things seemed to be good between them again. There'd been tension since Haydn had agreed Richie should go and visit his mother. Now Richie was away, and for a couple of weeks it would be just the two of them.

'Coffee?' she said, as he held her close, burying his face in her hair and breathing deeply.

'Yes, why not?' He kept hold of her hand as they made their way down the steps to the kitchen.

323

'Did Richie get off OK?'

'Yes, fine. The flight was on time and I do think there's a good deal to be said in favour of these small airports; so much less faffing around.'

'I don't think Edinburgh likes to think of itself as a *small* airport, but I know what you mean.' She made coffee for them both in a cafetière and brought some of Malcolm's rock buns to the table.

They chatted for a while about Haydn's journey and how much more talkative Richie had become. 'Although he's been quiet again the last few days,' said Haydn with a frown.

'I think all kids are a bit moody. At least he's developing his own interests.'

'Like Gameboys.'

'Yes, and karting.'

'I hope his mother realises what she's let herself in for, promising to take him every day.'

'It's good she's willing to make the effort,' said Catherine. Privately, she thought that if Esme hadn't agreed to this, Richie would have refused to make the trip. Apparently, Malcolm had told him Spain was really big in karting and that was what had swung it with him.

'So, how've you been?' said Haydn, taking her hand and stroking the palm with his long slim fingers. 'You must be relieved to have that last lot of visitors off your hands? According to Malcolm, Mr Saunderson was a demanding so-and-so.'

'He wasn't the only one.' Catherine took a deep breath and let it out through her nose. 'But if I'm going to make a success of this, I'm going to have to get used to handling people like that. And he went off happily enough in the end. He was even talking about enrolling for the Geology course next year.'

'I bet you were delighted about that.'

Catherine pulled a face. 'I need all the bookings I can get. In fact, I think I'm going to stop having so many gaps between courses. It was OK to begin with when we were just getting used to everything.'

'And you had your father under your feet.'

'And we had Father and Phyllida here. But now I think we need to run a bit of a tighter ship.'

'Sweat the assets and all that?'

'Make use of the house to its full potential.' Catherine frowned. 'And the staff.' She didn't think Mhairi would have any problem stepping up a gear, but she wasn't so sure about Malcolm. He was coping – admirably – with providing meals for some rather demanding guests, but she wasn't sure how he would manage without the gaps in between, even with an assistant. He seemed to need this time to perfect any new recipes, and to sleep.

'I don't want to interfere, but I'd be more than happy to go over any plans with you, if you wanted. After all, as you informed me not so long ago, I am your resident entrepreneur. You might as well make use of me.'

'Mmm,' said Catherine. It was all very well getting him to give talks to the community, which he had done brilliantly, but she didn't want to take advantage of him for her personal benefit. And she wasn't sure she wanted him to know she wasn't yet running at a profit. 'It's very kind of you...'

'But I should mind my own business.'

'I didn't mean that,' she said quickly, not wanting him to think she resented interference. She wasn't the one who was like that.

'It's just a thought. You have many skills, Catherine, but one wouldn't say making money was in your genes. There are advantages to knowing one of the *nouveau riche* like myself. Why not use it?'

'Thanks,' she said, doubtfully.

'There's something else I wanted to talk to you about,' he said. He had still been holding her left hand and now he turned it over and stretched out the third finger. 'When are you going to let me buy you a ring for here?'

'Oh.' Catherine could feel herself blushing. He had a way of introducing topics when she least expected them. 'I don't know.'

'I love you, Catherine,' he said gently. 'And maybe I'm a little old fashioned but I want everyone to know that I love you. I want to be able to tell Richie that you have agreed to be my wife.'

'You do?' Catherine felt a warm glow inside, that he really loved her. But there was fear there, too. She kissed his lips briefly. 'I think I love you too. Yes, I do, I do. It's just...'

'Just?'

She took a deep breath. She couldn't agree to taking such a big step when there was still problems unresolved. 'Sometimes I don't think you trust me.' He frowned and she paused, but she couldn't stop now. 'Like with Richie going to his mother's. You didn't want to discuss it with me. You don't want me to get – close. You've said more than once how bossy I am, and I am, you're right. But if you can't accept that, well...'

'I love you,' he said again, but although the

words were spoken softly she could see irritation in his green eyes.

'I know you do,' She paused and realised that she did believe him, did trust him on that at least. 'But do you really want me under your feet every day, involved in your life, making helpful suggestions as no doubt I will, trying to take over?'

'You think I can't cope with that?'

'I think it makes you cross, and then you withdraw from me, and I don't know if I can handle that.'

Haydn let go of her hand and sat back. She saw he hadn't expected her to refuse him. He had given her these weeks to get used to their relationship and when he had been ready to take it a step further he had expected her to fall in with him. And this despite his recent coolness.

'You're not very good at talking things through,' she said, forcing a smile. 'Like now. Are you going to get up and leave because I've annoyed you?'

'I thought you'd agree it was for the best. I'm sorry I was angry with you about Richie, but you don't know how hard it was for me to get custody. And *she* left *me,* you know, left both of us, why does she suddenly have the right to come back in to our lives?'

His eyes flashed, totally angry now, and Catherine felt cold. There was still so much emotion tied up in his relationship with Esme, with Richie. Until that was sorted out, was there really room for her?

'She's not asking a lot, to see her son for two weeks a year.'

'How do you know it'll stop there?'

'Why shouldn't it? She hasn't asked for anything more, has she?' Catherine realised that Haydn had told her very little about his marriage and still less about the divorce. Apart from the day he had first asked her to marry him, he hadn't mentioned it. She wondered what had happened to make him distrust his wife so much. 'Really, it is best for Richie to have a father *and* a mother. I truly believe that.'

'I've let him visit Esme, haven't I? As you all wanted. But if we married, you would be his mother, he wouldn't need to see her.'

Catherine stared at him in amazement. One minute you're resenting my taking an interest in the boy, the next you're asking me to be his mother. He has a mother, Haydn, and I could never take her place. I like the boy and hope, well, whatever happens, I hope we'll have a good relationship, but I can never be his *mother.*'

'So you're saying you won't marry me?'

'I'm saying I'm not sure. And if I'm not sure, I suppose I should say no.' Catherine felt dread seep into her. How could this be happening? 'We don't know each other well enough.'

'You're not willing to take the chance.'

Was that really the problem? Catherine was shaken by his words. 'I just need time.'

'You've had time,' said Haydn. He rose to his feet, his face pale and fixed. 'I've asked you twice now. Don't expect me to ask you again.' And he left the room.

Idiot, shouted Catherine in her head. She picked up her mug then put it down again; her hands were shaking too much. The argument had come out of nowhere. If she had seen it coming she would have prepared, reacted differently. Why did Haydn have to be so impatient? Fool. Imbecile. At first the words were directed at Haydn, but maybe they were more suited to herself. Why couldn't she decide? She felt lost, confused. Had she done the right thing?

She *hated* not to be sure. Maybe she had been right at the beginning. Getting involved with Haydn Smith was never going to be a good idea.

Chapter Thirty-six

Malcolm waited at the bottom of the short track that led from Annat House to the loch. Mhairi would have to pass this way on her bike. She was definitely keeping her distance. The only way to speak to her seemed to be to accost her physically. He sat on the wiry grass at the road side, keeping below the level of the rough stone wall so that she wouldn't be forewarned of his presence. He looked out across the water and scowled.

He only realised how happy he had been during those weeks with Mhairi now they were over. He had had girlfriends before, plenty of them, but no one who lit up his world when she was there, who he wanted to talk to just as much as he wanted to make love with. And he had thought Mhairi cared for him, too. When he was with her he had felt special, not the baby of the family, not the son who wasn't quite up to scratch. So why had it suddenly all gone wrong? It was her father who'd been ... ill, for Godssake, not either of them. Why did her father have to make such a difference?

He heard the bicycle tyres on the track and waited until almost the last moment before jumping up. Mhairi braked abruptly and almost fell.

'Wha-at?' she said. 'You fool, you gave me a fright! What on earth are you doing?' Then she remembered she was keeping her distance and tried to put her foot on the pedal again.

Malcolm took hold of her handlebar. 'Why are you avoiding me?' He couldn't be bothered with preamble. 'You haven't spoken to me properly for weeks.'

The expression on Mhairi's slim face became closed.

'I'm not. I've been a bit busy, but I see you around the house, don't I? Hard not to, actually.'

'You know what I mean.' Malcolm scowled. 'Look, if you want to stop going out with me you could at least tell me so to my face.'

He held his breath and watched her, instantly regretting the words. Why did he have to be so blunt, leave her no way out? When she said nothing he quickly said, 'I hope your dad's a bit better?' Maybe that was how he should have started this conversation.

'He does seem better,' said Mhairi cautiously.

'That's good.'

They stood in silence. Malcolm held the bike so tightly his knuckles were white. At least she hadn't said she didn't want to go out with him. He just needed to think of a way to retrieve the conversation.

Then they both spoke at once.

'Mhairi...'

'Look...'

'You go first.' As soon as he said it, Malcolm wished he hadn't. She was looking away from him, a bad sign.

She rubbed her eyes. 'I think I just need a bit of time. I don't know... Well, I just don't know.'

'But you're not saying you want us to finish?' Malcolm's spirits lifted. He touched her chin, so that she raised her head to meet his gaze. She looked wary, and very tired.

'What's the problem?'

'There isn't a... I don't know. I don't seem able to think properly just now.'

'I can wait,' he said. 'We'll just be friends for a while, how about that?'

Mhairi smiled at him, for what seemed like the first time in ages. 'Are you sure we can manage that?'

''Course we can,' said Malcolm. 'We can manage anything if we try.'

At that moment he really believed it. He walked along beside the bike for a little way, feeling immensely happy, because Mhairi was talking to him again. The late afternoon sun was sparkling on the water to their right and he could hear the small waves lapping on the pebbled shore. He hadn't noticed any of these things until a moment ago.

'Richie wasn't on the plane.'

'What?' said Catherine, stunned first to hear Haydn's voice on the phone and then by his words. 'What do you mean?'

331

'I mean he *wasn't on the plane*. I came to Edinburgh airport to meet him, and he's not here.'

Catherine could hear the shock in his voice and tried to suppress her own feeling of panic. There could be lots of reasons for this, surely? She made herself breathe slowly and tried to think.

'Have you phoned his mother? Maybe he just missed the flight.'

'I've tried but there's no answer at the house and her mobile is switched off.'

'Couldn't the airport people tell you anything? I mean, confirm he was booked on that flight?'

'I'm afraid that is confidential information,' said Haydn in the singsong voice of someone repeating words they have learnt by rote. 'The fact that I'm the boy's father... However. I'm going to wait for the next plane. There is another from Málaga but it's hours later. But if he is on that I can't see why they wouldn't have got a message to me by now.'

'It's hard to see why they wouldn't,' agreed Catherine, not wanting to think of sudden illnesses and car crashes and worse.

'She's abducted him,' said Haydn flatly.

'Wha-at? No, surely not. You can't know that. There are a lot of other possibilities.'

'It's happened before.'

As he said the words Catherine felt the ground fall away beneath her. She felt a sick horror wash over her. This had happened before? Her thoughts spun, the shock confused with anger. Why had he never mentioned it? It changed everything

But now wasn't the time to go into that. 'Is there anything I can do to help?'

There was a pause and she was afraid he was

going to reject her offer. This was the first time they had spoken in a fortnight. Then he said, 'Yes please. That's why I phoned. Could you go down to the cottage, check the answerphone there for me, and my e-mails? Do you still have your key?'

'Yes.' She had held on to it. Giving it back would have made everything seem final. 'I'll go straight down.'

'Call me when you're there. I'll need to give you the password for the computer.'

He rang off and Catherine stood for a moment, looking out at the soft drizzle, seeing nothing. If any harm had come to Richie... Haydn had never wanted the child to go. Now she understood why. She shuddered. *She* had been the one who persuaded him. Refusing to let her thoughts continue in that direction, she shouted to Mhairi that she was going out, and left at a run.

There were no messages from Esme at the cottage. They waited, Catherine at Annat House and Haydn at the airport. Richie was not on the next plane. Catherine wanted to drive down to Edinburgh to be with Haydn but he refused. He said he would get on to the police and then come home. His voice was bleak. If there was no news in the next twenty-four hours he would fly out to Spain himself.

'But what could have happened?' asked Malcolm plaintively, when she told him the news. She couldn't keep still, wandering all over the house from the kitchen to the attics and back.

Catherine swallowed hard. 'He's worried that Esme is keeping the child with her. If there had been an accident or something we would probably have heard. This looks more ... deliberate.'

'Gosh.' Malcolm stared at her. 'Like kidnapping, you mean?'

'It's not kidnapping exactly. I think. I don't know. I mean he was allowed by Haydn to go to his mother, it's just that she should have let him come back now. And she hasn't.' Catherine felt icy. Malcolm's horrified expression didn't help. What would happen if Richie didn't reappear? The child really seemed to be getting better, to be settling in Scotland.

Oh God, Haydn would never forgive her for this.

Haydn's phone rang for the twentieth or thirtieth time that day. Forty-eight hours had passed since Richie's disappearance. The Spanish police had called at Esme's house but found it empty. No one appeared to have any idea where they had gone.

To begin with, Haydn had snatched up the phone every time it rang, desperately hoping for good news, but now he was less keen. One of the London papers had got hold of the story and the last thing he needed was to fend off snooping, smarmy journalists. The caller's number did not display on his phone, making it all the more likely it was unwanted.

'Yes, hello?'

'Dad? It's Richie.' The boy's voice wavered. Haydn's heart gave a massive lurch of joy.

'Richie! Where are you? Are you OK?'

'I don't know.' The boy's voice was soft, possibly tearful.

Haydn made himself pause, not scream out all the questions that were racing through his mind. 'I'm so glad you've phoned. I've been worried. It's great to hear your voice.'

'Mum wouldn't let me come back.'

'I thought that might be the case.' He tried to keep the fury from his voice. 'I've been trying to call you on your mobile.'

'They took it away. I'm using the phone in the hotel. They think I'm asleep.'

'You've done really well to phone.'

'I thought I would never get through. I didn't know the right codes or anything...' The child sniffed.

'You don't need to worry now. I'm coming to get you.'

'But I don't know where we are. And we're moving again tomorrow, first thing.' The boy began to cry in earnest. Haydn cursed his stupid, selfish ex-wife.

'Tell me what you do know,' he said, trying to sound patient.

'We've been driving. We've passed B ... Bar ... they've got a really good football team.'

'Barcelona?' said Haydn, who had never thought he would be glad of his son's interest in football.

'Yeah. And I think we might be going to France. But they won't tell me anything and I don't understand Spanish.'

'Can you remember the name of the hotel?' Haydn's spirits had soared when he realised the child was still in Europe. He could get to him in hours, if only he knew where he was.

335

'I don't know. It's Spanish. Please come and get me, Dad.'

'I will. Just try and think...'

'Someone's coming. I have to go.' And the line went dead.

Chapter Thirty-seven

Haydn phoned Catherine to tell her he had spoken to Richie and she dashed down to the cottage.

By the time she arrived he had out a massive road atlas of Europe and was trying to guess where Esme might be.

'They'll be in a smart hotel. Somewhere between Barcelona and the border with France.'

'There must be an awful lot of posh hotels there. He didn't give you any other clues?' Catherine's heart ached to see the strain on Haydn's face, the restless tapping of his fingers.

'No. There was no time. Oh God.' For a moment, Haydn buried his face in his hands.

Catherine put her arms around him and held him close. There was nothing she could do to help. 'Have you told the police?'

'Of course, straight away. I'm hoping they can trace the call, but they'll have to be quick. And we don't know if Esme will realise Richie has contacted us. If she does, she'll move on straight away...' His voice tailed off. 'I'm going to get a flight immediately.'

Catherine could see why he would want to do so, to do something, but she wasn't sure it was the right thing. If he had flown to Malaga that morning, as he had considered doing, he would have missed this call and been at entirely the wrong end of Spain. She said this, tentatively, knowing she was not the right person to give advice.

'But I have to do something,' he said desperately.

'I know, I know. I just think maybe you should wait, see what the police say...'

'He's my *son*.'

'I know,' said Catherine.

He turned away. She didn't have children of her own, how could she possibly understand what he was feeling? He didn't say the words but she was sure that was what he was thinking and it hurt. But this was no time to think about herself.

'I'm going to book a flight.' He reached for the phone and then paused. 'I'll do it on the internet, I don't want to block the line.' He paused again. 'Should I fly to Barcelona or Perpignan on the other side of the border?'

Catherine had never seem him indecisive before. 'Let's check possibilities on the internet.' It would give him something to do.

He nodded in relief then, as he turned to go up to his office, the phone rang. They both jumped and he snatched it up.

'Yes? Yes? Who? Get off the bloody line!' He slammed the receiver down. 'Journalists,' he said, and sat down on the settee. 'I can't stand this.'

'Idiots,' said Catherine. 'You go upstairs and I'll make you some coffee. Go on, you might as well.'

Her tone was bracing and after a moment he responded to it, pushing himself out of the seat and setting off once again for the study.

As she arrived with the two steaming mugs, the phone rang again. Haydn picked it up. 'Yes? Yes, it is. Thank you.' There was a pause while he was put through to someone else and he whispered to Catherine, 'It's the police. They've traced the call.'

She put down the drinks and squeezed his shoulder encouragingly. Surely there would be good news?

'Yes, Haydn Eddlington-Smith speaking... Yes, so I understand. That's excellent. Have you contacted the Spanish police? You have? That's great. *What?* They won't? Why not?'

Haydn began arguing with the policeman at the other end of the line about the best course of action. After five minutes, he put down the receiver with a bang.

Catherine waited.

'They've traced the hotel and passed the information to their Spanish counterparts. But they've now informed me that it is "not normal practice" of the Spanish authorities to go in and pick up a child at short notice. They would prefer to have all the paperwork in place and then it has to be lodged with the local courts and then... Shit! We haven't got time for this.'

'I thought you said they were signatories to some convention or other.'

'The Hague Convention. Yes, they are. But as the police officer so patiently pointed out they have to think of the "best interests of the child" and it can be "very upsetting" if police suddenly

338

swoop in. And he is with his mother, so that makes it fine, apparently.' Haydn closed his eyes for a moment. 'Don't they think it's upsetting for Richie to be dragged off around the continent in this cloak and dagger way? By a woman he's hardly set eyes on in years? This is absurd!'

'What are you going to do?'

Haydn took a long drink of his coffee, now almost cold. The restless indecision was gone. His face was set and his voice calm. 'I'm going out there. They said they weren't able to tell me the name of the hotel but – I don't know if it was accidentally or on purpose – I heard them mention it in the background. Casa Bellavista. All I need to do is track down exactly where that is and get the next flight out.'

Catherine watched as he began his search on the internet. She had known he was good at this kind of thing but even so, hadn't expected results so soon. Within five minutes he had discovered three hotels of this name in Spain. One was in the south, one on Majorca, and one near Girona, close to the Spanish-French border.

'Got it,' he said. He called up the website which showed a beautifully proportioned Spanish villa set in sumptuous grounds. 'Yep, that's definitely it. Exactly what Esme would have chosen. Can't she even realise how obvious she is? Now, let's just hope they don't leave before I get there.'

'We could try and phone...' said Catherine cautiously.

'And give them warning they've been found? Not likely. I'm already petrified they'll realise Richie phoned me, but I've got to take the

339

chance they didn't. Right, now for flights.'

Thirty minutes later, he was gone. He had booked a flight from Glasgow to Barcelona which would get him in to that city at 5 a.m. local time. Then he had lined up a hire car and, if all went well, he would be at the hotel before breakfast. All Catherine could do now was hope Esme, Harold, and the child were there too.

It was still dark and just pleasantly cool as Haydn stepped out of the airport and made his way to the hire car. Everything had gone smoothly, more smoothly than he could have hoped. Now all he needed to do was get safely onto the autopista north, and find the damn hotel. He had sat nav and directions. He just needed to concentrate on driving on the wrong side of the road and dream of seeing Richie once again.

His mother had taken him to church often as a child and as he drove he prayed for help from a God he no longer believed in. The bells of a lone church began to ring for morning mass and it was as though he had been heard. It's going to be all right, he said to himself, as the car sped north through the dawn light.

But it wasn't.

A Señor and Señora Ca-va-narr? With a child? *Si,* they were here last night, but I am sorry, they have already departed.'

Haydn gripped the polished wooden counter to stop himself from falling. The receptionist was a young, very handsome man who was more than eager to help. He was devastated that Haydn had missed his friends, they had been gone less than an hour, perhaps he could phone ahead, or would señor like a room himself, he looked a little fatigued…

Haydn tried to think through the panic spinning in his mind. He might be exhausted, but fear spurred him on. He had been so close to finding Richie; he couldn't lose him now. He asked the clerk to find someone who could describe Harold's car to him, tipped him heavily, and set off again. He had to believe that they were heading for the border, and to hope that he could catch them before they reached it. What he would do when he found them he had no idea.

But he had promised Richie that he would come and get him, and so he would.

It was still early when Haydn reached the border post, but the sun was beating down with almost unbearable brightness. It had taken longer than he expected. He had felt the need to scan every wayside café for signs of Harold's cream Mercedes and twice had thought he had seen it. Both stops had been to no avail and now he was in the short queue for the border crossing. He scanned the vehicles ahead and there was nothing to raise his hopes. A couple of lorries, a few businessmen, and one or two family cars. Nothing large and cream. With a muttered exclamation of frustration, he pulled his own car out of the line and parked in a layby. He needed time to think.

This was all his fault. What a fool he had been. He should never have let the child out of the country. Who better than he knew what Esme was really capable of? He would never forgive her, never, for doing this to Richie.

But that wasn't what he needed to think about now.

He rubbed a hand over his tired eyes and examined the map once again. Should he cross the border and count on catching up with them on the French side? There were no obvious turn offs until north of Perpignan. He could pursue them up to that junction. If he hadn't come across them by then he would have to give up. The chances of finding them on one straight road were not great, but once the road divided his hopes were gone.

Or should he just stay in Spain? He had no proof that they had crossed the border and by continuing the chase on his own he might be missing contact from the police.

He hit the steering wheel hard. It was lucky Esme or *Sir* Harold, with his dyed hair and receding chin, weren't around. He wasn't sure he could resist punching them if they were.

He took out his mobile phone. Thinking of contact from the police made him realise it wasn't switched on. As soon as it found a network connection, the phone began to beep. Why hadn't he thought to turn it on before?

There was a message asking him to phone John Hugo and giving a mobile number. Now Haydn was really perplexed. What could John Hugo possibly want? He almost didn't bother. Yet the man had said it was urgent.

The phone was picked up at the other end as soon as it began to ring.

'Haydn? Thank God.'

'Is that John Hugo...?'

'Yes, John Hugo McDonald. Catherine's brother.'

'Yes, yes, I know that. But why are you phoning? I'm in Spain and...'

'I'm in Spain too,' said John Hugo triumphantly. 'And – well, to cut a long story short, I have someone here who wants to talk to you.'

None of this made sense. Haydn must be more tired than he realised. And then Richie's voice came on the line and his heart soared. The boy was safe!

'Dad? Hi, Dad. It's me.'

'Richie! Oh, God! Where are you? Are you all right?'

'Yeah, I'm OK. Now John Hugo's here.'

The wave of relief made Haydn feel almost faint. He rubbed his eyes and said, 'I'm so glad. Where are you?'

'I'm still in Spain. Where are you? John Hugo says you're here too.'

'I am, I am.' Haydn slumped back into the soft support of the driver's seat. 'I was just going to go over the border into France. I came to get you but you'd already left the hotel.'

'Mmm. Mum was mad when she found out that I'd phoned you. I didn't tell her, but it was on the bill.'

'Oh, Richie... Not to worry about that now. Look, where exactly are you? I want to see you with my own eyes as soon as possible.' Haydn drew in a ragged breath.

'I don't know. Do you want to talk to John Hugo again?'

'Please. I'll see you soon, Richie. I love you.'

'Oh,' said the child, sounding surprised for the first time in the conversation. 'Here's John Hugo.'

Catherine's brother gave succinct directions to the restaurant where he had caught up with Esme, less than ten kilometres south of the border. Lucky he had happened to be in the right place at the right time, he said, sounding very pleased with himself. Haydn was quite happy to feel pleased as well. He turned the car quickly and headed back south. He wanted to hear the full story, but most of all he wanted to see Richie.

John Hugo booked a room for Haydn and Richie in the hotel where he and a group of friends were staying in the little coastal resort of Sitges. Haydn slept most of the afternoon, exhaustion finally catching up with him. John Hugo offered to take the boy to the beach but Richie had declined. He wanted to stay with his dad and lay on the bed, reading quietly in their shared room.

In the evening, John Hugo took them to a select little fish restaurant and, after a couple of glasses of very good white wine, Haydn was finally able to relax. He had his arm resting loosely along the back of his son's chair, so he could brush the child's hair every so often with his hand.

'I can't thank you enough,' he said. 'I hate to think what would have happened if they'd crossed into France.'

'It was nothing,' said John Hugo complacently.

'You were brilliant,' said Richie, not for the first time.

'Your dad would have caught up with them in the end,' said John Hugo. 'But then I would have missed out on the excitement. Haven't had such fun in years.'

'It was great,' said Richie, his face was alive with the thrill of it all. "Course, Mum and Harold didn't know you, so when you came in to the restaurant they never thought to run or anything.'

'Not that they would have got far if they had,' said John Hugo. 'I'd checked out all the exits and had them covered.'

'You should have seen Harold's face,' said Richie with a giggle. 'He looked like a fish. And then Mum began to cry.' His face fell.

Esme had still been in tears when Haydn arrived. He thought she and her husband might have left in order to avoid him, but Harold tried to brazen it out.

'We've as much right to the child as you,' he had said.

'You have no rights,' Haydn had hissed, trying to keep the conversation from Richie's hearing. 'The only person with any rights here is Richie, and you have certainly gone against his wishes.'

As the child was clinging limpet-like to his father's side, Harold could hardly deny this. He spent the rest of the brief conversation trying to persuade Haydn that he really didn't need to involve the police any further in the matter. He wouldn't want to make trouble for Esme, would he? It might affect her residence permit... All Haydn wanted to do was to see the back of them, and eventually, when he said he probably wouldn't press charges, they left.

Haydn was still bemused as to how John Hugo had got involved in the whole affair.

'Apparently it was Malcolm's idea to contact me. Sometimes that boy is quite sensible,' said John Hugo.

'I didn't even know you were in Spain.'

'Malcolm remembered I was at Sitges. It was about two in the morning when he got hold of me. We'd been out, I'd not bothered to check my phone until then. We got the maps out and found where Richie's hotel was. Then I phoned ahead and spoke to the night porter. I know a bit of Spanish, which if I say so myself came in very handy. He told me they were still there, and what car they drove. He didn't know why I was asking, of course.'

'I can't thank you enough,' said Haydn.

'Then I set off,' John Hugo continued. 'A couple of my mates came too. The plan was to stake out the place and make sure they didn't leave before you arrived. But when they did leave all we could do was follow them. Would have been easier if you hadn't had your phone switched off.'

Haydn shook his head apologetically. 'Can't believe I was so stupid. I was just concentrating on getting there as fast as I could.'

'That's what I thought. The restaurant where you found us was their first stop. We decided at that point we couldn't risk them going any further, too close to the border.'

'So then John Hugo came in and found me,' said Richie, splashing vinegar over his chips. 'It was so cool.'

'I was worried Richie might not remember me,' said John Hugo.

'Phoo, 'course I would. I remember...' Richie

glanced at his rescuer and then decided not to say whatever it was he had remembered. Haydn recalled his son hadn't exactly warmed to John Hugo at Gordon's wedding and suppressed a smile.

'The lady tried to bluff her way out of it, claiming there'd been a misunderstanding.' John Hugo smiled. 'It didn't really matter what she said, I wasn't going to let the boy out of my sight until you got there. And the rest you know.'

Haydn hugged the child to him, and Richie, who even as a baby had not been keen on cuddles, hugged him in return. He said again, 'We can't thank you and your family enough.' If John Hugo hadn't been on holiday here... If Malcolm hadn't thought to phone him... It didn't bear thinking of.

Chapter Thirty-eight

It was the last week of September and the weather was pretending that summer had returned. The sun was high and hot and although some leaves had begun to fall and the bracken on the high hill was turning to rust, it was a beautiful evening. Far too nice to be sitting in Kinlochannat village hall.

'Maybe no one will come,' said Malcolm hopefully, giving the door its usual bang to open it.

'Tommy McAllister is definitely coming. I saw him in the shop earlier. And there'll be others, don't worry.'

'I'm not worrying.'

'I know.' Mhairi grinned. She had almost regained her easy humour and they were spending more time together again. That was good, but Malcolm wanted to be alone with her, not surrounded by half the youths of the village. He pulled her towards him, meaning to kiss her, but at that moment the outer door opened and she pulled away. He hoped that was the reason she pulled away.

She smiled at him. She seemed happy enough. 'I can't believe we've really got the money.'

'It was Father putting up half of it that got the ball rolling.' Malcolm couldn't keep the sneer from his voice. 'Who would have thought he'd get so community-minded all of a sudden?'

'He'd never have done it if you hadn't made that announcement at the wedding.'

Malcolm smiled. He liked having her approval. 'Maybe. Although, to be honest, if Father really hadn't wanted to do it he could have wriggled out of it. In the long run he always does what he wants.'

The door banged again and the village youngsters began to drift in. Private conversation was no longer possible but Malcolm was optimistic about later in the evening. He'd been patient for long enough.

'Come for a drink with me after?' he said softly.

'Maybe.'

Malcolm settled down to make himself as helpful as possible during the meeting.

At first, everything went well. The audience were suitably impressed that the skate/bike park looked like it was becoming a reality, so much so that even the most sceptical were smiling and clapping as Mhairi explained the progress that had been made. The final piece of the puzzle, the land they needed, had fallen into place that week when the council agreed to them using the field beside the school.

Then she went on to list all the things they needed to do now. She wanted the community to be as involved as possible. Firstly, because it would save money and secondly, because it was their project and they would feel more ownership if they were involved. Malcolm was amazed at how good she was with the jargon.

'The first thing we need to do is clear the field. I don't see why we can't do that ourselves, especially if we get some of your parents or older brothers and sisters to help.'

The crowd looked doubtful and Malcolm couldn't blame them. 'Not everyone has spare time on their hands,' he said, forgetting he was being supportive.

'And not everyone is fully employed, either,' said Mhairi. 'I'm not asking much. A few hours here and there, at evenings or weekends.'

'We wouldnae ken what to do,' said one of the youths.

'That's OK. Someone will show you.'

'You need people who are willing to work,' said Malcolm, looking around at the guarded expressions.

Mhairi scowled. 'We might have to twist a few arms, but I think we can get people to help.'

For once, Malcolm thought she was making a mistake. This project would have to be done professionally, meet health and safety criteria, and all the other rules and regulations, surely she realised that? He said, 'Do you really want to have to rely on the village layabouts for the success of this thing?'

Mhairi swung round to face him and he saw she had turned pale. He added hastily, 'I didn't mean...'

'*You* may think Kinlochannat consists of no good *layabouts*,' she said icily. 'But we know differently, don't we?' She turned to the rows of teenagers who were looking at one another uneasily. 'Tommy, I've already spoken to your dad and he says he'll drive his digger for us one Saturday. And the forestry people said they'd lend us a supervisor for a day or two if some of you lot would labour to him. Which, of course, I said you would. Wouldn't you?'

It took only a moment or two of restless shifting before one girl said, 'Aye, I would.' And then they all wanted to be included.

Malcolm was pleased for Mhairi that they were volunteering but he still had his doubts.

'That's excellent,' said Mhairi, smiling encouragingly at them. Malcolm was the only one close enough to see the cold glint in her eye. 'I know I can rely on the villagers,' she said.

Then he realised. She thought he'd meant her father. He hadn't, but he was sure she wouldn't believe him.

'Drink?' he said as soon as the meeting began to break up. He made sure he stayed at her side so she couldn't make a quick escape.

'I don't think so.'

350

'Mhairi, don't be like that. I didn't mean what I said...'

'Did you say something? I didn't notice.' She turned to talk to a couple of the girls but he wasn't to be avoided that easily. He kept beside her as she headed for the door. He knew she had to return the hall key to old Miss Murphy and with a bit of luck the youngsters wouldn't want to walk all the way with her.

He was right. By the time they had reached to top of the narrow lane that led up to Miss Murphy's tiny, tidy cottage, the youths had drifted away and Mhairi and he were alone.

He tried again. 'Look, Mhairi, I'm sorry. It just came out.' Why, oh why, had he had to use that word layabout?

Mhairi stared straight ahead. She had jewellery in all her piercings this evening, a diamond in her nose and three different coloured rings in each ear. She should have looked jaunty, with her short hair brushed back and her strange cat eyes dark with make-up, but instead she looked grim. After a while, when he thought she wasn't going to respond, she said abruptly, 'It doesn't matter whether you're sorry or not. It shows the way you think.'

'But it doesn't!' That was better, at least they were talking now. 'I just open my big stupid mouth and the words come out.'

'Words don't come from nowhere. It's the way you've been brought up, Malcolm, you can't help it. Those in the big house have always thought that those of us at the bottom of the pile are just some lazy scum and things haven't really changed.'

'Of course they've changed. Mhairi, you're being ridiculous.'

She turned on him then, eyes flashing. 'I am not being ridiculous. I've seen the way your father and your brothers look at me and people like me. Oh, I'm good enough to come and work in the house if Catherine wants me there, but I'm not one of you and I never will be.'

'No, thank God, you're not.' Malcolm caught her hand and made her pause. At least she hadn't included him in the list of people who looked down on her. 'My father is a useless snob way past his sell-by date. Ignore him, what does he matter? It's you and me that matter.'

'No, it's not. Family matters too. I'm not disowning *my* father, he's part of what I am.'

Malcolm had known this was the real issue. 'Well, he's lucky, isn't he? He's got you and your mum. You've got a family that stick together. I haven't, so why the hell should you hold them against me?'

'Oh, you all stick together when it comes down to it.' Mhairi sighed and pulled her hand away. She began walking up the hill again.

'I don't know what your problem is,' said Malcolm, hurrying to keep up. 'You're beautiful and clever and could do anything you wanted with your life. Why do you have such a chip on your shoulder about where you come from?'

'Because it is where I come from and you don't like it.'

'I never said I didn't like it!' He couldn't help raising his voice. 'It's you who've got all these idiotic ideas in your head. Look, why can't we forget it and start again?'

'We can never forget it. It's staring us in the face every day. Me in my ex-council house, you with a choice of not one but two swanky places to live. And your use of the family cars, and your trust fund and all the rest. It's not going to go away, Malcolm.'

Malcolm kicked viciously at the rosebay willow-herb that crowded the edge of the road, setting the downy seeds floating everywhere. Why couldn't she see sense, that none of this mattered? He couldn't understand how someone so bright could be so blind.

'You stay there,' said Mhairi as they came to the picket fence that surrounded Elizabeth Murphy's cottage. 'If you come in she'll want to talk for ever. She thinks you're wonderful. If I'm on my own it won't take a minute.'

Malcolm didn't like being told what to do, but Mhairi had a point. Miss Murphy did seem to have a soft spot for him and he really couldn't be bothered with her chatter just now. He slumped down on the verge.

Mhairi was optimistic in thinking it would only take her a minute to drop off the key. It was nearer ten by the time she returned and Malcolm had had the chance to calm down. He pushed himself back to his feet, brushing off the grass and seeds, and fell into step beside her. Initially, he said nothing.

His heart was sore. He had never understood that expression before but that was how he felt, hurting inside. He had to find the right words to explain to Mhairi. She might still reject him, refuse to take this relationship any further, but he had to try. They came to a turn in the road where a rough wooden bench had been sited to take full advantage of the view over the village to the loch. It had suffered from the attentions of the local teenagers, but it was still usable.

Malcolm touched Mhairi's arm. 'Sit here for a minute.'

She sighed but did as requested. She stared down over the scattered houses of the village, the few rows of traditional stone houses, the small council estate at the far side, and the bigger detached homes spilling out along the country roads. Malcolm was relieved that the shoulder of a hill hid Annat House and the Lodge from their sight.

'Mhairi, look. If it's me, if you don't like me and don't want any more to do with me I'll leave you alone, OK? But if it's just because of this thing you have about our families then I can't accept that. Truly, it doesn't matter one bit to me.'

'It's not *a thing I have*. It's the way it is.'

He looked at her for a long time. She was still looking at the view. 'I think I love you,' he said doubtfully, and then stopped. God, he couldn't be saying this. This was *serious*. Mhairi was still staring away from him, but he could see a faint pink seeping across her cheek. 'Mhairi, please, give me a chance.'

She turned and looked at him as though she had never seen him before. 'I can't believe you said that.'

'It's just asking for a chance...'

'About love.'

'Oh. That.' He took a deep breath and said. 'It's

354

true.' It was. He felt a great joy just looking at her, and hope because she wasn't turning away, and terror because she still said nothing.

She put up a hand and touched his cheek. 'You can't love me.'

'Oh yes I can.' He caught her hand and held it tight.

'You're crazy,' she said, but she was starting to smile.

'And if you give me the chance, I'm going to try and make you love me, too.'

'You are, are you?'

'Yes. So are we going to give this thing a go?'

She shook her head. The smile was widening but a frown remained between her brows. He wished he knew what was going on inside that head. He wished she'd say something.

'The thing is,' she said slowly and his heart beat frantically as he waited. 'The thing is, I already love you.' She leant forward very slowly and pressed her lips to his. 'That's what's so scary. Malcolm McDonald, I've loved you for as long as I can remember.'

'Jesus. Why didn't you say?'

He kissed her back. Not mad, crazy kisses, but gentle ones, hopeful. He could scarcely believe this. If she had loved him for ever, why had she been so difficult? He really didn't understand her. He had been so close to losing her, and they still hadn't resolved everything. But they would, they would.

Chapter Thirty-nine

Haydn had said he wouldn't ask Catherine to marry him again. They were friendly once more, rejoicing in Richie's safe return. Haydn hadn't said one word about it being Catherine's fault the boy had gone to Spain. He had refused to let her apologise, when she had tried, awkwardly, to do so. They had even shared ironic laughter when they saw the full-page spread in one of the gossip magazines about how Esme's love for her child had led her to make a terrible mistake and how she hoped that one day Richie would forgive her,

'Bet she got a pretty penny for that,' said Haydn. 'I wonder if Harold's money is running out.'

'Maybe she just likes the publicity,' said Catherine.

Haydn had considered this, his green eyes narrowed. 'You know, maybe you're right. And, God, how I hated it.'

'I'd hate it too. But you know publicity does have its uses. One of the Scottish papers phoned up last week wanting to do an article on Annat House and I think I might agree.'

'Using the press when it suits you is an entirely different matter,' he had said.

He seemed quite happy to spend time in her company. But they weren't sleeping together and Catherine was coming to realise that if she didn't do something to break the barrier between them, it would stay there. It might be pride on Haydn's part, or it might be that he simply didn't want her any more. If she didn't ask, she would never find out.

She was happier with her life in many ways. She still thought of her mother with sadness, and of Jean, but those were things she couldn't change. Just as she couldn't change her charming, selfish father. Accepting all that had been a big step. The thing was, it shouldn't stop you doing the things you could do.

On Richie's first weekend home from his new school, he came round to Annat House. He seemed happier than she had ever seen him. Somehow, Haydn coming to rescue him had changed the relationship between the two of them forever. Haydn obviously realised how much the child meant to him, and maybe Richie realised that too.

Catherine was flattered by the visit. 'Are you in the same class as Miles?' she asked, smiling fondly at him. He was growing and his awkward features seemed to be settling into his face, making him look more like his father.

'Nah. He's left, he's a year older.'

'And Antonia?'

'She's in the class below. And she's a girl.'

Catherine suppressed a smile. 'True.' When he didn't offer any more information she asked, 'So, have you made any friends?'

'I sit next to a Chinese boy called Aidan.'

'That's good. Is he nice?'

'He's all right. Is Malcolm around?'

'He's in the kitchen, of course. You can go down

and see him if you like.'

'OK.' The child hesitated, his shoulders drooping so that Catherine realised he didn't often sit in that hunched way these days. He said to the floor, 'My dad's at home, if you wanted to go and see him.'

'Ah. Thanks.' Catherine wondered if Haydn had put him up to this. That made her feel nervous. 'I've got work to do just now.'

'OK.'

The boy went down to the kitchen and Catherine returned to her computer. Perhaps it *was* time to visit his father and sort things out. Once, she had thought her mother was the only person she could trust. Now she was willing to rely on others – Malcolm and Mhairi for a start. Not her father, of course. She could never quite forgive him for keeping Jean a secret. But he was still her father and despite everything, she supposed she still loved him.

And Haydn? He wasn't like her father, or like any other man she had known. He was Haydn and she needed to tell him that – but she wasn't sure she felt up to it just now. She would wait until Richie was back at school and the coast was clear, then she would tackle Haydn head on.

She leant over to get another tissue from the box on the window sill. Her nose hadn't stopped running all day. That was probably why she was being so indecisive. She wasn't prone to illness and she would surely have shaken off this cold in a day or so.

But instead of getting better, she grew worse. The streaming nose developed into a raging sore throat, an aching head, and, worst of all, a fever that made her hot one moment and shivering the next.

'I've no time for this,' she said to Mhairi on the Monday morning, between sneezes. 'The next lot of visitors are due to arrive before lunch. I need to be here to meet them.'

'I don't think you want them to see you looking like that,' said Mhairi, eyeing her up and down. 'Best go to bed. You'll only spread the infection if you hang around.'

'You sound just like your mum.'

'Exactly. And I know what she'd say. Bed, with a hot water bottle and two Paracetamol. You're suffering from a virus and the only thing to do is rest and wait it out.'

'I've got too much to do...'

'We can manage without you, you know.' Mhairi's cheeks reddened slightly and she tossed her head. 'What do you think you employ us for? I'll get Mrs McWhirter and Susan to stay longer this afternoon, and I'll take over your side of things.'

'Are you sure you'll be OK?' Catherine thought of the visit she was going to make to Haydn. She sneezed three times in a row, shivered violently, and gave in. 'Yes, of course you will. You're a good girl, Mhairi.'

'Off you go to bed.'

'OK, OK. But don't forget the Arthurs specifically asked for a room at the front, and that Mrs Arthur has a gluten allergy?'

'No, Catherine, I won't forget. You know, you might be better off down at the Lodge.'

'No way. I'm staying in my room here. That way you can come up and keep me informed of everything that's going on. It's not that I don't think you can do it, but it is *my* business. I need to know what's happening.'

'Of course. Now, off you go. I'll bring you a hot drink in a wee while.'

Catherine was glad to do as she was told, which made her realise quite how ill she felt. She snuggled down in the bed, grateful for the hot water bottle, shivering and sniffing and listening to the sounds of activity in the house below, but having neither the energy nor the inclination to get involved.

Her thoughts turned more than once to Haydn, but if she didn't have the strength for work, she certainly wasn't up to facing him. He would have to wait. He probably wouldn't even miss her.

To her dismay, on the following day she was no better. Mhairi was so worried she talked of calling out the doctor, and even Malcolm said he'd never seen her look so bad. He said this from the doorway to her bedroom. He wasn't good with ill people. Perhaps they reminded him of their mother. Thinking of her mother brought tears to Catherine's eyes; ridiculous to be so weak. But her mother had been the only one who had ever looked after Catherine, and now she wasn't here. Not that Catherine needed looking after, really. She'd be fine in a day or two.

She turned her head away from Malcolm's anxious face, and slept.

The next time she woke it was evening, with the light fading at the window. Pip was snoring on the bed beside her and Haydn was sitting in the old armchair. From the look of him, legs stretched out, head resting on one of the wings, he had been there a while.

'What are you doing here?' she said. At least, that was what she meant to say. Most of the words were lost in a bout of coughing.

Haydn waited calmly until she had finished, then handed her a glass of water.

'I only heard this afternoon that you were ill.' He frowned down at her. 'You look awful.'

'Thanks.' Catherine found a handkerchief under her pillow and blew her nose. Seeing him there, so calm and collected, made her feel weepy. So stupid.

'Why didn't you get someone to phone me?'

'I've been OK. Mhairi and Malcolm have been looking after me. I'll be better soon.'

Haydn leant over and put a hand on her forehead. 'You're very hot.'

'I know. I've got a temperature. That's what happens.'

He smiled fleetingly and she felt annoyance rising. It was all right for him, looking beautiful and in control, while she felt – and looked – an utter mess.

'You'd better not stay. You don't want to catch whatever it is I've got.'

'I'll take the risk,' he said, smiling. 'Malcolm said he'd made soup. You look like you haven't been eating. I'll go down and get you some.'

'I'd prefer Mhairi to bring it up. I need to speak to her about how the course is going.'

'Mhairi is coping perfectly well. The only

difficulty I'm aware of is that the IT buff leading the course is showing an, er, decided preference for young Mhairi's company. And that isn't going down too well with Malcolm.'

'Oh, for goodness sake...'

'It's OK, they're keeping their arguments to the privacy of the kitchen. Won't do them any harm at all.' He paused in the doorway. 'Now you stay where you are, I won't be a moment.'

As soon as Catherine heard his footsteps disappearing down the thinly carpeted attic stairs, she jumped out of bed and made for her small bathroom. She needed to use the toilet, but her main concern was to wash her face and comb her hair. It was impossible to look wonderful in her present condition, but she didn't need to look a total wreck.

Even this small effort exhausted her, and when Haydn returned she was lying back on the pillows she had piled up behind her.

'I told you to stay put,' he said severely.

'Hmmph.' The soup smelt good and Catherine pushed herself upright and took the tray on her lap. Lentil and bacon soup, her favourite. And there was a glass of fresh orange and a pot of tea. 'Thanks,' she said grumpily, hating to be a nuisance. Then, remembering her manners, 'What about you? Aren't you having anything?'

'I ate with Malcolm and Mhairi earlier. That's why I'm so *au fait* with their arguments.'

'Oh. Well, don't feel you need to stay.'

Haydn said nothing but sat down once more in the battered armchair. He was dressed, as so often, in black jeans and a soft, dark jersey, and looked out of place in the untidy room, with the faded velvet curtains and scattered clothes. The light was almost gone now and he turned on the lamp beside the bed, drawing them closer in the pool of gold.

Catherine pulled her dressing gown around her. True, she had lain naked in his arms many times, but now she felt shy and awkward. She took up her spoon and began to eat the soup, initially with enthusiasm, but after a few mouthfuls her appetite faded. She took a bite of bread and butter then pushed that away too.

'Drink the orange juice, at least,' said Haydn, his tone gentle.

'I don't need anyone to look after me,' she said between sniffs.

'No, I can see that. Here.' He picked up the glass of juice and she suspected he might actually have held it to her lips if she hadn't taken it. Their fingers touched fleetingly but it meant nothing.

Catherine sipped the cold liquid and it soothed her throat. 'I hate being ill,' she said, after a while.

'Yes. Most inconvenient.'

'I hate being at a disadvantage,' she said, and glared at him.

'You are never at a disadvantage, my love.'

Her heart did a little flip at the words, but the smile on his lips remained faintly amused. They were just words.

'Malcolm and Mhairi are doing an excellent job. You need to trust them.'

'I know. I do trust them.'

She sipped the juice until the glass was empty, then Haydn picked up the tray and put it to one side. He didn't try and nag her to finish the soup or tea, as Mhairi would have done, and she was grateful for that. She shrugged off the fleecy, unsexy dressing gown and slid down under the covers.

'I think I'll try and sleep now,' she said. Then hopefully he would leave her alone. She couldn't relax while he watched her in that patient way. She didn't want his sympathy.

She closed her eyes and after a few minutes he said, 'Would you like me to go?'

'Yes please,' she said in a small voice.

He leant over and kissed her forehead, pushing her hair gently away. It was not a lover's touch.

She heard him leave the room and cross the small attic landing.

'Haydn!' she said, pushing herself up. What if he didn't come back? 'Haydn!'

He was at her side in a moment. 'It's OK, I won't go if you don't want. I was only going to sit in the kitchen for a while. I was coming back.'

Catherine sniffed and took a deep breath. She kept her gaze on his face, on the warm green eyes and the mouth that for once was not curved in a mocking smile.

'I need to ask you something.'

'Go ahead.' His eyes didn't leave hers.

She sat up properly, pushing her hair back, taking a deep breath. It was a risk, but she had to take it. 'Haydn Eddlington-Smith,' she said quietly. 'Will you marry me?'

The smile broadened. There was no mockery in it. 'Yes,' he said. 'Oh, yes.' He sat down on the bed beside her and pulled her into his arms. She held on to him. It was as though they had never been apart. This was right, where she should be. 'I thought you'd never ask.'

He began to kiss her and, with a strength she didn't think she had, she kissed him back.

'Do you think you should be doing this?' he said after a while.

She grinned at him. 'I feel better than I have in days.'

'That's wonderful. But we don't want to tire you out, do we? Move over a bit.' She did so and he slid under the covers beside her, still fully clothed. He put his arm around her and held her so her head could rest on his shoulder.

Neither of them spoke for a while. Then he dropped a kiss on her hair and said, 'Are you sure you're in your right mind? It's not the temperature talking? You, expressing a desire to get married.'

'Only as long as it's to you.' She gave a long sigh of contentment. She felt she had come home. Why had it taken her so long to make this step? She remembered what Georgie had said, about needing to know what she wanted for *herself*. Sometimes that was the hardest thing of all. 'I'll still be bossy, you know.'

'And I'll still resent interference.' He held her close, resting his face against her hair. 'What made you change your mind?'

'When you're not here, I'm not happy. It's more than love. I need you.' Her voice quivered as she spoke. She had never thought she would make that admission to anyone.

'Thank God,' he said. 'I need you too. And if I stay here much longer, I'm going to, er, want you right now. And I really don't think any more exertion is a good idea.' He pulled her close and kissed her so she hoped he might change his mind, but his self control was, as ever, formidable. 'We've got the rest of our lives,' he said severely when she was reluctant to release him. 'Now take your Paracetamol and get some sleep. And tomorrow you'll probably feel much better and we can start feeding you up.'

'Who's bossy now?' She smiled at him, drugged by happiness.

When he left the room she was sure she wouldn't even be able to close her eyes. There was so much to think about. They should get married as soon as possible, Haydn would like that. In the little Kinlochannat kirk, of course, and... She slept.

Chapter Forty

Catherine and Haydn's marriage was indeed celebrated in Kinlochannat kirk. The Reverend John somehow managed once again to overcome his concerns about conducting marriages of divorcees and lead the service himself.

It was a small but very happy ceremony. Richie was allowed the day off school, Georgie brought her youngest Labrador with a bow around his neck, and John Hugo came up from Edinburgh. Even Kerr, after complaining about the short notice, managed to make his way up from London. It was, of course, too far for Gordon and

Phyllida to come at short notice but they had sent an enormous bouquet of exotic flowers and a very generous cheque, so their approval was clear. Phyllida had wanted them to travel to Texas for their honeymoon, and Catherine had promised to bear it in mind at a later date.

As Catherine and Haydn emerged from the church into a misty autumn afternoon, Mhairi threw handfuls of pink and white confetti.

'Don't do that,' said Catherine in horror. 'I promised the Reverend. No confetti.'

Mhairi snorted. 'You think I care?'

Malcolm was taking pictures and said he had got an excellent one of the argument. Haydn just smiled and brushed confetti from his hair, giving it a ruffled look that made him more gorgeous than ever. She reached up and kissed him. 'I love you,' she whispered.

'I'm glad about that.' His tone was light but his smile warm. 'Now, are the cars here to take us to the reception?'

For once, Malcolm was excused cooking duties and the small reception was to be held at the Glentoul Hotel, where Haydn had taken Catherine for their first meal out together. That was not much more than six months ago, but it seemed so much longer. How could Catherine have imagined herself this happy, then?

In the lull after the toasts and the speeches, Mhairi and Malcolm pulled up two chairs beside Catherine and Haydn. Catherine smiled across at them.

She was not the only one who had changed in the last year. Mhairi still looked younger than her twenty-three years, but the exotic disguise of dyed hair and multiple piercings were long gone. The one diamond in her nose was modest, her hair was sleeked back in a very chic style, and the cream sheath dress was quietly elegant. Malcolm's hand stroked her bare arm, as though he couldn't get enough of her.

'We've got something to tell you,' he said. Mhairi frowned.

'You're not getting married?' said Catherine. It was the first thought that came into her head.

'Oh no,' said Mhairi, blushing.

'We're a bit young at the moment,' said Malcolm. 'What I wanted to say was...'

Mhairi nudged him. 'I really don't think we need to discuss this now.'

'Why not? The sooner they know the better, surely?' Malcolm was looking very handsome in his McDonald tartan kilt, but clearly had had rather a lot to drink. He grinned happily. 'We've decided to leave Annat at the end of the year.'

Mhairi added quickly, 'We'll stay until the end of the season and help you train up new staff and everything. We won't leave you in the lurch. It's just that we feel, well, we want to go away for a while.'

'Why? Where?' Catherine was dismayed. Just when she had come to realise that she *could* rely on other people, they were going away and leaving her.

'We don't really know,' said Malcolm, waving a hand vaguely. 'Europe. Maybe Thailand. Australia.'

'We've got some money saved, and when that's

used up we'll have to find jobs. Malcolm thinks we'll be able to.'

'I'm sure you will,' said Catherine, trying to shake herself into responding sensibly.

'I think it's an excellent idea,' said Haydn. 'You've no ties and there's a big wide world out there waiting to be explored. Go for it.'

'Thanks,' said Mhairi, then to Catherine, 'You really don't mind?'

'Of course not,' said Catherine, not quite truthfully. 'I've been very lucky to have you, both of you, to help out in this first year. It's a bit of a shock to hear that you're leaving, but I'm sure I'll cope.'

'We will,' said Haydn. Catherine pressed her lips together. He needn't think she expected him to help out. He was quite busy enough with his own project, which seemed to have taken on a life of its own.

And besides, she didn't like interference.

'You'll find other locals and train them up,' said Malcolm confidently. 'Wasn't that your plan all along?'

'As long as you don't go too soon,' she said. 'I'll miss you.'

'We're not going for ever,' said Mhairi. 'My dad is much better now, thank goodness, and Mum is encouraging me to go. We just think it's something we should do.' Catherine found she agreed. Neither Malcolm nor Mhairi would truly find their feet until they had left Kinlochannat. Later, if they chose, they could return.

The band struck up a tune and she and Haydn took the floor for the first dance of their married lives. She looped her arms loosely around his neck and smiled into his eyes.

'This is fun,' she said. Others might be leaving, but she and Haydn had discovered just where they were meant to be. Without him, she had been lost. It was only now she understood that.

'Isn't it just.' He pulled her to his chest and rested his cheek against her hair.

The publishers hope that this book has given you enjoyable reading. Large Print Books are especially designed to be as easy to see and hold as possible. If you wish a complete list of our books please ask at your local library or write directly to:

Magna Large Print Books
Magna House, Long Preston,
Skipton, North Yorkshire.
BD23 4ND